CULHWCH AND OLWEN

CULHWCH AND OLWEN

An Edition and Study of the
Oldest Arthurian Tale

edited by
Rachel Bromwich and D. Simon Evans

UNIVERSITY OF WALES PRESS
Cardiff
1992

ISBN 0–7083–1127–X

A catalogue record for this book is available from the British Library

Typeset by BP Integraphics Ltd., Bath, Avon
Printed in Great Britain by Billing and Sons Ltd, Book Plan, Worcester
Jacket design by Design Principle, Cardiff

Preface

The initial impetus for this book arose from our preparatory work for the Welsh edition of *Culhwch ac Olwen*, which we undertook in 1985 at the invitation of the Language and Literature Committee of the Board of Celtic Studies, and which was published in 1988 by the University of Wales Press under the title *Culhwch ac Olwen: Testun Syr Idris Foster wedi ei olygu a'i orffen gan Rachel Bromwich a D. Simon Evans.* Our commitment as editors of the preparatory material for an edition of this tale, which was left unfinished by the late Sir Idris Foster at his death, allowed us to add little to a work whose main purpose was to make the text of *Culhwch ac Olwen* available with the minimum of delay for study by students in the University of Wales. This restriction prevented us from offering the full critical apparatus and discussion which we had prepared in readiness, and which was plainly required by the central importance of *Culhwch ac Olwen* for all students of medieval Welsh literature. We therefore welcomed the opportunity to prepare this extended study, to which we have supplied a full glossary, a revised edition of the notes already assembled for the Welsh edition, and a newly-written introduction. The text of the tale here printed corresponds line-by-line with that of the Welsh edition, with the exception only that we have substituted English subtitles for those which we supplied previously in Welsh, and we have made a few minor corrections to the text. We hope that this English edition of *Culhwch ac Olwen* may reach a wider readership among students and scholars than has its predecessor.

Any study of *Culhwch ac Olwen* must remain profoundly indebted to the pioneer investigations of Sir Idris Foster, as these are to be found in his various published articles which we have listed in the bibliography, and in his unpublished MA dissertation 'Astudiaeth o Chwedl Culhwch ac Olwen' completed in 1935 and preserved in the Library of the University College of North Wales at Bangor and in the National Library of Wales. These works have deeply influenced generations of students in Wales, while others have spoken of their indebtedness to the ever-renewed zest and

perspicacity with which, year after year, Sir Idris unfolded his interpretation of the tale and its many problems to the students who
attended the seminars which he held regularly at Oxford. We have
followed Sir Idris's conclusions in associating the date of the tale in
what was perhaps its earliest written redaction, with the latter years
of the eleventh century, a time when certain historical events took
place in west Wales which seem to find their echo in the narrative.
We are also indebted to much of Sir Idris's discussion concerning
cognates in early Irish sources and in international folklore, though
we are as fully aware as he was that a number of enigmas in the tale
still remain for future scholars to unravel. In both the introduction
and the notes we have frequently referred to points of detail on which
Sir Idris had previously cast light. Yet the passing of the years has
inevitably seen changes of emphasis and major advances in the study
of both the language and the literature of medieval Wales and Ireland,
not least in regard to the study of the two great manuscripts in which
Culhwch ac Olwen is to be found. In the present work we have tried to
take account of all such developments more thoroughly than was
possible in our preparation of the earlier edition.

We are indebted to a number of friends who have given us assist-
ance of many kinds, and from whose observations we have profited.
In particular we are indebted to the members of the seminar held by
the Centre for Advanced Welsh and Celtic Studies at Aberystwyth
during the winter sessions of 1988–9, with whom we studied a part
of the tale. From this seminar we derived a number of valuable
insights, which we here acknowledge collectively rather than in-
dividually. We would also express our thanks to Dr Brynley
Roberts who read and commented upon a part of the introduction,
and to Dr Dafydd Huw Evans who gave invaluable help towards
the identification of certain places named in the account of Arthur's
great chase across south Wales in pursuit of the giant boar Twrch
Trwyth, and who provided us in addition with bibliographical
references relevant to the area of the hunt. Dr Evans and Mr Trevor
Harris kindly prepared the map located as the frontispiece to the
volume. Our thanks go to Ned Thomas and to Susan Jenkins of the
University of Wales Press, and to the printers for their care and
accuracy.

December – 1991   *Rachel Bromwich*
                                                       D. Simon Evans

Contents

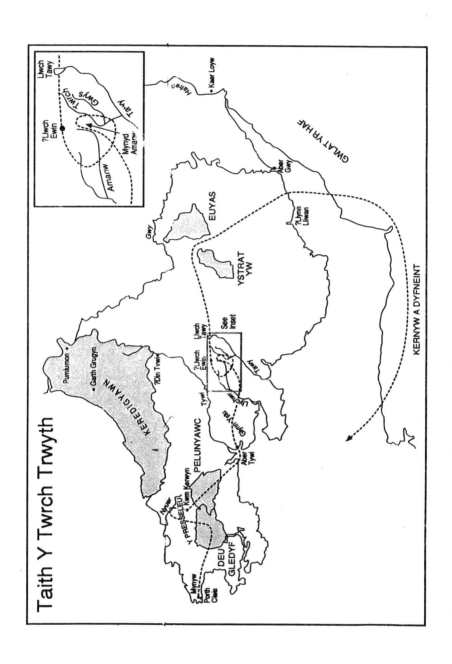

Taith Y Twrch Trwyth

Introduction

1. THE MANUSCRIPTS AND THE TEXT

Culhwch ac Olwen is preserved in two manuscripts, one of which belongs to the middle and the other to the end of the fourteenth century: the White Book of Rhydderch (P 4, cols.452–88), and the Red Book of Hergest (J 111, cols.810–44). The White Book (W, WM) is the earlier of the two, but unfortunately it contains only the first two thirds of the story, down to line 823 of the present edition. *The White Book Mabinogion* was printed and published by J. Gwenogvryn Evans (Pwllheli, 1907), and the text was republished in 1973 by the University of Wales Press, *Llyfr Gwyn Rhydderch: Y Chwedlau a'r Rhamantau*, with a new introduction by R. M. Jones. According to Mr Daniel Huws, Keeper of Manuscripts in the National Library of Wales, the P 4 section of the White Book is the work of several scribes working concurrently about the year 1350:[1] the text of *Culhwch* being in the same hand as that of *Chwedl Gereint fab Erbin*, which immediately precedes it in the manuscript. The Red Book of Hergest is a large compendium of medieval prose and verse, from which the tales and romances were edited by J. Rhŷs and J. G. Evans in *The Text of the Mabinogion and other Welsh tales from the Red Book of Hergest* (Oxford, 1887) (R, RM). The Red Book is the work of three professional scribes who worked in collaboration between 1382 and *c.*1410:[2] their work having been commissioned by an *uchelwr* or

[1] Daniel Huws, 'Llyfr Gwyn Rhydderch', CMCS 21 (Summer 1991, 1–37. See also the entry on the White Book of Rhydderch in *A Companion to the Literature of Wales*, ed. Meic Stephens (Oxford, 1986), 637, and CO(1) ix and n.2. For the make-up of the manuscript see B. F. Roberts, 'Dosbarthu'r Chwedlau Cymraeg Canol', YB xv (1988), 19–46. For earlier views see J. G. Evans's introduction to his edition, WM xii; and RWM i, 305; N. Denholm Young, *Handwriting in England and Wales* (Cardiff, 1954), 40.

[2] G. Charles-Edwards, 'Scribes of the Red Book of Hergest', *NLW Journal*, xxi (1980), 246–56; D. Huws, *NLW Journal*, xxii (1981), 1. Three later copies of *Culhwch* were made from the Red Book by Moses Williams in the early eighteenth century. These are contained in C 36, Ll

nobleman of Glamorgan named Hopcyn ap Thomas ab Einion
(*c.*1330–*post* 1403). There is some reason to associate the origin of
both these manuscripts with the abbey of Strata Florida,[3] though
there can be no absolute certainty on this point, and the evidence is
much stronger for the White Book than for the Red Book.

The main scribe of the Red Book was a certain Hywel Fychan,
whose hand has been identified in a number of other manuscripts. In
one of these he names himself as 'Hywel Fychan fab Hywel Goch o
Fuellt', and refers to his 'master' as 'Hopcyn ap Thomas ab Einion'
of Ynys Dawe.[4] Hywel Fychan inscribed the Red Book text of
Culhwch ac Olwen, and also that of *Gereint fab Erbin*, which
immediately precedes *Culhwch* in this manuscript, as it does also in
the White Book. (The potential significance of the juxtaposition of
these two tales will appear later in this introduction, in the section
on 'The Arthurian Court List'.) Not only did Hywel Fychan
inscribe both *Culhwch* and *Gereint*, but his hand has also been
conclusively identified in a brief passage in the WM text of *Culhwch*
(cols.467–8, ll.324–6 below), where the scribe had left a blank
space.[5] It is significant, therefore, to know that Hywel Fychan, the
scribe of the Red Book, at some point had access also to the White
Book.

But the few lines in WM which are in the hand of Hywel Fychan
fall far short of determining the relationship of WM and RM to each
other, more specifically as concerns the two texts of *Culhwch*. A
close comparison makes it impossible to maintain the view that the

90; and Ll 126 (RWM ii, 231, 562, 662). The earliest printed transcript is
that made from the Red Book by J. Jones (Tegid) and published in Lady
Charlotte Guest's *Mabinogion* in 1838–49.

[3] R. M. Jones, introduction to *Llyfr Gwyn Rhydderch*, xii–xiii; N.
Denholm Young, op.cit., 43.

[4] On Hywel Fychan see B. F. Roberts, 'Un o Lawysgrifau Hopcyn ap
Tomas o Ynys Dawy', B xxii (1968), 223–8; on Hopcyn ap Thomas see
further G. J. Williams, *Traddodiad Llenyddol Morgannwg* (Gwasg Prifysgol Cymru, 1948), 11–13; Prys Morgan, 'Glamorgan and the Red
Book', *Morgannwg* xxii (1978). 42–60.

[5] G. Charles-Edwards, 'White Book and Red Book', *NLW Journal*,
xxi (1980), 427–8; J. G. Evans, introduction to WM, viii; R. M. Jones,
Llyfr Gwyn Rhydderch, vi. However, it may be noted that although the
hand is that of Hywel Fychan, there are minor differences between the
wording of this and the corresponding passage in RM: *Gwastat/Gwestat*;
gellyngei/gollyngei; *yn bennguch/yn pennguch*.

RM text of the tale is a direct copy of that in WM: the only possible explanation of the undoubtedly close relationship between them is to conclude that both derive, with greater or less fidelity, from a common original, and possibly through one or more intermediaries.[6] The closeness of the two texts to each other is proved by their agreement in reproducing, on more than one occasion, mistakes which are common to both: the triple repetition of *merch* for *mab* in 341–2; of *rongomyant* for *rongomynyat* in 160, and of *gouynynat* for *gouynnyat* in 183; of *(b)aryf twrch* for *(b)aryf trwch* in 224; of *dissull* for *Dillus* in 700, and in the incorrect inversion of the relative in *yssyd yssit* in 504 (GMW 63, 142, cf. TC 281); and in the two glosses which both incorporate *gleif penntirec* 63, and *ae warthafleu sangnarwy* 79 (see notes). It will be seen from the *varia lecta* that in spite of minor variants in the forms of the names in the Arthurian Court List[7] (175–373), these names are preserved in identical order, and that there are very few instances in which either manuscript omits a name present in the other.

On the other hand both W and R preserve individual items— some of them highly significant—which are absent from the other text. In 149 each has incorporated a different word as a gloss on *gwrthrychyad*: W has *edling* where R has *teyrn*. In 632–3 W makes an addition to the list of the *anoethau* which is not found in R— *adar Rianhon y rei a duhun y marw ac a huna y byw a vynhaf*. In 436 R adds the telling words *vym brawt* to the name of Ysbaddaden Penkawr, in the passage in which Custennin is accounting for his dispossession from his land. But it is W alone which asserts Ysbaddaden's dominance over Arthur with the significant if ambiguous words, *dan uy llaw i y mae ef* (733) and W alone introduces Arthur's greeting to Culhwch with the solemn and legally-binding asseveration *Poet gwir Dyw, unben* 147, and in 807–8 W emphasizes the feat of Arthur's men in breaking into Wrnach's fortress with the added words *mal nat oed vwy no dim ganthunt*.

It is, however, far more usual to find R expanding the text by the

---

[6] See the discussion by R. M. Jones, introduction to *Llyfr Gwyn Rhydderch*, vi–xii, and cf. J. Vendryes, RC xlviii, 411; J. Loth, *Les Mabinogion* (Paris, 1913), i, 22–6. Ifor Williams was more guarded, PKM xi–xii; and some uncertainty was expressed in 1961 with respect to the texts of the Triads in W and R, TYP xxv–vi.

[7] The variants between the forms of the names in the Court List are listed in CO(1) xvi. See the *varia lecta*.

addition of words, phrases, and even whole sentences: *yn y ueiscawn 322*; *dim y wrth 375*; *Ar eildyd ar trydyd dyd y kerdassant ac o vreid y doethant hyt yno 415*; *llawer dyd yth rygereis 501*; *onyt dy uarw a uynny 546*; *ac onys rody ti a geffy dy angheu ymdeni 561*; *ac or gwenith hwnnw y mynnaf i gwneuthur bwyt a llyn tymeredic yth neithawr di ti am merch i 575*; *oll or anoethau . . . yn ueu itt 757–8*; *geyr bron gwrnach 788*; *ti a orugost hynn 810*. In 376–7 R allots to Culhwch himself the words which restrict to a year the period allowed to Arthur for finding Olwen, and expands the passage: *Y mab a dywawt rodaf yn llawen or nos heno hyt y llall ympenn y vlwydyn. Ac yna y gyrrwys arthur y kennadeu y bop tir yn y deruyn y geissaw y uorwyn honno, ac ympenn y vlwydyn y doeth kennadeu arthur drachevyn heb gaffel na chwedyl na chyuarwydyt y wrth olwen mwy nor dyd kyntaf.*

There are many differences between W and R in respect of individual words. Sometimes these can be accounted for as deliberate modernizations on the part of R, as appears in the consistent substitution of W's archaic *amkawd*, *amkeudant*, either by *y dywat*, *y dywawt*, *y dywedassant*, or (less frequently) by *heb y*. On p. xvi below we have drawn attention to R's modernizations of the more archaic prepositional and verbal forms employed by W. In the following instances R substitutes the more usual MW words for those given in W (those in W are here given first) *kwt ynt . . . am rydyallas/ble mae . . . am llathrudawd 37*; *ac ystrodur/a chyfrwy 62*; *kerth/kylch 96*; *rac dy deulin/rac dy vronn 98*; *didawl/didlawt 145*; *ath cret/ath glot 147*; *vyneb/agclot 154*; *hyt yr etil/y treigyl 158*; *yscwyt/ taryan 161*; *seith vrhyt/seith cuppyt 348*; *or/ol 416*; *douot/bud 446*; *pan at pawb eu damsathyr/pan aeth pawb allan y chware 468*; *y gam/y drwc 471*; *y falueu/y dwylaw 492*; *meglyt/ymauael 521*; *deu yskyuarn/deu glust 669*; *kyfret/kyn ebrwydet 689*; *ar mil/ar lwdyn 729*. Occasionally R gives mistaken equivalents: *ac ays/a chroes 67*; *lloring/llugorn 68* (see n. to l. 68).

In other instances there are word-changes for which there is little apparent reason, as they can hardly be called modernizations: *mwyhaf/teckaf 413*; *kymryt/kyuurd 127*; *kymryt/kyfret 395*; *gwynnach/ tegach 491*; *amrant/ael 518*; *kyfret/kyn ebrwydet 689*; *gallel/gwybot 782*; *gallel/y gwdost 789*; *na hanbwyllei/yny debycko 745*. R's surprising substitution of *ynys y kedyrn* for *ynys Prydein* in 368 can perhaps be accounted for by the scribe's familiarity with the text of *Mabinogi Branwen*, found in the same two manuscripts as those which contain *Culhwch*. R's tendency to update the language appears in a preference for 3rd. sing. forms in -*awd* over those in -*wys* (GMW 125, for exx. see p. xxi below), and in pres. subjunctives in -*o*, -*ont* over those in -*wy*, -*wynt* (GMW 128–9), as in *am crettwy/am cretto* 484; *mal na bwynt/mal na bont* 110; and in pres. indic. impers. in -*er*, -*ir* over those in -*(h)awr* (with future meaning): *pan agorawr/ pan agorer* 98; *nyn lladawr/nyn lledir* 475; *nyn hyscarhawr/nyt yscarwn* 383. The perfective prt. *ry*- tends to be superseded by finite forms in R: *rydyallas /llathrudawd* 37; *ry syrthwys/a syrthwys* 548. The two texts frequently employ variant forms of the verbs *gwneuthur* and *dyuot* (GMW 130, 133), substituting *gwnaeth/goruc; dyuu/doeth* etc. There are differences in copula-formations,[8] in which W's forms are markedly the more archaic. Frequently both manuscripts omit to lenite initial consonants, but this tendency is even more pronounced in R than in W: *teulu Gleis/cleis* 123; *y gar gysseuin/ kysseuin* 694; *oed well/gwell* 795; *yn bennguch/yn pennguch* 326.

Taken together, all these minor variations between the two texts are indicative of an accepted mode of copying in which to paraphrase was as acceptable, and far more usual, than to reproduce the original word-for-word. The frequent (and often insignificant) substitution of words and phrases for those in the text being copied enforces the conclusion that medieval scribes frequently wrote from dictation rather than from direct visual contact. This would account for R's many departures from W, if we are to conclude that both were following the same archetype with varying degrees of fidelity. But there are occasional indications that the scribes of W may also have worked in this way (see n. to *ti a merch* 574–5 and to 772–3 below).

We have followed the text of W until it ends at line 823, noting R's variants at the foot of the page. R continues from 823 until the end of the tale.

---

[8] See A. Watkins and P. Mac Cana, 'Cystrawennau'r Cyplad mewn Hen Gymraeg', B xviii (1960), 1–25.

II. ORTHOGRAPHY AND LANGUAGE

Some general features of the orthography and language of the text are described here. Features which are unusual or distinctive are referred to in the Notes and Glossary.

ORTHOGRAPHY

We find here in general the characteristics which belong to the White Book of Rhydderch (*c.* 1350) and to the Red Book of Hergest (*c.* 1400). The letters *u*, *v*, (less often *f*) occur for [*v*] at the beginning and in the middle of a word: *verch*, *uynnei*, *ouyn*; but at the end of a word we invariably find *f*: *ef*, *uydaf*, *sef* (*arnaw*=arnaf in 558 is an exception). *ff* [ɸ] is denoted by *f* and *ff*, *f* usually at the beginning of a word: *frwyn*, *ford*, *a ffan*, *porfor*, *caffel*, *Affric*. For [ŋ(*h*)] both *ng(h)* and *g(h)* are found: *ng(h)*: *angerd*, *anghen*, *angheu*, *anghleuach*, *anglot*, *kynghor*, *dangosset*, *deng milltir a deugeint* 348 (cf. *dec aradyr ar ugeint* 319), *dienghis*, *di(h)engis*, *dihengy*, *Dygyflwng*, *edling*, *enghi*, *engyl*, *eingon*, *ellwng*, *ellwngwyt*, *ellynghaf*, *gauylgygwng*, *gellwng*, *gellyngei*, *llong*, *lloring*, *llwng*, *ongyl*, *ranghei*, *Penpingyon*, *(y) rwng*, *sangharwy*, *tangneued(u)*, *yng Kelli Wic*, *yng Kernyw*, *yghongyl*, *ymgynghori*; *g(h)*: *aghengaeth*, *agheu*, *aghred*, *kyfrwg*, *kyuyg*, *kyghor*, *eglyn*, *ellygwr*, *estwg*, *uyg gwreic*, *uyghyuarws*, *uygkyueillt*, *Mygdwn*, *rwg*, *tyghaf*, *tyghet*, *tygwys*, *y gyt a*, *yg Kaer Loyw*, *yg carchar*, *yg Kelli Wic*, *yg Kernyw*, *yg kyuenw*, *yg gordwy*, *yg gwaelawt Dinsol*, *yg gwrthtir*, *yg gwrys*, *yg gwyllt*, *ygder*, *yGhaer Brythwch*, *yGhaer Neuenhyr*, *yGhaer Oeth*, *yGhaer Se*, *yGhamlan*, *yGherniw*, *ygwylldawc*.

t and *c* occur for *-d* and *-g*: *kymryt*, *mynet*, *gwlat*, *gwledic*, *gwreic*, *ygwylldawc*; *b* is usually found for *-b* as in *achub*, *atteb*, *kib*, *heb*, *hob*, *hub*, *mab*, *neb*, *pawb*, *pob*, *wyneb*; instances of *p* are rare: *crip*, *o bop tu*. *d* occurs for [ð] in all positions: *Kilyd*, *etiued*, *gwedi*. There is, however, evidence of orthographic features which are different, and which are earlier. *t* occurs for [ð]: *keyryt*, *defnyt*, *cwt*, *dyt*, *egweti*, *Goleudyt*, *gorsetua*, *gwarthegyt*, *gweti*, *itaw*, *iti*, *utunt*, *Ieithoet*, *llemidit*, *nawt*, *oet*, *roti*, *trydydyt*, *trydyt*, *yssyt*; and *d* for [d]: *aghred*, *berwid*, *bid*, *bod*, *bwyd*, *cennad*, *cleuydawd*, *cred*, *kyd*, *diwarnawd*, *ducpwyd*, *dyuod*, *dywawd*, *dywedud*, *gorucpwyd*, *gwlad*, *hacred*, *hyd*, *llysuwyd*, *meichad*, *nod, nyd, offeirad, pechawd, y gyd, ysgafned.* This reminds us of the practice in some earlier manuscripts, in particular the Black Book of Carmarthen. It is worth noting that *t* for [d] and *d* for [d] is found in the first part of *Culhwch*. The last instance of this occurs in 575 (*dyt* 'day') in a description of the first of the *anoethau*. This is doubtless a fact of some significance, although it is not now easy to determine the precise nature of this significance. It may be noted also that *t* for [d] and *d* for [d] is not evidenced in R, except in two instances: *methawd* 108, and *ymchoelawd* 109. Certain other features in the orthography of *Culhwch* are paralleled in the Black Book of Carmarthen: *w* alternates with *f* (*yscawin* (=*ysgafn*) LlDC 25,5; *kewin* (=*cefn*) ibid. 13,9); in *Culhwch h* is found for *ch* in some instances: *kyuerheis* (=*kyuercheis*) 146, *ymhoelwch* 178, *ymhoylwn* 479 (see p. xix below). In 459 we find *oheni* (=*ohonei*) as in LlDC 12,82; 17,38 (also *imdeni* (=*amdanei*) ibid. 12,50). See further LlC, 14 (1983–4), 210–15.

Consonantal *i* is generally not denoted in MW prose, or—for that matter—in the spoken language of south Wales today. But it does occur in *Culhwch*, denoted by *y*; *brychyon*. There are, however, examples where it is missing, especially in a final syllable: *anniueileit, anreitheu, arwydon, beichawc, bydydaw, keibedic, keissaw* (also *keisswch, keisswys*), *kydymdeithon, kyfreitheu, kytbreinhawc, datrithaw, deiuaw, dispeilaw, diffeithaw, Edeinawc, eillaw, eillwyt, eingon, einon, eiroet, eisseu, golwython, gweisson, gweitheu, gwichaw, gwreichon, meibon, meichad, meillonen, neithawr, neithawrwyr, peinawc, rithwys, syrthwys, treissaw, treulaw, troedawc, weithon, wyron, ymdiredaf, ymeneinaw, ymrithaw.* Cf. GMW 6.

LANGUAGE

In the part of the tale found in the White Book there are sections in which the language is markedly more archaic than in others: at the beginning, in the story of the Jealous Stepmother, in the description of Culhwch on his way to Arthur's court, in the account of Culhwch's dialogue with Glewlwyd Gafaelfawr, in the meeting with Custennin and his wife, in the description of Olwen, in the confrontation between Arthur's men and Ysbaddaden, in the quest for Wrnach's sword. There are a number of significant correspondences betwen the language of *Culhwch* and that of the

Cynfeirdd and the early Gogynfeirdd. In particular there are in *Culhwch*, as in the Black Book of Carmarthen, examples of *cw(d)* (*kwt* 29, 37, 515): LlDC *cv(d)* 29,26; 29,30, *pyr* occurs for 'why?' in 83 and 771 (for the latter R has *py rac*): both forms occur in LlDC (16,31; 16,42). There is one ex. of *ty* as a form of the prep. *y* 'to' (LlDC 8,13), cf. *dy* in *Culhwch* l.10. As in *Culhwch* (470, 490–1, 496 etc.) *ys* 'is' and *oed* 'was' occur at the beginning of a sentence before a nominal predicate (LlDC 10,11; 31,68) and in the construction of the Mixed Order: *Oed Maelgwn a uelun in imuan* (1,5). In LlDC, as in *Culhwch* (see p. xiii above) there seem to be cases where the scribe was copying from what he heard rather than from what he saw: *othdiwod* (*o'th ddyfod*) 35,17, *ys truc* (*ys drwg*), 17,23. There are also some striking correspondences in vocabulary between *Culhwch* and the Black Book. The following words occur in both, and are only exceptionally found in other texts: *amsathir, anoeth, asswynaw, cafall, cyssevin* (as adv.), *diwlith, fion, goruit, gordwy, goryscalawc, gwallaw, gurthtir, retkyr, teithiawc, ymda.*

The Llywarch Hen and Heledd cycles also offer some striking parallels to *Culhwch*. Note especially Arthur's words to Culhwch: *Mae uyg kallon yn tirioni vrthyt. Mi a wn dy hanuot o'm gwaet,* which recall Llywarch's words to his estranged son Gwen, *Neut atwen ar vy awen/Yn hanuot o un achen,* CLlH i,2. The twenty-four sons of Custennin Heusawr are reminiscent of the twenty-four sons of Llywarch Hen: Goreu, like Gwen ap Llywarch, is the sole survivor of the twenty-four. Comparisons can also profitably be made with Old Welsh texts and with the Laws of Hywel Dda.

The language of W is noticeably more archaic than that of R. Differences in vocabulary, such as R's invariable substitution of *dywat, dywawd, heb* for W's *amkawd* have already been noted (p. xii above). The following examples illustrate the more important differences in prepositional and verbal forms: W *gorucpwyt*/R *gwnaethpwyt* 10, 12, etc.; W *amkawd*/R *dywat, dywawt,* 16, 43, 49 etc., *heb* 29, 38, etc.; W *amkeudant*/R *dywedassant* 430, 809; W *racdu*/R *racdunt* 513; W *onadunt*/R *o honunt* 510; W *ry*/R *a* 25, 55, 379, 548; W *ganthu*/R *gantunt* 32; W *ar*/R *at* 39, 58, 246, 444; W *dothyw*/R *deuth* 99; W *dothwyf*/R *deuthum* 152; W *dyuu*/R *doeth* 114, 139; W *dyuuost*/R *doethost* 129; W *tynhet*/R *tynnit* 303; W *hyd uydei*/R *y bydei* 386; W *yt uei*/R *y bydei* 390; W *dodywch*/R *doethawch* 477; W *dodym*/R *doetham* 477; W *crettwy*/R *cretto* 484; W *dyccwy*/R *dycko* 768, 774; W *ymdewch*/R *doethawch*

515; W *ymdawn* /R *doetham* 515; W *myn yd*/R *lle yd* 563; W *pyr*/R *py rac* 771.

There are in *Culhwch* words, forms, and constructions which appear to be generally limited to the kinds of works mentioned above, (namely the early poetry, Old Welsh texts, and the Laws). First, words which are found also in the works of the Cynfeirdd and the Gogynfeirdd (references and meanings are given in the Glossary); *affwys, aghengaeth, amsathyr* (LlDC 16,37; H 127,6, also WM 133,2–3), *anoeth* (not found in prose, but cf. *Anoeth byd brawt bwyn kynnull* CLlH v,28; *Anoeth bit bed y Arthur* LlDC 18,135; also compare *anoethach* in Prydydd y Moch; *Anoethach powys ae thir amddyfrwys*, (H 279,11); *ardwyat, asswynaw* (cf LlDC 123, G 45), *ays* (*aessaur* LlDC 34,11; 34,32), *kat* (cf LlDC 127), *cafall* (cf. GPC 387 and see nn. to 336–7, 1015); *cleheren, cw* (LlDC 131), *kytbrein(h)awc* (used by Gwynfardd Brycheiniog in his *awdl* to Saint David, H 198,23–4; see n. to ll.593–4); *kyfret* (BT 26–7; *kyfret a gwylan*, H 130,11), *kyndynnyawc, chwechach, diotta, distrych, diwlith* (LlDC 30,35 *dit diulith*); *dygredu* (CLlH ii,19 *Ny'm dygred na hun na'e ohen*), *ertrei, gordwy* (LlDC 22,14), *gorwyd* (cf. LlDC 16,71; 30,26; 30,69; G 578), *goryscalawc* (cf. LlDC 36,23 *ath uit guin gorysgelho*), *gowan, gwrthwan* (used once by Cynddelw H 135, 17), *hu* (LlDC 34,17), *par* (CLlH i,3a *llym vympar*; LlDC 30,38), *recdouyt* (found in poetry, but without -d-, H 10,14; 33,13; 127,i; 217,19; also LL127,20 *rec douid*; see nn. to ll.17,176, and cf. Loth, RC ix, 274–6, J. Lloyd-Jones, B xv, 198–200; also CO(1) xxiii–xxiii), *retkyr* (LlDC 17,2 *Na chlat dy redcir ym pen minit*), *tardu* (cf. AP l.25 and n.), *ymda* (cf. LlDC 29,29; 31,5). Words found in OW: *kythrymhet* (*cithremmet gl.bilance libra* GPC 827); in the Laws: *amwabyr, knithyaw, corfflan, edling* (see n. to 149), *enghi, grwmseit* (cf. D. Jenkins, B xxxv, 55–61), *gwallocau, mut.*

Next, words in *Culhwch* which are found both in poetry and in the Laws; *adoet* (also in SDR 118, etc.), *amws, buelin, kysseuin* (LlDC 18,128; 18,131; cf. G 137), *erhyl, gordwy* (rare in prose, but found in poetry (LlDC 22,14)): it is said of Gruffudd ap Cynan (the grandson) *bu gordwy ar allmyr*, H 299,26); *gwallaw* (LlDC 23,25); *gwest* (see n. to 3); *gwrthtir* (LlDC 17,17; 18,104; 104,177); *teithiawc* (CA 1095 *mab brenhin teithiawc*, LlDC 34,56 *mab goholeth teithiauc*; see n. to l.91). Words found in poetry and also in OW: *cusul* (cf. LlDC 131), *deon* (cf. G 312); *dryssien, fion* (LlDC 16,74; 16,81); *pressen(t)* (common in religious poetry, LlDC 7,22; 20,6; HGC 292, also CLlH 136).

There are a number of words in *Culhwch* which do not occur

elsewhere: *aeruawc, alafon, amkawd* (cf. however *amgyhud* ClIH i, 1), *amdiuwynwys, anllawd, kymibiawc, damsathyr, darware, defnyt* (in the sense of 'substance (to be), future', cf. Ir. *damnae*, and n. to l.518), *diednedic, dygrynnyaw, eirychu, gal pen, goranhed, gordibla, lloring, malkawn* (missing in R), *pebreit*. And there are words not attested anywhere else in MW, but which are to be found in some later sources: *anghleuach, arswydwys, bwyellic, bwyttal* (see n. to l.1065), *camse, carngragen, cleicaw, cnwch, cuan, cyllagwst, kymrwt, dafates, dygaboli, dyskymon, foc, frawdunyaw, godrwyth, gwchi, llysuwyd*.

The significance of these words can be variously interpreted, but in general they suggest close affinity with the Cynfeirdd, and (especially) with the Gogynfeirdd, with OW material, and with the Laws—rather than with later prose works. Other aspects of the language here, such as the occurrence of rare old forms, serve to prove that the text is early. Furthermore, we must take account of other features in it which are reminiscent of more modern times, features which still appear in the spoken language of areas of south Wales, and which are indicative of the geographical background of the tale in its present form. It is sufficient to say that dialect forms are often (indeed, usually) more resistant to change than literary, standard forms. These forms are modern, but they are also old, unaffected by the flow of time. It would be wrong to define the area of country where they occur with any firm precision, but in general the evidence seems to point more especially to parts of the South, to old Carmarthenshire and Glamorgan: that is, to some of the very areas through which the Twrch Trwyth passed on his journey through south Wales.

One can then cite certain words in *Culhwch* which still occur in these areas, although our present knowledge does not warrant limiting their use to these areas alone: *cleheren* 'gadfly' is still heard in parts of the South, as is *cludweir* 'wood-pile' in the form *clidwer, cledwer*, fem. (north Carmarthenshire); *golwc* is still used with the meaning 'eye, eyesight'. According to T. J. Morgan (TC 25; LlC ii, 189) *gwaelawt ty* (143) lies behind *glowty*, still used for 'cow-shed' in Pembrokeshire and parts of Glamorgan. In Carmarthenshire we hear *lluchet* (68) in the form *llyched* for 'lightning', and *lludu* (572) for 'ashes'; *llwdwn* (420) is quite common for 'animal, beast'. In B x (1940), 131 the late Henry Lewis noted that the word *ragot* (1174) 'waylay' was still used in the form *rhagod* and *rhacod* in Brynaman and Gwynfe, on both sides of the Black Mountain (where it has the

meaning 'stop, prevent'), and it is used also as a noun; *rachot* occurs
as a noun in the Privilege of Teilo in LL 120,15, and *ragot* is found as
a verbal noun in BD 174,8. The derivative *ragotvaeu* (pl. of *ragotva*) is
found in HGVK 22,20 (see n. ibid. 90). It is also instructive to look
at some forms and formations which likewise reflect dialectal
features in approximately the same areas. Notice how the vowel,
usually *a*, *e*, or *i* has become unclear in some forms, and is
represented by *y*. In some (though not in all) cases it has been
influenced by the following vowel; in others it occurs in an
unaccented syllable; *bydydyaw*, *klyuychu* (*cleuychu* R), *cryuangheu*,
kydenawc, *kyffy*, *dyallu* (*dyall* is still heard for *deall*), *hyly*, *llywenyd*,
trychan, *trychanherw*, *trychanllong*, *trychantref*, *trywyr*, *tybygu*, *ydrych*,
ymgyffret, *yskynuaen*, *ywythred* (*ewythred* R).

Note also some other tendencies and variations: *dala*, *hela*, cf.
GMW 10. In MW the epenthetic vowel, which developed in certain
groups of consonants, is usually represented by *y*; cf. ibid. 12–13. In
spoken ModW for the most part it developed into a full vowel. In
Culhwch we have such a form: *araf* 'weapon' (226), *baraf* 'beard' (327,
966), but apart from these forms the vowel is regularly *y*, e.g.
amsathyr, *amwabyr*, *anadyl*, *aradyr*, *banadyl*, *baryf*, *kenetyl*, *congyl*,
kyn(n)edyf, *damsathyr*, *dogyn*, *eithyr*, *ewythyr*, *gauylgygwng*, *gweuyl*,
gwychyr, *gwystyl*, *hagyr*, *hoedyl*, *mynwgyl*, *ongyl*, *paladyr*, *pedestyr*,
racllauyn, *seithlydyn moch*, *treigyl*.

There are some other phonetic features, evidenced also in the
spoken language of these parts of Wales. *(h)w*, *wh*, *h* occur for the
standard literary *chw-*, *-ch(w)-*, (GMW 11): *a wennych rei* 662
(=*chwennych*, possibly a lenited form of the alternative *gwennych*,
cf. *chware/gware*, and note *darware* 73), *whedleu* 784 (=*chwedleu*),
kychwhynnei 349 (=*kychwynnei*), *ymhoelawd* 109 (=*ymchoelawd*),
ymhoelwch 478, *ymhoylwn* 479 (= *ymchoelwn/ymchoelwch*) *kyuerheis*
146 (=*kyuercheis*). Forms with *h* are still used in north
Carmarthenshire, but with *-h-* occasionally dropped. *Moelid* means
'to upset, turn over', and is the verb used in some parts for 'to
plough, turn over the soil'.

In MW *f*[*v*] may have been more of a labial than in ModW, where
it is a labio-dental; consequently we find it alternating with *w*,
GMW 9. Forms with *-w-* still predominate in south Wales, and in
Culhwch also we find such forms: *ysgawn*, 'light' 1041 for *ysgafn*,
equat. *ysgawnhet* 80, with which may be compared *ysgawn/ysgon* in
the spoken language; also Scilti *Yscawntroet* 239.

wy alternates with *oe* in MW, *wyth*/*oeth*, 'eight', GMW 4. Along with *eissoes* we have in MW *eisswys*, 415, a form still surviving in the south Wales dialect as *ishws*. This latter form exemplifies another tendency, *wy>w*, of which there is evidence in the spoken language of these parts. Here we can further mention the form *trw* (<*trwy*) 'through' in *Culhwch* 27, which is also found in the spoken language. But this can with equal probability be explained as resulting from an incorrect division of words, as they were heard by the scribe: *trwy yt* being heard as *trw yt*. Note also *vt* 170 = *wyt* R.

The form *oheni* (3rd. sing. fem. of *o*), another dialect form, occurs here: 459 (twice), 470, 767, 817; but in all five instances R has *ohonei*. Also *deni* 1213 W and R.

The *a* in *diwarnawt* 'day' 385 can still be heard in some parts, cf. also PKM 78,3.

In 729 we have the form *ellwngwyt*, where one would expect *ellyngwyt* with vowel mutation of *w*. But non-mutation of *w* is a feature of the spoken language of these parts: *dwrn* 'fist', pl. *dyrnau*, but colloquially in some parts *dwrne*, also *pwnn* 'a load', pl. *pwnne*. Another dialect feature may be the adjectival use of *pwy* 44, 89, 772, where we have *pa*, *py* in R.

Next, some other features may be noted which distinguish *Culhwch* from other prose texts, showing closer affinity with early works, as we have already suggested. First, we may mention the expression *anghen yn anghen*, 'by sheer force' 1176, used also by Prydydd y Moch (*c.*1173–1220) in his poem to Rhys Gryg: *Anghen yn anghen yn angheu oth gaf* (H 287,3). Furthermore, there are some early forms and formations which serve to underline the unique nature of the language of *Culhwch* in comparison with later prose works:

dy, 'to' and 'from'. *dy*/*di* occurs regularly in OW, e.g. *nit egid di a*, 'it goes not to a' in the Computus fragment (B iii, 256), also in the Cynfeirdd; Taliesin in Trawsganu Cynan Garwyn: keith ynt *dy* gynan, 'They are captive to Cynan', PT i,25. In the Welsh of the Book of Llan Dav both *dy* and *y* occur: *di uinid* and *i uinid*, 'up' (lit. 'to a mountain'), but in the later prose texts *di* is not found. In *Culhwch* it occurs once, in 12: keuynderw *dy* Arthur oed, 'a cousin to Arthur was he' (=*y* R). We find also one ⸞x. of *dy* 'from', *dy* wrth y gaffel yn retkyr hwch, 'from his having been found in a pig-run', 10. It also occurs in the Book of Llan Dav: *di* ar ir allt—but is not found in later texts. Cf. B xiii (1950), 1–5; GMW 199–201.

The 3 pl. ending of the prep. is commonly -*unt*, as in other prose works, but there are three exx. of -*u*; *ganthu, ohonu, racdu*. The ending -*udd* [*u*] does not occur, as it does in Hendregadredd: *arnadut (ar), kyfryngthut (kyfrwng), ganthut (gan), racdut (rac), trostut (tros), utut (y* 'to'), *ymdanadut (am).* Cf. GMW 58–60.

Some archaic verbal forms are attested, forms which are lacking in other prose texts. The old independent ending -(*h*)*awd* (3rd. pres. sing. with future meaning) is found in forms such as *bydhawt, methawd, ymhoelawd.* It occurs in the Black Book and in the Gogynfeirdd; *cosbawd, kymerawd, gunahaud, gyrhawt, reddaud,* cf. GMW 119. Also the impers. pass. ending -(*h*)*awr* with future meaning; *agorawr (agerer* R), *lladawr (lledir* R), *ysgarhawr (yscarwn* R). Such forms are not infrequently found among the Cynfeirdd and Gogynfeirdd–Aneirin: *dygiawr, gattawr, purawr;* Taliesin: *argollawr, barnawr, llycrawr, tarnawr;* Llywarch Hen: *lladawr;* LlDC 7,27 *talhaur, guarwyaur* 16,10 etc; Hendregadredd: *canawr, edmycawr, gwasgarawr,* etc. (many other exx.). Cf. GMW 121.

In twenty-seven verbs -*wys* is employed as the ending of the 3rd. pret. sing.: *amdiuwynwys, anwaydwys, arswydwys, asswynwys, keisswys, kychwynnwys, kynnullwys, kyscwys, digribywys, dygwydwys, dygyrchwys, esgynnwys, gallwys, gouynnwys, gweryskynnwys, gyrrwys, llygrwys, mynnwys, olrewys, plygwys, rithwys, syrthwys, tyuwys, tygvys, tynnwys, ymyrrwys, yscarwys.* -*awd* occurs in six verbs: *gochelawd, lladawd, tardawd, ymauaelawd, ymladawd, ymordiwedawd.* With the latter cf. *go(r)diwawd* PKM 32,21; 91,6, and see GMW 125. In PKM there are over fifty instances of -*wys*, and eighteen of -*awd*. In four verbs both are used: *kerdwys* 6,15/*kerdaud* 6,25; *kyrchwys* 4,7/*kyrchawd* 43,14; *mynnwys* 27,11/*mynnawd* 27,24; *tygywys* 11,2/*tygyawd* 20,28. In PKM -*awd* seems to be beginning to encroach on -*wys*, whereas in *Culhwch* they are kept severely apart, although R substitutes -*awd* for -*wys* in *mynnawd* 2, *trigyawd, tyuawd* 248.

The use of certain particles is of interest and significance:

ry. There are fifteen instances of *ry* used before a verb, but only four in the Red Book text. In the *Gododdin* there are twenty, ten in the poetry of Taliesin, twenty-one in Hendregadredd. There are ten in the White Book text of PKM, and seven in that of the Red Book; two instances occur in the Book of Blegywryd, and thirty-seven in the Book of Iorwerth. In BD there are twenty-seven, and twenty-six in *Gwyrthyeu y Wynwydedic Veir* (*c.*1250; B ix (1939), 334–41); *ar* (*a* + *ry*) occurs once in *Culhwch* and once in Hendregadredd, but instances abound in later texts such as *Peredur* and BD. *neur* (*neu* + *ry*) occurs only once, and once also in the poetry of Taliesin, but six times in ClIH, four times in Hendregadredd, and three times in PKM. Cf. GMW 166-8.

The use of *ry-* with a verbal noun must have been a new development in Welsh (it is not attested in Irish). It does not occur in the Cynfeirdd, but there are seven exx. in Hendregadredd. In the early prose texts instances are rare: two in the Book of Blegywryd, sixteen in the Book of Iorwerth, eight in *Peredur*, one in *Owein*, and two in *Gereint fab Erbin*. In the text of *Gwyrthyeu y Wynvydedic Veir* we have eleven exx., and eighty-four in BD. Not one occurs in *Culhwch*.

yr is a variant of *ry*. It occurs once in the *Gododdin* (Gwarchan Kynvelyn), six times in Hendregadredd, four times in PKM, once in the Book of Iorwerth and once in *Gereint fab Erbin*, but sixty-three times in BD. Not once does it occur in *Culhwch*. Cf. GMW 169.

neu(t) (=Ir. *no*.) This affirmative particle occurs quite often in the works of the Cynfeirdd, and there are 145 instances in Hendregadredd; two are found in the Book of Iorwerth, one in the Book of Blegywryd, three in BD, six in PKM. In *Culhwch* we find one: *A minneu neut ydynt yn gynyon boneu vy esgyll* 878, 'And as for me, the roots of my wings are (mere) stumps'. On *neur* (*neu* + *ry*) see above under *ry*. Cf. further GMW 169-70.

yt. This affirmative particle disappeared quite early. It occurs before a consonant, and is followed by lenition. There are seven instances in *Culhwch*; *trw yt gaffei wteicca* 27, *ohonot ti yt gaffo* 41, *rwy yt werthey Arthur* 381, *dyrnued uch y law ... yt uyd yn sych* 389, *y foc yt uerwit yndi* 541, *yt uerwid* 556, *bei oll yt uei val hynn* 795. It is found quite commonly in the Cynfeirdd, and also in OW, for example in the Privilege of Teilo: *y pop mynnic yt uoy* LL 120. In the *Gododdin* there are twenty-two instances, twelve in the poetry of Taliesin, fourteen in ClIH, eighty-four in Hendregadredd. There appears to be only one ex. in prose, in the Book of Blegywryd: *am y deu ymwystlaw hynny yt uyd y dosbarth ar awdurdaut llythyrawl*, 'it is concerning these two giving of pledges that there will be settlement by written authority' 18,18-19. Cf. GMW 171-2.

cwt, *cw(d)* 'where ?', also 'whence?', 'whither?'. It occurs in early

MW, in the Black Book and in the Book of Taliesin; there are six exx. in Hendregadredd. In *Culhwch* we find three, as follows: mynet a oruc y brenhin yg kyghor *kwt* gaffei wreic 28–9, *kwt* ynt plant y gwr a'm rydyallas yg gordwy 37; neu chwitheu *kwt* ymdewch 515. It does not occur in later prose texts. Cf. GMW 79. Note R pa le y 29, ble 37, pan 515.

<h2 style="text-align:center">SYNTAX</h2>

There are two basic features of syntax in Welsh which merit attention here, and which may be described under the following heads: the copula and nominal predicate, and the verbal noun.

Arwyn Watkins and Proinsias Mac Cana dealt with the constructions of the copula in B xviii (1960), 1–25, and outlined two main types of sentence in OW, namely 'A' consisting of copula + predicate + subject: *is discirr micoueidid* 'mean is my company', and 'B' predicate + copula + subject; *enuein di Sibellae int hinn* 'these are the names of Sibellae'. 'A' is the more common order in OW, but it was in time superseded by 'B'. In the *Gododdin* there are fifty-three instances of 'A' and twenty of 'B', in CLlH there are ninety-eight of 'A' and twenty of 'B'. In *Culhwch* there are sixteen instances of 'A' and eighty-three of 'B', in PKM five of 'A' and 172 of 'B': so that in *Culhwch* the balance has changed, but not to anything like the same extent as in PKM. It is more in keeping with the practice in early poetry, although it differs from this quite considerably.

Note the use of *ys* and *oed*, especially at the beginning of a sentence before a nominal predicate. Both occur in this position in the early poetry: exx. in the Black Book *ys bud bartoni* LlDC 10,11, *oet* trum y dial 31,68, and (in the mixed order, GMW 146) *Oed* Maelgun a uelun in imuan 1,5. In Hendregadredd there are upwards of sixty exx. of *ys* thus employed, and 120 of *oed*. Later their use in that position becomes more rare. Of *ys* there is one ex. in the Book of Iorwerth, two in PKM, one in *Peredur*, one in *Owein*, four in *Gereint fab Erbin*, one in BD; of *oed* there is one in PKM, four in *Owein*. In *Culhwch* we have three exx. of *ys*: *Ys* dyhed a beth gadu dan wynt a glaw y kyfryw dyn 132–3, 'It is a shameful thing to leave in wind and rain such a man'; *Ys* gohilion hwnn 472, 'He is all that is left'; *Ys* hwy yr rei hynny 598, 'Those are they'; eight exx. of *oed*: *Oed* dyhed kelu y ryw was hwnn 470, 'It were a pity to hide such a lad as this'; and in the sequence of sentences 490–6 (see n. to ll.487–98) *oed melynach y fenn* ... 'Yellower was her hair ...'(R *melynach oed*, etc.); *oed gwynnach y chnawd* ... 'Whiter was her skin ...'; *oed gvynnach y falueu* ... 'whiter were her palms'; *oed gwynnach y dwy uron* ... 'whiter was her breast'; *oed kochach y deu rud* ... 'redder were her cheeks'—and again later; *Oed reit y mi wrth hwnnw* 783, 'I had need of him'; *Oed well gennyf* ... *bei oll yt uei val hynn* 795, 'I would prefer were the whole of it like this'. *Poet* (3rd. impers. sing.) also occurs in this position: *Poet emendigeit y gof a'y digones* 527, 'Cursed be the smith who fashioned it'; *Poet emendigeit y foc yt uerwit yndi* 541, 'Cursed be the forge on which it was heated', and the same phrase is repeated in 556.

Originally, the copula came first in the construction of the mixed sentence, that is the type of sentence in which emphasis was intended to be placed on some part other than the verb. The order of words in the mixed sentence consisted first of a form of the copula, corresponding in tense and mood to that of the main verb, then the part to be emphasized, which was followed by the remainder of the sentence. In its basic and original form the mixed sentence occurs in OW, for example in the Computus fragment: *is gurth ir serenn hai bid in eir cimeir.o.retit loyr ir did hinnuith* ... *Is aries isid in arcimeir aries*, 'it is opposite the constellation which faces *o* that the moon runs that day ... It is aries that is opposite ...' (B iii, 256, ll.10–13). Also in early poetry: *Bydei re ruthrwn y waew*, 'It was with haste that I would rush against a spear', CLlH i,12c; *Oed Maelgwn a welwn in imuan*, 'It was Maelgwn I could see fighting', LlDC 1,5. Later the pres. *ys* came to be employed, irrespective of the tense and mood of the main verb. Such is the situation in PKM: *ys glut a beth yd ymdidanyssam ni*, 'continually have we conversed' 7,16–17; *ys llaw gyffes y medrwys y Lleu ef*, 'with a deft hand has the Fair One hit it' 80,22. Ultimately the copula was dispensed with completely; cf. GMW 141. It is significant that in *Culhwch* we have examples of the early, primitive form, providing us once more with unmistakable evidence of closer affinity with the earlier literature—Old Welsh and early poetry—rather than with the later prose texts. Five exx. occur, and they are presented in full here: *bydhawt ragot ti gyntaf yd agorawr y porth* 99–100, 'it will be for you that the gate shall be opened first'; *Poet yn gystal y'th deon a'th niuer* ... *y bo y gwell hwnn* 144–5, 'May it be equally to your nobles and your retinue that this greeting be'; *bythawd o'th law pan y dechreuwyf* 151, 'it shall be at your hand that I will begin'; *Ys* mi a'e heirch 566, 'It is I who seek her'; *Oed* digawn o drwc a wnaethoed Duw ynni 1087–8, 'It was enough harm that God had wrought us'.

The verbal noun, because of its varied uses, constitutes one of the basic aspects and problems of Welsh syntax. We shall note here some of the more important constructions as they are exemplified in *Culhwch*, although they do not represent any unique feature. First, the use of a verbal noun in narrative in place of a finite verb: *mynet* y wlat y gwedi 3, 'the country went to prayer'. For exx. with other verbs see 4, 14, 22, 46, 164, etc.

When the verbal noun belongs to an intransitive verb, as in the case of *mynet* in 3 above, the subject immediately follows it in the form of a noun. For further exx. see 14, 22, 384, 469, 786, 802, 804, 990, 1053, 1102, 1104, 1110, 1232. When the subject is a pers. pron. a poss. pron is used, as follows: *uyn dyuot* 39, *a'e dyuot ynteu* 46, *y uot* 265, 970, *eu bot* 414, *y uynet* 456, *a'e dyuot hitheu* 461, 487, *y uot ef* 1028, *eu mynet heibaw* 1100. When the verbal noun belongs to a transitive verb, that is when it takes an object, the subject is governed by the prep. *o*: *A chaffael mab ohonu* 4, *Galw o Arthur ar Gyndylic Kyuarwyd* 399; also 175, 408, 413, 442, 459, 462, etc.

A common construction in MW is that of verbal noun + *a* +(*g*)*oruc*/(*g*)*wnaeth* 'did', usually equivalent in meaning to a simple form of the verb: *A chymryt y mab a oruc y meichad* 9, 'And the swineherd took the boy (lit. 'And take the boy the swineherd did'), cf. GMW 160. For further exx. with *goruc* (*gorucpwyd*, -*pwyt*, also *gwnaeth*(*ant*), -*pwyd*, -*pwyt*) in *Culhwch* see glossary.

A common construction in MW prose is the use of *sef* (*ys* + *ef*). It occurs in various combinations, of which the following may be noted as relevant to the construction described above. In this we find *sef* + *a* (rel. pron. obj.) + *goruc*/*gwnaeth*, followed by a verbal noun (cf. GMW 52), a construction which may be described as a variant of verbal noun + *a* + *goruc*. Note the following: *Sef a oruc Arthur dyuot a'e luoed* 1139, 'What Arthur did was bring his hosts' = *Dyuot a'u luoed a oruc Arthur*, 'Arthur brought his hosts'. Cf. further 23, 806, 894, 938.

III. THE STORY AND ITS CHARACTERS

Culhwch's quest for Olwen belongs to the tale-type known internationally as 'Six Go Through the World' (AT 513A) or, more popularly as 'The Giant's Daughter'. In stories of this kind the hero succeeds in accomplishing a number of apparently impossible tasks, placed as calculated impediments in his way by a giant who knows that he himself is fated to die when his daughter marries, and therefore he will be prepared to do all he can to prevent her marriage taking place.[9] The nucleus of this tale can be traced as related to the Greek story of the Argonauts, and a Celtic parallel, first pointed out by Idris Foster, is to be found in the Middle Irish saga *Tochmarc Emire*[10] 'The Wooing of Emer' which tells how Cú Chulainn won his wife Emer. In neither the Welsh nor the Irish tale is the hero in any way daunted by the tasks which the girl's hostile father imposes on him, and both Culhwch and Cú Chulainn are successful in winning their brides—though it is only with the help of Arthur and a selection of his magically-gifted followers that Culhwch is enabled to do so. Indeed, in the Welsh tale the hero's 'Helpers' take over such a large part of the action that Culhwch himself is almost entirely eclipsed: after his companions have assisted him in finding Ysbaddaden's fortress and have thus enabled him to meet with Olwen and to declare his love, Culhwch is not heard of again until at the end of the story he receives his bride. As Ysbaddaden does not fail to point out, this result is entirely due to the strength of Arthur and his men, who brought it about for Culhwch. If Culhwch's presence on the various adventures is to be taken as implied, this is nowhere explicitly stated.

The *tynged* or compulsion which Culhwch's evilly-motivated

[9] I. Ll. Foster, 'Astudiaeth o Chwedl Culhwch ac Olwen', MA thesis, University of Wales, Bangor (1935), and CO(1) xxxiii. Cf. ST and TPC under E 765.4.1; G 530.2; H 335,336; T 91.1; T 97; and IPT 72–5. The parallel between *Culhwch* and the story of the Argonauts is noted by Jackson; see also Stith Thomson, *The Folktale*, 54, 280; CO(1) xxxiii.

[10] LU 307–19. Ed. A. G. van Hamel, *Compert Con Culainn and Other Stories* (Dublin, 1933), 16–68. Cf. Doris Edel, *Helden auf Freiersfüssen* 'Tochmarc Emire und 'Mal y kavas Kulhwch Olwen'* (Amsterdam, 1980). The parallel was noted even earlier by John Rhŷs, HL 487 (1898).

stepmother[11] places upon him is that he shall never obtain any other wife than Olwen, daughter of the 'Chief Giant' Ysbaddaden. Culhwch's father therefore directs his son to go and seek the help of Arthur, because of the bond of kinship which exists between them: *Arthur yssyd geuynderw it*, 'Arthur is your cousin'. This is because Culhwch's dead mother was Goleuddydd, daughter of Anlawdd Wledig (see n. to l.2), and so too, according to *Brut y Brenhinedd* was Eigr, Arthur's own mother. In this, as in other details which recur throughout the story, such as the names of Gwenhwyfar and of Caledfwlch, it is not easy to discount the possibility of influence from *Brut y Brenhinedd* upon *Culhwch ac Olwen*, at some undefined stage in the story's development. This is hardly surprising, for it must be remembered that the texts of *Brut y Brenhinedd* go back to a period at least a century earlier than the White Book of Rhydderch.[12]

Even before the year 1100 Arthur's high status had become established, at least in theory, as that of a one-time ruler over the whole of Britain: in the Life of St Cadog he is *rex illustrissimus Britanniae* (VSB 68), and in the early poem on Geraint fab Erbin he is *amherawdr* 'emperor'(LlDC 21,24). In *Culhwch* Arthur is described as *Penteyrnedd yr Ynys hon* 'Chief of Princes of this Island', and his power, authority, and magnetism are implicit in all that he does, and in the response of others towards him. Arthur can make people do what they are told: a famous prisoner is released at his bare word, he can summon quarrelling men to come and be adjudicated by him, the saints of Ireland come to ask Arthur's protection on his arrival in the country—even the Oldest Animals appear to be under obligation to serve the messengers of Arthur. (The Twrch Trwyth and his retinue of pigs are almost alone in refusing to do anything at

---

[11] For the motif of the Jealous Stepmother see ST and TPC under S 31; H 913.1; P 282; M 411.1.1. There are many parallels in Irish; for refs. see CO(1) xxxv; K. Jackson, EC xi (1964–5), 92–4. For a Gaelic analogy to the linking in a single tale of the two motifs of the Jealous Stepmother and the Giant's Daughter see J. E. Caerwyn Williams, *Y Storïwr Gwyddeleg a'i Chwedlau* (University of Wales Press, 1972) 'Merch Brenin Dyffryn yr Unigedd', 229–36, and note pp. 252–6.

[12] First half of thirteenth century. On the Welsh *Brut* see B. F. Roberts, 'The Treatment of Personal Names in the Early Welsh Versions of *Historia Regum Britanniae*', B xxv (1973), 274; ibid. *Brut y Brenhinedd* (Dublin, 1971), xxix. Cf. TYP xviii.

all at Arthur's request.) The stages are obscure by which Arthur's name attained this eminence, but from at least the tenth century, if not earlier, it had begun to act as a matrix to which were drawn the names of a number of originally unrelated mythical and legendary figures. No doubt we should take with a grain of salt the rhetorical passage in which the gatekeeper, Glewlwyd Gafaelfawr, elaborates on the extent of Arthur's reputed exploits over a large part of the known and of the unknown world:[13] however, it is not easy to discount the likelihood that these allusions to Arthur's far-flung conquests owe something to the exalted status accorded to him in the *Historia Regum Britanniae* and in *Brut y Brenhinedd*.

In Wales the popular and the learned concept of Arthur was above all else that of a defender of his country against every kind of danger, both internal and external: a slayer of giants and witches, a hunter of monstrous animals—giant boars, a savage cat monster, a winged serpent (or dragon)—and also, as it appears from *Culhwch* and *Preiddeu Annwn*, a releaser of prisoners. This concept is substantiated from all the early sources: the poems *Pa Gur* and *Preiddeu Annwn*, the Triads, the Saints Lives, and the *Mirabilia* attached to the *Historia Brittonum*. In the Triads Arthur is the self-appointed guardian of his country against foreign invaders, and in HRB Arthur's great fight with the giant on Mont St. Michel reminds him of an earlier contest which he had fought with the giant Ritho on Snowdon. This episode in HRB and in the *Brut*, serves to recall a wealth of indigenous folklore concerning Arthur's fights with a number of giants on mountain-tops in Wales: traditions which by their very nature are dateless, but which are certainly indigenous, and can in no way be attributed to the single influence of the *Historia Regum*. In a significant lecture[14] published some years ago A. G van Hamel compared this concept of Arthur with that of Fionn mac Cumhaill as portrayed in early Irish sources and in folklore. Both are defenders, hunters, and slayers of monsters, and van Hamel enlarged on the comparison by noting that Arthur, like Fionn, is presented as an intercessor in conflicts between mythical beings: Arthur arbitrates between Gwyn ap

[13] On the passage see B. F. Roberts, 'Yr India Fawr a'r India Fechan', LlC xiii (1980-1), 281-3, and n. to lines 116-28. Cf. AoW 6.

[14] 'Aspects of Celtic Mythology', PBA xx (1934), 207-48; G. Murphy, *Duanaire Finn* iii, 213-17, 'Professor van Hamel's Views concerning the origin of the Arthurian Cycle and the Finn Cycle'.

Nudd and Gwythyr ap Greidawl, as does Fionn between the members of the Tuatha Dé Danann. Whatever Arthur's ultimate origins may be, in early literature he belongs, like Fionn, to the realm of mythology rather than to that of history.

It is the less surprising that Arthur's name and his growing prestige, both as a great king and as a slayer of monsters, should have attracted towards it the tale of another, and a no less formidable giant, when the folk-tale of 'The Giant's Daughter' came to be established in Wales. For Culhwch, in strong contrast to Arthur, is essentially an untraditional figure: outside *Culhwch ac Olwen* he is virtually non-existent. As is frequently the case with the heroes of folk-tales, he has his existence solely for the purpose of this one story. Apart from one later citation of Culhwch's name in *Englynion y Clyweit* (B iii, 13, 45), his name is attested once only, in a single *englyn* in *Canu Heledd: Kyndylan, Gulhwch gynnifiat llew/ Bleid dilin disgynnyat/Nyt atuer twrch tref y dat* (CLlH xi, 10), 'Cynddylan, a lion-warrior (like) Culhwch; a wolf, an attacker in pursuit, the boar (ie. Cynddylan) will not return to his patrimony'. (In the previous stanza Cynddylan has been described as *callon gwythwch*, 'heart of a wild boar'.) More than one parallel instance has been cited in these and other *englynion* in which there has been substitution among personal names, either one name in place of another, or a name in place of a common noun.[15] Against this background, it is not unreasonable to conclude that Culhwch's name in the *englyn* is a substitution. The names of Olwen and Ysbaddaden are equally untraditional: neither of them has any existence outside *Culhwch ac Olwen*. Anlawdd Wledig and Goleuddydd derive from the milieu of the Lives and Genealogies of

---

[15] In CLlH 1, 23b the texts of RB and copies of WB have substituted *llu kyndrwyn* for the Black Book's *lv kigrun* (=*cynghrwn*) 'a compact/orderly host'(= LlDC 18,49; see Ifor Williams's note). J. Rowland discusses the orthographic significance of this error, B xxix (1981), 518–19, and see her *Early Welsh Saga Poetry* 580. See also J. T. Koch, SC xx/xxi (1985–6), 52. Other instances are CLlH xi, 15a where Siôn Dafydd Rhys's copy of an *englyn* has substituted *Cyndhelw* for *Cyndelan* (Cynddylan), and n. ibid., 200. A further instance is LlDC 40, 8–10 where *Tri meib kynuarch* is accepted as a necessary emendation of *Tri meib llywarch*; see introduction to LlDC xv, and B xvii, 180. Some such word as *culwydd* 'lord, chief' may have been displaced by *Culhwch* in the stanza quoted. See CO(I) lxxxv.

the Welsh Saints; Culhwch's father Kilydd appears to be one of a group of names in the story which stem from the *Gododdin* poem. None of these names appear in any other of the tales or romances, nor in the Triads, nor are they cited in praise-poetry; Olwen's name does not figure as a paragon of beauty in poetry any earlier than the fifteenth century.[16]

It is true that Culhwch's name ('slender pigling') retains mythical reverberations which make it probable that his origin lies in the surviving memory of an ancient belief in animal transformations, a belief which is so pervasive in *Culhwch ac Olwen* as to constitute an underlying theme, and one which gains emphasis from a number of early Irish analogies (see below pp. lxviii–lix). But however momentous Culhwch's name may have once been in mythological terms, mythology can offer no satisfactory explanation for the choice of 'Culhwch' as the name of the hero of 'The Giant's Daughter', when this folk-tale came to be told in Wales. Culhwch's birth in a pigsty indicates that the author was at least partially aware of some of the layers of meaning which were embodied in his name (see n. to l. 10). These pig associations may in themselves have been sufficient to cause the gravitation of Culhwch's story into the established orbit of Arthur, the great slayer of giants and monsters, who was known already from the ninth century as the hunter of the monstrous boar, the Twrch Trwyth.

Yet there is a rival to Culhwch as hero of the tale or, more probably, a doublet of Culhwch. *Culhwch ac Olwen* is a story full of doublets, both in *personae* and in incidents, and Goreu son of Custennin offers striking points of similarity with Culhwch himself. Like Culhwch he is a cousin of Arthur, for his mother was yet another of the five daughters of Anlawdd Wledig (TYP 366); Goreu is therefore also a cousin to Culhwch himself. (Compare the doublet of prisoners, Eiddoel and Mabon, who are also presented in the story as cousins.) Goreu, too, is hardly less an anonymous figure than is Culhwch, since he is almost equally unknown and unrecognized in Welsh tradition (see nn. to ll.455, 811). Ysbaddaden is Goreu's uncle, his father Custennin being a brother to the giant (following R's text of l.436). Ysbaddaden has 'despoiled' (or 'dispossessed') his brother, and has brought about

---

[16] Cf. n. to *Olwen* l.498 below, and D. M. Lloyd, *Rhai Agweddau ar Ddysg y Gogynfeirdd* (University of Wales Press, 1977), 10.

the deaths of his twenty-three sons; Goreu is the last one remaining, hence he is reared in secrecy (as other well-known heroes, such as Peredur, are reputed to have been). Goreu first distinguishes himself in the attack on the fortress of the giant Wrnach, yet after this episode he is not heard of again, until he is named as one of the huntsmen engaged in the hunt for the Twrch Trwyth. Finally it is Goreu, not Culhwch, who cuts off Ysbaddaden's head and places it on a stake, thus avenging the 'despoilment' of his father and the deaths of his brothers. The name of Custennin, and perhaps Goreu's own name (see n. to l.811), fits well with the Cornish ambience which is indicated from time to time by elements dispersed throughout the tale. Goreu's inclusion in a triad contained only in the later (WM and RM) collection, *Tri Goruchel Garcharawr*, is discussed below (pp. lx-lxi).

On his father's advice, Culhwch proceeds to Arthur's court to ask for Arthur's help in his difficult and dangerous search for the Giant's daughter. After his initial altercation with the gatekeeper Glewlwyd Gafaelfawr, Culhwch makes a brash and aggressive entrance into the court, riding right into the hall on horseback— something which was contrary to royal custom and all the canons of good behaviour (though it is paralleled in the actions of other heroes, see n. to l.141). Arthur receives him with great courtesy, and agrees to his initial request, which is that the king should trim his hair. Arthur does this, employing a gold comb and scissors of silver. The significance of the hair-cutting, as a recognition and acceptance of consanguity, is made clear from a passage in the ninth-century *Historia Brittonum*[17], relating to Guorthegirn's treatment of his son (and grandson), a boy born by incest with Guorthigern's own daughter. The boy is placed in the care of St Germanus, who receives him with the following words:

> 'Pater tibi ero, nate; nec te dimittam donec mihi nouacula cum forcipe pectineque detur et tibi liceat haec patri tuo carnali dare'. Sicque factum est. Et infans sancto obediuit Germano, perrexitque ad auum suum—patrem scilicet carnalem—Guorthegirnum; et dixit illi puer, 'Pater meus es: capud meum tonde, et comam capitis mei! 'Et ille erubescens siluit, et infantulo respondere noluit, sed surgens iratus est ualde.

---

[17] *The Historia Brittonum: The Vatican Version*, ed. D. N. Dumville, 90; ed. F. Lot, ch.39.

'I will be a father to thee, and I will not let thee go until there be given to me a razor with scissors and a comb, and it is permitted to thee to give these to thy carnal father.' And thus it was done. And the child obeyed Germanus, and went to his grandfather—that is his carnal father—Guorthegirn, and the boy said to him, 'Thou art my father, shear my head and comb my hair.' And he was ashamed and remained silent, and would not reply to the child, but rose up, and was very angry.

Guorthegirn was evidently confounded and shamed by the publicity of this exposure, and the story implies that he did not accede to the request. In *Culhwch ac Olwen* the subject of cutting the hair of beards and head, and its necessary implements—razor, comb, and scissors—is so central a theme as to warrant the quotation of this important passage. Its relevance for the tale of *Culhwch* was pointed out long ago by Sir Ifor Williams.[18] But it appears that the narrator of the story was not entirely clear as to the ancient and symbolic significance of the hair-cutting, for Arthur grants Culhwch's request even before he questions the boy as to his name and parentage. Once his blood-relationship to the king has been confirmed, Culhwch then claims from Arthur, as his *pencenedl*, the *cyfarws* or privileged gift (see n. to l. 59) to which he is entitled on the occasion of his acceptance into the tribe. Culhwch's *cyfarws* is that the king should help him to discover Olwen. He invokes as his sureties the whole company who are present at the court, led by Cei and Bedwyr. With a select band of companions and helpers, Culhwch is then enabled to make his way to the fortress of Ysbaddaden.

The story of *Culhwch ac Olwen* falls into three parts.[19] The first part tells of the hero's birth and the quest imposed upon him by the ill-will of his jealous stepmother, and this brings him to Arthur's court. The second part describes the reception given to Culhwch and his companions at the fortress of Ysbaddaden, and it lists the *anoethau* or difficult tasks imposed on them by the giant. The final

[18] 'Hen Chwedlau', THSC 1946, 53–4; see also Idris Foster, ALMA 33. In both passages the implements—razor, comb, and scissors—are identical with those between the ears of the Twrch Trwyth. Noticeable also in the tale is the frequency of such personal epithets as *barfawc*, *barfdraws*, *barftrwch*, *keinfarfawc*.

[19] As pointed out by B. F. Roberts, Ast.H. 299–300; ibid., 'Middle Welsh Prose Narratives' in L. A. Arrathoon (ed.), *The Craft of Fiction* (Rochester, Michigan, 1984), 223–4.

part is made up of tales of the accomplishment of some ten of these tasks—tales which echo traditions of certain archetypal feats which were traditionally performed by Arthur and his men. Each of the first two sections ends with a long list: the first is the Arthurian Court List, and the second is the list of the *anoethau* imposed by the Giant. From the point of view of antecedent Welsh and Celtic tradition, the interest of *Culhwch ac Olwen* centres principally in the content of these two long lists, and in the tales which follow of the accomplishment of a selection of the *anoethau*. It will now be necessary to consider these two lists in greater detail, before passing on to consider the narratives of accomplishment.

IV. THE ARTHURIAN COURT LIST

(1)

The oldest list of the names of Arthur's companions—evidently they represent his *teulu* or personal retinue—appears in an unfinished poem, which has no title, in the Black Book of Carmarthen (LlDC no.31 = BBC 94–6). It begins with the line *Pa Gur yw y Porthaur*. This poem is the most significant among the identifiable sources or analogues of *Culhwch ac Olwen*. It proves that already between the ninth and eleventh centuries Arthur's name was becoming the great matrix to which the names of mythical and legendary figures were being drawn. Although the poem has many obscurities, there can be no doubt about a number of the personal names which are listed in it: these correspond with names in the Court List in *Culhwch*, and for these the reader is referred to the notes and index which follow the text of the tale below. In the poem a few of these names appear in more archaic forms—*Mabon (ap) Mydron, Guin Godybrion, Anguas Edeinauc, Lluch Llauynnauc*. As Dr Brynley Roberts has pointed out (Ast.H. 298), in the poem as in *Culhwch* these names appear in an Arthurian context, and in each case are listed as 'sureties' by a warrior seeking to forward his personal demand. The poem also provides a precedent for the dialogue between Culhwch and Glewlwyd Gafaelfawr the gatekeeper, and later for that between Cei and the guardian of the fortress of Wrnach Gawr. In addition it foreshadows other encounters by Arthur and his men with witches and hostile monsters. Owing to the poem's importance in relation to *Culhwch*, we subjoin a working translation, for convenience of reference, and to be studied alongside the original text in the Black Book. The poem opens with a verbal interchange between Arthur and Glewlwyd Gafaelfawr: Glewlwyd is presented here as the guardian—or perhaps the proprietor—of a hostile fortress into which Arthur and his men are seeking to gain admittance. But it rapidly develops into a monologue in which Arthur names his followers, giving precedence to Cei as leading hero. Arthur boasts of his followers' wonderful monster-slaying feats, in places as far apart as the vicinity of Edinburgh and the island of Anglesey.

Owing to the loss of a leaf from the manuscript, this monologue breaks off abruptly. We are indebted for our translation to the edition and notes to the poem by Dr Brynley Roberts (Ast.H. 296–309).[20] We have used italics for the lines, or half-lines, spoken by Glewlwyd—the remainder of the poem consists of Arthur's long speech:

(1) What man is the Gate-Keeper? *Gleuluid Gauaeluaur* ('G.Mighty Grasp).
What man asks it? Arthur and Cei Guin ('Fair Cei').
What (company) goes with you? The best men in the world.
Into my house you shall not come, unless you reveal(?) them.
(5) I will reveal(?) them, and you will see them.
The vultures of Elei(?) and wise men all three;
Mabon son of Mydron, the servant of Uthir Pendragon,
Kysceint son of Banon, and Guin Godybrion.
My servants were fierce in defending their claims;
(10) Manawidan son of Llŷr, profound was his council:
Manauid brought shattered shields from Tryfruid (or 'shattered and broken shields'):
and Mabon son of Mellt, he spattered blood on the grass,
and Anguas Edeinauc and Lluch Llauynnauc—
(15) they were defenders of Eidyn (Edinburgh) on the border.
A lord would cherish them . . .
Cei entreated them while he killed them by threes.
When Celli was lost, men endured savagery;
Cei mocked them as he cut them down;
(20) Though Arthur was laughing, the blood was flowing—
In the hall of Awarnach, fighting with a hag.
He smote Pen Palach ('Cudgel Head') in the settlements of Dissethach,

[20] Since going to press, the poem *Pa Gur* has been edited and discussed by P. Sims-Williams in chapter 2 of *The Arthur of the Welsh*, eds. R. Bromwich, A. O. H. Jarman and B. F. Roberts (Cardiff 1991). His translation differs from ours only in some points of detail. See also A. O. H. Jarman's notes and glossary to LlDC. Also useful will be found T. Jones, 'The Early Evolution of the Legend of Arthur', *Nottingham Mediaeval Studies* viii (1964), 16–17 (=B xvii, 247–8), and Jones and Jones, Mab xxiii–xxiv; ALMA 14–15; J. Lloyd-Jones, *Ériu* xvi, 123–4; TYP 304, 362.

on the mountain of Eidyn he fought with the *Cinbin* ('Dog-Heads');

They fell by the hundred, by the hundred they fell

(25) before Bedwyr Bedrydant ('of Perfect Sinew') . . .

on the banks of Tryfruid, fighting with a *garvluid* ('Rough Grey')

furious was his nature, with sword and shield,

a host was futile, compared with Cei in battle:

he was a sword in battle, pledges came from his hand—

(30) he was a steadfast leader of an army for a country's good,

Bedwyr and Brydlaw (or 'son of Brydlaw');

Nine hundred to listen, six hundred to scatter—

his onslaught would be worth.

I used to have servants—it was better when they were alive.

(35) Before the lords of Emrys (or 'splendid lords') I saw Cei in haste,

Lord of booty, the 'long man' was hostile (?)

heavy was his vengeance, fierce was his anger.

When he drank from a buffalo-horn, he drank for four,

When he came into battle, he slew for a hundred.

(40) Unless it were God who caused it, Cei's death were impossible.

Cei the Fair and Llacheu, they made slaughter

before the pang (i.e. 'death') from blue spears . . .

On the uplands of Ystafingun

Cei killed nine witches.

(45) Fair Cei went to Môn (Anglesey) to destroy lions—

his shield was shattered (or ?'polished') against Cath Paluc;

When people ask 'Who killed Cath Paluc?'

Nine score warriors would fall as her food,

nine score champions . . .[21]

---

[21] Here the poem breaks off. Some additional notes on obscure references may be added. The names in l.6 have not so far been satisfactorily explained: B. F. Roberts compares *Elei* with the River Ely in Glamorgan, Ast.H., 303. For *Uthir Pendragon* (7) see TYP 520–3. *Tryfruid* (26) is the name given in HB to one of Arthur's battles (ALMA 6,8). For *Awarnach* (21) see n. to *Wrnach Gawr*, l.747 below. The 'mountain of Eidyn' (23) must be either Arthur's Seat or the Castle Rock of Edin-

(II)

The long list of the men and women assembled at Arthur's Court occupies some 200 lines of the text of Culhwch ac Olwen (175–373), and more than nine columns of WM. These names are invoked by Culhwch as guarantors of the *cyfarws* or privileged gift which he demands from Arthur on the occasion of his acceptance by the king as his kinsman: a recognition which is symbolized by the act of Arthur's combing and cutting his hair. The *cyfarws* which Culhwch then demands from Arthur is that the king should obtain for him the Giant's daughter Olwen, with whom he has already fallen into 'absent love'.

Discounting patronymics, and allowing for the duplication of three names (Gormant mab Ricca, Gwyn mab Nwyvre, Llenlleawc Wydel), and of three others which recur in the list under variant forms (Gwawrdur/Gwaredur Kyruach; Anwas/Henwas Edeinawc; Gallcoit/Gallgoic); together with some names of animals, perhaps inadvertently included (the pups of the bitch Rhymhi, the boars Twrch mab Perif, and Twrch mab Anwas, the horses Call, Kuall, and Kauall)—the total count of the members of the Court amounts to just under 260 names. These evidently derive from a wide variety of sources: there are names belonging to the genealogies and regnal lists of the early Welsh kingdoms—Morgannwg, Dyfed, Powys and Erging, as well as those of Devon and Cornwall and of the 'Old North'—and names of legendary or mythical characters, such as those which appear in the poem *Pa Gur*, a group from the *Gododdin*,[22] and others which are recognizable variants of names in

burgh. The 'border' of Eidyn (15) may stand for the northern border between the Britons and the Picts. The *Cinbin* ('Dog-Heads') have been associated with the *cynocephali* of St Augustine (Cy xxviii, 110n.); they may also be compared with the mythical *Coinchenn* who figure in many early Irish sources (see G. Murphy, *Duanaire Finn* iii, 91n.). With *gar-vluid* (26) cf. n. to *Gwrgi Garwlwyd* TYP 391. For *Llacheu* (41) (son of Arthur) see idem 416–18; for *Cath Paluc* (46–7) see idem 484–7: *lleuon* 'lions' would not be inappropriate for the monster Cath Paluc of triad no. 26. *Ystafingun* (43) is an unknown place-name, (but see now AoW 45).

[22] *Bratwen, Gwawrdur, Moren Mynawc, Nwython, Clydno Eidin (sic), Greit, Cyndylic.* Elsewhere in the tale: *Kilyd* (Culhwch's father), *Cilyd Canhastyr, Cilyd Cyuwlch, Grugyn, Gwlgawt Gododin, Nwython.*

the *Mabinogi*.[23] Five names are those of leading figures in the Irish Ulster cycle of tales (178–80),[24] and one or two others are also Irish. Dispersed through the list are groups of men alleged to be Arthur's relatives, whether on the father's or on the mother's side (205, 222, 252 ,290). Farcical names such as Clust mab Clustfeinad 'Ear son of Hearer', Drem mab Dremhidydd 'Sight son of Seer', Neb 'Anybody', Drwg a Gwaeth a Gwaethaf Oll 'Bad and Worse and Worst of All' intermittently bring the long incantatory sequence down to earth. Alliteration is frequent between names of father and son (Greidawl Gallddofydd and Gwythyr fab Greidawl), between two brothers (Gwalchmai and Gwalhafed, Yskyrdaf and Yscudyd), or two sisters (Gwenhwyfar and Gwenhwyfach; compare Esyllt Vynwen and Esyllt Vyngul). There are also triads: Duach, Brathach, and Nerthach; Bwlch and Cyfwlch and Sefwlch; and three men named Gwyn (181–2) who all seem to be emanations of the legendary Gwyn ap Nudd. Triple unities of this kind are in fact a feature of Celtic mythology and iconography, and they have been perpetuated under a variety of forms in both early Welsh and early Irish literature.[25] There are also larger groups of names which may rhyme or alliterate, such as the four men named Gweir, the five sons of Seithfed, the five sons of Iaen, the five sons of Erim, or the nineteen sons of Caw—groups in which the personalities merge and at times seem to lack any but verbally distinguishing features, being multiplied solely for rhetorical effect. More arresting are the names of historical figures which belong to near-contemporaries who lived in the late eleventh and early twelfth centuries: Sulien, whose name commemorates that of the famous bishop of St

---

[23] *Teyrnon Twr Bliant, Gwarae Gwallt Eurin, Pwyll, Teliessin Pen Beird, Manawedan (sic) mab Llyr, Lluydeu mab Kelcoet (sic), Casnar Wledic, Hyueid Unllen(?)*. Elsewhere in the tale: *Rianhon (sic), Glinneu eil Taran, Gouannon mab Don, Glew mab Yscawt (=?Unic Glew Yscwyd* PKM 39,2).

[24] See notes to ll.178–80; add *Maylwys mab Baedan* (178), Scilti *Scawntroet* (234). For discussion see P. Sims-Williams, B xxix (1982), 607–14, and idem n. on *Brys mab Bryssethach*, 618.

[25] As was first emphasized by J. Vendryes, 'L'Unité en trois personnes chez les Celtes', *Comptes-rendus de l'Academie des Inscriptions et des Belles Lettres* (1935), 325 (reprinted in his *Choix d'Études Linguistiques et Celtiques*). See further M. L. Sjoestedt (trans. Dillon) *Gods and Heroes of the Celts* (London, 1949), 17, 31, 43 and *passim*; P. Mac Cana, *Celtic Mythology* 48; TYP 155–6.

David's; 'Sberin' son of the Breton Count Alan Fergant, and William the Conqueror himself, if indeed it is he who appears under the name of Gwilenhen/hin brenin Freinc. Inset in the list are intriguing fragments of narrative: the triad of the three men who escaped from the battle of Camlan (226–32), Sgilti and his two companions who were preternaturally light-footed (233–44), Teithi Hen whose lands were submerged by the sea (245), Cei's remarkable potentialities as described by his father (265–73), Osla Gyllellfawr and his marvellous bridge-building knife (279–83). Such diversions counteract any monotony in the long list and enhance its verisimilitude by directing attention to familiar narratives or—it may be, to narrative details which have been invented for this very purpose.

Names receive either a patronymic—only exceptionally a matronymic, as in Gwalchmei mab Gwyar, Mabon mab Modron— or an epithet, *Brenhin, Gouynnyat, Gwydel*, etc. Almost never are epithet and patronymic combined. D. Ellis Evans has shown (B xxiv (1972), 420–2; EC xiii (1972), 178–89) that a type of formation frequent in both Continental and Insular Celtic personal names is one in which a substantive precedes its adjective—*Taliesin* 'Radiant Brow' is a familiar example. In both Irish and Welsh such formations occur most frequently in epithets, and he notes the predominance in the first elements in such epithets of words denoting parts of the body, and this equally characterizes both languages. Examples from the Court List are *Barf Trwch* 'Cut Beard', *Garanhir* 'Long Shank', *Gwallt Eurin*, 'Golden Hair', *Tal Aryant* 'Silver Brow', *Mordwyt Twll* 'Mighty Thigh', *Pen Uchel* 'High Head'. Compounds of this kind are well illustrated both in the Court List and in names which appear elsewhere in CO. Lenition of epithets following personal names is not consistent in the tale: in CO, as in TYP, the radical is often retained in instances in which alliteration is best preserved by retaining it—we find Cyndelic *Kyuarwyd* (177), but Elidir *Gyfarwyd* (329).[26] In both texts of CO *mab* is only exceptionally lenited to *uab* when a patronymic follows a personal name. In 359–72 lenition of epithets after women's names is variable (Esyllt *Vynwen* but Gwenlliant *Tec*). There are examples in the iist which show the older usage by

[26] Non-lenition of epithets is the older usage, as was shown by Ifor Williams, CA lxxix–lxxx. There is a similar variation between lenition and non-lenition of epithets in the Triads, see TYP cxi,n.

which patronymics following *merch* are lenited, but there is no consistency in this.[27]

Though the Arthurian Court List is anticipated in a significant manner in the poem *Pa Gur*, yet the closest parallel to this category of names is to be found in the Triads. Thirty-five names belong in common to CO and to *Trioedd Ynys Prydein*: fifteen of these are of fairly frequent appearance (Cei, Bedwyr, Gwalchmei, Drystan, Gereint mab Erbin, etc), ten appear only in CO and in TYP, and the remaining ten are found only in these two sources and in one or all of three lists, each one quite clearly derived independently from *Culhwch ac Olwen*. These are the list of Arthur's counsellors in *Breudwyt Ronabwy*[28] (WM 159–60=BR 19–20), that of the hero's companions in *Chwedl Gereint fab Erbin* (WM 411–12 = GER), and the group of some twenty-five personal names derived from CO in *Englynion y Clyweit* (B iii (1927), 4–21 = Eng). The texts of all three of these lists have been dated to the late twelfth or early thirteenth centuries, and it is plain that each of them is separately derived from the list in CO. Each also includes a few names which appear elsewhere in CO, but which do not in all cases figure in the Court List as well: *Goreu uab Custennin* (BR and GER),[29] *Osla Gyllellvawr* (BR), *Gwryr Gwalstot (sic) Ieithoed* (BR) = *Gwrei Gwalstod Ieithoed* (GER)= *Gwrhir Gwalstawt (Eng)*, *Gwyn mab Tringat* (GER); *Eng* even has *Kulwch* (sic). These names place beyond doubt the dependence of the three lists on the tale of CO, rather than on some independent list of names drawn upon separately by each one of them. All three lists are supplemented by names which appear in TYP but which are absent from CO. A character named *mab Alun Dyuet* appears twice in CO; BR and GER both give this name in full as *Dyuyr mab Alun Dyuet* (see n. to l.185). This is but one of several indications which suggest that these lists derive from an earlier

[27] The Triads show a similar variation between lenition and non-lenition following *merch*; see TYP no.56 and n.; TC 101,1.

[28] The list in BR is usefully compared by J. K. Bollard with the lists in CO, GER, and TYP in LlC xiii (1980–1), 161–2.

[29] Significantly, the name of *Goreu m. Custennin* already appears in the corresponding passage in the text of GER in P 6, dated to *c*.1300 (see WM p. 206), which indicates that it was integrated into the list of Gereint's followers at least fifty years before the date of WM. (See p. x above on the close integration of *Culhwch* with GER in the texts of both W and R.)

recension of CO than that of either of the two manuscripts which have come down. Further evidence on this point—unless it is an editorial correction—is that *Eng* preserves the correct reading *mab* in place of *merch* in citing the three names in which this obvious mistake occurs (see n. to lines 341–2).[30] Yet BR shares a mistake which is common to both texts of the Court List in CO, by perpetuating the misreading *ac Adwy* for *a Cadwy* (182).

Each of the three derived lists gives in addition eight or nine names which do not appear either in CO or in the Triads. Four such names are common to BR and to GER: *Peredur Paladyr Hir/Peredur vab Eurawc; Riogan/Riogoned uab brenin Iwerdon; Gwilym uab rwyf Freinc; Hywel uab Emyr Llydaw.* (This last name can only be explained as derived from the *Brut*, see TYP 407). *Gwilym uab rwyf Freinc* may correspond to CO's *Gwilenhen brenin Freinc*, though there is no available evidence as to which of these is the earlier form (see n. to l. 720). A few of the farcical invented names have been adopted from CO: *Eng* has *Dremhidydd* in recollection of CO's *Drem mab Dremhidydd* 'Sight son of Seer', and the names of Arthur's servants *Hygwyd,Huarwar*, and *Hir Atrwm*; while BR reproduces *Nerth mab Kadarn.*

One or two triads, found only in the Early Version of TYP (P 16, P 45, P 47) contain rare names which are found also in CO: *Bytwini* (*Bitwini*) *Esgob, Drych eil Kibdar, Llawvroded Varvawc*, the oxen *Melyn Gwanhwyn* and the *Ych Brych* (who appear in *Culhwch* among the *anoethau*), *Keinvarvawc* as the epithet of Cei's father (264), *Dalldaf eil Cunin* (*Kimin*) *Cof, Moruyd uerch Uryen.* On the other hand there are some names in the Court List in CO (including *Gwenhwyfar* and her sister *Gwenhwyfach*)[31] which do not appear in the Early Version of TYP, but are prèsent only in the larger, and later, collection of Triads which is common to WM and RM. It may

---

[30] Yet another indication of miscopying in CO appears in ll. 182–3, where the epithet *gwledic* has clearly been transferred to Fflewdwr Flam from the following name in the list—Ru(v)awn Pebyr mab Dorath (Wledic). The occurrence of both names in TYP and in BR make plain that the epithet *gwledic* belongs properly to Dorath/Dewrarth Wledic, not to Fflewdwr Flam.

[31] For *Gwenhwyfar* and *Gwenhwy(f)ach* see notes to ll. 161, 359. The Triads in P 47 have some additional early names which are found in CO: *Myngrwn march Gwedw, Moruud uerch Uryen, Clydno Eidyn, Cadwy mab Geraint* (TYP nos. 46a, 70, 71, 75).

be noted also that the enigmatic triad *Tri Goruchel Garcharawr* 'Three Exalted Prisoners' (TYP 52) which is of particular relevance to *Culhwch*, appears only in WM and RM. This triad is fully discussed below (pp. lx-lxi).

Already in the Early Version of TYP there appears an incipient tendency to substitute the formula *Tri . . . Llys Arthur* in place of the more general *Tri . . . Ynys Prydein*, for example *Tri Vnben Llys Arthur: Gobrwy mab Echel Vordwytwll, a Chadreith mab Porthawr Gadw, a Fleudur Flam* (triad 9) which contains two names which occur in CO—it is tempting to surmise that the third name may have been dropped from the Court List by a careless copyist: here it is impossible to tell whether the triad underlies the text of *Culhwch*, or vice versa. Further instances of the *Llys Arthur* formula are found among the supplementary triads in WM and RM (nos. 18 and 65), and increasingly in the later collections, such as P 47 (cf. TYP lxxxi). Besides employing the 'Arthur's Court' formula, *Culhwch ac Olwen* resembles the Triads in its perpetuation of the wider (and older) *Ynys Prydein* formula, or—in the fuller form in which it appears in CO—*Teir Ynys Prydein a'e Their Rac Ynys* (see n. to l.282). The Early Version of TYP, like *Brut y Brenhinedd*, appears to have been in existence before the middle of the thirteenth century:[32] evidently, therefore, the 'Arthur's Court' framework was an established convention by this date: indeed, the poem *Pa Gur* suggests that its origins may go back to a considerably earlier period. It would be impossible to claim that any one of the extant series of TYP underlies the Court List in CO, yet it is obvious that at some stage there has been considerable mutual influence between the two. The most probable conclusion to be drawn from this is that triads (but not necessarily in any of the existing groupings) formed a major constituent in the formation of the Court List. This must have occurred at a much earlier date than that of the text of CO as we now have it. Analogies for rhetorical categories of a similar kind are to be found in early Irish, as for instance in the lists of the names of warriors of Ulster and of Connacht in the epic *Táin Bó Cúailnge*.[33]

[32] Cf. B. F. Roberts, B xxv (1973), 274; ibid. B xxvii (1977), 332; TYP xviii.

[33] C. O'Rahilly, *The Táin Bó Cúailnge* (Recension 1), 3455–3497, trans. 218; and—for a long sequence of triadic groups—3946–3981, trans. 231–2; O'Rahilly *Táin Bó Cúailnge from the Book of Leinster* (Recension 2), 4054–4100, trans. 247–9, and ibid. *Ireland and Wales*, 116–17.

The court list in *Fled Bricrend* 'Bricriu's Feast' gives a list of the women of Ulster, led by Mugain, wife of Conchobar: unlike the list of the women at Arthur's Court, it gives the names of their husbands, as well as of their fathers.[34]

From the long list of the men and women at Arthur's Court there is abstracted a 'short list' of Six Helpers,[35] and these are the men who actually accompany Culhwch on his journey to Ysbaddaden's fortress, and subsequently in performing the tasks which the Giant requires from the hero. Cei appoints himself as the first of these Helpers, but Arthur nominates the other five. This makes up the conventional number of Six (Magic) Helpers, required by the tale-type 'Six Go Through the World' to which, as has been shown, the tale of Culhwch's quest for the Giant's Daughter belongs. The Six Helpers are Cei, Bedwyr, Gwrhyr Interpreter of Tongues, Menw fab Teirgwaed, Gwalchmei fab Gwyar, and Cyndylic the Guide. Each hero possesses an essential qualification for the undertaking, whether it be for path-finding,[36] liaison with men or animals, power of enchantment, or general warlike ability. All of the Six have been previously named in the Court List, and it is significant that both the long and the short lists begin with the names of Cei and Bedwyr. These two are Arthur's foremost companions in all sources, in the poem *Pa Gur*, in the Life of St Cadoc, in the *Historia Regum Britanniae*, and in *Brut y Brenhinedd*. Like Cei and Bedwyr, Gwalchmei fab Gwyar and Menw fab Teirgwaed are also known in TYP. Gwalchmei and Cyndylic receive no further mention in the tale, though their presence on the subsequent adventures is no doubt to be inferred, as is that of Culhwch himself, though his name is not

O'Rahilly compares the triple groups in CO with similar triple groups in the story of *Da Derga's Hostel* (TBDD ed. Stokes, 107–33, AIT 93–126).

[34] *Fled Bricrend*, LU lines 8405–8416; *Fled Bricrend: Bricriu's Feast* ed. G. Henderson, ITS vol. IV (London, 1899), 34.

[35] Or 'Skilful Companions'; see ST and TPC under F.601.0.1.; and further IPT 72, 101; Stith Thomson, *The Folktale*, 54.

[36] Several names in the long list bring out the necessity had by medieval travellers for guides, path-finders, and builders of impromptu bridges: besides the two guides Cyndylic and Elidir, there is Gwadyn Odeith who cleared the way for Arthur and his men (305), and Osla Gyllellfawr, whose remarkable knife served as a bridge for Arthur's whole army to cross a river.

mentioned again after the scene at Ysbaddaden's fortress, until his wedding takes place at the very end of the story. It is clear that these six men are the hero's original Helpers, and not the farcical group with fantastic powers who have been previously named in the Court List—Drem mab Dremhidydd, Ôl mab Olwydd, Medyr mab Methredydd, Clust mab Clustfeinad, Sucgyn mab Sucnedydd. None of these reappear in any of the adventures connected with the accomplishment of the tasks, nor are they ever mentioned again in the tale.

It would appear that the Court List has been successively inflated, probably at different stages in the evolution of the text of *Culhwch ac Olwen*. Nearly all of the names in the list are inessential to the story (their nominal role being merely that of guarantors): apart from the four special 'Helpers' alluded to above, individual members of the large concourse at Arthur's court play a barely minimal part in the development of the tale. About a dozen of these names do recur, a few of them among the *anoethau*, and more in the story of the hunt for the Twrch Trwyth—in the course of which a number of them are slain—including Osla Gyllellfawr, Gwilenhen brenin Freinc, and Arthur's 'uncles' Gwrbothu Hen and Llygatrudd Emys. Their recurrence in these later episodes indicates that there had been sufficient time for the contents of the Court List to have become integrated into the text of CO, at an earlier date in the tale's transmission than that which is represented by the two existing manuscripts. When these names do recur, they may reappear in a slightly variant form from that in which they were originally found in the Court List.[37]

We suggest that the whole of the Arthurian Court List is an accretion to *Culhwch ac Olwen*,[38] but an accretion made at a considerably earlier date in the transmission of the tale from that which is represented by the two manuscripts. It may have been based partly or wholly on some pre-existing list of heroic names, or

---

[37] Exx: *Gluydyn/Gwlydyn Saer; Garwyli eil Gwythawc Gwyr/Arwyli eil Gwydawc Gwyr; Kynedyr Wyllt mab Hettwn Tal Aryant/Kyledyr Wyllt mab Nwython; Reidwn mab Beli/Reidwn fab Eli Atuer; Cledyf Kyuwlch/Kilyd Kyuwlch.*

[38] Cf. the somewhat similar suggestions made by Sims-Williams, B xxix, 606, and P. L. Henry, SC iii, 34 'It seems to have little organic connection with the tale'.

on a collection of triads and of genealogies, and it is likely to have been added to progressively. The fact that none of the group of six Irish heroes in 178–80 reappears in any one of the three derived lists in BR, GER, and *Eng* suggests that these may be one such addition. In the extant text there has evidently been some degree of transference of names between the list and the later part of the tale. But if the whole series of names between lines 175–373 is excised, the sense of the tale runs on with greater clarity and smoothness: line 174 being followed immediately by 374: Culhwch specifies his *cyfarws*—that Arthur should help him to find and to win Olwen, and Arthur replies that he has never even heard of Olwen; messengers are then dispatched to search for her, and return after a year without success (like the similar fruitless year's search by the emperor's messengers in *Breudwyt Maxen*). The Six Helpers are then appointed, and it is principally these, with some additions, who are the hero's companions throughout the rest of the tale. Once the Six have been appointed, it appears that they have no further difficulty in finding Ysbaddaden's fortress and Olwen's home.

This conclusion in no way depreciates the very great interest of the Arthurian Court List, nor does it cast doubt on the antiquity of the materials from which it is composed. The list incorporates a wide conspectus of the names of traditional heroes, many of whom were known to poets of the twelfth and thirteenth centuries (a few even earlier), and a number appear also in the Triads and in early Welsh regnal lists. It may have received progressive accretions at the hands of successive copyists of the tale. Similar lists of the personnel of Arthur's Court became a recurrent feature of Continental Arthurian romances.[39] Either the Triads with their 'Arthur's Court'

[39] An example is the list of men assembled at Arthur's Court (ll. 1691–1750) and again later for the heroine's marriage (ll. 1934–2024) in Chrétien de Troyes' *Erec et Enide* (ed. W. Foerster, Halle, 1934). This list is placed differently in the story from its place in GER, and there is almost no correspondence between the names of the members of Arthur's court in the French and the Welsh lists (see AoW 278). Cf. also the account in HRB ix, 12 (=BD 157–8) of Arthur's Whitsuntide court held at Caerleon and attended by kings and bishops. Many of the names here given correspond closely with names preserved in OW in the Harleian Genealogies (EWGT 9–13) and bear no resemblances to the names in the *Culhwch* list, except for Cei and Bedwyr and Run mab Nwython (*Culhwch* l. 257).

framework, or the tale of *Culhwch ac Olwen* itself, could have been the pattern for these, or else—as the Irish analogies suggest[40]—there may have been similar lists incorporated in stories which have since been lost.

---

[40] There is some evidence that the Irish saga-lists originated in lists of titles which may have been recited orally by poets before their patrons. Cf. Myles Dillon, *The Cycles of the Kings*, 115; P. Mac Cana, *The Learned tales of Medieval Ireland*, 33–4, 50. The same might well have been true at one time of the triad sequences; TYP lxxi-lxxii. Cf. J. N. Radner, 'Irony in *Culhwch and Olwen*', CMCS 16 (1988), 49.

V. THE *ANOETHAU* OR TASKS

Ysbaddaden exacts forty *anoethau* ('things difficult to obtain, marvels') from Culhwch as the price of winning Olwen for his wife. These are:

(1) to uproot a thicket and burn the roots, manure and plough the ground with the ashes, sow and reap the whole within a single day, in order to make food for the wedding-guests;

(2) to obtain Amaethon son of Don to prepare the ground;

(3) Gofannon son of Don to make ready the plough-shares;

(4) the two oxen of Gwlwlydd Wineu to plough the land;

(5) the oxen Melyn Gwanwyn ('Yellow Spring') and the Ych Brych ('the Brindled Ox') to be in a single yoke together;

(6) the two horned oxen, Nyniaw and Peibiaw, under a single plough;

(7) to sow the ploughed land with the same amount of flax seed as the nine hestors which were sown when Ysbaddaden married Olwen's mother (but which have never grown) in order to get enough flax from it to make a white head-dress for Olwen for her wedding;

(8) honey nine times sweeter than the honey of a first swarm of bees, to make bragget for the wedding;

(9) the cup of Llwyr son of Llwyrion to contain the bragget;

(10) the *mwys* (hamper) of Gwyddneu Garanhir to contain the food;

(11) the horn of Gwlgawd Gododdin to serve the drink;

(12) the harp of Teirtu to entertain the Giant;

(13) the Birds of Rhiannon to entertain the Giant (absent from R);

(14) the Cauldron of Diwrnach the Irishman to cook food for the wedding feast;

(15) the tusk of Ysgithrwyn Chief of Boars to shave the beard of Ysbaddaden;

(16) Odgar son of Aedd to draw the tusk from the Boar's head while the Boar is still alive;

(17) Caw of Prydyn to guard (*cadw*) the tusk;

(18) the blood of the Black Witch to stiffen the Giant's beard for shaving;

(19) the bottles of Gwyddolwyn the Dwarf to keep the blood warm;

(20) the bottles of Rhynnon Stiff-bearded to hold milk for everyone;

(21) the comb and scissors[41] from between the two ears of the Twrch Trwyth, son of Taredd Wledig, to cut and comb the Giant's hair;

(22) Drudwyn, the pup of Greid son of Eri, to hunt the Twrch Trwyth;

(23) the leash of Cors Cant Ewin to hold Drudwyn;

(24) the collar of Canhastyr Canllaw to hold the leash;

(25) the chain of Cilydd Canhastyr to hold the collar;

(26) Mabon son of Modron to lead Drudwyn;

(27) Gwyn My(n)gdwn the horse of Gweddw, to be a horse for Mabon;

(28) Eiddoel son of Aer to search for Mabon;

(29) Garselid the Irishman, chief huntsman of Ireland, to hunt the Twrch Trwyth;

[(30) the two pups of the bitch Rhymhi;[42]]

(31) a leash of the beard of Dillus Farfawg ('the Bearded'') to hold the two pups;

(32) Cynedyr/Cyledyr Wyllt ('the Wild') to hold the two pups;

(33) Gwyn son of Nudd to hunt the Twrch Trwyth;

(34) Du, the horse of Moro Oerfeddawg, as a horse for Gwyn;

(35) Gwilenhin, king of France, to hunt the Twrch Trwyth;

(36) the son of Alun Dyfed to unleash the hounds;

(37) the hounds Aned and Aethlem to hunt the Twrch Trwyth;[43]

(38) Arthur and his huntsmen to hunt the Twrch Trwyth;

(39) Bwlch and Cyfwlch and Syfwlch, the sons of Cleddyf Difwlch, to hunt the Twrch Trwyth;

[41] Later a razor (*ellyn*) is added to these, ll. 1090, 1185. The razor has presumably been omitted from this item in the list of *anoethau* because the *ysgithr* or tusk of Ysgithrwyn had already been stipulated as the implement with which to shave Ysbaddaden.

[42] This item has fallen out of both texts, but it is clearly implied by the two following items 31 and 32 (see n. to ll.930–1). There is some confusion, since according to l.964 (see n.) the leash made from the beard of Dillus (no. 31) was required to hold Drudwyn. Clearly no. 32 relates to no. 30.

[43] Evidently this and the previous item should be transposed.

(40) the Sword of Wrnach the Giant to kill the Twrch Trwyth.

There are doublets in the list, of which the two most obvious were pointed out long ago by W. J. Gruffydd (Cy xlii, 137)—the two Boar Hunts for Ysgithrwyn Ben Beidd and for the Twrch Trwyth, and the two prisoners, Eiddoel and Mabon. Nos. 16 and 17 constitute another doublet: in the event it is Caw of Prydyn, not Odgar mab Aedd, who abstracts the tusk from the head of Ysgithrwyn (1020). There are triplets also, or triple groups,—the oxen in nos. 4, 5, 6, the items relating to Ysgithrwyn Ben Beidd in nos. 15, 16, 17, and the leash, collar, and chain required to hold Drudwyn, nos. 23, 24, 25. In effect, the essential contents of the list of *anoethau* could be more concisely summarized as follows:

Items 1–7 are concerned with preparing, ploughing, and cultivating a piece of land to grow food for the wedding-feast.[44] The task is endowed with the aura of mythical associations by its allusions to the sons of Don—names which call to mind the milieu of the *Mabinogi*. The oxen in items 4 and 5 derive from the 'Triads of Horses', as these appear in the Early Version of TYP. Item 7 is the culmination of this group of *anoethau*, but the incident of the Lame Ant seems singularly inappropriate here, and may be an addition or substitution, since the purpose of this *anoeth* was to cause flax-seed to grow which had hitherto refused to germinate. Ysbaddaden's words (606) 'I have that measure still' seem to indicate that the seed was already in the soil, and did not require ants to collect it: at the same time Ysbaddaden was not to be outwitted as to the amount of flax he expected from the seed. Items 8–14 and 20 are further concerned with the provision of food and drink and entertainment for the wedding. The vessels described have affinities with the magical food-producing vessels

[44] These items recall the episode in the Argonauts, a tale-type analogous to *Culhwch* (see IPT 73–5), in which Jason and his companions are required to plough with bulls a large field (and to sow it with dragons' teeth which will grow into armed men) as the price of obtaining the Golden Fleece (H. J. Rose, *Handbook of Greek Mythology* (1928), 202). Items 1–6 thus seem likely to reflect tasks original to this version of the Giant's Daughter tale, although a different orientation is given to the group of agricultural *anoethau* from that found in the Greek tale.

listed among the 'Thirteen Treasures of the Island of Britain'[45]—a list which was very popular with the poets in the fifteenth and sixteenth centuries, though items in it are obviously much older than this.

Items 15–19 list the 'razor' (the tusk of Ysgithrwyn Chief of Boars), and the men who are to obtain it, together with the primitive shaving-soap (the witch's blood) to be used for shaving Ysbaddaden for the wedding.

Item 21 is the most important of all the *anoethau*, and it is central to the whole story. It introduces the Twrch Trwyth, and names the treasures—the comb and scissors[46]—which must be obtained from between his ears. Items 22–39 supply the names of the men, hounds, horses and implements which are required for the hunt of the Twrch Trwyth. Interpolated among these is another triplet—items 30–2 which are concerned with the 'two pups of the bitch Rhymhi'—though their real purpose seems to be to introduce the story of Dillus the Bearded.

Item 40, the Sword of Wrnach, raises some special problems (see pp. liv–lv below). It has been long recognized that this task may well be an addition to the original list of the *anoethau*, and it is significant that after the Sword has been obtained, Arthur enquires of his men 'Which of these *anoethau* ought to be sought *first?*'

As W. J. Gruffydd observed (Cy xlii, 134), all the *anoethau* represent objects or actions or persons which are required, either to provide for the wedding-feast, or for the shaving of Ysbaddaden when this takes place. Items 1–14 and 20 are required for the first purpose, and except for no. 40, all the remaining items are required for the second: this second and larger group represents the tasks which are connected with the two boar-hunts. Such overlap as exists between the names of characters found in the Court List and those found among the *anoethau* is restricted to the names in the second group—that is, the men, hounds, horses, and their accoutrements which are required to take part in one or other of the

---

[45] See TYP cxxxiii-v, 240–1; EC x (1963), 434–77, LlC v (1958), 33–69. Items 10 and 14 constitute the earliest evidence for two of the magical treasures among the *Tri Thlws ar Ddeg*. See now AoW 85–8. Items 4, 5, 27, 34 betray an association with the 'Triads of Horses', a distinct and early group of TYP (see TYP xcviii-cvii and triads nos. 44–46a), and cf. n. to Llamrei, l.1016 below.

[46] See n.41 above.

two boar-hunts. Evidently there have been accretions to both groups of the *anoethau,* though these are most obvious in the second or larger group (see further pp. lxxii-lxxiii below). The presence of some twelve men from the Court List is noted among the huntsmen mentioned as participating in the great boar-hunt: half of these are merely listed as having been slain by the Twrch Trwyth. With the exception of Gwyn ap Nudd, Caw of Prydyn, and Gwythyr ap Greidawl, men who have been previously named in the Court List play little or no further part in the story.

The last part of the tale describes the achievement of ten of the tasks which were stipulated by Ysbaddaden. Most of these stories of achievement bear all the signs of incorporating genuine early traditions, whose antiquity is beyond all conjecture. For some of them there is supporting evidence in early poetry, in the Triads, and elsewhere. The titles of those which remain unaccomplished are suggestive of similar tales about mythical and legendary figures: how far these denote stories which actually existed, either orally or in writing, we can never know. In the following list the tasks are numbered in the order of their accomplishment: the order in which they were stipulated by the Giant is then sub-joined. In no way do these numbers correspond—the last task to be stipulated is the first to be performed:

  (i) the Sword of Wrnach (40);
 (ii) Eiddoel son of Aer (28);
(iii) Mabon son of Modron, with the tale of the Oldest Animals
      (26);
 (iv) the two pups of the bitch Rhymhi (30);
  (v) the nine hestors of flax-seed, with the tale of the Lame Ant
      (7);
 (vi) the Beard of Dillus the Bearded (31);
(vii) the tusk of Ysgithrwyn Chief of Boars (15);
(viii) the Cauldron of Diwrnach the Irishman (14);
 (ix) the comb and scissors from betwen the ears of the Twrch
      Trwyth (21)
  (x) the blood of the Black Witch (18).

In addition, four of the *anoethau* are stated to have been obtained, though no details are given. These are Drudwyn, the pup of Greid son of Eri (22), the leash of Cors Cant Ewin (23), Gwyn Myngdwn, the horse of Gweddw (27), and Cynedr/Cyledyr Wyllt (32). The obtaining of the two pups of the bitch Rhymhi (30) is also implied by the story, without specific mention at this point; as also is the achievement of two other tasks which were never even demanded by the Giant: these are the obtaining of the two hounds of Glythfyr Lydewic (1009), and that of Gwrgi Severi (1010). In addition to these, the names of six of the huntsmen (or groups of huntsmen) demanded by Ysbaddaden are cited as having taken part in subsequent adventures; evidently, therefore, these too must have been obtained. These are Caw of Prydyn (17), Garselid the Irishman (29), Gwyn son of Nudd (33), Gwilenhin king of France (35), Arthur and his men (although these are already present as Culhwch's companions) (38), the sons of Cleddyf Difwlch (39). To these can be added the hounds Aned and Aethlem (37), since at the end of the tale these are said to have disappeared into the Severn estuary in pursuit of the Twrch Trwyth. There remain eighteen of the *anoethau* to which the story makes no further allusion: these are items 1–6, 8–13, 19, 20, 24, 25, 34, 36.

The 'short list' of Arthur's warriors who are appointed to assist Culhwch on his quest has already been alluded to (p. xliii). The first four of these—Cei, Bedwyr, Gwrhyr the Interpreter, and Menw son of Teirgwaedd—accompany Culhwch on his journey to the fortress of Ysbaddaden and on subsequent adventures, while the other two, Gwalchmei and Cynddylig the Guide, are not mentioned again in the story. To the four 'Helpers' just mentioned the names of other heroes are successively added, in connection with one or other of the ensuing tasks. The following, therefore, are the hero's companions in the achievement of the ten tasks which are narrated:

(1) The attack on Wrnach Gawr: Cei, Bedwyr, Gwrhyr, Goreu fab Custennin.

(2) The release of Eiddoel: Arthur and his men (unspecified).

(3) The release of Mabon (after enquiry from the Oldest Animals) Cei, Bedwyr, Gwrhyr, and Eiddoel take part, but it is Cei and Bedwyr alone who go on the Salmon's back up the Severn to Gloucester to release the prisoner;

(4) The pups of the bitch Rhymhi: Arthur and his men (unspecified); the pups and their mother are disenchanted 'by God for Arthur'.

(5) The Lame Ant: Gwythyr son of Greidawl is the solitary achiever.

(6) Dillus the Bearded: Cei and Bedwyr (Cei then takes offence at Arthur's satirical *englyn*, and disappears from the story).

[At this point the story of Arthur's arbitration between Gwyn ap Nudd and Gwythyr ap Greidawl is interpolated.]

(7) The Hunt for the boar Ysgithrwyn: Arthur is accompanied by Mabon son of Mellt and Caw of Prydyn; Caw slays the boar and captures its tusk.

(8) The Cauldron of Diwrnach: Arthur is accompanied by Bedwyr, Llenlleawc the Irishman, and Arthur's *gwas* Hygwyd.

(9) The Hunt for the Twrch Trwyth: Arthur is accompanied by a general muster of men and horses and hounds from all his dominions. They are led by Bedwyr, Menw son of Teirgwaedd, Gwrhyr the Interpreter, and Gwarthegyd son of Caw. Eight additional huntsmen are here introduced, who have not previously appeared in the story: Tarawg of Allt Clwyd, Gwydre son of Arthur, Kynlas son of Cynan, Hir Peissawg king of Brittany, Madawg son of Teithion, Eiriawn Penlloran, Rhuddfyw Rhys, Gwyngelli.[47]

(10) The Black Witch: Arthur's companions are named as Gwyn ap Nudd and Gwythyr ap Greidawl, together with his servants Cacamwri and Hygwyd, Hir Amren and Hir Eiddyl. Arthur himself kills the Witch with a cast of his knife Carnwennan, and Caw of Prydyn collects the Witch's blood.

[47] Cf. J. Rhŷs, CF 529, for the suggestion that some of these names may conceal forgotten place-names.

VI. GIANTS AND WITCHES

Culhwch ac Olwen introduces three other Giants besides Ysbaddaden Pencawr. These are Wrnach Gawr, Dillus Farfawg, and Diwrnach Wyddel/Gawr.[48] All three are slain by Arthur's men. Witches are the female counterparts of Giants, and in the penultimate episode Arthur's companions attack the terrible Black Witch *yg gwrthtir Uffern*, 'in the uplands of Hell', and it is Arthur himself who gives her the *coup de grace* with his dagger Carnwennan. This episode is to some degree anticipated in the poem *Pa Gur*, where Arthur fights with a *gwrach* ('hag'), and where Cei is credited with having slain *naw widdon* 'nine witches'.[49] Similarly, the episode of Diwrnach Wyddel is in a manner prefigured in *Preiddeu Annwn*.[50] The *anoethau* which are now to be considered are all primary Arthurian traditions, which depict Arthur and his band of men as the defenders of their land against Giants and other *gormesoedd*, whether enemy invaders or hostile monsters.

The task of obtaining the Sword of Wrnach Gawr (see n. to l.747) is the last of the tasks demanded by Ysbaddaden from Culhwch, and the first to be accomplished. This task is only crudely aligned with the other *anoethau*, and does not properly belong with either of the two groups which are listed above. The intended purpose of the Sword was that it should be used to slay the Twrch Trwyth, but the purpose of hunting the boar was not, in any case, to kill him, but to obtain the valuable treasures from between his ears. In the event, Wrnach's Sword is turned upon the Giant himself, and at the end of the story the Twrch Trwyth escapes unharmed into the sea. As was indicated above (p. l), there is good reason to believe that the episode of Wrnach is an addition to *Culhwch ac Olwen*, and that it was attracted into the story by reason of Arthur's exalted reputation as the greatest of Giant Killers.

---

[48] Caw of Prydyn is yet another Giant, who appears to have been introduced into the story under the influence of the *Vita Cadoci* (see n. to l.647), but as an ally—not an opponent of Arthur, as is his son Hueil in the *Vita*. Cf. also Cynwyl Sant (n. to l.230), whom Siôn Dafydd Rhys lists among the Welsh Giants; see n. 52 below.

[49] See nn. to ll.652–3.

[50] BT 54–6. Ed. and trans. M. Haycock, SC xviii-xix (1983–4), 52–78.

In certain respects the whole episode duplicates earlier events in *Culhwch ac Olwen*. The journey to Wrnach's fortress is similar to the earlier journey to the fortress of Ysbaddaden: both are described as *mwyhaf ar keyryt y byt* 'the greatest of fortresses in the world' (413, 760); Cei is the protagonist on both expeditions, and Gwrhyr acts as his spokesman on both occasions—first with Custennin Heusawr, who directs the band to Ysbaddaden's territory, and then with the *gwr du* who fulfils the same role as guide to Wrnach's fortress. Both guides give to Arthur's men a portentous warning as to their danger. The dialogue with Wrnach's gatekeeper parallels that held previously by Culhwch with Glewlwyd Gafaelfawr before Arthur's gate. Arthur and Wrnach employ an identical formula in questioning their gatekeeper, *Chwedleu porth gennyt?* 'Have you news from the gate?'(115, 779). Feasting and carousal are in progress in the halls of both Arthur and of Wrnach, and no admittance is to be granted except to a king's son or to a craftsman; but whereas Culhwch reverses this situation and gains admittance by the potency of his threat to Glewlwyd, Cei wins entry to Wrnach's fortress by means of his claim to possess the very craft for which Wrnach has an immediate need. (The incident of the furbishing of Wrnach's Sword is obscure: why did not Cei use it to kill the Giant as soon as he had it in his hand, instead of waiting to obtain the scabbard?)

Both of these episodes have their prototype in the poem *Pa Gur*, in which Arthur is required to specify the qualifications of his men for admission into a hostile fortress guarded by Glewlwyd Gafaelfawr. In *Culhwch ac Olwen* Glewlwyd has been transmuted from the guardian of a hostile fortress into the gatekeeper of Arthur's own court. Yet in other respects the incident of Wrnach Gawr follows the outline of the poem more closely than does the account of Culhwch's arrival at Arthur's court; for here, as in the poem, Cei is the primary hero. In contrast, the account of Culhwch's arrival at Arthur's court seems to be a farcical burlesque of the situation presented in the poem.[51] A less immediate, but no less significant parallel for both these incidents is to be found in the early Irish saga *Cath Maige Tuired* ('The Battle of Moytura') which narrates how the god Lug (the

---

[51] Cf. TYP 362.

Welsh Lleu) applies for entry into the fortress of Tara,[52] to which admission is only allowed to the possessor of a distinctive craft. Since Lug was *samildanach* ('endowed with many arts together') he was admitted immediately, once his supreme qualifications were recognized. This story and the poem *Pa Gur* are likely to be antecedent compositions which in different ways are of equal relevance for *Culhwch ac Olwen*: in CMT the Irish giant Balor offers a unique parallel to Ysbaddaden (see n. to l.517) in that he, like Ysbaddaden, requires an attendant to lift up his eyelids so that he can obtain a clear view of his challenger (Lug or Culhwch). But it would be impossible to assert the priority of composition of either CMT or *Pa Gur* over the other. Both incorporate myths which are certainly older than *Culhwch* in the form in which we now have the story.

A main purpose of the Wrnach Gawr episode appears to have been to present Goreu son of Custennin as a hero who is second only to Cei. We have suggested above (pp. xxx-xxxi) that Goreu is in some measure a doublet of Culhwch himself. It will be recalled that it is Goreu, not Culhwch, who finally slays Ysbaddaden Pencawr. Surely this was the task for which the Sword of Wrnach was once intended, as the murder-weapon which duplicated the *ysgithr* or tusk of the giant Boar, which was destined to slay Ysbaddaden Chief Giant in an early version of *Culhwch ac Olwen*?

Dillus Farfawg ('the Bearded') is the next Giant to be introduced into the story. The incident concerning him is but one variant among a number of traditions about Giants who are associated with ancient sites (mainly hill-top *caerau* or *cestyll*) which are spread over a wide area of Wales, and each is precisely located. These Giant traditions were collected from oral sources by Siôn Dafydd Rhys at the beginning of the seventeenth century.[53] Arthur is said to have slain several of these Giants; and no other hero is credited with a similar achievement, except for Arthur's nephew Gwalchmei, who is said to have killed three witches, all of them sisters and wives of the Giants. It appears that at least one of these traditions of Giants associated with Welsh mountain-tops has come down from the twelfth century, in Geoffrey of Monmouth's allusion to the story of

---

[52] See CMT 38–41; AIT 35–6, and CO(1) xciii–iv.

[53] Ed. Hugh Owen, Cy 27 (1917), 115–52, from P 118, fos.829–837. See further C. R. Grooms, 'Giants in Welsh Folklore and Tradition', Ph.D. thesis, University of Wales (Aberystwyth), 1988.

the Giant Ritho/Rhita on Eryri (Snowdon), which is reproduced in *Brut y Brenhinedd*.[54] This Giant was engaged in the obnoxious pursuit of collecting the beards of kings in order to make for himself a mantle, and he wished to include Arthur's beard in it, and to give it precedence over all the others. Siôn Dafydd Rhys recapitulates this story in words which clearly recall those of the *Brut*, but which at the same time indicate that he knew of a number of variants of the tale, localized at several different places in Wales. He sets the tale in context among his other Giant stories:

> And all these Giants were of enormous size, and (they were) in the time of Idris Gawr, which Idris was king and chief over them. And in the land of Meirionydd also, and close to Pen Aran in Penllyn, and under the place called Bwlch-y-groes, is a grave of great size, where they say Lytta or Ritta or Rithonwy or Itto Gawr was buried; whose body some of the tribe of Giants removed from Eryri to somewhere near Mynydd Aran Fawr in Penllyn. This Ricca Gawr was the one with whom Arthur had fought and killed in Eryri. And this Giant made for himself a mantle (*pilis*) of the beards of the kings he had killed. And he sent to Arthur to order him to cut off his own beard and send it to him. And as Arthur was the chief of the kings, he would place his beard above the other beards as an honour to Arthur. And if he would not do that, he asked Arthur to come and fight with him, and that the strongest of them should make a mantle from the beard of the other. And when they went to fight, Arthur obtained the victory, and he took the Giant's beard and his mantle.[55] (Translation)

The story of Dillus, localized on Pumlumon, is clearly a loose variant of Geoffrey of Monmouth's tale, as told in *Brut y Brenhinedd*. But against the background of the widespread Giant stories which Siôn Dafydd Rhys gives in summary, it is barely conceivable that the *Brut* could have been his only source for the version which he gives. As given here, it differs from the story of Rhita Gawr in that Dillus did not himself collect the beards of kings, nor was his own beard required to make a king's mantle. Instead it was required to make a leash for a particular hound (Drudwyn),[56] and by this means it became an essential preliminary for the great central boar-hunt. The story is likely to be at least as ancient as that of Rhita Gawr: it is localized on Pumlumon, and it is

[54] HRB x,3 (ed. Wright, 119; trans. Thorpe, 240), = BD 170.
[55] Cy 27, 126–9.
[56] Either for the two pups of the bitch Rhymhi, or alternatively for the hound Drudwyn, see nn. to ll.701, 964.

linked to this day with place-names and natural features which are still identifiable in the area.[57]

Why Cei, rather than Arthur, should be the hero of this incident as it is told in *Culhwch* is beyond conjecture, though *Pa Gur* serves as a reminder that Cei, no less than Arthur, was renowned as a proficient slayer of monsters. On a purely functional level, the offence which Cei is said to have taken at Arthur's abusive *englyn* (978–80) may simply reflect the author's decision to remove Cei at this point from the main story, in order to clear the stage for his final sequence of incidents, each of which, from this point onwards appears to reflect an archetypal feat in which Arthur was the leader. The shaving of Dillus prefigures the shaving of Ysbaddaden, and it strikes a keynote in *Culhwch ac Olwen* owing to the story's recurrent preoccupation with the theme of the cutting and shaving of hair and beards, frequently underlined by the attachment to personal names of such epithets as *Barfawg*, *Barf Trwch*, *Barf Draws*, *Keinfarfawg*. The beard is an obvious symbol of virility, and there is ample evidence for the degrading nature of forcibly cutting the hair of another's head—as in the story of Samson and Delilah.[58]

One of these archetypal Arthurian feats was the winning of a magically endowed Cauldron from the 'Otherworld'. Diwrnach Wyddel ('D. the Irishman') can with assurance be identified with *Dyrnbhwch Gawr* (whom Siôn Dafydd Rhys locates in the district of Ewias), and with *Dyrnfwch/Dyrnog Gawr* whose food-producing and testing Cauldron is listed among the Thirteen Treasures of the Island of Britain (see n. to l.635). This in turn plainly descends from the *peir pen Annwn*, the 'Cauldron of the Chief of Annw(f)n' in the

---

[57] See n. to l.954, and CO(1), lviii, n.137. Siôn Dafydd Rhys (loc.cit.) cites the place-name *Rhiw y Barfau* in Cwm Cynllwyd near Bala, in one variant of the story. *Erwbarfe* is the name of a farm near Ponterwyd, Ceredigion.

[58] *Judges* xvi. Cf. ST and TPC under D 1831 (strength in beard), and F.531.1.6.13 (a Giant's strength in his beard). For an Irish parallel cf. *Aided Conroi maic Dairi*, ed. *Ériu* ii (1905), 22; AIT 329. According to the Welsh Laws, if a woman wished shame on her husband's beard, it gave him a right to strike her *am unau meuel ar e uaryf* 'for wishing shame on his beard', *Llyfr Iorwerth*, ed. A. R. Wiliam (University of Wales Press, 1960), 28; cf. WLW 52. There are a number of instances in the tales and in poetry of the asseveration *Mefl ar fy marf/dy farf* 'Shame on my/your beard'; PKM 47,10; WM 134, 17–18; CLlH xi,88c; GDG 108,26; 152,3.

poem *Preiddeu Annwn*[59]—and it thus appears to be a Cauldron of mythical antiquity. In the poem, this Cauldron was fetched from Annw(f)n (the Otherworld) by Arthur in his ship Prydwen (see n. to l.938). The story as we have it in *Culhwch* is a euhemerized version of the same myth, in which Ireland has taken the place of Annw(f)n. Yet another reminiscence of the magic Cauldron which was brought from Ireland to Wales (and later returned to Ireland) is to be found in *Mabinogi Branwen*,[60] where Bendigeidfran's invasion of Ireland, like Arthur's raid on Annw(f)n, is portrayed as a tragic expedition which had disastrous consequences, emphasized in both cases by the meagre number of the seven survivors. Arthur's triumphant return from Ireland in *Culhwch* with his ship Prydwen carrying Diwrnach's Cauldron 'full of the treasures of Ireland' is in contrast to these two tragic presentations of the basic myth. Diwrnach Wyddel is slain with Arthur's sword Caledfwlch, although the act of killing him is attributed, rightly or wrongly, to another Irishman, Llenlleawc Wyddel. The localization of the story in Ireland is sufficient in both cases to account for the epithet *Gwyddel*, and an Irish derivation is unlikely for either *Llenlleawc* or *Diwrnach* (see nn. to ll.253, 635).

---

[59] BT 55,2; SC xviii/xix, 60, l.15.
[60] PKM 34–5,45; Mab 29–30, 37. Cf. T. Jones, 'Early Evolution' 14 (=B xvii 246).

VII. THE TWO PRISONERS AND
THE OLDEST ANIMALS

The two Prisoners are Eiddoel fab Aer and Mabon fab Modron.
Both are imprisoned at Gloucester, and the tales of their release by
Arthur's men have long been regarded as variants of a single story,[61]
linked by the transparent device of representing Eiddoel and Mabon
as cousins. The release of Mabon is made to depend upon previously
freeing Eiddoel, so that he may join with the others in obtaining the
release of Mabon. The name of Eiddoel's captor *Gliui*, derives from
a written form of the Latin *Glevi, and represents the genitive of the
Roman name for Gloucester, as surely as does Caerloyw, the place
of Mabon's imprisonment (see nn. to ll.831, 923). Yet all that we
know of Mabon fab Modron indicates that his mythical origins
belong far away from Gloucester: dedications to the god *Maponos*
son of *Mātrona* are found on sites in the neighbourhood of Hadrian's
Wall, and there is evidence that the centre of his cult lay in south-
west Scotland (see n. to l.685).

In 913–16 Mabon fab Modron describes himself as a notorious
prisoner, yet no previous suggestion of a tradition of imprisonment
has come down in connection with the god *Maponos*. We learn of his
imprisonment only from *Culhwch ac Olwen* and from a triad—TYP
no. 52. This is a triad of especial interest and relevance for the
subject-matter of our tale:

> Tri Goruchel Garcharavr Ynys Prydein: Llŷr Lledyeith a uu gan
> Euroswyd yg karchar, a'r eil Mabon ap Modron, a'r trydyd Gweir ap
> Geirioed.
>   Ac vn a oed goruchelach no'r tri, a uu deirnos yg karchar yg Kaer
> Oeth ac Anoeth, ac a uu deir nos yg karchar gan Wen Bendragon, ac a
> uu deir nos yg karchar hut a dan Lech Echemeint. Ac y sef oed y
> Goruchel Garcharavr hvnnv, Arthur. A'r un gwas a'e gollygavd o'r tri
> charchar hynny. Ac y sef oed y gvas hvnnv, Goreu vab Kustenin y
> geuynderv.

> (Three Exalted Prisoners of the Island of Britain: Llŷr Half-Speech,
> who was imprisoned by Euroswydd, and the second, Mabon son of
> Modron, and the third, Gweir son of Geirioedd.
>   And one (Prisoner) was more exalted than the three of them; (he)
> was three nights in prison in Caer Oeth and Anoeth, and three nights

[61] Cy xlii, 137, 139–40. See above p. xlix.

imprisoned by Gwen Pendragon, and three nights in an enchanted prison under the rock of Echeifyeint. This Exalted Prisoner was Arthur. And the same lad released him from each of these three prisons—Goreu son of Custennin, his cousin.)

Mabon fab Modron is the only name to appear in both versions of the triad. The other names in the *Culhwch* version—Lludd Llaw Ereint and Greid son of Eri—are both alluded to elsewhere in the story (in the episode of Creiddylad, 988–1004)—where Greid son of Eri does actually appear as a prisoner. In support of the TYP version there is corroborative evidence in *Preiddeu Annwn*[62] for the antiquity of a tradition of Gweir's imprisonment in Caer Sidi: here Arthur figures as a releaser of prisoners, as in *Culhwch*. But in the triad Arthur's role is reversed, and here he is himself a *goruchel garcharawr*, a prisoner more exalted than any one of the other three.

Significantly, the triad TYP no. 52 appears for the first time in the text of TYP which is common to WM and RM. It is not found in the 'Early Version'. Several of the triads in the WM-RM collection have additional notes appended to them similar to the one found here, and these additional notes betray the influence upon them of the text of the *Mabinogi*, which is contained in the same two manuscripts (see TYP xxvii-xxviii). It seems most probable that the text of *Culhwch ac Olwen* has similarly influenced the text of the triad, since the tale is also contained in WM-RM. This deduction is further enforced by the allusion in the appended note to Arthur's 'cousin' Goreu fab Custennin—a character who is virtually unknown outside the tale of *Culhwch*, and it is the tale of *Culhwch* alone which explains this relationship (see p. xxx above).

Variants of a name which is not dissimilar to that of Eiddoel are attested in HRB and in BD, where they are used to denote a duke and a bishop of Gloucester. In the *Historia Brittonum* also the names *Eldat/Eldoc* are found among the descendants of Gwrtheyrn, himself a descendant of the eponym *Gloyw* (see n. to l.694). Two allusions in poetry further substantiate the belief that there could have been an ancient traditional hero who bore some such name as Eiddoel. Perhaps all the variants of this name which have been cited derive from an original famous prisoner who was incarcerated at

[62]BT 54, ed. M. Haycock, SC xviii/xix, 52–78. (On *Llech Echemeint*—perhaps Harlech—see Elin Jones and Nerys Ann Jones, *Gwaith Llywarch ap Lleywelyn*, I, 109 and n.) and Glyn Jones, LlC x (1969), 243–4.

Gloucester in Roman or sub-Roman times, as Sir Idris Foster believed.[63] If this is so, the story of Eiddoel's release is the earlier of the two prisoner stories, although in *Culhwch ac Olwen* as we have it, this tale is hastily and summarily passed over, and all the prominence is given to the story of Mabon, the 'Immemorial Prisoner' as W. J. Gruffydd considered him to be[64]—and the episode of Mabon's delivery is focused into high relief by prefixing to it the folk-tale of the 'Oldest Animals'.

Various scholars[65] have indicated the antiquity and the widespread distribution of the international tale of the 'Oldest Animals', which has been adapted in different ways in different countries. The version of 'The Oldest Animals' in *Culhwch* is the earliest to be recorded in Wales, but several independent popular versions have come down from later times. The earliest of these so far known was published by Thomas Jones from a manuscript in the hand of the seventeenth-century Thomas Wiliems of Trefriw.[66] Here the Oldest Animals are the Eagle, Stag, Salmon, Blackbird and Owl: the Owl is the oldest of them all. In most of the popular versions the subject of the tale is the marriage of the Owl with one of the other birds, and in several of them an additional creature *'Llyfant* (the Toad of) *Cors Fochno'* is added. A triad preserved in a few late manuscripts (TYP no. 92) gives *Tri Hynaif Byd: Tylluan Gwm Kowlwyd, Eryr Gwern Abwy, a Mwyalchen Gelli Gadarn*. It is interesting to find that the place-names with which the Oldest Animals are associated remain remarkably stable throughout all the Welsh versions of the tale, although these names denote places which are either remote or not certainly identifiable (see nn. to ll. 847, 859, 871).[67] This could be taken to imply either that the folk-versions have taken the names from *Culhwch ac Olwen*, or that

[63] This matter is treated more fully in CO(1) xlviii–xlix.

[64] Cy xlii, 142; W. J. Gruffydd, *Rhiannon*, 91–102. Cf. CO(1) xliv–xlv.

[65] E. B. Cowell, 'The Legend of the Oldest Animals', Cy v (1892), 169–72; IPT 76–9. Cf. CO(1) l–liv.

[66] NLW Journal vii (1951), 62–6. Two other versions have been published by Dafydd Ifans, B xxiv (1972), 461–4. See further T. Jones, 'Y Stori Werin yng Nghymru', THSC 1970, 22–4.

[67] These place-names are briefly discussed by M. Richards, 'Arthurian Onomastics', THSC 1969, 256. See further D. Machreth Ellis, B xxi (1966), 30–7 (on *Cilgwri*), and HL 555n. (on *Gwernabwy*).

the 'Oldest Animals' in *Culhwch* was itself taken from a pre-existing folk-tale. It is highly doubtful whether the redactor of *Culhwch* had any but an indistinct notion as to the location of the places with which the 'Oldest Animals' were associated. Various of the *cywyddwyr* wish for their patrons a longevity comparable with that of one or other of the Oldest Animals—Stag, Salmon, Eagle, or (occasionally) the oak-tree. These allusions[68] make plain that the story of the 'Oldest Animals' was widely known, at least from the late fourteenth century.

Animal Helpers—usually 'Grateful Animals' alternate with the human Helpers endowed with magical gifts, who belong to stories of the type AT 513A to which *Culhwch ac Olwen* belongs. In one sense, therefore, the 'Oldest Animals', who give essential help to Arthur and his men, are duplicated further on in *Culhwch ac Olwen* by the episode of the Lame Ant (942–52), who belongs very clearly to the folk-tale motif listed in the category of 'Grateful Animals'.[69]

Several Irish parallels have been pointed out to the story of the Oldest Animals, including the tales of Tuan mac Carill and of Fintan mac Bochra.[70] Here the emphasis is slightly different from that in the Welsh versions: the two protagonists are presented as types of longevity who have survived from a remote pagan past in order that they may transmit the heroic record of that past to certain early Irish saints, in a newly Christianized Ireland. To make this credible they are said to have passed through successive animal transformations—Stag, Boar, Hawk, Salmon. These stories imply the concept of unimpeded transference between human and animal form—a concept which continually recurs in *Culhwch ac Olwen*. In Irish, as in *Culhwch*, the Salmon is characteristically presented as the oldest of all living creatures.

---

[68] For refs. see CO(1) liii–liv.

[69] See ST and TPC under B.365.2.1; B.481.1; H.1091.1. Cf. IPT 79; Stith Thomson, *The Folktale*, 54–5; CO(1) lv–lvi.

[70] LU 42–6 (Tuan); LU 305 (Fintan). See further CO(1) l–lii; J. Carey (ed. and trans.) 'Scél Tuain meic Chairill', *Ériu* xxxv (1984), 93–111; EIHM 318–19.

VIII. THE TWO BOAR HUNTS

'The Boar is massive and ugly, black in appearance and character, the archetype of unrelenting ferocity. Completely fearless, unmoved by pain, it is capable of killing dog, horse, or man. In imaginative literature it is the quarry of the epic hero . . . It is depicted as huge, as big as a horse; its eyes are wide and malevolent; the horrific mouth bristles with teeth: most awful are the curved, gleaming tusks.'[71]

The story of Arthur's great Boar Hunt, like that of the release of the Prisoners, has come down in two versions.[72] The tusk of the boar Ysgithrwyn Ben Beidd 'White Tusk Chief of Boars' was required to shave Ysbaddaden for Olwen's wedding (638–40), and the comb and scissors from between the ears of the Twrch Trwyth were required to trim the Giant's hair in celebration of the same occasion (667–70). The two boar hunts are separated by the story of Diwrnach Wyddel (Gawr), in a manner comparable to that in which the release of the two Prisoners is separated by the tale of the Oldest Animals. Sir Idris Foster believed (CO(1) lxiv) that the shorter and simpler narrative of the hunt to obtain the tusk (*ysgithr*) of Ysgithrwyn Ben Beidd was 'indigenous' to the story in the sense that it belonged to the original series of tasks imposed when the tale of the 'Giant's Daughter' came to be developed on Welsh soil. Subsequently a narrative which existed independently and was more widely known—that of the hunt for the Twrch Trwyth— became superimposed upon the story of Ysgithrwyn, and this development was facilitated by the fact that the Twrch Trwyth story had previously been assimilated into the cycle of Arthur's growing fame. This caused the narrator of *Culhwch* to make some adjustments in order to synchronize the two stories: a razor (*ellyn*) became added to the Twrch Trwyth's treasures (1090, 1185), though this was not originally listed among the *anoethau*, since Ysgithrwyn's tusk was first intended as the sole instrument with which the Giant was to be 'shaved' (i.e. to be killed). In the story as we now have it, it is Caw of Prydyn who wins Ysgithrwyn's tusk and splits the boar's head, and it is he who finally 'shaves'

---

[71] John Cummins, *The Hound and the Hawk: The Art of Medieval Hunting* (London, 1988), 96.

[72] Cf. Cy xlii, 136–7.

Ysbaddaden Pencawr, presumably with the tusk of Ysgithrwyn. In the case of the Two Boars, as in that of the Two Prisoners, the earlier and the more 'authentic' version is summarized and quickly passed over, in order to give the greater amplification and prominence to the second version—the events leading to the release of Mabon, and the hunt for the Twrch Trwyth.

The following allusions in poetry make it clear that traditions of the Twrch Trwyth, the mythical Giant Boar, were current over a wide area of Wales (and perhaps even beyond), and that they were known from a very early period:

CA 1340 (Gwarchan Cynfelyn): Gweilging *torch trychdrwyt*/ trychinfwrch trychethin;[73]

H 104,19–20 (Cynddelw): Keffitor ymdwr am *drwyd* hevelyt/ *Twrch* teryt y ar uwyd;

RP 1219,19 (Gr. ap Maredudd) milwr torch trin mal *aerdwrch trwyt*;

GIG no.2, 19–20: A gŵr gwynllwyd, *Twrch Trwyd* trin,/ Nawswyllt yn rhoi farneiswin;

IGE(2), CIV (Rhys Goch) p.317, A wnai Wilym, dreiddlym drafn/*Dwrch Drwyd*, â ffleimlwyd fflamlafn;

LGC 75,3–4: Tori y trevi trwy wŷth, ac archoll/Trychau tyrau oll val y *Twrch Trwyth*;

Ibid. (quoted in DD): Y tro a aeth i'r *Twrch Trwyd*/I Ddafydd a oddefwyd.

Trwyd is the boar's name in all the examples except for the penultimate one, and the fifteenth-century Lewys Glyn Cothi is late enough for his allusion to have been derived from a knowledge of the written text of *Culhwch ac Olwen*. If there were need for corroborative evidence that *trwyd* (see n. to ll.669–70) is the authentic form of the boar's name, it is to be had from the famous reference to Arthur's boar hunt in the *Mirabilia* appended to the ninth-century *Historia Brittonum*:[74]

---

[73] See CA 363. As Jackson points out (OSPG 155), if this allusion is contemporaneous with the earliest text of the *Gododdin*, it may be even older than the allusion to the Twrch Trwyth cited below from the *Historia Brittonum*.

[74] On the *Historia Brittonum* see HW 223–6; Wendy Davies, *Wales in the Early Middle Ages*, 205–6; D. N. Dumville, 'Nennius and the Historia Brittonum', SC x/xi (1975–6), 78–95; ibid., 'Sub-Roman Britain: History and Legend' *History*, 62 (June 1977), 176–7.

Est aliud mirabile in regione quae dicitur Buelt. est ibi cumulus lapidum et unus lapis superpositus super congestum cum vestigio canis in eo. quando venatus est porcum Troit, impressit Cabal, qui erat canis Arthuri militis, vestigium in lapide, et Arthur postea congregavit congestum lapidum sub lapide, in quo erat vestigium canis sui, et vocatur Carn Cabal. et veniunt homines et tollunt lapidem in manibus suis per spatium diei et noctis et in crastino die invenitur super congestum suum.[75]

(There is another marvel in the region which is called Buellt. There is a pile of stones there, and one stone with a dog's paw-mark on it is placed on top of the pile. When he hunted the boar Troit, Cabal—who was the dog of Arthur the warrior—left the imprint of his paw on the stone, and Arthur afterwards collected a heap of stones beneath the stone on which was the paw-mark of his dog, and it is called Carn Cabal. And men come and take the stone away in their hands, for the space of a day and a night, and on the next day it is found again upon the pile.)

The name of this mountain-top cairn has survived to the present day as Corn Cafallt[76] (*Carn Cafall*) near Rhayader (Powys), to give onomastic justification for this 'marvel'. It looks as though the tradition which purports to explain the name was already ancient by the ninth century, when the author of HB set it down in an imperfectly understood version. OW *Cabal<caballus* means a horse, and *Cafall* actually appears elsewhere in *Culhwch* as a horse's name (337, 739). The most acceptable meaning of *carn* in this place-name is that of a mountain 'cairn', but among the other meanings of *carn* is a horse's hard hoof: in no way can it denote a dog's softer paw.

[75] Ed. F. Lot, ch. 73 (p. 216) from Harleian MS 3859 (*c*. 1100). We have adopted the reading *Troit* in accordance with four MSS of this passage, in place of Harleian's *Troynt*. *Troit=Trwyd* with *wy<oe<oi* and *-t* misread at some stage by a copyist of CO as *-th* (see n. to ll. 669–70). For further discussion of the Twrch's name see Idris Foster in G. Murphy, (ed.), *Duanaire Finn* iii, 200; P. Sims-Williams in D. Whitelock *et al. Ireland and Medieval Europe* (Cambridge, 1982), 239. We retain *Trwyth* in the text (even though derived from an orthographical mistake) since WM and RM are in accord in employing it. On this passage see B. F. Roberts, AoW 90–1.

[76] On the site see Thomas Jones, 'Early Evolution', 11 (=B xvii (1958), 243). Cf. Lady Charlotte Guest's account of a visit to the place in her note on the Twrch Trwyth; Guest, *Mabinogion* 331–2. For a *Rhos Gafallt* some fifteen miles away in Ceredigion, see R. J. Thomas, B viii (1937), 125.

'The horse's cairn' is thus most probable as the original meaning of
Carn Cabal.

This seminal passage is the earliest and the only source outside
Culhwch which associates the story of the Twrch Trwyth with the
name of Arthur. Even though the detailed place-names given in the
story of the hunt for the Twrch Trwyth indicate that the author of
Culhwch was drawing for his story on popular folk-tradition from a
wide area of Wales, covering Pembroke, Glamorgan, Ceredigion
and Brycheiniog,[77] yet it is difficult to believe that he did not also
know of the *Mirabilia* in HB, which had already associated the story
of the Giant Boar with Arthur's monster-slaying feats. This
supposition is further supported by the fact that the author of
Culhwch perpetuated the name of *Cafall* as that of Arthur's dog (see
n. to l. 1015). If current onomastic tradition had been his only
source, he would perhaps have been less likely to have mistaken the
meaning of the name *Carn Cabal*.

It is difficult to judge how to estimate another story, which may
be related to that of the Twrch Trwyth, since it concerns another
magically-endowed pig—the sow *Henwen* ('Old White'). In an
extended version of a triad (TYP no. 26), Henwen is pursued by her
keeper from Cornwall across the Bristol Channel and lands in
Gwent (thus reversing the itinerary of the Twrch Trwyth), after
which her journey over much of Wales is traced with some degree of
onomastic precision. In the south of the country she gives symbolic
birth to a grain of wheat, and a grain of barley, and to a bee, but on
reaching Gwynedd she produces instead a wolf, an eagle, and the
ferocious Cath Palug 'one of the Three Scourges of Anglesey'. It is
only in the WM-RM version that Henwen is hunted by Arthur and
his men, but the triad is preserved in a simpler form in the Early
Version of TYP (see n. to *Datweir Dallpenn*, l. 197 below). The
incident may be based on a story of comparable antiquity to that of
the Twrch Trwyth, or it may be a farcical adaptation of the Giant
Boar's story.

That the Twrch Trwyth was a divine being in animal form is
borne out by Arthur's words in reply to his men's question as to the
meaning and significance (*ystyr*) of the Twrch 'He was a king, and

---

[77] In *Culhwch* the Twrch Trwyth does not actually visit Buellt, as he
does in the *Mirabilia*, but he passes close to this region in traversing
Brycheiniog.

God transformed him for his sins into a pig' (1075–6). Two early Irish sources preserve the Twrch's name in its exact cognate Irish form, and thus they have an immediate relevance for his significance or *ystyr*. A list of the members of the mythical *Tuatha Dé Danann* ('People of the Goddess Dana') in the *Lebor Gabála Érenn*[78] ('Book of the Taking of Ireland') gives: *Brigid banfile . . . is aicci ro bhai Fé a Menn, da righ-damhraidhi . . . Ocus is aco ro bai Torc Triath.i.righ torcraidhi Érenn agus is de ata Magh Triath-airne . . .*'[79] ('Brigid the woman-poet, it is she who possessed Fé and Menn, the two royal oxen . . . And with them was Torc Triath, king of the boars of Ireland, from whom Magh Triathairne is named.') Again, in *Cormac's Glossary*[80] the term *Orc Treith* is explained as *nomen do mac rig . . . Triath enim rex vocatur, unde dixit poeta, Oinach n-uire treith.i.biadh agus edach loghmar . . .*' ('Name for a king's son . . . a king is called *triath*, hence the poet said 'Feast for a king's son, food and precious clothes . . .''). These two sources are at least as old as the *Mirabilia* in HB.

An echo of a similar belief in the exalted status and supernatural character of the boar persists in the story of the semi-divine hero Diarmaid Ui Dhuibhne,[81] who was killed by an enchanted boar who had been reared as his foster-brother, hence it was *geis* or taboo, throughout his life, for Diarmaid to kill boars. The *Dindshenchas* (Irish poems or prose notes with stories purporting

---

[78] R. A. S. Macalister, (ed.), *Lebor Gabála Érenn* (ITS vol. xli, Dublin, 1941), 196. According to O'Rahilly, EIHM 193–5, the origins of the *Lebor Gabála* go back to the eighth century.

[79] That is, Treitheirne in Munster; E. Hogan, *Onomasticon Goedelicon*, 645. The 'two royal oxen' are reminiscent of Nynniaw and Peibyaw among the *anoethau* (ll. 599–600).

[80] *Sanas Cormaic* ed. J. O'Donovan and Whitley Stokes, (Calcutta, 1868), 179. *Orc* according to DIL (N-O-P, col.153) has two meanings a) 'a young pig' (archaic and poetic), and b) 'of the young of other animals' referring to *Sanas Cormaic*. *Torc* means i) 'boar', ii) 'hero, chieftain', DIL (to-tu col.259). For *triath* see ibid. 307 'lord, chieftain. Given in the Laws as highest of 26 titles of dignity'—again with reference to *Sanas Cormaic*.

[81] Nessa Ni Sheaghdha, (ed. and trans.), *Toruigheacht Dhiarmada agus Ghrainne* (ITS vol. xlviii, Dublin, 1967), xxiv, 85–7; G. Murphy, *Duanaire Finn* iii, xxxv-vi.

to give onomastic explanations of place-names)[82] preserve a number of anecdotes in which men and women are transformed into boars or sows, often with accompanying sex-transition. One of these tales relates to a certain *Caelcheis*, a name which is significantly similar to that of *Culhwch* (see n. to l. 10). And we have seen that the divine *Torc Triath* was thought to be commemorated in the place-name *Treitheirne*. The itinerary of the Twrch Trwyth from his arrival at Porth Clais in Dyfed to his final immersion in the Severn estuary off Cornwall, is similarly regarded in the story as commemorated in place-names spread widely over the southern half of Wales. The Twrch's companion Grugyn is said to have been slain at *Garth Grugyn* in Ceredigion (see nn. to ll. 1083, 1160). These traditions are paralleled in the *Mabinogi*, where each *Mochtref* and *Mochnant* throughout the country is said to record a place through which Pryderi passed when he brought his pigs from Dyfed to Gwynedd. In the main these stories have usually been regarded as *post hoc* attempts to explain pre-existing place-names.[83]

All the evidence goes to show that the concept of a mythical Giant Boar, who was in reality a god or a king under enchantment, goes back for many centuries, and has its origins in pagan Celtic religious belief. The comb, razor, and scissors between the ears of the Twrch Trwyth appear to symbolize his regal status (he was son of Taredd *Wledig*), and may have held a profound significance for the author of the story—whether or not it was he, or a predecessor, who endowed the Twrch with these *anoethau*. They cannot be divorced from the identical implements used by Arthur when he confirms his kinship with Culhwch by trimming his hair, or again from those with which St Germanus intended that Guorthigirn (Gwrtheyrn) should perform the same act for his own son (see above, pp. xxxi-xxxii). There is no reason to conclude that either Wales or Ireland borrowed the concept of the royal boar *Trwyd/Triath* from the other country; both language and iconography prove that zoomorphism of this kind was a prominent feature of

---

[82] See E. J. Gwynn, *The Metrical Dindshenchas* (5 vols., Dublin 1903–35) iii, 386–94; *The Rennes Dindshenchas*, RC xv (1894), 470–2. For relevant material from the *Dindshenchas* see further CO(1) lxix-lxx.

[83] Cf. W. J. Gruffydd, *Math fab Mathonwy*, 335, and CO(1) lxxii. Lady Charlotte Guest speculates interestingly on this matter in the introduction to her *Mabinogion*. See also *Met.Din.* v, 91–2, on the importance of onomastic knowledge for the learned orders in Ireland.

pagan Celtic belief, and one which has come down in both countries from the remote past on the European continent. The boar has been described as 'the cult-animal *par excellence*',[84] and the divine boar was represented in the Gaulish swine-god *Moccus*. A deity in the form of a boar is very fittingly and strikingly typified by a sculpture from pre-Roman Gaul[85] which depicts a crude human figure wearing a torque, and with a boar engraved across its torso. The story of *Culhwch ac Olwen* is fully charged with survivals of a faith in the credibility of frequent and easy interchange between human and animal form.

[84] See Anne Ross, PCB 308–21.
[85] PCB 310 and plate 79a (from Euffigneix, France).

IX. STYLE, STRUCTURE AND INFLUENCE

The framework of *Culhwch ac Olwen* is that of a pre-existing folk-tale, containing a variety of international themes. Celtic folklore, and legendary matter are drawn upon as the story proceeds. Yet as it stands *Culhwch* is a literary composition: the work of an unknown author. It is likely that the story was primarily intended for reading aloud to a receptive audience—whether this was courtly or monastic—an audience which shared with the author a common cultural inheritance, common beliefs, assumptions, and expectations.

The variations in style which the story displays are deeply indebted to the craftsmanship of the oral storyteller. The short, abrupt sentences of the opening section and the concise treatment given to such later episodes as that of the Lame Ant, the release of Eiddoel and the final release of Mabon, have a good deal in common with the summary style which characterizes a number of Old Irish tales. These have been characterized as 'artistic compositions in their own right', and as demonstrating by their form that their author was fully aware of the different requirements of oral and of written literature.[86] In Welsh, as in Irish, this terse style of narration allows nevertheless for the frequent verbatim reporting of conversations and descriptions. The pace of the story quickens and takes on a heroic dimension with Culhwch's departure for Arthur's court, and the style is heightened at this point by two rhythmical rhetorical passages, the one describing the hero's splendid appearance and equipment as he rides on his way, and the other

[86] Cf. Gearóid Mac Eoin, *Studia Hibernica* 4 (1964), 245, 'The short sagas seem to be the result of an attempt to achieve an artistically satisfying form based on the invariable elements in the tales. For this dialogue, descriptions, and other such matter was included. This ... seems to have led the writers to an appreciation of the different requirements of oral and written literature, for the consistent style of the short sagas shows that their authors were aware of this difference.' Dr B. F. Roberts regards this 'crisp, brisk style' in Welsh as 'one element in the passage from an oral to a literary medium': 'Middle Welsh Prose Romances' p. 221 in *The Craft of Fiction* ed. Leigh A. Arathoon (Rochester, Michigan, 1984).

reporting Glewlwyd's extended boast about Arthur's far-flung conquests. Later variations in style and tempo include the harsh comedy of Ysbaddaden's reception of Arthur's emissaries, contrasted with the dramatic, even majestic style of the successive visits made in turn by these same emissaries to the Oldest Animals, the representatives of the primeval world. Subsequent episodes are narrated in varying amounts of detail, until they culminate in the riotous sweep across Wales with which the story reaches its climax in the great boar hunt. Primitive and rather slapstick humour frequently appears: as in the account of Cei's reception by Custennin's wife, and above all in the violent final episode in the cave of the Black Witch. Burlesque elements recur throughout the Arthurian Court List, and irony is never far absent,[87] including ironic understatement. Yet at this distance of time it is virtually impossible for us to appreciate the finer shades of this irony, since the basic assumptions of both author and audience are too far removed from us, and too remote from our own culture.

Dr B. F. Roberts has drawn attention to the triple structure of the story,[88] in which each of the first two sections terminates with an extended list. The first section recounts the hero's early life, and brings him to Arthur's court; it ends with the long list of court members who are named as Culhwch's sureties; the second brings Culhwch and his companions to the fortress of Ysbaddaden, and concludes with the list of *anoethau* stipulated by the Giant; while the remainder of the story recounts the achievement of the *anoethau*, and leads up to the Giant's death. Each of the two lists has been considerably inflated, probably at different periods and at the hands of successive scribes. In view of these obvious accretions, the failure of the author to fulfil in detail the expectations aroused by the long list of *anoethau* is apparent rather than real, for evidently the selection of the tasks completed is intended to be representative, and to imply the achievement of all of them. This is made clear in Arthur's question which introduces the final task 'Is there any of the tasks *still* not obtained?' Indeed one might venture to suggest that in the original folk-tale three great tasks alone were specified: an agricultural task of ploughing, sowing, and reaping a field (as in the Argonauts) in order to provide food and drink for the wedding-

[87] See J. N. Radner, 'Interpreting Irony in Medieval Literature: the Case of *Culhwch ac Olwen*', CMCS 16 (1988), 41–59.

[88] B. F. Roberts, loc.cit. 218–19; ibid. Ast.H. 299–300.

feast; the task of obtaining one of the (Thirteen?) Otherworld Treasures (the cauldron of Diwrnach is the one which is narrated in full), and the task of obtaining the tusk of a dangerous boar, with which to 'shave' Ysbaddaden, (a euphemism for killing him). These tasks were not only duplicated and triplicated in the list as we have it, but they became further inflated by the addition of more names of men and animals not previously mentioned, and of feats which earlier tradition had associated with Arthur and his men, comprising two more giant stories (Dillus and Wrnach), Arthur's release of a famous prisoner, Arthur's fight with a hag, and Arthur's contest with the giant boar Twrch Trwyth—an episode which became superimposed upon the earlier story of Ysgithrwyn Chief of Boars (see above p. lxiv). However this may be, from the author's point of view the story was fully rounded off and drawn to its logical conclusion with the terse account of Ysbaddaden's horrific end.

The lyrical description of Olwen in the second of the tripartite divisions (487–98) counterbalances the description of Culhwch in the first (60–81), even down to the detail of the 'four white trefoils' left in her track, which purposely recall the four sods cast up by Culhwch's horse. These two passages are early instances of rhetoric or *araith* (Latin *oratio*): passages of heightened prose in rhythmical periods, in which substantives may be welded into unfamiliar compounds and governed by a series of alliterating compound adjectives. This rhetorical style bears some resemblance to the elaborate diction of the Gogynfeirdd, the court poets of medieval Wales. Melville Richards[89] traced its origins in Middle Welsh prose texts, and showed that these origins appear already in sporadic collocations in the Four Branches of the *Mabinogi* (*gwas gwineu mawr teyrneid, march drythyll llamsachus,* etc.). They become increasingly prominent in the later tales *Peredur, Gereint fab Erbin,* and *Breuddwyd Rhonabwy,* but none of these later tales have such striking and prominent passages of rhetorical description as those in *Culhwch.*

This style reaches its final development in the *Areithiau Pros* ('Prose Rhetorics') which come to light in manuscripts towards the middle of the sixteenth century, though undoubtedly their origins

---

[89] Melville Richards, *Breudwyt Ronabwy* (University of Wales Press, 1948), Rhagymadrodd.

go back to a very much earlier date.[90] Not only do these passages contain echoes of *Culhwch* and of the other 'Mabinogion' tales, but Dr B. F. Roberts has pointed out the survival in them of a similar rhythmical pattern to that which is found also in the two rhetorical passages in *Culhwch* to which we have just referred.[91] Both in their earliest and in their latest manifestations these passages of *araith* reflect the manner of delivery of the *cyfarwydd* or oral storyteller, and they clearly demand an oral delivery to do them full justice. They are significantly paralleled in the inflated rhetorical style which characterizes the later Middle Irish sagas, such as Recension II (the Book of Leinster) version of the *Táin*. It is subsequently reflected in the descriptive passages known as 'runs' which have remained a constant feature of Gaelic folk-tales down to modern times.[92] These 'runs' are employed as markers to signify the arrival of a significant point in the story, such as the hero's preparations for battle or for a sea-voyage, or the description of a heroine's beauty, or they are employed for the imposition of a *geis* or taboo (cf. Ysbaddaden's imposing of the *anoethau*). All the evidence suggests that this kind of rhetorical prose arose independently in Irish and in Welsh, and that in both languages it derives from a common Celtic inheritance which long antedates its appearance in written form. Sir Idris Foster envisaged the Welsh passages of *araith* as having originated at a time when the division between poetry and prose was not so clearly differentiated, nor so decisively marked as it was normally to become in later times.[93]

It is in the nature of the folk-tale framework of *Culhwch* that the 'primary' characters (though not necessarily the principal ones) in this story—Culhwch and his family, Olwen, Ysbaddaden, Custennin—are untraditional, and have almost no existence outside the story itself. Cognate versions of the tale 'Six Go

[90] D. Gwenallt Jones, *Yr Areithiau Pros* (University of Wales Press, 1934).

[91] B. F. Roberts, 'Tales and Romances' in A. O. H. Jarman and Gwilym Rees Hughes (eds.), *A Guide to Welsh Literature I* (Swansea, 1976), 241.

[92] Cf. Alan Bruford, 'Gaelic Folktales and Mediaeval Romances', *Bealoideas: The Folklore of Ireland Society*, xxxiv (Dublin, 1966), esp. pp. 36–40; CO(1), xcv.

[93] I. Ll. Foster, 'Y Cefndir' in *Y Traddodiad Rhyddiaith* I (Llandysul, 1970), 20–1. See further CO(1) xciv–xcvi.

Through the World' show it to be an entity which could, and probably did, exist quite separately from the Arthurian complex onto which it became subsequently grafted. In early British tradition Arthur was the most notorious of Giant Slayers, hence 'Arthur's Court' provided a fitting context for Culhwch's search for Olwen, and Arthur's followers were pressed into service as Culhwch's companions on his quest. It is possible also that the legendary fame of Arthur's great boar hunt caused the attraction to it of Culhwch's name ('slender pigling', see n. to l.10): otherwise this name seems an arbitrary choice for that of the hero who wooed the 'Giant's Daughter'. The names of Arthur's immediate followers—Cei, Bedwyr, and Gwalchmei—are names of general currency throughout early Welsh sources, and are equally familiar in the Triads and in poetry, in the romances and in the *Brut*.

Although these familiar Arthurian names appear in *Trioedd Ynys Prydein*, it is not easy to regard the 'Early Version' of the Triads either as a source for *Culhwch ac Olwen*, or as a work derived from the tale—at any rate in its final form. The two appear to be independent developments of Welsh Arthurian story, indebted similarly to both written and unwritten sources, and each containing names not found in the other. The same cannot be claimed for the collection of Triads in the White Book and the Red Book of Hergest: since in several instances this collection is suspect of having been influenced by written texts contained in the same two manuscripts (cf. *Tri Goruchel Garcharawr*, pp. lx–lxi). In discussing the parallel (though incomplete) versions of the Arthurian Court List which are found in both *Breuddwyd Rhonabwy* and *Gereint fab Erbin* it was proposed (p. xl) that these two lists derive from the Court List in *Culhwch*, but apparently from an earlier text of the tale from that which has come down, and the same appears to be true of the even lengthier list of names derived from *Culhwch* in *Englynion y Clyweit* (see idem). Actual verbal borrowings from *Culhwch* are found both in *Peredur* (see nn. to ll.69, 522) and in *Breuddwyd Rhonabwy* where, as in *Culhwch*, the battle of Camlan is said to have been 'woven' or 'plotted' (*estoui/ystoui*; see n. to l.297): in *Culhwch* this was done by nine plotters together, and in *Breuddwyd Rhonabwy* by the single character Iddawg Cordd Prydein.

The description of Peredur's boorish entry into Arthur's court and his uncouth appearance is an obvious parody of Culhwch's splendid arrival at the court, and his aggressive behaviour there.

Another echo of the tale—though in this case it is not a parody—occurs in *Seith Doethon Rufein*,[94] where a stepmother holds a conversation with an old hag in words which almost exactly reproduce the conversation between Culhwch's stepmother and the *hen wrach* whom she questions about her husband's offspring. (This incident is only found in the Welsh version of *Seith Doethon Rufein*, and in no other.) Among the *Areithiau* or 'Prose Rhetorics' the parody *Araith Iolo Goch* is the one most obviously indebted to *Culhwch ac Olwen*:[95] apart from verbal echoes it includes the names of Olwen and Ysbaddaden, together with a number of other names from the Court List.

Among the poets it seems virtually certain that Dafydd ap Gwilym was the earliest to quote from the actual written text of *Culhwch ac Olwen*, (as he appears also to have done when he quotes names from the *Mabinogi*).[96] He recalls the *dau ychen Fannog* (GDG 130,15–16) and he reproaches Gruffudd Gryg with the taunt that if forks were to be had to raise his eyelids (recalling those of Ysbaddaden) it would be possible for words, like a poisoned spear, to make an impact on him (GDG 154,15–20). These allusions are the less surprising since there is ample evidence for Dafydd's acquaintance with much of the story material which has come down in the White Book, and his evident familiarity with Rhydderch ab Ieuan Llwyd,[97] its apparent owner, may quite possibly have given him access to the White Book itself. More then one copy of the written text of *Culhwch ac Olwen* was certainly in circulation after the mid fourteenth century, and thereafter the allusions made by poets to *Culhwch* and to the other native and foreign tales become too numerous to need any accounting for.

[94] H. Lewis (ed.), *Chwedleu Seith Doethon Rufein* (University of Wales Press 1925, 1967),esp. pp. 23, 44–5.

[95] *Yr Areithiau Pros* pp. 12–17. Preserved only in a late manuscript Mostyn 133 (RWM i,114) in the hand of the copyist John Jones Gellilyfdy.

[96] R. Bromwich, 'Cyfeiriadau Dafydd ap Gwilym at Chwedl a Rhamant', YB xii (1982), 59–60.

[97] On Rhydderch ab Ieuan Llwyd and his connection with the White Book see introduction by R. M. Jones to WM (2), xiii–xiv, and Daniel Huws, 'Llyfr Gwyn Rhydderch', CMCS 21 (1991), 19–22.

X. DATE AND PROVENANCE OF THE TALE

The world envisaged by the author of *Culhwch ac Olwen* extended from St David's westwards to Ireland and through Pembrokeshire, Brycheiniog, Ceredigion, and Glamorgan to Devon, Cornwall, and Brittany. Evidently the author was also vaguely aware of places in north Britain—*Penn Blathaon* (262), *trugein cantref Pryd(y)n* (647), *Y Gogled* (997, 1012, 1208), *Dunart brenhin y Gogled* (254). And he had at least *heard* of countries further afield—Normandy, France, Llychlyn (Scandinavia), Europe, India, and Africa. He may have heard stories concerning some of the more exotic legendary places in which Glewlwyd locates Arthur's far-flung adventures (117–26). But his detailed local knowledge of places and their geographical relation to each other was confined to the area of south Wales traversed by the Twrch Trwyth and his attendant boars when they were hunted across the country by Arthur and his men. Traces of the cults of several of the Welsh saints are manifested over the whole area of the great hunt, from Ireland through Wales and across to Cornwall. The influence of these saints must have been long felt as a living force in these areas between the ninth and eleventh centuries: the very period when the traditions which made up *Culhwch ac Olwen* were being assembled. For early audiences many of the places and people alluded to in the story would have held resonances which they can no longer hold for us: their names would have evoked familiar landmarks by land or by sea, and they would have recalled other stories, familiar to these early audiences but now irretrievably lost to us.

The story takes us back to an archaic world whose primitive manners lie beyond our sympathy and comprehension.[98] Very little emotion or human response is in any way expressed, and there is a total absence of compassion. No apology or explanation is either given or expected for deeds of unprovoked violence: King Doged is killed and his wife is forcefully abducted, Wrnach the Giant is slain with his own sword, and for no apparent reason, Nwython is killed and his son is compelled to eat his father's heart, Ysbaddaden is violently decapitated and his dismembered head is placed on a stake

[98] Cf. D. S. Evans, YB xiii (1985), 101–13.

before his own fortress. Such crude barbarities outdistance anything—even the atrocities of Efnisien—which is in the least comparable in the Four Branches of the *Mabinogi*. There is a complete lack of moral perspective in *Culhwch*. But the same is true, if only to a lesser degree, in the miracle-working Lives of the Welsh saints.

In contrast to all this savagery *Culhwch ac Olwen* bears the signs of having been shaped by an author familiar with Christian customs and practices. There is mention of prayer: Cilydd's countrymen pray that he shall have an heir, and when Culhwch is born, he is baptized (10). Though the custom of baptism is alluded to in the Four Branches, it is distanced from the author's own world by the explanation *o'r bedyd a wneit yna* 'with the baptism which was used then', and God's presence is recognized only in the frequent greetings and asseverations *Duw a ro da it, Y rof a Duw*, etc. These are partly paralleled in *Culhwch* by the greetings *Nawd Duw ragoch* (438), *Henpych well . . . o Duw ac o dyn* (513–14), and the asseveration *Gwir Dyw* (147, 162, 172), though these occur less frequently than in PKM. The Arthurian Court List includes both a bishop (Bitwini Escob) and a priest (Kethtrwm Offeirad), and reference is made to a guardian angel (*engyl canhorthwy*, 230), and to a saint (Cynwyl sant)—as having been present at the battle of Camlan. The existence of both saints and devils is recognized: the saints of Ireland come to ask Arthur's protection on his arrival in the country (1062), and the mythical Gwyn ap Nudd is said to possess the nature of *dieuyl Annwuyn* 'the devils of Hell'.[99] The number of references in the tale to *Duw, Dyw* (God) is both distinctive and significant. Both the Stag and the Blackbird direct Arthur's men to 'a tribe of animals God created before me' (857, 870). On more than one occasion God is perceived to have intervened in human affairs by transforming men into animals as a punishment for their unspecified sins: the Twrch Trwyth was a king who had been transformed into a boar

[99] See n. to l.714. *Annwfn*, normally the Celtic 'Otherworld', here clearly denotes hell, just as *gwrthdir Uffern* 'the uplands of hell' is employed on three occasions in the tale (ll.189, 653, 1207) as a euphemism for the pagan Otherworld. In l.409 there is reference to a *gwlat aghred*, an 'unbelieving' or pagan country. In l.715 the world is described as *pressen*, a word which recalls the early religious *englynion* in the Juvencus MS (BWP 101), and is found in religious verse in the Black Book and elsewhere (see p. xvii above).

(1075–6), as had his accompanying pigs (1081–2); Nynnyaw and Peibyaw, kings of Erging, had been metamorphosed into oxen (599–600), and the bitch Rhymhi had (presumably) been turned into the form of a she-wolf (935). Such direct divine intervention is unparalleled in the other Welsh tales: Math fab Mathonwy can unaided transform his errant nephews into the alternating shapes of stag, boar, and wolf (with accompanying sex-changes)—before causing the offspring of these strange unions to be baptized (PKM 75,25).

Culhwch ac Olwen is unique among the medieval Welsh tales in respect of its author's evident familiarity with the native learning of the Welsh church, comprising the Lives and genealogies of the saints, the Bucheddau and Bonedd y Saint. The Life of St Cadog by Lifris of Llancarfan[100] and the Life of St David by Rhigyfarch of Llanbadarn[101] are the two earliest, as well as the two most important of these Lives in relation to Culhwch ac Olwen. Both were written in Latin by Welsh (as distinct from Norman) ecclesiastics, and are believed to have been originally composed at some date during the last decades of the eleventh century, though the original manuscripts have not come down.[102] Both show points of contact with the Irish church, and with the traditions of Irish saints. They are the only two Lives of Welsh saints which certainly antedate the publication of Geoffrey of Monmouth's Historia Regum Britanniae in 1138. This fact gives an especial interest to the Life of St Cadog, as one of the small group of Welsh saints' Lives in which Arthur—rex illustrissimus Britanniae—plays the part of a rex tyrranus who is

[100] Ed. and trans, VSB 24–141. See H. D. Emanuel, 'An Analysis of the Composition of the 'Vita Cadoci'', NLW Journal vii (1952), 217–26.

[101] Ed and trans. J. W. James, Rhigyfarch's Life of St David (University of Wales Press, 1967).

[102] Recensions of the Life of St David date from the mid twelfth century (James, op.cit. xi–xiv; WLSD xli; cf. D. P. Kirby, 'A Note on Rhigyfarch's Life of David', WHR 4 (1969). The earliest MS of the Life of St Cadog (Cot. Vesp. A. xiv), dates from c.1200 (VSB viii; Emanuel, op. cit. 217). The date of the two Lives relative to each other has not yet been satisfactorily established. See further W. Davies, Wales in the Early Middle Ages (Leicester, 1982), 208; C. N. L. Brooke, 'St. Peter of Glou-cester and St. Cadog of Llancarfan', ch.III in C. N. L. Brooke, The Church and the Welsh Border in the Central Middle Ages (Boydell and Brewer, 1986) (=revised version of chapter first published in N. K. Chadwick (ed.) Celt and Saxon (Cambridge, 1963).

obliged to submit to St Cadog's higher authority and to make restitution to the saint for his misdeeds. It is only in the Life of St Cadog that Cei and Bedwyr are named, and play their traditional part as Arthur's companions, appearing with him in two episodes which purport to explain archaic place-names in south-east Wales— *Boch Rhiw Carn*[103] and *Rhyd Gwrthebau*.[104] The frequency of such onomastic stories—which explain place-names by reference to events which are believed to have occurred at them—is but one of the features which indicate that the Life of St Cadog draws on a traditional background which is in some ways closely similar to that of *Culhwch ac Olwen*.

The existence of a special relationship between *Culhwch* and the Life of St Cadog is further borne out by the prominence in both of the character of Caw of Prydyn (see n. to l.647), and of certain other names which appear in the Court List—Samson, Sawyl Penn Uchel, Brys mab Bryssethach (see nn. to ll.214, 332 and 344). These references add weight to the strong suggestion which is offered by the occurrence in *Culhwch* of the two place-names *Dinsol* and *Mynyd Bannawc* (ll.106, 597, see nn.) to the effect that the text of the *Vita Cadoci* was actually available and known to the final author of *Culhwch ac Olwen*.

Caw of Prydyn was to become a legendary figure in Wales, but he is recorded first in the earlier of the two Lives of Gildas, written in the ninth century by a monk of Ruys in Brittany. Both here and in the later Life by Caradog of Llancarfan, Caw is presented as the father of St Gildas and of a number of other sons, some of whose names appear in the Arthurian Court List (see nn. to ll.206–13). There is evidently some connection between these names and one or both of the Lives of Gildas. Another figure who forms a fundamental link between *Culhwch* and the Lives and genealogies of the Welsh saints is *Anlawd/Amlawd Wledig* (see p. xxx above, and n. to l.2), the grandfather of Arthur, Culhwch, and Goreu fab Custennin, as well as of St Illtud. The Life of St Illtud appears to provide the earliest instance of his name—*Anlaud Britannie rex*. Anlawd(d)is an untraditional figure, in the sense that he is known only from ByS, the Life of St Illtud, and from *Brut y Brenhinedd*, rather than from poetry or Triads. But his name proved convenient

[103] 'The cheek of the cairn's slope'(?), VSB 26.
[104] 'The Ford of Responses'(or 'Objections'), VSB 72. On Lifris's fondness for giving explanations of place-names see Brooke, loc.cit. 86.

as that of the progenitor of the mothers of all these secular and
religious heroes. We have seen above (pp. lxv-lxvi) that an additional
document of ecclesiastical provenance which may have been known
to the author of *Culhwch ac Olwen* was one which contained the
Mirabilia attached to the *Historia Brittonum*.

The chief significance for *Culhwch* of the Life of St David lies in
the evidence it provides for cultural links with Ireland during the
very period in which the story was taking shape. Rhigyfarch, the
author of the Life, was one of the sons of Sulien, the famous scholar
of Llanbadarn and bishop of St David's, who had spent years of
study in Ireland and was in a position to transmit the fruits of this
study to his sons. *Sulien*—a rare name—is even included in the
Arthurian Court List (203). The close proximity of Ireland and of
Irish ecclesiastical learning (together with a suspicion of national
rivalry) is made apparent from the very beginning of the Life of St
David, when an angel warns St Patrick against settling on the site
which was later to become Mynyw or St David's, on the grounds
that the place was to be reserved for a more holy saint who was yet
to be born. David is baptized by Ailbe, a bishop from Munster, and
later he has several Irish disciples, including St Aidan of Ferns. A
number of Irish saints are said to have visited St David, and the
allusions to journeys by ecclesiastics between Ireland and St David's
are corroborated by references in the Irish Lives of saints. St David's
local conflict with the pagan Irishman Boia is a reminiscence of the
strong Irish presence in Dyfed in the early centuries. There is
evidence that the area covered by the cult of St David corresponded
approximately and significantly with the route of the Twrch
Trwyth through Wales after he landed at Porth Clais, close to St
David's—a place from which roads led through south Wales, and
continued as far as Devon and Cornwall. As in the Life of St Cadog,
there are references which are evocative of names in *Culhwch*—a
Constantine king of Cornwall (see n. to l.435), and 'Proprius' a
Latinization of the name of Peibyaw king of Erging (599), more
correctly named as *Pebiawc* in the Welsh version of the Life of St
David. It is tempting to discern a covert reference to the ascetic
practices of St David's monks in the allusion to the *ychen bannawg*
(see nn. to ll.593-6).

All the evidence we have surveyed points to the last decades of the
eleventh century, perhaps the turn of the century, *c.*1100, as the
most likely period for the redaction of *Culhwch* in a form

approaching that in which we now have it. The linguistic evidence, though by its nature it cannot be precise, is in general conformity with this dating. Obviously *Culhwch* has received subsequent accretions in the course of its long transmission between the eleventh century and the date of the two fourteenth-century manuscripts in which the text is preserved. In particular, additions have surely been made both to the Arthurian Court List and to the list of *anoethau*. The relative dating of *Culhwch* to elements in *Brut y Brenhinedd* also poses some virtually insoluble problems (see nn. to *Gwalchmei, Gwenhwyfar, Caledfwlch*). Sir Idris Foster[105] stressed the historical events of the year 1081 as significant for the dating of *Culhwch*, and these events point to a period of composition similar to that indicated by the ecclesiastical sources. In 1081 Gruffudd ap Cynan came across from his exile in Ireland and landed (like the Twrch Trwyth) at Porth Clais near St David's, where he joined with Rhys ap Tewdwr, the ruler of Deheubarth, and won the battle of Mynydd Carn.[106] In the same year William the Conqueror is said to have visited St David's, where it is most likely that he made peace with Rhys ap Tewdwr.[107] It is not unlikely that these happenings were in the mind of the author of *Culhwch*, and that they had an influence on his portrayal of certain events in the story.

This seems to be as far as we can go in determining the probable historical, geographical, and cultural background of the author of *Culhwch ac Olwen*. Where could the story have been committed to writing? Everything points to the south-west of Wales, to an important monastic centre such as St David's, Carmarthen, or Llandeilo Fawr. In Wales, and particularly in the south, there took place between the ninth and the eleventh centuries a revival of interest in the country's past, together with the cultivation of a new genre of prose, and these together amounted to a cultural renaissance. We have seen that *Culhwch ac Olwen* shares a similarity of intellectual background and betrays certain common interests with more than one of the Lives of the saints. In south Wales there was a continual awareness of closeness to Ireland, with Porth Clais and St David's as places from which passage between the two countries was both frequent and relatively easy. The famous bishop Sulien must have taken this route when he travelled to Ireland, and

[105] ALMA 38–9; CO(1) lxxxix.
[106] HW 384–5; HGVK xvi, 77–8.
[107] HW 393–4.

it is difficult to avoid seeing in the Twrch Trwyth's arrival at Porth Clais a reverberation of Gruffudd ap Cynan's return to the same place after the first of his two periods of exile in Ireland.

It has been seen above (pp. xv-xxv) that the language of *Culhwch ac Olwen* is archaic and belongs to the end of the OW period, and that it shows a greater similarity to the language of the early poetry and that of the Gogynfeirdd, as well as to the earliest fragments of OW prose preserved in the Laws and other documents, than to the language of the later prose tales. It has been seen also that certain comparisons can be made with the language spoken today in certain areas of south Wales: with the speech of Pembroke and west Glamorgan, and more particularly with that of Y Cantref Mawr in north Carmarthenshire. It is tempting to set *Culhwch ac Olwen* against the background of the spoken language of this area, and to relate it to a centre where such Old Welsh documents as the *Surexit* Memorandum and possibly the Computus fragment were produced and preserved.

We have also considered in detail the significant correspondences between the language of *Culhwch* and the language of the Black Book of Carmarthen, together with some of its contents, particularly the poem *Pa Gur yw y Porthaur*. This manuscript was inscribed at the priory of Carmarthen in the mid thirteenth century.[108] Linguistic evidence indicates that *Culhwch* was produced at some monastic centre which lay close to the route taken by the Twrch Trwyth. We do not know exactly where this was, but there seems to be a good case for believing that *Culhwch ac Olwen*, like the Black Book itself, belongs to Carmarthen.

---

[108] LlDC xvii. See further A. O. H. Jarman, 'Llyfr Du Caerfyrddin/ The Black Book of Carmarthen', PBA lxxi (1985), 333–56, and AoW 7–8.

Culhwch ac Olwen

Culhwch's Birth: His Jealous Stepmother

[WM. col. 452]

Kilyd mab Kyledon[1] Wledic a uynnei wreic kynmwyd ac ef.
Sef gwreic a uynnwys[2], Goleudyt merch Anlawd Wledic.
Gwedy y west genti,[3] mynet y wlat y gwedi malkawn a
geffynt etiued. A chaffael[4] mab ohonu[5] trwy weti y wlad.
5 Ac o'r awr y delis beichogi, yd aeth hitheu ygwylldawc heb
dygredu anhed. Pan dyuu y thymp idi, ef a dyuu y iawn
bwyll iti. Sef y dyuu myn yd oed meichad[6] yn cadw kenuein
o uoch. A rac ouyn y moch enghi a oruc y urenhines. A
chymryt y mab a oruc y meichad hyt pan dyuu y'r llys. A
10 bydydaw y mab a orucpwyt,[7] a gyrru Kulhwch arnaw dy[8]
vrth y gaffel yn retkyr hwch. Bonhedic hagen oed y mab;
keuynderw dy Arthur[9] oed. A rodi y mab a orucpwyd[10] ar
ueithrin.

A gwedy hynny klyuychu[11] mam y mab, Goleudyt merch
15 Anlawd Wledic. Sef a oruc hi galw y chymar attei, ac
amkawd hi[12] vrthaw ef, 'Marw uydaf i o'r cleuyt hwnn, a
gwreic arall a uynny ditheu. A reedouyd ynt y gwraged
weithon. Drwc yw iti hagen llygru dy uab. Sef y harchaf it
na mynnych wreic hyt pan welych dryssien deu peinawc ar
20 uym bed.'[13] Adaw a oruc ynteu hynny idi. Galw y hathro
attei a oruc hitheu ac erchi idaw amlymu[14] y bed pob [453]
blwydyn hyd na thyffei[15] dim arnaw. Marw[16] y urenhines.
Sef a wna[e]i[17] y brenhin gyrru gwas pob bore y ydrych
malkawn[18] a dyffei dim ar y bed. Gwallocau a oruc yr athro
25 ym penn y seith ulwydyn y ryn ry adawsei[19] y'r urenhines.

[1]Kelydon.
[2]ffynnwys W., vynnawd R.
[3]genthi.
[4]a chaffel.
[5]ohonunt.
[6]myn yd ydoed y meichat.
[7]wnaethpwyt.
[8]*om.*
[9]y arthur.
[10]wnaethpwyt.
[11]cleuychu.
[12]yna y dywat hi.
[13]vym bed i.
[14]amlynu.
[15]nathffei W., na thyuei R.
[16]marw uu.
[17]a wnaei.
[18]*om.*
[19]seith mlyned yr hynn a adawssei.

Diwarnawd yn hyly yr brenhin;[1] dygyrchu y gorfflan[2] a
oruc;[3] gweled y bed a uynnei trw yt gaffei wreicca. Gwelet y
dryssïen a oruc. Ac mal y gwelas mynet a oruc y brenhin yg
kyghor kwt gaffei[4] wreic. Amkawd[5] un o'r kyghorwyr,
30 'Mi a wydwn wreic a[6] da it a wedei. Sef yw honno gwreic
Doget Urenhin.' Kyghor uu ganthunt[7] y chyrchu, A llad y
brenhin a dwyn y wreic atref ganthu[8] a orugant ac un uerch a
oed idi gyd a hi. A gwereskyn[9] tir y brenhin a wnaethant.

Dytgweith[10] yd aeth y wreicda allan y orymdeith. Y deuth
35 y dy hen wrach a oed yn y dref heb dant yn y fenn. Amkawd[11]
y urenhines, 'Ha wrach, a dywedy di imi y peth a ouynnaf it,
yr Dyw? Kwt ynt[12] plant y gwr a'm rydyallas[13] yg gordwy?'
Amkawd[14] y wrach, 'Nyd oes plant itaw.' Amkawd[14] y
urenhines, 'Gwae uinheu uyn dyuot ar[15] anuab.' Dywawt[16] y
40 wrach, 'Nyt reit iti hynny. Darogan yw itaw kaffel ettiuet;
ohonot ti yt gaffo ef kanys ry gaffo[17] o arall. [454] Na wna
tristit heuyt; un mab yssyd itaw.'

Mynet a oruc y wreicda yn llawen atreff, ac amkawd hi[18]
vrth y chymmar, 'Pwy ystyr[19] yw gennyt ti kelu dy blant
45 ragof i?' Amkawd[20] y brenhin, 'A mineu nys kelaf.'[21]
Kennatau y mab a orucpwyt, a e dyuot ynteu[22] y'r llys.
Dywedut a oruc y lysuam wrthaw, 'Gwreicca yssyd da iti, a
mab.[23] A merch yssyd imi gwiw y bob gwrda yn y byt.'
Amkawd[24] y mab, 'Nyt oet y mi etwa wreicca.' Dywawd
50 hitheu,[25] 'Tyghaf tyghet it na lath[o][26] dy ystlys vrth wreic
hyt pan geffych Olwen merch Yspadaden Penkawr.'
Lliuaw[27] a oruc y mab, a mynet a oruc serch y uorwyn ym

[1]yn hely y brenhin.
[2]gordlan.
[3]+y brenhin.
[4]pa le y kaffei.
[5]Heb.
[6]wreica W.; wreicka R.
[7]gantunt.
[8]y wreic gantunt.
[9]goresgyn.
[10]Dydgweith.
[11]ac y dywawt.
[12]ble mae.
[13]am llathrudawd.
[14]heb y.
[15]dyuot at.
[16]ac yna y dywawt.
[17]o honat ti. yr nas kaffo.
[18]y dywawt hi.
[19]pa ystyr.
[20]Heb.
[21]+weithon.
[22]a dyuot ac ef.
[23]gwreic yssyd da itti y chael.
[24]y dywawt.
[25]Ac yna y dywawt hitheu.
[26]Mi a tynghaf dynghet itt na chyflado.
[27]lliwaw.

pob aelawt itaw kyn nys rywelhei eiroet.[1] Amkawd[2] y dat
vrthaw, 'Ha uab, py liuy ti? Py drwc yssyd arnat ti?' 'Uy
55 llysuam ry dygyys[3] im na chaffwyf wreic byth hyt pan
gaffwyf Olwen merch Yspadaden Penkawr.'[4] 'Hawd it
kaffel hynny, uab,'[5] heb y tat vrthaw. 'Arthur yssyd
geuynderw it. Dos titheu ar[6] Arthur y diwyn dy wallt, ac
erchych hynny idaw yn gyuarws it.'

Culhwch goes to Arthur's Court

60   Mynet a oruc y mab ar orwyd pennluchlwyt pedwar gayaf
gauylgygwng carngragen, a frwyn eur kymibiawc yn y
penn. Ac ystrodur[7] eur anllawd y danaw, a [455] deu par
aryanhyeit lliueit yn y law. Gleif (ennillec)[8] yn y law,
kyuelin dogyn gwr yndi[9] o drum[10] hyt awch. Y gwaet y[11] ar
65 y gwynt a dygyrchei, bydei kynt[12] no'r gwlithin kyntaf o'r
konyn hyt y llawr, pan uei uwyaf y gwlith mis[13] Meheuin.
Cledyf eurdwrn ar y glun a racllauyn eur itaw, ac ays[14]
eurcrwydyr arnaw, a lliw lluchet nef yndi, a lloring[15] elifeint
yndi. A deu uilgi uronwynyon urychyon racdaw,[16] a
70 gordtorch rudeur am uynwgyl pob un o cnwch[17] yscwyd hyt
yskyuarn. Yr hwn a uei o'r parth asseu a uydei o'r parth
deheu, a'r hwnn a uei o'r parth deheu a uydei o'r parth
asseu, mal dwy morwennawl[18] yn darware yn y gylch.
Pedeir tywarchen a ladei pedwar carn[19] y gorwyd, mal pedeir
75 gwennawl yn yr awyr uch y benn, gweitheu uchtaw,
gveitheu istaw.[20] Llenn borfor[21] pedeir ael ymdanaw, ac aual
rudeur[22] vrth pob ael iti. Can mu oed werth pob aual.
Gwerth trychan mu o eur gwerthuawr a[23] oed yn y archenat
a'e warthafleu (sangharwy),[24] o benn y glun hyt ym blayn y
80 uys. Ni chwyuei ulaen blewyn arnaw[25] rac ystwawnet tuth y

[1] yr nas gwelsei eiryoet.
[2] Ac yna y dywawt.
[3] a dynghwys.
[4] Yspadaden benn kawr.
[5] hawd yw itti hynny.
[6] dos att.
[7] a chyfrwy.
[8] gleif penntirec W. R.
[9] om.
[10] drwm.
[11] yr W.; om. R.
[12] gynt.
[13] vis.
[14] a chroes.
[15] llugorn.
[16] tu racdaw.
[17] gwrd torch rudem ... o gnwch.
[18] dwy uorwennawl.
[19] bedwarcarn.
[20] uchot ... issot.
[21] o borffor.
[22] aual eur wrth bop ael.
[23] om.
[24] ae warthafleu sangnarwy W.R.
[25] ny chrymei ... y danaw.

gorwyd y danaw[1] yn kyrchu porth llys Arthur.
[456] Amkawd[2] y mab, 'A oes porthawr?'[3] 'Oes. A
thitheu, ni bo teu dy benn, pyr y kyuerchy di? Mi a uydaf
porthawr[5] y Arthur pob dyw[6] kalan Ionawr, a'm
85 raclouyeit, hagen, y ulwydyn eithyr hynny; nyt amgen
Huandaw a Gogigwr[7] a Llaeskemyn,[8] a Ffenpingyon a
ymda ar y penn yr eiryach[9] y draet, nyt vrth nef nyt vrth
dayar, mal[10] maen treigyl ar lawr llys. Agor y porth.' 'Nac
agoraf.' 'Pwy[11] ystyr nas agory ti?' Kyllell a edyw ymwyt, a
90 llynn ymual, ac amsathyr y[12] neuad Arthur. Namyn mab
brenhin gvlat teithiawc, neu y gerdawr[13] a dycco y gerd, ny
atter y mywn. Llith y'th gwn ac yd y'th uarch,[14] a golwython
poeth pebreit i titheu, a gwin goryscalawc, a didan gerdeu
ragot. Bwyt degwyr a deugeint[15] a daw attat y'r yspytty.
95 Yno y bwyta pellenigyon a mabyon gwladoed ereill nyd
ergyttyo kerth[16] yn llys Arthur. Ny byd gwaeth it[17] yno
nocet y[18] Arthur yn y llys. Gwreic y gyscu gennyt,[19] a didan
gerdeu rac dy deulin.[20] Yuory, pryt anterth, pan agorawr y
porth rac y niuer a dothyw hediw yma,[21] bydhawt ragot ti
100 gyntaf yd agorawr[22] y porth. A chyueisted a wnelych yn y lle
a dewissych yn neuad Arthur, o'e gwarthaf hyd y
gwaelawd.' Dywedut a oruc y mab, 'Ny wnaf i dim [457] o
hynny, Ot agory y porth, da yw. Onys agory, mi a dygaf
anglot y'th arglwyd a drygeir y titheu. A mi a dodaf[23] teir
105 diaspat ar drws y porth hwnn hyt na bo anghleuach[24] ym
Penn Pengwaed yg Kernyw ac yg gwaelawt Dinsol yn y
Gogled, ac yn Eskeir Oeruel yn Iwerdon. Ac yssyd o wreic
ueichawc yn y llys honn, methawd eu beichogi, ac ar nyd

[1] oed y danaw.
[2] y dywawt.
[3] borthawr.
[4] byrr.
[5] borthawr.
[6] duw.
[7] gogigwc W.R.
[8] llaeskenym.
[9] ar y benn yr arbet.
[10] namyn ual.
[11] py.
[12] om. y R.
[13] y gerdawr W.R.
[14] ac yth ueirch; om. yd.
[15] degwy[r] ar d[e]ugeint—r in red and d[e] deleted.
[16] kylch.
[17] in, W.; inn, R.
[18] noc et W.; no chyt ac R.
[19] genthi.
[20] rac dy vronn.
[21] pan agerer y porth rac y niuer a deuth yma hediw.
[22] agorir.
[23] ad a dodaf W.
[24] agheuach.

beichawc onadunt, ymhoelawd eu calloneu yn yrthtrwm[1]
110 arnadunt mal na bwynt[2] ueichawc byth o hediw allan.
Amkawd[3] Glewlwyt Gauaeluawr, 'Py[4] diaspettych ti
bynhac am gyfreitheu llys Arthur, ny'th atter ti y mywn
hyny elwyf ui y dywedud y Arthur gesseuin.'[5]
Ac y dyuu Glewlwyt y'r neuad. Amkawd[6] Arthur
115 vrthaw, 'Chwedleu porth genhyt?' 'Yssydynt genhym.[7]
Deuparth uy oet a dodyw,[8] a deuparth y teu ditheu. Mi a
uum gynt yGhaer Se ac Asse, yn Sach a Salach, yn Lotor a
Fotor. Mi a uum gynt yn yr India Uawr a'r India Uechan. Mi
a uum gynt yn ymlad deu Ynyr pan ducpwyt y deudec
120 gwystyl o Lychlyn. A mi a uum gynt yn yr Egrop, a mi a
uum yn yr Affric, ac yn ynyssoed[9] Corsica, ac yGhaer
Brythwch a Brythach[10] a Nerthach. Mi a uum gynt pan
ledeist ti teulu Gleis[11] mab Merin, pan ledeist Mil Du [458]
mab Ducum. Mi a uum gynt pan wereskynneist Groec[12] vrth
125 parth y dwyrein. Mi a uum gynt yGhaer Oeth ac Anoeth, ac
yGhaer Neuenhyr Naw Nawt[13]: teyrndynyon tec a welsam
ni yno, ny weleis i eirmoet dyn kymryt[14] a'r hwnn yssyd yn
drws y porth yr awr honn.'[15] Amkawd[16] Arthur, 'Or bu ar dy
gam y dyuuost[17] y mywn, dos ar dy redec allan. A'r sawl a
130 edrych y goleu ac a egyr y lygat ac a e kae, aghengaeth idaw.
A gvassanaethet rei a buelin[18] goreureit ac ereill a golwython
poeth pebreit[19] hyt pan uo goranhed[20] bwyt a llynn idaw. Ys
dyhed a beth gadu dan wynt a glaw y kyfryw dyn a dywedy
di.' Amkawd[21] Kei, 'Myn llaw uyghyueillt, bei[22] gwnelhit
135 uyg kyghor i ny thofrit kyfreitheu llys[23] yrdaw.' 'Na wir,
Kei wynn. Ydym wyrda hyt tra yn dygyrcher. Yd ytuo
mwyhaf y kyuarws a rothom, mwyuwy uyd yn gwrdaaeth

[1]yn wrthrwm heint.
[2]bont.
[3]heb y.
[4]pa.
[5]nyth ellyngir di . . . gysseuin.
[6]ac yna y doeth . . . ac y dywawt.
[7]om.
[8]ys ethyw gennyf deuparth vy oet .
[9]ynyssed.
[10]brytach W.; brythach R.
[11]di deulu Cleis.
[12]oresgynneist roec.

[13]naw nawd.
[14]eiryoet dyn kyuurd.
[15]y porthawr awr honn W., y porth yr awr honn R.
[16]ac y dywawt.
[17]os ar dy gam y doethost.
[18]o vuelin.
[19]pybreit.
[20]parawt.
[21]heb y.
[22]pei.
[23]kyfreitheu y llys.

ninheu ac an cret[1] ac an hetmic.'

Ac y dyuu[2] Glewlwyd y'r porth, ac agori y porth racdaw.
140 Ac a goryw pawb[3] diskynnu vrth y porth ar yr yskynuaen,
nys goruc ef,[4] namyn ar y gorwyd y doeth y mywn.
Amkawd[5] Kulhwch, 'Henpych gwell, Penn Teyrned yr Ynys
honn. Ny bo gwaeth y'r gwaelawt ty [459] noc y'r gwarthaf
dy.[6] Poet yn gystal y'th deon a'th niuer a'th catbritogyon[7] y
145 bo y gwell hwnn. Ny bo didawl[8] neb ohonaw. Mal y mae
kyflawn y kyuer[c]heis i well i ti, boet kyflawn dy rat titheu a'th
cret[9] a'th etmic yn yr Ynys honn.' 'Poet gwir Dyw, unben.[10]
Henpych gwell titheu.[11] Eisted kyfrwg deu o'r milwyr, a
didan gerd ragot[12] a breint edling (gwrthrychyad teyrnas)
150 arnat[13] byhyt bynnac y bych yma. A ffan ranhwyf uyn da y
ospeit a ffellennigyon, bythawd o'th law[14] pan y dechreuwyf
yn y llys honn.' Amkawd y[15] mab, 'Ny dothwyf[16] i yma yr
frawdunyaw bwyt a llynn. Namyn or kaffaf uyghyuarws, y
dalu a'e uoli a wnaf. Onys caffaf, dwyn dy vyneb[17] di a wnaf
155 hyt y bu dy glot ym pedryal[18] byt bellaf.' Amkawd Arthur,
'Kyn ny thriccych ti[19] yma, unben, ti a geffy [y] kyuarws[20] a
notto dy benn a'th tauawd,[21] hyt y sych gwynt, hyt y gwlych
glaw, hyt yr etil[22] heul, hyt yd ymgyffret mor, hyt yd ydiw
dayar,[23] eithyr uy llong a'm llen, a Chaletuwlch uyg cledyf, a
160 Rongomynyat[24] uyg gvayw, ac Vyneb Gwrthucher uy
yscwyt,[25] a Charnwenhan uyg kyllell, a Gwenhvyuar uyg
gwreic.' 'Gwir Dyw[26] ar hynny?' 'Ti a'e keffy yn llawen. Not
a nottych.' [460] 'Nodaf.[27] Diwyn uy gwallt a uynaf.' 'Ti a

---

[1]cret *perhaps half-changed to* clot
W., clot R.
[2]doeth.
[3]ac yr y pawb disgynnu.
[4]nys disgynnawd ef.
[5]ac y dywawt Kulwch.
[6]gwaelaw tty ... gwarthaf dy.
[7]ath gatwridogyon.
[8]didlawt.
[9]crot W., ath glot R.
[10]*om.*
[10]*om.*
[11]+heb yr Arthur.
[12]a geffy rac dy uron.
[13]breint edling arnat gwrthrychyad
teyrnas W.; breint teyrn arnat

[ ]gwrthrychyat teyrnas R.
[14]bint yth law.
[15]heb y.
[16]ny deuthum.
[17]agclot.
[18]pedryual.
[19]Heb yr arthur yna. Kan ny thrigyy
di.
[20]kyuarws W.; y kyuarws R.
[21]ath dauawt.
[22]treigyl.
[23]y dayar.
[24]ron gom yant W., rongomyant R.
[25]uyn taryan.
[26]duw.
[27]*om.*

gyffy hynny.' Kymryt crip eur o Arthur, a gwelliu[1] a doleu
165 aryant itaw, a chribaw y benn a oruc. A gouyn pwy oet a
oruc.[2] Amkawd Arthur,[3] 'Mae uyg kallon yn tirioni vrthyt.
Mi a wn dy hanuot o'm gvaet. Dywet[4] pwy vyt.'
'Dywedaf.[5] Kulhwch mab Kilyd mab Kyledon Wledic o
Oleudyt merch Anlawd Wledic, uy mam.' Amkawd
170 Arthur, 'Gwir yw hynny.[6] Keuynderw vyt[7] titheu y mi.
Not a nottych, a thi a'e keffy, a notto dy benn a'th dauawt'.[8]
'Gwir Dyw im ar hynny, a gvir dy deyrnas?' 'Ti a'e keffy yn
llawen.' 'Nodaf arnat kaffel im Olwen merch Yspadaden
Penkawr; a'e hasswynaw a wnaf ar dy uilwyr.'

Culhwch invokes his Sureties from the Court

175 Asswynaw y gyuarws ohonaw ar Kei[9] a Bedwyr, a
Greidawl Galldouyd, a Gwythyr uab Greidawl, a Greit mab
Eri, a Chyndelic Kyuarwyd, a Thathal Twyll Goleu, a
Maylwys[10] mab Baedan, a Chnychwr mab Nes a Chubert m.
Daere, a Fercos m. Poch, a Lluber Beuthach, a Chonul
180 Bernach.[11]

A Gwyn m. Esni, a Gvynn m. Nwywre,[12] a Gwynn m.
Nud, ac Edern mab Nud, a Cadwy[13] m. Gereint, a Fflewdwr
Flam Wledic, a Ruawn Pebyr. Dorath, a Bratwen m.
Moren Mynawc[14] a Moren Mynawc e hun, a Dalldaf eil
185 Kimin Cof, a mab Alun Dyuet, a mab Saidi, a mab Gwryon, ac
Vchdryt Ardwyat[15] Kat, a Chynwas Curyuagyl,[16] a Gwrhyr
Gwarthecuras, ac Isperyr Ewingath, [461] a Gallcoit
Gouynnyat,[17] a Duach a Brathach[18] a Nerthach, meibon
Gwawrdur Kyruach—o vrthdir Uffern pan hanoed y gwyr.[19]
190 A Chilyd Canhastyr, a Chan[h]astyr Canllaw, a Chors
Cant Ewin, ac Eskeir Gulhwch Gonyn Cawn,[20] a Drustwrn
Hayarn, a Glewlwyt Gauaeluawr, a Lloch Llawwynnyawc,

[1]gwelleu.
[2]+arthur.
[3]om.
[4]dywet im.
[5]Dywedaf heb y mab.
[6]Gwir yw hynny heb yr arthur.
[7]vt W.; wyt R.
[8]athdauawt (d in a later hand) W.; ath R. dauawt R.
[9]ar gei.
[10]maelwys.
[11]choruil beruach W.R.
[12]nwyfure.
[13]ac adwy W. R. . . . a fflewdur.
[14]mynac W.; mynawc R.
[15]uchtrut ardywat.
[16]curuagyl.
[17]gouynynat W.; gallcoyt gouynynat R.
[18]grathach.
[19]y gwyr hynny.
[20]gouynkawn.

ac Anwas Edeinawc,[1] a Sinnoch mab Seithuet, a Watu mab
Seithuet, a Naw mab Seithuet,[2] a Gwenwynwyn mab Naw
195   mab Seithuet,[3] a Bedyw mab Seithuet, a Gobrwy mab Echel
Uordvyt Twll, ac Echel Uordvyt Twll[4] e hun, a Mael mab
Roycol, a Datweir Dallpenn, a Garwyli eil Gwythawc
Gwyr, a Gwythawc Gwyr e hun, a Gormant mab Ricca, a
Menw mab Teirgwaed, a Digon mab Alar, a Selyf mab
200   Sinoit, a Gusc mab Achen,[5] a Nerth mab Kadarn, a Drutwas
mab Tryffin, a Twrch mab Perif, a Thwrch mab Anwas,[6] a
Iona urenhin Freinc, a Sel mab Selgi, a Theregut mab Iaen, a
Sulyen mab Iaen, a Bratwen mab Iaen, a Moren mab Iaen, a
Siawn mab Iaen, a Chradawc mab Iaen—gwyr Kaer Tathal
205   oedynt, kenetyl[7] y Arthur o pleit y tat.

Dirmyc mab Kaw, a Iustic mab Kaw, ac Etmic mab Kaw, ac
Angawd mab Kaw, ac Ouan mab Kaw, a Chelin mab Kaw, a
Chonnyn [462] mab Kaw a Mabsant mab Kaw, a Gwyngat
mab Kaw, a Llwybyr mab Kaw, a Choch mab Kaw, a Meilic
210   mab Kaw, a Chynwal[8] mab Kaw, ac Ardwyat mab Kaw, ac
Ergyryat mab Kaw, a Neb mab Kaw, a Gildas[9] mab Kaw, a
Chalcas mab Kaw, a Hueil mab Kaw—nyd asswynwys
eiroet yn llaw arglwyd.

A Samson Uinsych, a Theliessin[10] Penn Beird, a
215   Manawedan[11] mab Llyr, a Llary mab Casnar Wledic, ac
Sberin[12] mab Flergant brenhin Llydaw, a Saranhon mab
Glythwyr, a Llawr eil Erw, ac Anynnawc[13] mab Menw mab
Teirgwaed, a Gwynn mab Nwywre a Fflam mab Nwywre, a
Gereint mab Erbin ac Ermit mab Erbin[14] a Dyuel mab Erbin,
220   a Gwynn mab Ermit a Chyndrwyn mab Ermit, a Hyueid
Unllenn, ac Eidon Uawrurydic, a Reidwn Arwy, a Gormant
mab Ricca—brawt y Arthur o barth y uam; Pennhynef
Kernyw y tat. A Llawurodet Uaruawc,[15] a Nodawl Uaryf
Trwch,[16] a Berth mab Kado, a Reidwn mab Beli, ac Iscouan
225   Hael, ac Yscawin mab Panon, a Moruran eil Tegit—ny

[1]Annwas Adeinawc.
[2]a Watu ... Seithuet *om.*
[3]mab Seithuet *om.*
[4]uordyttwll W.
[5]gusc m. atheu.
[6]a thwrch m. perif a thwrch m.
annwas.
[7]kenedyl ... o bleit.

[8]a chynwas.
[9]gilda.
[10]a theleessin.
[11]mamawydan.
[12]ysperin.
[13]annyannawc.
[14]ac e W.; *marg.*, ac erinit m erbin R.
[15]Llawnrodet.
[16]twrch W.R.

dodes dyn y araf yndaw yGhamlan[1] rac y haccred, pawb a
tybygynt[2] y uod yn gythreul canhorthwy; blew a oed arnaw
mal blew hyd. A Sande Pryt Angel[3]—ny dodes neb y wayw
yndaw yGhamlan[1] [463] rac y decket, pawb a debygynt y
230 uod yn engyl[3] canhorthwy. A Chynwyl Sant—y trydygwr
a dienghis o Gamlan;[4] ef a yscarwys diwethaf ac Arthur y ar
Hengroen y uarch.

Ac Uchdryt mab Erim ac Eus mab Erim a Henwas
Edeinawc mab Erim a Henbedestyr mab Erim a Scilti
235 Scawntroet[5] mab Erim. Teir kynedyf a oed ar y trywyr
hynny: Henbedester ny chauas eiroet a'e kyfrettei o dyn nac
ar uarch nac ar droet; Henwas Edeinawc[6] ni allwys mil
pedwar troedawc eiroet y ganhymdeith hyd un erw,
anoethach[7] a uei bellach no hynny; Scilti Yscawntroet, pan
240 uei wyn hwyl[8] kerdet yndaw vrth neges y arglwyd, ny
cheisswys ford eiroet am gwypei py le yd elei; namyn tra uei
coet,[9] ar uric y coet y kerdei, a thra uei uynyd, ar ulaen y
kawn y kerdei,[10] ac yn hyt y oes ny flygwys konyn dan y
draet, anoethach[11] torri rac y yskafned.[12]

245 Teithi Hen mab Gwynhan a weryskynnwys[13] mor y
kyuoeth, ac y dihengis ynteu o ureid ac y doeth ar Arthur[14]—
a chynedyf a oed ar y gyllell: yr pan deuth ymma ny
thrigwys[15] carn ar [464] nei uyth, ac vrth hynny y tyuwys[16]
heint yndaw a nychdawt hyt tra uu uyw, ac o hynny y bu
250 uarw. A Charnedyr mab Gouynyon Hen, a [Gwenwynwyn
mab Naf],[17] gysseuin ryssswr Arthur, a Llygatrud Emys a
Gwrbothu Hen—ewythred Arthur oedynt, brodyr y uam.

Kuluanawyt mab Goryon, a Llennleawc Vydel o Bentir
Gamon, a Dyuynwal Moel, a Dunart brenhin y Gogled.
255 Teyrnon Twr Bliant,[18] a Thecuan Glof, a Thegyr Talgellawc.
Gwrdiual mab Ebrei, a Morgant Hael, Gwystyl mab

---

[1] yg kat gamlan.
[2] a debygynt.
[3] agel.
[4] o gat kamlan.
[5] ac sgilti yscawntroet.
[6] Henwas adeinawe.
[7] yghwaethach.
[8] wynhywl W.; wyn hwyl R.
[9] tra uei y mewn coet.
[10] a thra ... y kerdei om.
[11] yghwaethach.
[12] ysgawnet.
[13] oresgynnwys.
[14] att arthur.
[15] ny. thrigyawd.
[16] y tyuawd.
[17] om. W.
[18] +oedynt W.; Teirnon twryf bliant R.

[Nwython] a Run mab Nwython[1] a Lluydeu mab
Nwython, a Gwydre mab Lluydeu, o Wenabwy merch Kaw
y uam—Hueil y ewythyr a'e gwant, ac am hynny y bu gas
260   rwg Arthur a Hueil[2] am yr acholl.

Drem mab Dremidyd, a welei o Gelli Wic yGherniw hyt
ym Penn Blathaon ym Predein pan drychauei[3] y gwydbedin
y bore gan yr heul. Ac Eidoel[4] mab Ner, a Gluydyn Saer[5] a
wnaeth Ehangwen neuad Arthur. Kynyr Keinuaruawc—
265   Kei a dywedit y uot yn uab itaw. Ef a dywawd vrth y wreic,
'Osit rann imi o'th uab ti,[6] uorwyn, oer uyth uyd y galon, ac
ny byd gwres yn y dwylaw. Kynedef arall a uyd arnaw:[7]
[465] os mab y mi uyd, kyndynnyawc uyd. Kynedyf arall a
uyd[8] arnaw: pan dycco beich, na mawr na bychan uo, ny
270   welir uyth na rac vyneb na thra'e geuyn.[9] Kynedyf arall a
uyd arnaw: ny feit neb dwuyr a than[10] yn gystal ac ef.
Kynedyf arall a uyd arnaw: ny byd gwasanaythur[11] na
swydvr mal ef.'

Henwas a Hen Vyneb a Hengedymdeith,[12] Gallgoic[13] un
275   arall—y dref y delhei idi,[14] kyt bei trychant tei[15] yndi, or
bei eisseu dim arnaw ny adei ef hun uyth ar legat[16] dyn tra uei
yndi. Berwynn mab Kyrenyr, a Fferis[17] brenhin Freinc—ac
am hynny y gelwir Kaer Paris.[18] Osla Gyllelluawr, a
ymdygei Bronllauyn Uerllydan; pan delhei Arthur a'e luoed
280   y uron llifdwr, y keissit lle kyuyg[19] ar y dwuyr, ac y dodit y
gyllell yn y gwein ar draws y llifdwr—digawn o bont
uydei y lu Teir Ynys Prydein a'e Their Rac Ynys ac
eu hanreitheu. Gwydawc mab Menester, a ladawd Kei,
ac Arthur a'y lladawd[20] ynteu a'e urodyr yn dial Kei.
285   Garanwyn mab Kei, ac Amren mab Bedwyr, ac Ely a Myr
a Reu Rwyddyrys, a Run Rudwern, ac Eli a Thrachmyr,

---

[1]Gwystyl mab. Run m. nwython.
[2]rwng hueil ac arthur.
[3]ym prydein pan dyrchauei.
[4]eidyol.
[5]Glwydyn Saer.
[6]oth uab di.
[7]kynnedyf arall arnaw.
[8]heuyt a uyd.
[9]nac rac y wyneb na thraegeuyn R.;
na thaegeuyn W.
[10]a dwuyr ac a than.

[11]gwasanythur W.; gwassanaethwr R.
[12]+arthur *above line.*
[13]Gwallgoyc.
[14]Y dref y dref W.; idi *om.* R.
[15]trychan*tref* (*del.*) W.; trychant tei
R.
[16]ar lygat.
[17]gerenhir a pharis.
[18]kaer baris.
[19]kyuing.
[20]a lladawd.

penkynydyon Arthur. [466] A Lluydeu mab Kelcoet, a
Hu[n]abwy[1] mab Gwryon, a Gwynn Gotyuron, a Gweir
Dathar Wenidawc, a Gweir mab Kadellin Tal Aryant, a
290   Gweir Gwrhyd Enwir, a Gweir Gwyn Paladyr[2]—ywythred[3]
y Arthur, brodyr y uam; meibon Llwch Llawwynnyawc o'r
tu draw y Uor Terwyn.

    Llenlleawc Vydel ac ardyrchawc Prydein, Cas mab Saidi,
Gwruan Gwallt Auwyn, Gwilenhen[4] brenhin Freinc,
295   Gwittart mab Aed[5] brenhin Iwerdon, Garselit Vydel,
Panawr Penbagat, Atleudor[6] mab Naf, Gwynn Hyuar maer
Kernyw a Dyfneint—nawuet[7] a estoues Cat Gamlan. Kelli a
Chuel,[8] a Gilla Goeshyd—trychanherw a lammei yn y un
llam,[9] pen llemidit Iwerdon.[10]

300   Sol a Gwadyn Ossol a Gwadyn Odeith[11]—Sol, a allei
seuyll un dyt ar y un troet; Gwadyn Ossol, pei saf hei ar benn
y mynyd mwyaf yn y byd ef a uydei yn tyno gwastat dan y
droet;[12] Gwadyn Odeith, kymeint a'r uas twym pan dynhet[13]
o'r eueil oed tan llachar y wadneu pan gyuarfei galet ac ef;[14] ef
305   a arllwyssei ford y Arthur yn lluydd.[15] Hir Erwm a Hir
Atrwm, y dyd y delhynt y west, trychantref a achubeint yn
eu kyuereit;[16] gwest hyt nawn [467] a diotta hyt nos. Pan
elhynt y gyscu, penn y pryuet[17] a yssynt rac newyn mal pei
nat yssynt uwyt eiroet. Pan elhynt y west nyd edewynt[18] wy
310   na thew na theneu, na thwym nac oer, na sur na chroyw, nac
ir na hallt.[19]

    Huarwar mab Halwn,[20] a nodes y wala ar Arthur yn y
gyuarws; trydyt gordibla Kernyw[21] a Dyfneint[22] pan gahad
idaw y wala; ny cheffit gwyn gwen arnaw uyth[23] namyn tra

---

[1]hunabwy.
[2]gweir baladyr hir.
[3]ewythred.
[4]-hin *changed to* hen W.; gwyllennhin R.
[5]+oed.
[6]a fflendor.
[7]y nawuet gwr a ystoues.
[8]Keli a chueli.
[9]llan. penn llemhidyd.
[10]+oed hwnnw.
[11]gwadyn odyeith.
[12]y traet.

[13]tynnit.
[14]gyuarffei galet ac wynt.
[15]yny llud.
[16]a achubit yn eu kyfueir.
[17]a wneynt a diotta hyt pan vei nos pan elynt y gysgu. Ac yna penneu y pryuet.
[18]ny dywe nyd edewynt W.
[19]+na brwt nac of.
[20]aflawn.
[21]kernyw vu.
[22]*om.*
[23]vyt.

315 uei lawn. Gwarae[1] Gwallt Eurin, deu geneu Gast Rymhi,
Gwydrut a Gwyden[2] Astrus, Sucgyn mab Sucnedut, a
sugnei y morawl y bei trychanllong arnaw hyt na bei namyn
traeth sych; bron llech rud a oed yndaw. Caccymuri[3] gwas
Arthur—dangosset itaw yr yscubawr,[4] kyt bei rwyf dec
320 aradyr ar ugeint[5] yndi ef a'y trawei a fust heyernyn[6] hyt na
bei well y'r rethri a'r trostreu a'r tulatheu noc y'r man geirch
ygwaelawt yr yscubawr.[7] Llwng[8] a Dygyflwng ac Anoeth
Ueidawc a Hir Eidyl a Hir Amren—deu was Arthur[9]
oedynt, [a Gweuyl mab Gwastat[10]—y dyd y bei drist y
325 gellyngei[10a] y lleill weuyl idaw y waeret hyt y uogel a'r llall
a uydei yn bennguch[11] ar y benn].

[468] Vchdryt Uaryf Draws, a uyryei y uaraf[12] goch
seuydlawc a oed arnaw dros dec trawst a deugeint[13] oed yn
neuad Arthur. Elidir Gyuarwyd, Yskyrdaf ac Yscudyd—
330 deu was y Wenhwyuar oedynt; kynhebrwydet oet eu traet
vrth eu neges ac eu medwl.

Brys uab Bryssethach o dal y Rydynawc[14] Du o Brydein, a
Grudlwyn Gorr; Bwlch a Chyuwlch a Seuwlch,[15] meibion
Kledyf Kyuwlch, vyron Cledyf Diuwlch. Teir gorwen gwen
335 eu teir yscwyt, tri gouan gwan eu tri gwayw; tri benyn
byneu eu tri chledyf; Glas, Glesic, Gleissat eu tri chi; Call,
Kuall, Kauall eu tri meirch; Hwyr Dydwc a Drwc Dydwc a
Llwyr Dydwc eu teir gwraged; Och a Garym[16] a Diaspat eu
teir vyryon; Lluchet a Neuet ac Eissywed eu teir merched;
340 Drwc a Gwaeth a Gwaethaf Oll eu teir morwyn.

Eheubryt mab[17] Kyuwlch, Gorascwrn mab[17] Nerth,
Gwaedan mab[17] Kynuelyn Keudawc,[18] Pwyll Hanner Dyn,
Dwnn Diessic Unben, Eiladar[19] mab Penn Llarcan,
Kynedyr[20] Wyllt mab [469] Hettwn Tal Aryant, Sawyl Penn

[1]Gware.
[2]gwydneu.
[3]Racymwri.
[4]dangossit yr yscubawr a uynnit idaw.
[5]dec eredyr ar hugeint.
[6]hayarn.
[7]+yn y ueiscawn.
[8]om.
[9]y Arthur.
[10]gwestat. [ ] om. W.
[10a]gollyngei.
[11]yn pennguch.
[12]uaryf.
[13]idaw dros wyth drawst a deugeint a.
[14]redynawc.
[15]Sefwlch.
[16]ac arym W.; a garym R.
[17]merch W.R.
[18]keudawc W.; keudawt R.
[19]Eiladyr.
[20]Kyuedyr W.; Kyvedyr R.

345 Uchel, Gwalchmei mab Gwyar, Gwalhauet mab Gwyar,
Gwrhyr Gwalstawd Ieithoed—yr holl ieithoed a wydat'[1]—a'r
Kethtrwm Offeirad. Clust mab Clustueinat—pei cladhet
seith vrhyt[2] yn y dayar, deng milltir a deugeint y clywei y
morgrugyn y bore pan gychwhynnei y ar lwth.[3] Medyr mab
350 Methredyd—a uedrei y dryw yn Eskeir Oeruel yn Iwerdon
trwy y dwy goys[4] yn gythrymhet o Gelli Wic. Gwiawn
Llygat Cath[5]—a ladei ongyl ar lygat y gwydbedyn heb
argywed y'r llygat.[6] Ol mab Olwyd—seith mlynet kyn no'e
eni a ducpwyd moch y dat, a ffan drychauwys[7]ynteu yn wr
355 yd olrewys y moch ac y deuth attref[8] ac vynt yn seith
kenuein. Bitwini[9] Escob, a uendigei uwyt a llyn[10] yr mwyn
merchet eurtyrchogyon[11] yr Ynys honn.

Y am Wenhwyuar, Penn Rianed yr Ynys honn, a
Gwenhwyach y chwaer, a Rathtyen[12] merch Vnic Clememyl,
360 Kelemon[13] merch Kei, a Thangwen[14] m. Weir Dathar
Wenidawc, Gwen Alarch m. Kynwal[15] Canhwch, Eurneit
merch Clydno Eidin, Eneuawc merch Uedwyr, Enrydrec
merch Tutuathar, Gwenwledyr merch Waredur[16] Kyruach,
Erduduyl[17] merch Tryffin, Eurolvyn[18] merch [Wdolwyn
365 Gorr],[19] Teleri [470] merch Peul, Indec merch Arwy Hir,
Moruyd[20] merch Uryen Reget, Gwenlliant Tec,[21] y uorwyn
uawruredic,[22] Creidylat merch Llud Llaw Ereint, y uorwyn
uwyaf y mawred a uu yn Teir Ynys Prydein[23] a'e Their Rac
Ynys—ac am honno y may[24] Gwythyr mab Greidawl a
370 Gwynn mab Nud yn ymlad pob dyw kalan Mei uyth hyt dyt
brawt; Ellylw merch Neol Kyn Croc—a honno a uu teir
oes gvyr yn uyw; Essyllt Vynwen ac Essyllt Uyngul.[25]
Arnadunt oll y hasswynwys Kulwch mab Kilid[26] y gyuarws.

[1]Gwastawt . . . a wydyat.
[2]cledit seith cuppyt.
[3]pan gychwynnei . . . y lwth.
[4]goes.
[5]Lygat Cath.
[6]yr llygat om.
[7]dyrchauawd.
[8]adref.
[9]Betwini.
[10]vwyt a llyn arthur.
[11]eur dyrchogyon.
[12]Rathtyeu merch unic clememhill.
[13]a relemon.
[14]a thannwen.

[15]kynnwyl.
[16]waledur.
[17]Erdutuul.
[18]Eurolwen.
[19]Wdolwyn Gorr om. W.
[20]Moruud.
[21]Dec.
[22]uawr vrydic.
[23]teir ynys y kedyrn.
[24]y mae.
[25]Essyllt vinwen ac Esyllt vingul.
[26]y hasswynwynwys Kulwch mab Kilyd.

The Quest for the Giant's Daughter

Arthur a dywawd,[1] 'Ha unben, ny rygiglef i eirmoet[2] [y
375 wrth][2] y uorwyn a dywedy di na'e rieni. Mi a ellynghaf
genhadeu o'e cheissaw yn llawen.'[3] O'r nos honno hyt y llall
ym penn y ulwydyn y bu y kenhadeu yn krwydraw. Ympen
y ulwydyn, hyny uyd kenhadeu Arthur heb gaffel dim.
Dywawd yr unben,[4] 'Pawb ry gauas[5] y gyuarws ac yd vyf i
380 ettwa yn eissywet.[6] Mynet a wnaf i, a'th wyneb di a dygaf i
genhyf.' Dywawd Kei, 'Ha unben, rwy yt werthey Arthur.
Dygyrch ti genhym ni. Hyd pan dywettych ti nat oes hi[7] yn y
byt, neu ninheu a'e caffom, ny'n hyscarhawr[8] a thi.'

Kyuodi yna Kei. Angerd oed ar Gei: naw nos a naw
385 diwarnaw[t][9] hyt y anadyl y dan dwuyr; naw [471] nos a naw
dieu hyd uydei[10] hep gyscu. Cleuydawd[11] Kei ny allei uedyc y
waret. Budugawl[12] oed Kei.[13] Kyhyt a'r prenn uchaf yn y
coet uydei pann uei da ganthaw.[14] Kynnedyf arall oed arnaw:
pan uei uwyaf y glaw, dyrnued uch y law ac arall is y law yt
390 uyd [ei][15] yn sych yr hynn a uei yn y law, rac meint y angerd; a
ffan uei uwyaf y anwyd ar y gydymdeithon, dyskymon[16]
vydei hynny utunt y gynneu tan.

Galw a oruc Arthur ar Uedwyr, yr hynn nyt arswydwys[17]
y neges yd elhei Gei idi.[18] Sef a oed ar Uedwyr,[19] nyt oed neb
395 kymryt[20] ac ef yn yr Ynys honn namyn Arthur a Drych eil
Kibdar. A hynn heuyt, kyt bei unllofyawc nyt anwaydwys
tri aeruawc kyn[21] noc ef yn un uaes ac ef. Angerd arall oed
arnaw: un archoll a uydei yn y wayw[22] a naw gwrthwan.

---

[1] a dywawt yna.
[2] + dim y wrth.
[3] + dyro ym yspeit y cheissaw; Y mab a dywawt rodaf yn llawen or nos heno hyt y llall ympenn y vlwydyn. Ac yna y gyrrwys arthur y kennadeu y bop tir yn y deruyn y geissaw y uorwyn honno. ac ympenn y vlwydyn y doeth kennadeu arthur drachevyn. heb gaffel na chwedyl na chyuarwydyt y wrth olwen mwy nor dyd kyntaf.
[4] Ac yna y dywawt kulwch.
[5] a gauas.
[6] yn eissywedic ettwa.
[7] nat ydiw y uorwyn honno.
[8] nyt yscarwn.
[9] diwarnaw W.; diwarnawt R.
[10] y bydei.
[11] cleuydawd W.; cleuydawt R.
[12] budugal W.; budugawl R.
[13] oed Gei.
[14] gantaw.
[15] yt uei W; y bydei R.
[16] gedymdeithon diskymon.
[17] + eiryoet.
[18] y delei gei idi vynet.
[19] om.
[20] kyfret.
[21] yn gynt.
[22] y waew.

Galw o Arthur ar Gyndylic[1] Kyuarwyd. 'Dos ti im[2] y'r
400 neges honn y gyt a'r unben.' Nyt oed[3] waeth kyuarwyd yn y
wlad ny rywelei[4] eiroet noc yn y wlad e hun.

Galw Gwrhyr Gwalstawt[5] Ieithoed:[6] yr holl ieithoed a
wydat.[7]

Galw Gwalchmei mab Gwyar, cany deuth attref[8] eiroet
405 heb y neges yd elhei o'e cheissyaw.[9] Goreu pedestyr oed a
goreu marchawc. Nei y Arthur, uab [472] y chwaer a'y
gefynderw oed.

Galw o Arthur ar Uenw mab[10] Teirgwaed, kanys o
delhynt[11] y wlat aghred[12] mal y gallei yrru lleturith
410 arnadunt,[13] hyt nas gwelei neb vynt ac vyntvy a welynt
pawb.

Custennin the Shepherd and Ysbaddaden Chief Giant

Mynet a orugant hyd pan deuuant[14] y uaestir mawr, hyny
uyd kaer[15] a welynt, mwyhaf[16] ar keyryt y byt. Kerdet[17]
ohonu y dyt hwnnw. Pan debygynt vy eu bot yn gyuagos y'r
415 gaer nyt oydynt[18] nes no chynt. Mal[19] y deuant eisswys ar un
maes a hi, han ny uyd dauates uawr a welynt heb or[20] a heb
eithaf iti, a heusawr yn cadw y deueit ar benn gorsetua a
ruchen o grwyn amdanaw, a gauaelgi kydenawc[21] ach y law
noc amws naw gayaf oed mwy.[22] Deuawt oet arnaw ny
420 chollet oen eiroet[23] ganthaw anoethac[h][24] llwdwn mawr.
Nyd athoed kyweithyd[25] hebdaw eiroet ny wnelei ae anaf ae
adoet arnei. Y sawl uarw brenn a thwympath a uei ar y
mays[26] a loskei y anadyl hyt y prid dilis.

Amkawd[27] Kei, 'Gwrhyr Gwalstawd Ieithoed, dos y

[1]gyndelic.
[2]dos di; om. im.
[3]achaws nyt oed.
[4]nys rywelsei.
[5]gwas (del.) gwalstawt W.; gwall-
tawt R.
[6]+achaws.
[7]a wydyat.
[8]adref eiryoet.
[9]y cheissaw.
[10]uab.
[11]ot elynt.
[12]angkret.
[13]lletrith arnadunt a hut.
[14]deuthant.
[15]yny uyd kaer uawr.

[16]teckaf o geyryd.
[17]a orugant ... +hyt ucher.
[18]oedynt nes nor bore.
[19]Ar eildyd ar trydyd dyd y
kerdassant ac o vreid y doethant hyt
yno. a phan deuant ym bronn y gaer
yny vyd ....
[20]ol.
[21]kedenawc.
[22]oed vwy noc amws naw gayaf.
[23]eiryoet.
[24]anoethac W.; agwhaethach llwdyn
R.
[25]gyweithyd.
[26]maes a losgei.
[27]yna a dywawt.

425   gyfrwch a'r dyn racco.' 'Kei,[1] nyt edeweis uynet namyn hyd
      yd elhut titheu.' 'Down[2] y gyt yno.' Amkawd[3] Menw mab
      Teirgwaed, 'Na uid amgeled genhwch mynet yno. Mi a
      yrraf lledrith ar y ki hyd na wnel argywed y neb.'
      Dyuot a wnaethont[4] [473] myn yd oed yr heusawr.
430   Amkeudant,[5] 'Berth yd ytwyt,[6] heusawr.' 'Ny bo berthach
      byth y boch chwi no minheu.' 'Myn Dyw, can wyt penn.'
      'Nyd oes anaf y'm llygru namyn vym priawt.' 'Pieu y deueit
      a getwy di, neu pieu y gaer?'[7] ['Meredic a wyr ywch].[8] Dros y
      byt y gwys pan yw Yspydaden Penkawr bieu y gaer.'[9] 'Neu
435   titheu, pwy wyt?' 'Custenhin Amhynwyedic vyf i,[10] ac am
      uym priawt y'm ryamdiuwynwys Yspydaden Penkawr.[11]
      Neu chwitheu, pwy ywch?' 'Kenhadeu Arthur yssyd yma yn
      erchi Olwenn.'[12] 'Vb, wyr. Nawd Dyw ragoch. Yr y byt na
      wnewch hynny. Ny dodyw neb[13] y erchi yr arch honno a
440   elhei a'e uyw ganthaw.'[14] Kyuodi a oruc yr heusawr y uynyd.
      Mal[15] y kyuyt, rodi modrwy eur a oruc Culhuch[16] itaw.
      Keissaw gwiscaw y uodrwy ohonaw[17] ac nyd a[e]i[18] idaw, a'y
      dodi a oruc ynteu ymys y uanec, a cherdet a oruc adref a roti y
      uanec ar y kymhar.[19] A chymryt a oruc hitheu y uodrwy o'r
445   uanec. 'Pan yr [doeth][20] y ti, vr, y uodrwy honn? Nyt oed
      uynych it caffel douot.'[21] 'Mi a euthum[22] y'r mor y geissaw
      moruwyt. Nachaf gelein[23] a welwn yn dyuot gan yr ertrei[24] y
      mywn.[25] Ny weleis i eirmoyt gelein gymryt a hi,[26] ac am[27] y
      uys ef y keueis [474] y uodrwy hon.' ' Oia wr, cany at [y]

[1] +heb ef.
[2] +ninheu.
[3] +heb y menw mab T.
[4] a orugant.
[5] amkeudawt W.; ac y dywedassant
wrthaw R.
[6] yd wyt.
[7] bieu . . . +racko.
[8] om. W.
[9] . . . pan yw caer yspydaden penkawr
bieu y gaer, W . . .; pan yw kaer yspadaden penkawr yw R.
[10] Custennin yn gelwir uab dyfnedic.
[11] am uym priawt ym ryamdiuwyn-
wys uym priawt yspadaden penkawr, W.; ac am vym priawt ym
rylygrwys vym brawt yspadaden
pen kawr R.

[12] +merch yspadaden penn kawr.
[13] ny doeth neb eiryoet y erchi yr
arh.
[14] ae vywyt gantaw.
[15] ac ual.
[16] culhwch.
[17] gwisgaw y uodrwy honno ohonaw.
[18] nyt ai W.; nyt aei R.
[19] att y gymhar y gadw.
[20] om. W.
[21] pan ryattei y dywawt hitheu. gwr y
uodrwy hon nyt oed vynych itt
gaffel bud.
[22] +heb ef.
[23] kelein.
[24] gan y tonneu.
[25] om.
[26] kelein degac no hi.
[27] om.

450 mor[1] marw dlws yndaw, dangos imi y gelein honno.' 'Ha
wreic, y neb pieu y gelein ti a'y gwelho[2] yma ochwinsa.'[3]
'Pwy ef[4] hwnnw?', heb y wreic. 'Kulhwch mab Kilid mab
Kelydon Wledic, o Oleudyt merch Anlawd Wledic, y uam, a
doeth y erchi Olwen.'[5] Deu synhwyr a oed genthi: llawen a
455 oed genthi[6] dyuot y nei uab y chwayr[7] attei, a thrist oed
genthi kany rywelsei[8] eiroet y uynet a'e eneit ganthaw a
delhei y erchi y neges honno.

Kyrchu a orugant vy porth llys Custenhin heusawr.
Clybot oheni[9] hitheu eu trwst[10] yn dyuot. Redec oheni yn eu
460 herbyn o lywenyd.[11] Goglyt a oruc Kei ym prenn o'r
gludweir,[12] a'e dyuot hitheu yn eu herbyn y geissaw mynet
dwylaw mynwgyl udunt. Gossot o Gei eiras kyfrwg[13] y
dwylaw. Gwascu ohonei hitheu yr eiras hyt pan yttoed[14] yn
vden diednedic. Amkawd Kei, 'Ha wreic, pei mi ry wascut
465 uelly,[15] ny oruydei ar arall uyth rodi serch im. Drwc a serch
hwnnw.'[16]

Dyuot a orugant hwy y'r ty a gvneuthur eu gwasanaeth.
Ym penn gwers, pan at pawb eu damsathyr, agori kib a oruc
y wreic yn tal y pentan,[17] a chyuodi gwas pengrych [475]
470 melyn oheni. Amkawd Gwrhyr, 'Oed dyhed[18] kelu y ryw
was hwnn. Gwn nat y gam[19] e hun a dielir arnaw.'
Amkawd[20] y wreic, 'Ys gohilion hwnn tri meib ar ugeint ry
ladawd[21] Yspydaden Pen Cawr imi. Nyd oes oueneic[22] imi o
hwnn mwy noc o'r rei ereill.' Amkawd[23] Kei, 'Dalet
475 gydymdeithas a mi, ac ny'n lladawr[24] namyn y gyd.'

Bwyta ohonunt. Amkawd[25] y wreic, 'Pa neges y

[1]mor W.; y mor R.
[2]gwely.
[3]y chwinsaf.
[4]pwy yw.
[5]+ yn wreic idaw.
[6]genti.
[7]chwaer
[8]kany welsei.
[9]o honei.
[10]+ wy.
[11]lewenyd.
[12]glutweir.
[13]y rwng.
[14]yny yttoed.

[15]Ha wreic heb y kei pei mi a wascut
uelly.
[16]y serch arnaf. drycserch oed
hwnnw.
[17]pan aeth pawb allan y chware. agori
kib uaen a oed yn tal y penntan a oruc
y wreic.
[18]heb y gwrhyr ys oed gryssyn.
[19]y drwc.
[20]heb y.
[21]a ladawd.
[22]o uenic W.; oueneic R.
[23]ac yna y dywawt.
[24]nyn lledir.
[25]ac yna y dywawt.

dodyvch¹ yma chwi?' 'Y dodym y erchi Olwen.'² 'Yr Dyw,
canywch rewelas³ neb etwa o'r gaer, ymhoelwch.'⁴ 'Duw a
vyr nat ymhoylwn hyt pan welhom y uorwyn.⁵ A daw
480   hitheu yn teruyn⁶ y gweler?' 'Hi a daw yma pob dyw
Sadwrn y olchi y fenn, ac yn y llestyr yd ymolcho yd edeu y
modrwyeu oll. Nac hi⁷ na'e chennad ny daw byth
amdanunt.' 'A daw hi yma o chenneteir?'⁸ 'Duw a wyr na
ladaf i uy eneit. Ny thwyllaf ui a'm crettwy.⁹ Namyn o
485   rodwch cret na wneloch gam iti, mi a'e kennattaaf.'¹⁰ 'As
rodwn.'¹¹

Olwen and her Father

Y chennatau a orucpwyd. A'e dyuot¹² hitheu a chamse
sidan flamgoch amdanei, a gordtorch rudeur am y mynwgyl
y uorwyn,¹³ a mererit gwerthuawr [476] yndi a rud
490   gemmeu.¹⁴ Oed melynach¹⁵ y fenn no blodeu y banadyl.
Oed gwynnach¹⁶ y chnawd no distrych y donn.¹⁷ Oed
gvynnach y falueu¹⁸ a'e byssed no chanawon¹⁹ godrwyth o
blith man grayan²⁰ fynhawn fynhonus.²¹ Na golwc hebawc
mut, na golwc gwalch trimut, nyd oed olwg tegach²² no'r
495   eidi. No bronn alarch gwynn oed gwynnach y dwy uron.²³
Oed kochach²⁴ y deu rud no'r fion.²⁵ Y sawl a'e gwelei
kyflawn uydei o'e serch. Pedeir meillonen gwynnyon a dyuei
yn y hol myn yd elhei.²⁶ Ac am hynny y gelwit hi Olwen.

Dygyrchu y ty²⁷ a oruc, ac eisted kyfrwg²⁸ Kulhwch a'r
500   dalueinc. Ac ual y gwelas yd adnabu.²⁹ Dywawt Kulhwch

---

¹... y doethawch chwi yma oe hachaws.
²Ni a doetham y erchi Olwen yr gwas hwnn. Heb y wreic yna. ...
³canych gwelas.
⁴ymchoelwch dracheuyn.
⁵+heb y kei.
⁶yn theruyn W.; yn teruyn R.
⁷na hi.
⁸ony chennetteir.
⁹na thwyllafi am cretto...gret.
¹⁰rodwch gret ... idi ... kannattaaf.
¹¹As redwn [the e *is uncertain and may be an* o]. W., Rodwn heb wynteu R.
¹²Dyuot a oruc.
¹³gwrd dorch rud eur am vynwgyl y uorwyn.
¹⁴rud emeu.
¹⁵Melynach oed.
¹⁶Gwynnach oed.
¹⁷distrych tonn.
¹⁸Tegach oed y dwylaw.
¹⁹no channawan.
²⁰gaean.
²¹ffynhonws.
²²olwc degach.
²³Gwynnach oed y dwyuron no bronn alarch gwynn.
²⁴Cochach oed.
²⁵ffuon cochaf.
²⁶a uydei yn y hol pa fford bynnac y delhei.
²⁷Dyuot yr ty.
²⁸geyr llaw.
²⁹gwel y hadnabu. +Ac y ...

vrthi, 'Ha uorwyn, ti a gereis. A dyuot a wnelych genhyf?'
'Rac eirychu pechawd iti ac i minheu, ny allaf ui dim o
hynny.[1] Cret a erchis uyn tat im nat elwyf heb y gyghor,
kanyt oes hoedyl itaw namyn hyny[2] elwyf gan vr. Yssit,[3]
505   hagen, cussul a rodaf it, os aruolly. Dos y'm erchi[4] y'm tat, a
ffa ueint bynnac a archo ef iti, adef ditheu y gaffel,[5] a minheu
a geffy.[6] Ac ot amheu dim, mi ny cheffy,[7] a da yw it o
dihengy a'th uyw genhyt.'[8] 'Mi a adawaf hynny oll, ac a'e
caffaf.'[9]
510   Kerdet a oruc hi y hystauell. Kyuodi onadunt[10] vynteu
[477] yn y hol hi y'r gaer, a llad naw[11] porthawr a oed ar naw
porth heb disgyrryaw gwr,[12] a naw gauaelgi heb wichaw un.
Ac y kerdassant racdu a'r neuad.[13] Amkeudant,[14] 'Henpych
gwell, Yspadaden Penkawr, o Duw ac o dyn.' 'Neu
515   chwitheu, kwt ymdewch?'[15] 'Yd ymdawn[16] y erchi Olwen
dy uerch y Gulhwch mab Kilid'[17] 'Mae uy gweisson drwc
a'm direidyeit?'[18] heb ynteu. 'Drycheuwch[19] y fyrch y dan
uyn deu amrant[20] hyt pan welwyf defnyt uyn daw.'
Gorucpwyt hyn[n]y.[21] 'Dowch yma auory. Mi a dywedaf
520   peth atteb iwch.'[22]
Kyuodi[23] a orugant vy, a meglyt[24] a oruc Yspadaden
Penkawr yn un o'r tri llechwayw gwenhwynic a oed ac[h] y
law a'e odi[25] ar eu hol. A'e aruoll a oruc Bedwyr a'e odif
ynteu, a gwan Yspadaden Penkawr trwy aual y garr yn
525   gythrymhet. Amkawd[26] ynteu, 'Emendigeit anwar daw,
hanbyd gwaeth[27] yd ymdaaf gan anwaeret. Mal dala cleheren

---

[1]dyuot a wnelhych gennyf. rac eirychu pechawt itti ac y minneu, llawer
dyd yth rygereis. Ny allaf i dim o
hynny.
[2]kanyt hoedel idaw namyn hyt pan.
[3]Yssyd yssit W.R.
[4]Dos di ym erchi i.
[5]a phob peth or a notto ef arnat ti y
gael adef y gel.
[6]a gey.
[7]ot amheu ef dim mi nys keffy.
[8]or dihengy ath uywyt gennyt.
[9]+heb ynteu.
[10]o honunt.
[11]y naw.
[12]un gwr.
[13]a dyuot racdunt a orugant ac yr

neuad.
[14]amkeudawt W.; Henpych gwell
heb wy R.
[15]pan doethawch.
[16]neur doetham.
[17]mab kilyd mab kelydon wledic.
[18]direitwyr.
[19]dyrcheuwch.
[20]vyn dwy ael a dygwydawd ar vy
llygeit.
[21]Hynny a wnaethpwyt.
[22]chwi a geffwch atteb.
[23]+ymeith.
[24]ac ymauael.
[25]ac W.; oed geir y law ae dodi R.
[26]y dywawt ynteu, Ymendigeit...
[27]gwaeth byth.

y'm tostes yr hayarn gwenwynic.[1] Poet emendigeit y gof a'y digones a'r einon[2] y digonet arnei, mor dost yw.'

Gwest a orugant vy[3] y nos honno[4] yn ty Gustenhin.[5] 530 A'r eil dyt gan uawred a gyrru gwiw grip y mywn gwallt[6] y doeth[478]ant y'r neuad.[7] Dywedut a orugant, 'Yspadaden Penkawr, doro[8] in dy uerch dros y hegweti a'e hamwabyr iti a'e dwy garant.[9] Ac onys rody, dy agheu a geffy ymdanei.'[10] 'Hi a'y ffedeir gorhenuam a'e fedwar gorhendat yssyd uyw 535 ettwa—reit yw im ymgyghori[11] ac vynt.' 'Dypi[12] iti hynny,' heb vy.[13] 'Awn y'n bwyt.' Mal y kyuodant, kymryt a oruc ynteu yr eil llechwayw a oed ach[14] y law a'e odif ar eu hol. A'e aruoll a oruc Menw mab Teirgveth,[15] a'e odif ynteu a'e wan yn alauon y dwyuronn, hyt pan[16] dardawd y'r mein gefyn 540 allan. 'Emendigeit anwar daw,[17] mal dala gel bendoll y'm tostes yr hayarn dur. Poet emendigeit y foc yt uerwit yndi.[18] Pan elwyf yn erbyn allt hatuyd ygder dwy uron arnaf,[19] a chyllagwst, a mynych lysuwyd.' Kerdet a orugant wy y eu bwyd.

545 A dyuod y trydydyt[20] y'r llys. Amkeudant,[21] 'Yspadaden Penkawr, na saethutta ni bellach. Na uyn anaf ac adoet a'th uarw arnat.' 'Mae uyg gweisson? Drycheuwch[22] y fyrch— uy aeleu ry syrthwys[23] ar aualeu uy llygeit—hyt pan gaffwyf edrych ar defnyd uyn daw.' Kyuodi a orugant,[24] ac mal y 550 kyuodant kymryt[25] y trydyt llechwayw gwenwynic a'e[26] odif [479] ar eu hol. A'e aruoll a oruc Kulhwch a'e odif yn [teu] mal[27] y rybuchei a'e wan ynteu yn aual y lygat hyt pan

[1]+hwnn.
[2]eingon.
[3]om.
[4]+heuyt.
[5]+heussawr. Yr eil dyd.
[6]gwall.
[7]yr gaer ac y mywn yr neuad.
[8]dyro.
[9]hengwedi ae hamwabyr y titheu. ae dwy gares.
[10]+Y dywawt ynteu.
[11]ymgyghor.
[12]Dybi itti.
[13]wynt.
[14]awch W.; ach R.
[15]teirgwaed.

[16]hyn W.; hyt R.
[17]+heb ynteu.
[18]y berwit yndi ar gof ae digones mor dost yw.
[19]+weithon.
[20]y trydyt dyd.
[21]amkeudawt W.; Y dywawt yspadaden penkawr. Na saethutta vi bellach onyt dy uarw a uynny R.
[22]dyrcheuwch.
[23]a syrthwys.
[24]+hwy.
[25]a oruc yspadaden pennkawr.
[26]ac.
[27]yn W., ynteu ual R.

aeth y'r gwegil allan.[1] 'Emendigeit anwar daw, hyt tra y'm
gatter yn uyw hanbyd gwaeth drem uy llygeit. Pan elwyf yn
555 erbyn gwynt berw[2] a wnant; atuyd gal penn a ffendro
arnaw[3] ar ulaen pob lloer. Poet emendigeit foc yt uerwid[4]
yndi. Mal dala ki kyndeiravc[5] yw genhyf mal y'm gwant yr
hayarn gwenwynic.'[6] Mynet onadunt y eu bwyt.

Tranhoeth y deuthant[7] y'r llys. Amkeudant,[8] 'Na
560 saethutta ni.[9] Na uyn[10] adoet ac anaf a merthrolyaeth[11] yssyt
arnat, ac a uo mwy os mynhy. Doro in dy uerch.'[12] 'Mae y
neb y dywedir vrthaw[13] erchi uy merch?' 'Mi a'e heirch,
Kulhwc[h] mab Kilyd.'[14] 'Dos yma myn yd[15] ymwelwyf a
thi.' Kadeir a dodet y danaw, vyneb yn vyneb ac ef.

Ysbaddaden stipulates the *Anoethau*

565 Dywawt Yspadaden Penkawr, 'Ae ti a eirch uy merch?'
'Ys mi a'e heirch.'[16] 'Cred a uynhaf y genhyt, na wnelhych
waeth no gwir arnaf.' 'Ti a'e keffy.'[17] 'Pan gaffwyf inheu[18] a
nottwyf arnat ti, titheu a geffy uy merch.'[19] 'Nod a
nottych.'[20]
570 'Nodaf.[21] A wely di y garth mawr draw?' 'Gwelaf.' 'Y
diwreidyaw o'r dayar a'e losci ar vyneb y tir hyt pan uo glo
hwnnw a'e ludu a [480] uo teil itaw a uynhaf; a'e eredic a'y heu
hyd pan uo y bore erbyn pryt diwlith yn aeduet,[22] hyd pan uo
hwnnw a wnelit yn uwyd a llynn y'th neithawrwyr ti a
575 merch. A hynny ol[l] a uynaf y wneuthur yn un dyt.'[23]
'Hawd yw genhyf gaffel[24] hynny, kyd tybyckych na bo
hawd.'

[1] ae wan trwy aual y lygat hyt pan aeth trwy y wegil allan.
[2] berwi.
[3] arnaf.
[4] gweirwyt.
[5] kanderawc.
[6] +hwnn.
[7] doethant.
[8] amkeudawt W.; ac y dywedassant R.
[9] +bellach.
[10] namyn.
[11] anaf ac adoet a merthyrolyaeth.
[12] Dyro inn dy uerch. ac onys rody ti a geffy dy angheu ymdeni.
[13] y dywir W.; yssyd yn erchi vy merch i R.
[14] om.
[15] lle yd.
[16] uy merch i. Mi heb y kulhwch.
[17] om.
[18] om.
[19] +ti a gehy yn llawen heb y Kulhwch.
[20] notta yr hyn a vynnych.
[21] +heb ynteu.
[22] Diwreidaw hwnnw or dayar a uynnaf ae loski ar wyneb y tir. hyt pan uo yn lle teil idaw ae eredic ae heu yn undyd ae uot yn aeduet.
[23] a hynny gouot undyd. ac or gwenith hwnnw y mynnaf i gwneuthur bwyt a llynn tymeredic yth neithawr di ti am merch i.
[24] kaffel. kyt tybyckych di.

'Kyt keffych hynny, yssit[1] ny cheffych. Amaeth a
amaetho y tir hwnnw nac a'e digonho, onyt[2] Amaethon
580   mab Don. Ny daw ef o'e uod genhyt ti,[3] ny elly ditheu treis
arnaw ef.'

'Hawd yw genhyf gaffel hynny[4] kyt tybycckych ti na bo
hawd.'

'Kyt keffych hynny, yssit ny cheffych.[5] Gouannon mab
585   Don y dyuot yt ym penn[6] y tir y waret yr heyrn. Ny wna ef
weith o'e uod namyn y urenhin teithiawc, ny elly ditheu
treis arnaw ef.'

'Hawd yw genhyf.'

'Kyt keffych.[7] Deu ychen Gwlwlyd Wineu, yn deu
590   gytbreinawc[8] y eredic y[9] tir dyrys draw yn vych.[10] Nys ryd ef
o'e uod, ny elly ditheu treis arnaw.'

'Hawd yw genhyf.'

'Kyt keffych.[11] Y Melyn Gwanhwyn a'r Ych Brych yn deu
gytbreinhawc a uynhaf.'[12]
595   'Hawd yw genhyf.'[13]

'Kyt keffych.[14] Deu ychen bannawc, y lleill yssyd o'r parth
hwnt y'r Mynyd Bannawc a'r llall o'r parth hwnn,[15] ac eu
dwyn y gyt y dan yr un aradyr.[16] Ys hwy yr rei [481] hynny,
Nynhyaw a Pheibyaw,[17] a rithwys Duw yn ychen am eu[18]
600   pechawd.'

'Hawd yw genhyf.'[19]

'Kyt keffych.[20] A wely di y keibedic rud draw?'

'Gwelaf.'

'Pan gyuaruum gyseuin a mam y uorwyn honno yd hewyt
605   naw hestawr llinat yndaw; na du na gwynn ny doeth ohonaw

---

[1]yssyd W.R..
[2]+mor dyrys yw nyt oes. namyn.
[3]y gennyt ti. Ni elly ditheu dreis.
[4]hawd y kaffaf i hynny ... di.
[5]Kyt keffych ditheu hynny yssit. nas
keffych ... gouannon uab.
[6]y penn.
[7]kyt keffyc W.; Kyt keffych di hynny
yssit nas keffych R.
[8]gyt preinyawc.
[9]W. y *om.*
[10]yn wych.
[11]kyt keff. W.; kyt keffych hynny yssit
nas kaffy Y melyn gwannwyn R.

[12]gyt breinawe a uynnaf a uynnaf.
[13]Hawd yw gen W.; Hawd yw
gennyf kaffel hynny R.
[14]Kyt keffych yssit nas
keffych.
[15]yma.
[16]aradry W.; aradyr R.
[17]sef yw y rei hynny. nynnyaw a
pheibaw.
[18]y pechawt.
[19]Hawd yw gen. W.; Hawd yw
gennyf kaffel hynny R.
[20]kyt kef W. Kyt keffych hynny yssit
nas keffych R.

etwa, a'r messur hwnnw yssyd gennyf ettwa. Hwnnw a
vynnaf inheu y gaffel[1] yn y tir newyd draw, hyt pan vo ef a
uo pennlliein guynn am penn vym merch[2] ar dy neithawr.'
'Hawd yw genhyf.'[3]

610 'Kyt keffych.[4] Mel a uo chwechach naw mod no mel
kynteit heb wchi heb wenyn[5] y vragodi y wled.'
'Hawd yw genhyf.'[6]

'Kyt keffych.[7] Kib Lwyr[8] mab Llwyryon, yssyd pennllat[9]
yndi; canyt oes lestyr yn y byt a dalhyo y llyn cadarn hwnnw
615 namyn hi. Ny cheffy ti hi o'e uod ef, ny elly titheu treis[10]
arnaw.'
'Hawd yw genhyf.'[3]

'Kyt keffych.[11] Mwys Gwydneu Garanhir: pob tri nawyr
pei delhei y byt oduchti, bwyt[12] a uynho pawb wrth y uryt a
620 geiff yndi. Mi a uynnaf uwytta o honno y nos y kysco vy
merch genhyt. Nys ryd ef o'e uod y neb, ny elly titheu y
dreissaw ef.'
'Havd yw genhyf.'[13]

'Kyt keffych.[14] Corn Gwlgawt Gododin[15] y wallaw arnam
625 y nos honno. Nys ryd ef o'e uod, ny elly titheu y treissaw ef.'
'Hawd yw genhyf.'[16]

[482] 'Kyt keffych.[17] Telyn Teirtu y'm didanu y nos
honno. Pan uo da gan dyn, canu a wna e hunan; pan uynher
idi, tewi a wna.[18] Nys ryd ef o'e uod, ny elly titheu treis
630 arnaw ef.'

---

[1]ar llinat hwnnw a uynnaf i y gaffel y
heu.
[2]uym merch i.
[3]hawd yw genh' W.; Hawd yw
gennyf kaffel hynny kyt tebyckych
di na bo hawd R.
[4]Kyt keffych di hynny yssyd nas
keffych.
[5]heb wychi ac heb wenyn yndaw a
vynnaf.
[6]hawd yw W.; Hawd yw gennyf
kaffel hynny. kyt tebyckych di na bo
hawd R.
[7]om.
[8]llwyr uab llwyryon.
[9]bennllat.
[10]nys keffy di . . . ni elly ditheu dreis.

[11]kyt keff' W.; kyt keffych hynny.
yssit nas keffych R.
[12]kyt delei y byt y gyt bop trinaw
wyr. y bwyt.
[13]havd yw genh' W.; Hawd yw
gennyf kaffel hyny kyt tybyckych di
na bo hawd R.
[14]kyt W.; Kyt keffych hynny yssit
nas keffych R.
[15]gogodin.
[16]hawd yw W.; Hawd yw gennyf
kaffel hynny kyt tebyckych na bo
hawd R.
[17]kyt keff' W. Kyt keffych hynny
yssit nas keffych R.
[18]idi tewi hi a teu. a honno.

'Hawd yw genhyf.'[1]

'Kyt keffych.[2] Adar Rianhon y rei a duhun y marw ac a huna y byw a vynhaf y'm didanu y nos honno.'[3]

'Hawd yw genhyf.'[4]

635   'Kyt keffych.'[5] Peir Diwrnach Wydel, maer Odgar mab Aed brenhin Iwerdon y verwi bwyt dy neithawrwyr.'[6]

'Hawd yw genhyf.'[7]

'Kyt keffych.[8] Reit yw ym olchi vym penn ac eillaw vym baryf. Yskithyr Yskithyrwyn Penn Beid[9] a uynnaf y eillaw

640   ym. Ny hanwyf well ohonaw onyt yn vyw y tynnir[10] o'e pen.'

'Hawd yw genhyf.'[11]

'Kyt keffych.[12] Nyt oes yn y byt a'e tynho o'e penn namyn Odgar mab Aed brenhin Iwerdon.'

645   'Hawd yw genhyf.'[13]

'Kyt keffych.[14] Nyt ymdiredaf y neb o gadw yr yskithyr namyn y Kaw[15] o Prydein. Trugein cantref Prydein yssyd [y]danaw ef. Ny daw ef o'e uod o'e teyrnas, ny ellir[16] treis arnaw ynteu.'

650   'Hawd yw genhyf.'[17]

'Kyt keffych.[18] Reit yw ym estynnu vym blew wrth eillaw ym. Nyt estwg uyth ony cheffir guaet y Widon Ordu merch y Widon Orwen o Pennant Gouut yg gwrthtir Uffern.'

'Hawd yw genhyf.'[19]

655   'Kyt keffych.[20] Ny mwynha y gwaet onyt yn dwym y keffir.[21] Nyt oes lestyr yn y byt a gattwo gwres y llyn a dotter

---

[1] hawd W.; Hawd yw gennyf kaffel hynny kyt tebyckych na bo hawd R.
[2] kyt keff W.; Kyt keffych hynny yssit nas keffych R.
[3] Adar ... honno *om.*
[4] hawd W.; Hawd yw gennyf kaffel hynny kyt tebyckych na bo hawd R.
[5] kyt keff W.; Kyt keffych hynny yssit nas keffych R.
[6] neithawr.
[7] hawd W.; Hawd yw gennyf kaffel hynny kyt tebyckych na bo hawd R.
[8] kyt W.; Kyt keffych hynny yssit nas keffych R.
[9] Beird.
[10] tinnir.
[11] hawd W.; Hawd yw gennyf kaffel hynny kyt tebyckych na bo hawd R.
[12] kyt W.; kyt keffych hynny yssit nas keffych R.
[13] hawd W.; Hawd yw gennyf kaffel hynny R.
[14] kyt W.; kyt keffych hynny yssit nas k' R.
[15] y kadw W.; y gado R.
[16] ny elly ditheu dreis.
[17] hawd W.; Hawd yw gennyf kaffel hynny kyt tebyckych na bo hawd R.
[18] kyt W.; Kyt keffych hynny yssit nas keffych R.
[19] hawd W.; Hawd yw gennyf kaffel hynny. kyt tebyckych na bo h'a R.
[20] kyt W.; Kyt k' R.
[21] Ny mynnaf ... y keffych.

yndaw namyn botheu Guidolwyn Gorr, a gatwant gures
yndunt pan [483] dotter yn y dwyrein yndunt y llyn hyt pan
dyffer y'r go[r]llewin.[1] Ny ryd[2] ef o'e vod, ny elly titheu y
660   treissaw.'
    'Hawd yw genhyf.'[3]
    Kyt keffych.[4] Llefrith a wennych rei; nyt aruaeth[5] kaffel
lleurith y bawb nes kaffel botheu Rinnon Rin Baruawc.[6] Ny
surha uyth llyn yndunt. Nys ryd ef o'e uod y neb, ny ellir
665   treis arnaw.'[7]
    'Hawd yw genhyf.'[8]
    'Kyt keffych.[9] Nyt oes yn y byt crib a guelleu y galler
gwrteith vyg uallt ac wy,[10] rac y rynhet, namyn y grib a'r
guelleu yssyd kyfrwg deu yskyuarn[11] Twrch Trwyth mab
670   Tared Wledic. Nys ryd ef o'e uod et cetera.'
    'Hawd yw genhyf.[12]
    'Kyt keffych.[13] Ny helir Twrch Trwyth hyny gaffer
Drutwyn, keneu Greit mab Eri.'
    'Hawd yw genhyf.'[14]
675   'Kyt keffych.[15] Nyt oes yn y byt gynllyuan a dalhyo
arnaw, namyn kynllyuan Cors[16] Cant Ewin.'
    'Hawd yw genhyf.'[17]
    'Kyt keffych.'[18] Nyt oes torch yn y byt a dalhyo y
gynllyuan, namyn torch Can[h]astyr[19] Canllaw.'
680   'Hawd yw genhyf.'[20]
    'Kyt keffych.[21] Cadwyn Kilyd Canhastyr y daly y torch[22]
gyt a'r gynllyuan.'
    'Hawd yw genhyf.'[23]
    'Kyt keffych.[24] Nyt oes yn y byt kynyd a digonho

---

[1]hyt pan deler yr gorllewin.
[2]nys ryd . . . ditheu y dreissaw ef.
[3]Hawd W.; 'Hawd yw gennyf et cetera R.
[4]kyt W.; Kyt k' R . . . a whennych.
[5]arllaeth W.; aruaeth R.
[6]baruawt W.; barnawt R.
[7]ny elly ditheu dreis arnaw ef.
[8]hawd W.; Hawd yw gennyf k' R.
[9]kyt W.; Kyt keffych h' R.
[10]uyg gwallt ac wynt.
[11]y rwng deuglust.
[12]hawd W.; Hawyd yw gennyf k'.R.
[13]kyt W.; Kyt keffych et cetera R.

[14]hawd W.; Hawd yw R.
[15]kyt W.; Kyt keff R . . . kynllyuan R.
[16]cwrs W.; kwrs R.
[17]hawd W.; Hawd yw g' R.
[18]kyt W.; Kyt keff'. h' R.
[19]canhastyr.
[20]hawd W.; Hawd et cetera R.
[21]kyt W.; Kyt keffych hynny yssit nas keffych R.
[22]y dorch.
[23]hawd W.; Hawd yw R.
[24]kyt W.; Kyt k' et cetera R.

685 kynydyaeth ar y ki[1] hwnnw, onyt Mabon mab Modron, a
ducpwyt yn teir nossic y wrth y vam. Ny wys py tu[2] y mae,
na pheth yw, ae byw ae marw.'
'Hawd yw genhyf.'[3]
'Kyt keffych.[4] Guyn Mygtwn,[5] march Gwedw—kyfret a
690 thon yw[6]—dan Vabon y hela Twrch Trwyth.[7] Nys ryd[8] ef
o'e vod et cetera.'
Hawd yw genhyf.'[9]
'Kyt keffych.[10] Ny cheffir Mabon vyth, [484] ny wys py
tu[11] y mae, nes kaffel Eidoel y gar gysseuin[12] mab Aer, kanys
695 diuudyawc uyd yn y geissaw. Y geuynderw yw.'
'Hawd yw genhyf.'[13]
'Kyt keffych.[14] Garselit[15] Wydel, penkynyd Iwerdon yw.
Ny helir Twrch Trwyth uyth hebdaw.'
'Hawd yw genhyf.'[16]
700 'Kyt keffych.[17] Kynllyuan o uaryf Dillus[18] Varchawc,
canyt oes a dalhyo y deu geneu hynny namyn hi. Ac ny ellir
mwynyant a hi onyt ac ef yn vyw y tynnir o'e varyf, a'e
gnithyaw a chyllellprenneu. Ny at neb[19] o'e vywyt
gwneuthyr hynny idaw. Ny mwynha hitheu yn uarw canys
705 breu vyd.'
'Hawd yw genhyf.'[20]
'Kyt keffych.[21] Nyt oes kynyd yn y byt a dalhyo y deu
geneu hynny, namyn Kynedyr Wyllt mab Hettwn
Clauyryawc. Guylltach[22] naw mod yw hwnnw no'r
710 gwydlwdyn guylltaf yn y mynyd. Ny cheffy ti ef byth, a
merch[23] inheu nys keffy.'
'Hawd yw genhyf.'[24]
'Kyt keffych.[25] Ny heli[r][26] Twrch Trwyth nes kaffel Guynn

[1]ar ki . . .
[2]pa du.
[3]hawd W.; Hawd yw R.
[4]kyt W.; Kyt k' et cetera R.
[5]mygdwn.
[6]kynebrwydet yw a thonn y dan.
[7]y twrch trwyth.
[8]ryd om. W.
[9]hawd W.; Hawd yw g'. R.
[10]kyt W.; Keffych h'.R.
[11]kany wys pa tu.
[12]kysseuin.
[13]hawd W.; Hawd et cetera R.
[14]kyt W.; Kyt k'. R.

[15]Garsclit W.R.
[16]hawd W.; Hawd yw R.
[17]kyt W.; Kyt k'. R.
[18]dissull W.R.
[19]neb om.
[20]hawdd W.; Hawd yw R.
[21]kyth W.; Kyt keffych hynny et cetera R.
[22]Glafyrawc, gwylltall.
[23]Nys keffy . . . na merch.
[24]hawd W.; Hawd yw g. R.
[25]kyt W.; Kyt keff' Ny helir. R.
[26]heli W. helir R.

mab Nud ar dodes[1] Duw aryal dieuyl Annwuyn yndaw rac
715 rewinnyaw y bressen. Ny hebcorir ef odyno.'
'Hawd yw genhyf.'[2]
'Kyt keffych.[3] Nyt oes uarch a tyckyo[4] y Wynn y hela
Twrch Trwyth, namyn Du march Moro Oeruedawc.'
'Hawd yw genhyf.'[5]
720 'Kyt keffych.[6] Nes dyuot Guilenhin brenhin Freinc,[7] ny
helir Twrch Trwyth uyth hebdaw. Hagyr yw idaw adaw y
teyrnas,[8] ac ny daw[9] uyth yma.'
'Hawd yw genhyf.'[10]
'Kyt keffych.[11] Ny helir Twrch Trwyth vyth heb caffel
725 mab Alun Dyuet. Ellygywr da yw.'[12]
'Hawd yw genhyf.'[13]
'Kyt keffych.[14] Ny helir [485] Twrch Trwyth uyth nes
kaffel Anet ac Aethlem. Kyfret[15] ac awel wynt oedynt;[16] ny
ellwngwyt eiroet ar mil nys lladwynt.'[17]
730 'Hawd yw genhyf.'[18]
'Kyt keffych.'[19] Arthur a'e gynydyon y hely[20] Twrch
Trwyth. Gwr kyuoethawc yw ac ny daw genhyt;[21] sef yw yr
achaws, dan uy llaw i y mae ef.'[22]
'Hawd yw genhyf.'[23]
735 'Kyt keffych.[24] Ny ellir hela Twrch Trwyth vyth nes kaffel
Bwlch a Chyuwlch a Syuwlch, meibyon Kilyd Kyuwlch,
wyryon[25] Cledyf Diuwlch. Teir gorwen guen eu teir yscwyt;
tri gouan guan eu tri guayw;[26] tri benyn byn eu tri chledyf;
Glas, Glessic, Gleissat,[27] eu tri chi; Call, Cuall, Cauall, eu tri
740 meirch; Hwyr Dydwc, a Drwc Dydwc, a Llwyr Dydwc, eu

---

[1] a ry dodes.
[2] hawd W.; Hawd yw R.
[3] kyt W.; Kyt k'. R.
[4] yn y byt a dycko.
[5] hawd W.; Hawd yw R.
[6] kyt W.; Kyt. k', h'. R.
[7] gilennhin urenhin ffreinc.
[8] y deyrnas + yrot ti.
[9] daw ef.
[10] hawd W. Hawd yw R.
[11] kyt W. Kyt k'. et cetera R.
[12] heb gaffel ... gell llyngwr da yw hwnnw.
[13] hawd W.; Hawd yw R.
[14] kyt W.; Kyt. et cetera R.

[15] kynebrwydet.
[16] ynt.
[17] ny ellyngwyt eiryoet ar lwdyn nys ledynt.
[18] hawd W.; Hawd et cetera R.
[19] kyt W.; Kyt keffych h'. R.
[20] gedymdeithon y hela.
[21] ef yrot ti. ny elly ditheu dreis arnaw ef.
[22] om.
[23] hawd W.; Hawd et cetera R.
[24] kyt W.; Kyt. k'. et cetera R.
[25] wryon W.; wyryon R.
[26] gwaew.
[27] Gleissic Gleissac.

teir guraged; Och a Garam[1] a Diaspat, eu teir gureichon:
Lluchet a Neuet[2] ac Eissywet, eu teir merchet; Drwc a
Gwaeth a Guaethaf Oll, eu teir morwyn. Y trywyr[3] a ganant
eu kyrn, a'r rei ereill oll a doant y diaspedein, hyt na
745 hanbwyllei neb pei dygwydei[4] y nef ar y dayar.'
     'Hawd yw genhyf.'[5]
     'Kyt keffych.[6] Cledyf Wrnach Gawr. Ny ledir uyth
namyn ac ef. Nys ryd ef y neb[7] nac ar werth nac yn rat, ny
elly titheu treis arnaw ef.'
750 'Hawd yw genhyf.'[8]
     'Kyt keffych.[9] Anhuned heb gyscu nos a geffy yn keissaw
hynny, ac nys keffy, a merch inheu nys keffy.'
     'Meirych a gaffaf inheu a marchogaeth. A'm harglwyd gar
Arthur a geiff imi hynny oll. A'th verch titheu a gaffaf ui,
755 a'th eneit a golly titheu.'
     [486] 'Kerda nu ragot. Ny oruyd arnat na bwyt na dillat y
merch i.[10] Keis hynny.[11] A ffan gaffer hynny,[12] vym merch
inheu a geffy.'[13]

The Sword of Wrnach the Giant, and the naming of Goreu

     Kerdet a orugant wy y dyd hwnnw educher, hyny vyd
760 kaer uaen gymrwt a welasit, uwyhaf ar keyryd y byt.[14]
Nachaf gwr du, mwy no thrywyr y byt hwnn, a welant yn
dyuot o'r gaer.[15] Amkeudant wrthaw, 'Pan doy ti, wr?'[16]
     'O'r gaer a welwch chwi yna.'[17] 'Pieu y gaer?'[18] 'Meredic a
wyr ywchi. Nyt oes yn y byt ny wyppo pieu y gaer honn.
765 Wrnach[19] Gawr pieu.' 'Py uoes yssyd y osp a phellenhic y
diskynnu yn y gaer honn?' 'Ha vnben, Duw a'ch notho. Ny
dodyw neb guestei[20] eiroet oheni a'e uyw ganthaw.[21] Ny edir
neb idi namyn a dyccwy y gerd.'[22]

[1]acaram W.; agaram R.
[2]auynet W., a vynet R.
[3]y trywyr hynny.
[4]a phawb or rei ereill a diaspedant
yny debycko pawb dygwydaw.
[5]hawd W.; yw *et cetera* R.
[6]kyt W.; Kyt. k'. R.
[7]nys ry ef oe uod.
[8]hawd W.; Hawd yw *et cetera* R.
[9]Kyt W., Kyt keffych R.
[10]ym merch i tra geissych hynny.
[11]*om.*
[12]a phan geffych hynny oll or

anoetheu.
[13]+ yn ueu itt.
[14]kaer uawr a welynt vwyhaf or byt.
[15]wr du mwy oed no thrywyr yn y
byt hwnn yn dyuot or gaer.
[16]ac y dywedassant wynteu wrthaw.
Pan deuy di wr.
[17]racco.
[18]+ heb wynt.
[19]wrnac gawr bieu.
[20]nodho. ny deuth gwestei.
[21]vywyt gantaw.
[22]dycko y gerd gantaw.

Kyrchu y porth a orugant. Amkawd[1] Gwrhyr Gualstawt
770 Ieithoet, 'A oes porthawr?'[2] 'Oes. A titheu, ny bo teu dy
penn, pyr y kyuerchy dy?'[3] 'Agor y porth.' 'Nac agoraf.'
'Pwy ystyr[4] nas agory ti?' 'Kyllell a edyw ym mwyt a llynn
ymual, ac amsathyr yn neuad Vrnach.[5] Namyn y gerdawr a
dyccwy y gerd,[6] nyt agorir.'[7] Amkawd Kei,[8] 'Y porthawr,
775 y mae kerd genhyf i.' 'Pa gerd yssyd genhyt ti?' 'Yslipanwr
cledyueu goreu yn y byt wyf ui.' 'Mi a af y dywedut hynny y
Vrnach Gawr, ac a dygaf atteb yt.'
Dyuot a oruc y porthawr y mywn. Dywawt Wrnach
Gawr,[9] [487] 'Whedleu porth y genhyt?' 'Yssydynt
780 genhyf.[10] Kyweithyd yssyd yn drws y porth ac a uynnynt[11]
dyuot y mywn.' 'A ouynneist ti a oed gerd ganthunt?'[12]
'Gouynneis.[13] Ac vn onadunt a dywawt gallel yslipanu
cledyueu.'[14] 'Oed reit y mi[15] wrth hwnnw. Ys gwers yd wyf
yn keissaw a olchei vyg cledyf; nys rygeueis.[16] Gat hwnnw y
785 mywn, cans oed[17] gerd ganthaw.'
Dyuot[18] y porthawr ac agori y porth, a dyuot Kei y mywn
e hun. A chyuarch guell a oruc ef y Wrnach Gawr. Kadeir a
dodet y danaw.'[19] Dywawt Wrnach, 'Ha wr, ae gwir a
dywedir arnat,[20] gallel[21] yslipanu cledyueu? 'Mi a'e
790 digonaf.'[22] Dydwyn y cledyf attaw a orucpwyt.[23] Kymryt
agalen gleis a oruc Kei y dan y gesseil.[24] 'Pwy well genhyt
arnaw, ae guynseit ae grwmseit?' 'Yr hwnn a uo da genhyt ti,
malpei teu uei, gwna arnaw.' Glanhau a oruc hanher y lleill
gyllell idaw, a'e rodi yn y law a oruc, 'A reinc dy uod di
795 hynny?' 'Oed well[25] genhyf noc yssyd y'm gwlat bei oll yt uei

[1] heb y.
[2] borthawr.
[3] dy dauawt yth benn py rac y.
[4] pwystyr W. Py ystyr R.
[5] wrnach gawr.
[6] dycko y gerd y mywn.
[7] yma heno bellach.
[8] Heb y kei yna.
[9] ac y dywawt wrnach wrthaw.
Chwedleu.
[10] Ys ydynt gennyf.
[11] yn drws y porth a uynnynt.
[12] +hwy.
[13] +heb ef.
[14] gwybot yslipanu cledyueu o
honaw yn da.

[15] as oed reit ynni (with attempt to correct
ynni i ymi).
[16] ac nys keueis.
[17] kan oes.
[18] +a oruc.
[19] +geyr bron gwrnach. Ac y
dywawt wrnach wrthaw.
[20] arnat ti.
[21] y gwdost.
[22] Mi a wnn hynn yn da heb y kei.
[23] Dwyn cledyf wrnach a wnaethpwyt attaw.
[24] +a gouyn or deu pwy oed oreu
gantaw.
[25] oed gwell.

val hynn.[1] Dyhed a beth bot gwr kystal a thi heb
gedymdeith.' 'Oia wrda, mae imi gedymdeith kyny
dygo[n]ho[2] y gerd honn.' 'Pwy yw hwnnw?' 'Aet y porthawr
allan, a mi a dywedaf ar arwydon idaw.[3] Penn y wayw a daw
800   y ar y baladyr, ac yssef a dygyrch y guaet y ar y guynt, ac a
diskyn ar y baladyr.'[4] Agori y porth a wnaeth [488] pwyt, a
dyuot Bedwyr y mywn. Dywawt[5] Kei, 'Budugawl yw
Bedwyr, kyn ny digonho[6] y gerd hon.'
      A dadleu mawr a uu ar y gwyr hynny allan. Dyuot[7] Kei a
805   Bedwyr y mywn, a guas ieuanc a doeth gyt ac wynt y
mywn[8]—vn mab Custennhin heussawr. Sef a wnaeth ef a'e
gedymdeithon a glyn[9] wrthaw, mal nat oed vwy no dim
ganthunt mynet dros y teir catlys a wnacthant hyt pan
dyuuant y mywn y gaer.[10] Amkeudant y gedymdeithon wrth
810   vab Custenhin, 'Goreu dyn yw.' O hynny allan y gelwit[11]
Goreu mab Custenhin. Guascaru a orugant wy y eu llettyeu
mal y keffynt llad eu llettywyr heb wybot y'r Cawr. Y cledyf
a daruu y wrteith, a'e rodi a oruc Kei yn llaw Wrnach Kawr[12]
y malphei y edrych a ranghei y uod idaw y weith[13] Dywawt[14]
815   y Kawr, 'Da yw y gweith, a ranc bod yw genhyf.' Amkawd[15]
Kei, 'Dy wein a lygrwys dy gledyf. Dyro di imi y diot y
kellellprenneu oheni,[16] a chaffwyf inheu gwneuthur rei
newyd idaw.'[17] A chymryt y wein ohonaw, a'r cledyf[18] yn y
llaw arall. Dyuot ohonaw vch pen y Kawr malphei y cledyf a
820   dottei yn y wein. Y ossot a oruc ymphen y Kawr, a llad y
penn y ergyt y arnaw. Diffeithaw y gaer a dwyn a vynnassant
o tlysseu.[19] Yg kyuenw yr vn dyd[20] ymphen y vlwydyn y
deuthant[*] [R. col. 833] y lys Arthur, a chledyf Wrnach
Gawr gantunt.

---

[1]pei bei oll ual hynn.
[2]dygoho W.; dycko R.
[3]idaw y arwydon.
[4]+eilweith.
[5]ac y dywawt.
[6]wypo.
[7]Dadleu mawr a uu gan y gwyr a oed
allan am dyuot . . .
[8]A dyuot gwas ieuanc oed gyt ac
wynt y mywn.
[9]yg glyn R. mal . . . ganthunt *om.* R.
[10]dyuot dros y teir katlys hyt pann
yttoed y mywn y gaer.
[11]Y dywedassant y gedymdeithon

wrth uab Custennin. ti a orugost
hynn. goreu dyn wyt. Ac o hynny
allan y gelwit ef . . .
[12]Wrnach gawr.
[13]y gweith.
[14]ac y dywawt.
[15]y dywawt kei dy wein di.
[16]o honei.
[17]Ac y wneuthur ereill o newyd
idaw.
[18]chedyf W.
[19]or da ar tlysseu.
[20]hwnnw *del.* W.
[*W *fin.*, R. *henceforth*].

The Freeing of Eiddoel fab Aer

825 Dywedut a wnaethant y Arthur y ual y daruu udunt.
Arthur a dywawt, 'Pa beth yssyd iawnaf y geissaw gyntaf o'r
annoetheu hynny?' 'Iawnaf yw,' heb wynteu, 'keissaw
Mabon uab Modron, ac nyt kaffel arnaw nes kaffel Eidoel
uab Aer y gar yn gyntaf.' Kyuodi a oruc Arthur a milwyr
830 Ynys Prydein gantaw y geissaw Eidoel, a dyuot a orugant
hyt yn rackaer Gliui yn y lle yd oed Eidoel yg karchar. Seuyll
a oruc Gliui ar vann y gaer, ac y dywawt, 'Arthur, py holy di
y mi pryt na'm gedy yn y tarren honn? Nyt da im yndi ac nyt
digrif, nyt gwenith, nyt keirch im, kyn ny cheissych ditheu
835 wneuthur cam im.' Arthur a dywawt, 'Nyt yr drwc itti y
deuthum i yma namyn y geissaw y karcharawr yssyd
gennyt,' 'Mi a rodaf y carcharawr itti, ac ny darparysswn y
rodi y neb. Ac ygyt a hynny vy nerth a'm porth a geffy di.'

The Oldest Animals

Y gwyr a dywawt wrth Arthur, 'Arglwyd, dos di adref.
840 Ny elly di uynet a'th lu y geissaw peth mor uan a'r rei hynn.'
Arthur a dywawt, 'Gwrhyr Gwalstawt Ieithoed, itti y mae
iawn mynet y'r neges honn. Yr holl ieithoed yssyd gennyt, a
chyfyeith wyt a'r rei o'r adar a'r anniueileit. Eidoel, itti y
mae iawn mynet y geissaw, dy geuynderw yw, gyt a'm gwyr
845 i. Kei a Bedwyr, gobeith [834] yw gennyf y neges yd eloch
ymdanei y chaffel. Ewch im y'r neges honn.'

Kerdet a orugant racdunt hyt att Vwyalch Gilgwri.
Gouyn a oruc Gwrhyr idi, 'Yr Duw, a wdost ti dim y wrth
Uabon uab Modron, a ducpwyt yn teir nossic ody rwng y
850 vam a'r paret?' Y Uwyalch a dywawt, 'Pan deuthum i yma
gyntaf, eingon gof a oed yma, a minneu ederyn ieuanc
oedwn. Ny wnaethpwyt gweith arnei, namyn tra uu
uyg geluin arnei bob ucher. Hediw nyt oes kymmeint
kneuen ohonei heb dreulaw. Dial Duw arnaf o chigleu i
855 dim y wrth y gwr a ovynnwch chwi. Peth yssyd iawn,
hagen, a dylyet ymi y wneuthur y gennadeu Arthur, mi
a'e gwnaf. Kenedlaeth[1] vileit yssyd gynt rithwys[2] Duw no
mi. Mi a af yn gyuarwyd ragoch yno.'

Dyuot a orugant hyt yn lle yd oed Karw Redynure. 'Karw

[1] kenedlaeth[h].
[2] gynt a rithwys: 'a' *in a later hand.*

860 Redynure, yma y doetham ni attat, kennadeu Arthur, kany
wdam aniueil hyn no thi. Dywet, a wdost di dim y wrth
Uabon uab Modron, a ducpwyt yn deir nossic y wrth y
uam?' Y Karw a dywawt, 'Pan deuthum i yma gyntaf, nyt
oed namyn vn reit o bop tu y'm penn, ac nyt oed yma goet
865 namyn un o gollen derwen, ac y tyfwys honno yn dar can
keing, ac y dygwydwys y dar gwedy hynny, a hediw nyt oes
namyn wystyn coch ohonei. Yr hynny hyt hediw yd wyf i
yma. Ny chigleu i dim o'r neb a ouynnwch chwi. Miui hagen
a uydaf gyfarwyd ywch, [835] kanys kennadeu Arthur ywch,
870 hyt lle y mae aniueil gynt a rithwys Duw no mi.'

Dyuot a orugant hyt lle yd oed Cuan Cum Kawlwyt.
'Cuan Cwm Kawlwyt, yma y mae kennadeu Arthur. A
wdost di dim y wrth Vabon uab Modron a ducpwyt yn teir
nossic y wrth y uam?'[1] 'Pei as gwypwn, mi a'e dywedwn.
875 Pan deuthum i yma gyntaf, y cwm mawr a welwch glynn
coet oed, ac y deuth kenedlaeth o dynyon idaw, ac y
diuawyt, ac y tyuwys yr eil coet yndaw. A'r trydyd coet yw
hwnn. A minneu, neut ydynt[2] yn gynyon boneu vy esgyll.
Yr hynny hyt hediw ny chiglef i dim o'r gwr a ouynnwch
880 chwi. Mi hagen a uydaf gyuarwyd y genadeu Arthur, yny
deloch hyt lle y mae yr anniueil hynaf yssyd yn y byt hwnn, a
mwyaf a dreigyl, Eryr Gwern Abwy.'

Gwrhyr a dywawt, 'Eryr Gwern Abwy, ni a doetham,
gennadeu Arthur, attat y ouyn itt a wdost dim y wrth Vabon
885 uab Modron a ducpwyt yn teir nossic y wrth y uam?'[3] Yr
Eryr a dywawt, 'Mi a deuthum yma yr ys pell o amser, a
phann deuthum yma gyntaf maen a oed ym, ac y ar y benn ef
y pigwn y syr bop ucher. Weithon nyt oes dyrnued yn y
uchet. Yr hynny hyt hediw yd wyf i yma, ac ny chiglef i dim
890 y wrth y gwr a ouynnwch chwi. Onyt un treigyl yd euthum
y geissaw uym bwyt hyt yn Llynn Llyw, a phann deuthum i
yno y lledeis uyg cryuangheu y mywn ehawc, o debygu bot
vym bwyt yndaw wers vawr, ac y tynnwys ynteu ui hyt yr
affwys, hyt pann uu abreid im ymdianc y gantaw. Sef a
895 wneuthum inheu, mi a'm [836] holl garant, mynet yg gwrys
wrthaw y geissaw y diuetha. Kennadeu a yrrwys ynteu y

---

[1] a ducpwyt et cetera.   [3] a duc et cetera.
[2] ydydynt.

gymot a mi, a dyuot a oruc ynteu attaf i, y diot dec tryuer a
deugeint o'e geuyn. Onyt ef a wyr peth o'r hynn a geisswch
chwi, ny wnn i neb a'e gwypo. Mi hagen a uydaf gyuarwyd
900 ywch hyt lle y mae.'

Dyuot a orugant hyt lle yr oed. Dywedut a oruc yr Eryr,
'Ehawc Llyn Lliw, mi a deuthum attat gan gennadeu
Arthur y ouyn a wdost dim y wrth Vabon uab Modron, a
ducpwyt yn teir nossic y wrth y uam?' 'Y gymeint a wypwyf
905 i, mi a'e dywedaf. Gan bob llanw yd af i ar hyt yr auon uchot
hyt pan delwyf hyt ymach mur Kaer Loyw, ac yno y keueis i
ny cheueis eirmoet o drwc y gymeint. Ac mal y crettoch,
doet un ar uyn dwy ysgwyd i yma ohonawch.' Ac ysef yd
aeth ar dwy ysgwyd yr Ehawc, Kei a Gwrhyr Gwalstawt
910 Ieithoed. Ac y kerdassant hyt pann deuthant am y uagwyr
a'r karcharawr, yny uyd kwynuan a griduan a glywynt am y
uagwyr ac wy. Gwrhyr a dywawt, 'Pa dyn a gwyn yn y
maendy hwnn?' 'Oia wr, yssit le idaw y gwynaw y neb yssyd
yma. Mabon uab Modron yssyd yma yg carchar,[1] ac ny
915 charcharwyt neb kyn dostet yn llwrw carchar a mi, na
charchar Llud Llaw Ereint, neu garchar Greit mab Eri.' 'Oes
obeith gennyt ti ar gaffel dy ellwng ae yr eur ae yr aryant ae yr
golut presennawl, ae yr catwent ac ymlad?' 'Y gymeint
ohonof i a gaffer, a geffir drwy ymlad.'

The Freeing of Mabon fab Madron

920 Ymchoelut ohonunt wy odyno, a dyuot hyt [837] lle yd
oed Arthur. Dywedut ohonunt y lle yd oed Mabon uab
Modron yg karchar. Gwyssyaw a oruc Arthur milwyr yr
Ynys honn, a mynet hyt yg Kaer Loyw y lle yd oed Mabon yg
karchar. Mynet a oruc Kei a Bedwyr ar dwy yscwyd y pysc.
925 Tra yttoed vilwyr Arthur yn ymlad a'r gaer, rwygaw o Gei y
uagwyr a chymryt y carcharawr ar y geuyn, ac ymlad a'r
gwyr ual kynt.[2] Atref y doeth Arthur a Mabon gantaw yn
ryd.

The bitch of Rhymhi and her Pups

Dywedut a oruc Arthur, 'Beth iawnhaf weithon y geissaw
930 yn gyntaf o'r annoetheu?' 'Iawnhaf yw keissaw deu geneu
Gast Rymhi.' 'A wys,' heb yr Arthur, 'pa du y mae hi?' 'Y
mae,' heb yr un, 'yn Aber Deu Gledyf.' Dyuot a oruc Arthur

[1]ygcarch.   [2]ar gwyr ual kynt ar gwyr.

hyt yn ty Tringat yn Aber Cledyf, a gofyn a oruc wrthaw, 'A
glyweist ti y wrthi hi yma? Py rith y mae hi?' 'Yn rith
935 bleidast,' heb ynteu, 'a'e deu geneu genthi yd ymda. Hi a
ladawd vy ysgrybul yn vynych, ac y mae hi issot yn Aber
Cledyf y mywn gogof.'

Sef a oruc Arthur, gyrru ym Prytwenn y long ar uor, ac
ereill ar y tir, y hela yr ast, a'e chylchynu uelly hi a'e deu
940 geneu. Ac eu datrithaw[1] o Duw y Arthur yn eu rith e hunein.
Gwascaru a oruc llu Arthur bob un bob deu.

The Lame Ant

Ac ual yd oed Gwythyr mab Greidawl dydgweith yn
kerdet dros vynyd, y clywei leuein a gridua girat, a
garwson[2] oed eu clybot. Achub a oruc ynteu parth ac yno, ac
945 mal y deuth yno [837b] dispeilaw cledyf a wnaeth, a llad y
twynpath wrth y dayar, ac ev diffryt uelly rac y tan. Ac y
dywedassant wynteu wrthaw, 'Dwc uendyth Duw a'r
einym gennyt, a'r hynn ny allo dyn uyth y waret, ni a down y
waret itt.' Hwyntwy wedy hynny a doethant a'r naw
950 hestawr llinat a nodes Yspadaden Pennkawr ar Culhwch yn
uessuredic oll, heb dim yn eisseu ohonunt eithyr un
llinhedyn, a'r morgrugyn cloff a doeth a hwnnw kynn y nos.

The Beard of Dillus the Bearded

Pan yttoed Gei a Bedwyr yn eisted ar benn Pumlumon ar
Garn Gwylathyr, ar wynt mwyaf yn y byt, edrych a
955 wnaethant yn eu kylch, ac wynt a welynt vwc mawr parth a'r
deheu, ym pell y wrthunt heb drossi dim gan y gwynt. Ac
yna y dywawt Kei, 'Myn llaw vyng kyueillt, syll dy racco
tan rysswr.' Bryssyaw a orugant parth a'r mwc, a dynessau
parth ac yno dan ymardisgwyl o bell, yny uyd Dillus
960 Uarruawc yn deiuaw baed coet. Llyna, hagen, y rysswr
mwyaf a ochelawd Arthur eiryoet. Heb y Bedwyr yna wrth
Gei, 'A'e hatwaenost di ef?' 'Atwen,' heb y Kei, 'Llyna
Dillus Uarruawc. Nyt oes yn y byt kynllyuan a dalyo
Drutwyn keneu Greit uab Eri namyn kynllyuan o uaryf y
965 gwr a wely di racko. Ac ny mwynhaa heuyt onyt yn vyw y

[1]dat rithaw.
[2]garscon.

tynnir a chyllellprenneu o'e uaraf, kanys breu uyd yn uarw.'
'Mae an kynghor ninneu wrth hynny?' heb y Bedwyr.
'Gadwn ef,' heb y Kei, 'y yssu y wala o'r kic, a gwedy hynny
kyscu a wna.' Tra yttoed ef yn [837c] hynny, y buant wynteu
970 yn gwneuthur kyllellbrenneu. Pan wybu Gei yn diheu y uot
ef yn kyscu, gwyneuthur pwll a oruc dan y draet, mwyhaf yn
y byt, a tharaw dyrnawt arnaw anueitrawl y ueint a oruc, a'e
wascu yn y pwll hyt pan daroed udunt y gnithiaw yn llwyr
a'r kyllellbrenneu y uaryf. A gwedy hynny y lad yn gwbyl.
975   Ac odyna yd aethant ell deu hyt yg Kelli Wic yg Kernyw, a
chynllyuann o uaryf Dillus Uaruawc gantunt a'e rodi a oruc
Kei yn llaw Arthur. Ac yna y kanei Arthur yr eglyn hwnn:
              Kynnllyuan a oruc Kei
              O uaryf Dillus uab Eurei.
980   Pei iach dy angheu uydei.
Ac am hynny y sorres Kei hyt pan uu abreid y uilwyr yr Ynys
honn tangneuedu y rwng Kei ac Arthur. Ac eissoes, nac yr
anghyfnerth ar Arthur nac yr llad y wyr, nyt ymyrrwys Kei
yn teit gyt ac ef o hynny allan.

Gwyn ap Nudd and Gwythyr and Creiddylad

985   Ac yna y dywawt Arthur, 'Beth iawnaf weithon y geissaw
o'r annoetheu?' 'Iawnaf yw keissaw Drutwyn keneu Greit
uab Eri.'
       Kyn no hynny ychydic yd aeth Creidylat uerch Lud Law
Ereint gan Wythyr mab Greidawl, a chynn kyscu genthi
990 dyuot Gwynn uab Nud a'e dwyn y treis. Kynnullaw llu o
Wythyr uab Greidawl, a dyuot y ymlad a Gwynn mab Nud,
a goruot o Wyn, a dala Greit mab Eri, a Glinneu eil Taran, a
Gwrgwst Letlwm, a Dyfnarth y uab. A dala o Penn uab
Nethawc, a Nwython, a Chyledyr Wyllt y uab, a llad
995 Nwython a oruc a diot y gallon, a chymhell ar Kyledyr yssu
callon y dat, ac am hynny yd aeth Kyledyr yg gwyllt. Clybot
o Arthur hynny, a dyuot hyt y Gogled, a dyuynnv a oruc ef
Gwynn uab Nud attaw, [837d] a gellwng y wyrda y gantaw
o'e garchar, a gwneuthur tangneued y rwng Gwynn
1000 mab Nud a Gwythyr mab Greidawl. Sef tangneued a
wnaethpwyt, gadu y uorwyn yn ty y that yn diuwyn o'r dwy
barth, ac ymlad bob duw kalan Mei uyth hyt dyd brawt o'r
dyd hwnnw allan y rwng Gwynn a Gwythyr, a'r un a orffo
onadunt dyd brawt, kymeret y uorwyn.

1005   A gwedy kymot y gwyrda hynny uelly, y kauas Arthur
Mygdwn march Gwedw, a chynllyuan Cors[1] Cant Ewin.

The Slaying of Ysgithrwyn Chief of Boars

Gwedy hynny yd aeth Arthur hyt yn Llydaw, a Mabon
uab Mellt gantaw, a Gware Gwallt Euryn, y geissaw deu gi
Glythmyr Ledewic.[2] A gwedy eu kaffel yd aeth Arthur hyt
1010   yg gorllewin Iwerdon y geissaw Gwrgi Seueri, ac Odgar uab
Aed brenhin Iwerdon gyt ac ef. Ac odyna yd aeth Arthur y'r
Gogled, ac y delis Kyledyr Wyllt, ac yd aeth [y geissaw]
Yskithyrwynn Penn Beid. Ac yd aeth Mabon mab Mellt a
deu gi Glythuyr Ledewic yn y law, a Drutwyn geneu Greit
1015   mab Eri. Ac yd aeth Arthur e hun y'r crhyl, a Chauall ki
Arthur yn y law. Ac yd esgynnwys Kaw o Brydein ar Lamrei
kassec Arthur, ac achub yr kyfuarth.[3] Ac yna y kymerth
Kaw o Brydein nerth bwyellic, ac yn wychyr trebelit y doeth
ef y'r baed, ac y holldes y benn yn deu hanner. A chymryt a
1020   oruc[4] Kaw yr ysgithyr. Nyt y kwnn a nottayssei Yspadaden[5]
ar Gulhwch[6] a ladawd y baed, namyn Kauall ki Arthur e
hun.

Menw fab Teirgwaedd in Bird's Form

A gwedy llad Ysgithyrwyn Benn Beid, yd aeth Arthur
a e niuer hyt yng Kelli [837e] Wic yng Kernyw.[7] Ac odyno y
1025   gyrrwys Menw mab Teirgwaed y edrych a uei y tlysscu y
rwng deuglust Twrch Trwyth, rac salwen oed uynet y
ymdaraw ac ef, ac ony bei y tlysseu gantaw. Diheu, hagen,
oed y uot ef yno. Neur daroed idaw diffeithaw traean
Iwerdon. Mynet a oruc Menw y ymgeis ac wynt. Sef y
1030   gwelas wynt yn Esgeir Oeruel yn Iwerdon. Ac ymrithaw a
oruc Menw yn rith ederyn, a disgynnu a wnaeth uch penn y
gwal, a cheissaw ysglyffyaw un o'r tlysseu y gantaw. Ac ny
chauas dim, hagen, namyn un o'e wrych. Kyuodi a oruc
ynteu yn wychyrda, ac ymysgytyaw hyt pan ymordiwedawd
1035   peth o'r gwenwyn ac ef. Ac odyna ny bu dianaf Menw uyth.

---

[1] Cwrs.
[2] lewic.
[3] kyfuarch.
[4] aorc.
[5] yspaden.
[6] gwlhwch.
[7] yngkernyw—r in a later hand.

The cauldron of Diwrnach Wyddel

Gyrru o Arthur gennat gwedy hynny ar Odgar uab Aed
brenhin Iwerdon, y erchi peir Diwrnach Wydel, maer idaw.
Erchi o Otgar idaw y rodi. Y dywawt Diwrnach, 'Duw a
wyr, pei hanffei well o welet un olwc arnaw nas kaffei.' A
1040 dyuot o gennat Arthur a nac genthi o Iwerdon. Kychwynnu
a oruc Arthur ac ysgawn niuer genthaw a mynet ym Prytwen
y long, a dyuot y Ywerdon, a dygyrchu ty Diwrnach Wydel a
orugant. Gwelsant niuer Otgar eu meint, a gwedy bwyta
onadunt, ac yuet eu dogyn, erchi y peir a oruc Arthur. Y
1045 dywawt ynteu pei as rodei y neb, y rodei wrth eir Odgar
brenhin Iwerdon. Gwedy lleueryd nac udunt, kyuodi a
oruc Bedwyr ac ymauael yn y peir a'e dodi ar geuyn [838]
Hygwyd, gwas Arthur (brawt oed hwnnw vn uam y
Gachamwri gwas Arthur). Sef oed y swyd ef yn wastat
1050 ymdwyn peir Arthur a dodi tan y danaw. Meglyt o
Lenlleawc Wydel yg Kaletvwlch a'e ellwg ar y rot, a llad
Diwrnach Wydel a'e niuer achlan. Dyuot lluoed Iwerdon ac
ymlad ac wy. A gwedy ffo y lluoed achlan, mynet Arthur a'e
wyr yn eu gwyd yn y llong, a'r peir yn llawn o swllt Iwerdon
1055 gantunt. A diskynnu yn ty Llwydeu mab Kel Coet ym Porth
Kerdin yn Dyuet. Ac yno y mae messur y peir.

Hunting the Twrch Trwyth

Ac yna y kynnullwys Arthur a oed o gynifwyr yn Teir Ynys
Prydein a'e Their Rac Ynys, ac a oed yn Freinc, a Llydaw, a
Normandi, a Gwlat yr Haf, ac a oed o gi gordethol[2] a march
1060 clotuawr. Ac yd aeth a'r niueroed hynny oll hyt yn Iwerdon,
ac y bu ouyn mawr ac ergryn racdaw yn Iwerdon. A gwedy
disgynnu Arthur y'r tir, dyuot seint Iwerdon attaw y erchi
nawd idaw. Ac y rodes ynteu nawd udunt hwy, ac y
rodassant wynteu eu bendyth idaw ef. Dyuot a oruc gwyr
1065 Iwerdon hyt att Arthur a rodi bwyttal idaw. Dyuot a oruc
Arthur hyt yn Esgeir Oeruel yn Iwerdon, yn y lle yd oed
Twrch Trwyth, a'e seithlydyn moch gantaw. Gellwng kwn
arnaw o bop parth. Y dyd hwnnw educher yd ymladawd y
Gwydyl ac ef. Yr hynny pymhet ran y Iwerdon a wnaeth yn
1070 diffeith. A thrannoeth yd ym [839]ladawd teulu Arthur ac ef;

---

[1]achan.   [2]gicwr dethol.

namyn a gawssant o drwc y gantaw, ny chawssant dim o da.
Y trydyd dyd yd ymladawd Arthur e hun ac ef, naw nos a
naw nieu. Ny ladawd namyn un parchell o'e uoch.
Gouynnwys y gwyr y Arthur peth oed ystyr yr hwch
1075 hwnnw. Y dywawt ynteu, 'Brenhin uu, ac am y bechawt y
rithwys Duw ef yn hwch.'

Gyrru a wnaeth Arthur Gwrhyr Gwalstawt Ieithoed y
geissaw ymadrawd ac ef. Mynet a oruc Gwrhyr yn rith
ederyn, a disgynnv a wnaeth vch benn y wal ef a'e seithlydyn
1080 moch. A gouyn a oruc Gwrhyr Gwalstawt Ieithoed[1] idaw,
'Yr y Gwr a'th wnaeth ar y delw honn, or gellwch dywedut,
y harchaf dyuot un ohonawch y ymdidan ac Arthur.'
Gwrtheb a wnaeth Grugyn Gwrych Ereint—mal adaned
aryant oed y wrych oll—y fford y kerdei ar goet ac ar uaes y
1085 gwelit ual y llithrei y wrych. Sef atteb a rodes Grugyn, 'Myn
y gwr a'n gwnaeth ni ar y delw honn, ny wnawn, ac ny
dywedwn dim yr Arthur. Oed digawn o drwc a wnathoed
Duw ynni, an gwneuthur ar y delw hon, kyny delewch
chwitheu y ymlad a ni.' 'Mi a dywedaf ywch yd ymlad
1090 Arthur am y grib a'r ellyn a'r gwelleu yssyd rwng deu glust
Twrch Trwyth.' Heb y Grugyn, 'Hyt pann gaffer y eneit ef
yn gyntaf, ny cheffir y tlysseu hynny. A'r bore auory y
kychwynnwn ni odyma, ac yd awn y wlat Arthur, a'r meint
mwyhaf a allom ni o drwc a wnawn yno.'

1095 Kychwyn a orugant hwy ar y mor parth a Chymry, ac yd
aeth [840] Arthur a'e luoed a'e ueirch a'e gwn ym Prytwen, a
tharaw [l]lygat ymwelet ac wynt. Disgynnu a wnaeth Twrch
Trwyth ym Porth Cleis yn Dyuet. Dyuot a oruc Arthur hyt
ym Mynyw y nos honno. Trannoeth dywedut y Arthur eu
1100 mynet heibaw, ac ymordiwes a oruc ac ef yn llad gwarthec
Kynnwas Kwrryuagyl, a gwedy llad a oed yn Deu Gledyf o
dyn a mil kynn dyuot Arthur.

O'r pan deuth Arthur y kychwynnwys Twrch Trwyth
odyno hyt ym Presseleu. Dyuot Arthur a lluoed y byt
1105 hyt yno. Gyrru a oruc Arthur y wyr y'r erhyl, Ely, a
Thrachmyr, a Drutwyn keneu Greit mab Eri yn y law e hun,
a Gwarthegyt uab Kaw yghongyl arall, a deu gi Glythmyr
Letewic yn y law ynteu, a Bedwyr a Chauall ki Arthur yn y

---

[1] These words are written above the line.

law ynteu. A restru a oruc y milwyr oll o deu tu Nyuer.

1110 Dyuot tri meib Cledyf Divwlch, gwyr a gauas clot mawr yn llad Ysgithyrwyn Penn Beid. Ac yna y kychwynnwys ynteu o Lynn Nyuer, ac y doeth y Gwm Kerwyn, ac y rodes kyuarth yno. Ac yna y lladawd ef bedwar rysswr y Arthur— Gwarthegyd mab Kaw, a Tharawc Allt Clwyt, a Reidwn

1115 uab Eli Atuer, ac Iscouan Hael. A gwedy llad y gwyr hynny, y rodes yr eil kyuarth udunt yn y lle, ac y lladawd Gwydre uab Arthur, a Garselit Wydel, a Glew uab Yscawt, ac Iscawyn uab Panon. A'e doluryaw ynteu yna a wnaethpwyt.

A'r bore ym bronn y dyd drannoeth yd ymordiwedawd rei

1120 o'r gwyr ac ef. Ac yna y lladawd Huandaw, a Gogigwr, a Phen Pingon, tri gweis Glewlwyt Gauaeluawr, hyt nas gwydyat Duw was yn y byt ar y helw ynteu, eithyr Llaesgemyn¹ e hunan, gwr ny hanoed well neb ohonaw. Ac y gyt a hynny y lladawd llawer o wyr y wlat, a Gwlydyn

1125 Saer, pensaer y Arthur. Ac yna yd ymordiwedawd Arthur ym Pelunyawc² ac ef, ac yna y lladawd ynteu Madawc mab Teithyon, a Gwyn mab Tringat mab Neuet, [841] ac Eiryawn Pennlloran. Ac odyna yd aeth ef hyt yn Aber Tywi. Ac yno y rodes kyuarth udunt, ac yna y lladawd ef Kynlas

1130 mab Kynan, a Gwilenhin brenhin³ Freinc. Odyna yd aeth hyt yg Glynn Ystu, ac yna yd ymgollassant y gwyr a'r cwn ac ef.

Dyuynnu a oruc Arthur Gwyn uab Nud attaw, a gouyn idaw a wydyat ef dim y wrth Twrch Trwyth. Y dywawt

1135 ynteu nas gwydyat. Y hela y moch yd aeth y kynnydyon yna oll, hyt yn Dyffryn Llychwr. Ac y digribywys Grugyn Gwallt Ereint udunt a Llwydawc Gouynnyat, ac y lladassant⁴ y kynnydyon hyt na diengis dyn yn vyw onadunt namyn un gwr. Sef a oruc Arthur dyuot a'e luoed hyt lle yd

1140 oed Grugyn a Llwydawc, a gellwng yna arnadunt a oed o gi ry nodydoed yn llwyr. Ac wrth yr awr a dodet yna, a'r kyuarth, y doeth Twrch Trwyth ac y diffyrth wynt. Ac yr pan dathoedynt dros uor Iwerdon, nyt ymwelsei ac wynt hyt yna. Dygwydaw a wnaethpwyt yna a gwyr a chwn arnaw.

1145 Ymrodi y gerdet ohonaw ynteu, hyt ym Mynyd Amanw, ac

---

¹llaesgenym.   ³brein.
²pelumyawc.   ⁴lladass.

yna y llas banw o'e uoch ef. Ac yna yd aethpwyt eneit dros
eneit ac ef, ac y lladwyt yna Twrch Llawin. Ac yna y llas arall
o'e voch, Gwys oed y enw. Ac odyna yd aeth hyt yn
Dyffrynn Amanw, ac yno y llas Banw a Bennwic. Nyt
1150 aeth odyno gantaw o'e uoch yn vyw namyn Grugyn Gwallt
Ereint a Llwydawc Gouynnyat.

O'r lle hwnnw yd aethant hyt yn Llwch Ewin, ac yd
ymordiwedawd Arthur ac ef yno. Rodi kyuarth a wnaeth
ynteu yna. Ac yna y lladawd ef Echel Uordwyt Twll, ac
1155 Arwyli eil Gwydawc Gwyr, a llawer o wyr a chwn heuyt. Ac
yd aethant odyna hyt yn Llwch Tawy. Yscar a wnaeth
Grugyn Gwrych Ereint ac wynt yna, ac yd aeth Grugyn
odyna hyt yn Din Tywi. Ac odyna yd aeth hyt yg
Keredigyawn, ac Eli[1] a Thrachmyr gantaw, a lliaws gyt ac
1160 wynt heuyt. Ac y doeth hyt yg Garth Grugyn,[2] ac yno [842]
y llas Grugyn yn y mysc,[3] ac y lladawd Ruduyw Rys, a llawer
gyt ac ef. Ac yna yd aeth Llwytawc hyt yn Ystrat Yw, ac yno
y kyuaruu gwyr Llydaw ac ef, ac yna y lladawd ef Hir
Peissawc brenhin Llydaw, a Llygatrud Emys, a Gwrbothu
1165 ewythred Arthur, vrodyr y uam. Ac yna y llas ynteu.

The Twrch Trwyth is driven into the sea

Twrch Trwyth a aeth yna y rwng Tawy ac Euyas.
Gwyssyaw Kernyw a Dyfneint o Arthur yn y erbyn hyt yn
Aber Hafren, a dywedut a oruc Arthur wrth vilwyr yr
Ynys honn, 'Twrch Trwyth a ladawd llawer o'm gwyr. Myn
1170 gwrhyt gwyr, nyt a mi yn uyw yd aho ef y Gernyw. Nys
ymlityaf i ef bellach, namyn mynet eneit dros eneit ac ef a
wnaf. Gwnewch chwi a wnelhoch.' Sef a daruu o gyghor
gantaw, ellwng kat o uarchogyon, a chwn yr Ynys gantunt,
hyt yn Euyas. Ac ymchoelut odyno hyt yn Hafren, a'e ragot
1175 yno ac a oed o vilwyr prouedic yn yr Ynys honn, a'e yrru
anghen yn anghen yn Hafren. A mynet a wnaeth Mabon uab
Modron gantaw ar Wynn Mygdwn march Gwedw yn
Hafren, a Goreu mab Custennin, a Menw mab Teirgwaed, y
rwng Llynn Lliwan ac Aber Gwy. A dygwydaw o Arthur
1180 arnaw, a rysswyr Prydein gyt ac ef. Dyneissau a oruc Osla
Gyllelluawr, a Manawydan uab Llyr, a Chacamwri[4] gwas

[1]eil.
[2]gregyn.
[3]y llas llwydawc gouynnyat yn y mysc.
[4]a chacmwri.

Arthur, a Gwyngelli, a dygrynnyaw yndaw. Ac ymauael yn
gyntaf yn y traet, a'e gleicaw ohonunt yn Hafren, yny yttoed
yn llenwi ody uchtaw. Brathu amws o Uabon uab Modron
1185 o'r neil[l]parth, a chael yr ellyn y gantaw, ac o'r parth arall y
dygyrchwys Kyledyr Wyllt y ar amws arall gantaw, yn
Hafren, ac y duc y gwelleu y gantaw. Kynn kaffel diot y grib,
kaffel dayar ohonaw ynteu a'e draet, ac o'r pan gauas y tir
ny allwys na chi na dyn na march y ganhymdeith hyt pan
1190 aeth y Gernyw. Noc a gaffat o drwc yn keissaw y tlysseu
hynny y gantaw, gwaeth a gaffat yn keissaw diffryt y
deu wr rac eu bodi. Kacamwri,[1] ual y tynnit ef y uynyd, y
tynnei deu uaen ureuan ynteu [843] y'r affwys. Osla Gyllelluawr, yn redec yn ol y twrch, y dygwydwys y gyllell o'e
1195 wein ac y kolles; a'e wein ynteu gwedy hynny yn llawn o'r
dwfyr, ual y tynnit ef y uynyd y tynnei hitheu ef y'r affwys.
Odyna yd aeth Arthur a'e luoed[2] hyt pan ymordiwedawd
ac ef yg Kernyw. Gware oed a gafat o drwc gantaw kyn no
hynny y wrth a gaffat yna gantaw yn keissaw y grib. O drwc
1200 y gilyd y kaffat y grib y gantaw. Ac odyna y holet ynteu o
Gernyw, ac y gyrrwyt y'r mor yn y gyueir. Ny wybuwyt
vyth o hynny allan pa le yd aeth, ac Anet ac Aethlem gantaw.
Ac odyno yd aeth Arthur y ymeneinaw ac y uwrw y ludet y
arnaw hyt yg Kelli Wic yg Kernyw.

The Very Black Witch

1205 Dywedut o Arthur, 'A oes dim weithon o'r anoetheu heb
gaffel?' Y dywawt vn o'r gwyr, 'Oes, gwaet y Widon Ordu,
merch y Widon Orwen o Penn Nant Gouut yg gwrthtir
Uffern.' Kychwyn a oruc Arthur parth a'r Gogled, a dyuot
hyt lle yd oed gogof y wrach. A chynghori o Wynn uab Nud
1210 a Gwythyr uab Greidawl gellwng Kacamwri[3] a Hygwyd y
urawt y ymlad a'r wrach. Ac ual y deuthant y mywn y'r ogof
y hachub a oruc y wrach, ac ymauael [a oruc] yn Hygwyd
herwyd gwallt y benn, a'e daraw y'r llawr deni. Ac ymauel
o Gacamwri[4] yndi hitheu herwyd gwallt y phenn, a'e
1215 thynnu y ar Hygwyd y'r llawr, ac ymchoelut a oruc hitheu ar
Kacamwri,[5] ac eu dygaboli yll deu ac eu diarui, a'e gyrru[6]

---

[1] Kacmwri.
[2] a lluoed.
[3] kacmwri.
[4] gacmwri.
[5] kacmwri.
[6] *above the line.*

allan dan eu hub ac eu hob. A llidyaw a oruc Arthur o welet y
deu was hayachen wedy eu llad,[1] a cheissaw achub yr ogof.
Ac yna y dywedassant Gwynn a Gwythyr wrthaw, 'Nyt dec
1220   ac nyt digrif genhym dy welet yn ymgribyaw a gwrach.
Gellwng Hir Amren a Hir Eidil y'r ogof.' A mynet a
orugant. Ac or bu drwc trafferth y deu gynt, gwaeth uu
drafferth y deu hynny, hyt nas gwypei Duw y vn ohonunt ell
pedwar allu mynet o'r lle, namyn mal y dodet ell pedwar ar
1225   Lamrei kassec Arthur. Ac yna achub a oruc Arthur drws yr
ogof, ac y ar y drws a uyryei y wrach a Charnwennan y
gyllell, a'e tharaw am y hanner yny uu yn deu gelwrn hi. A
[844] chymryt a oruc Kaw o Brydein gwaet y Widon a'e
gadw ganthaw.

Ysbaddaden's Death: Culhwch marries Olwen

1230   Ac yna y kychwynnwys Kulhwch, a Goreu uab Custennin
gyt ac ef, a'r sawl a buchei drwc y Yspadaden Pennkawr, a'r
anoetheu gantunt hyt y lys. A dyuot Kaw o Brydein y eillaw
y uaryf, kic a chroen hyt asgwrn, a'r deu glust yn llwyr. Ac y
dywawt Kulhwch, 'A eillwyt itti, wr?' 'Eillwyt,' heb ynteu.
1235   Ae meu y minheu dy uerch di weithon?' 'Meu,' heb ynteu.
'Ac nyt reit itt diolwch y mi hynny, namyn diolwch y
Arthur y gwr a'e peris itt. O'm bod i nys kaffut ti hi vyth.
A'm heneit inheu ymadws yw y diot.' Ac yna yd ymauaelawd Goreu mab Custennin yndaw herwyd gwallt y
1240   penn, a'e lusgaw yn y ol y'r dom, a llad y penn a'e dodi ar
bawl y gatlys. A goresgyn y gaer a oruc a'e gyuoeth.

A'r nos honno y kyscwys Kulhwch gan Olwen. A hi a uu
un wreic idaw tra uu vyw. A gwascaru lluoed Arthur, pawb
y wlat.

1245   Ac uelly y kauas Kulhwch Olwen merch Yspadaden
Pennkawr.

[1] wedy eu llad *on the edge of the page.*

Notes

1. **Kilyd**: *Cilydd* (Ir. *céle*) 'comrade, companion', GMW 96–7. This is one of a group of personal names in CO which are paralleled in the *Gododdin*: according to CA l.120 *Kilyd* was the name of the father of *Tudfwlch Hir*, a warrior from Eifionydd, to whom the *Gorchan Tudfwlch* is dedicated. Another descendant of Kilydd (perhaps a brother of Tudfwlch, CA lviii) was Gorthyn Hir, described as *mab brenhin teithiawc/ud gwyndyt gwaet kilyd gwaredauc*, CA 1095–1100 (see n. to l.586 below). For other names from the *Gododdin* in CO see introduction p. xxxvii. n. 22 above.

Kyledon: (R: *Kelydon*) *Wledic*. The name corresponds to that of the Coed Celyddon, first mentioned in HB ch. 56 as the site of *Cat Coit Celidon*, one of Arthur's battles. The *silva Caledonii* extended over a large part of the south-west of Scotland, and was within easy reach of both Carlisle and Glasgow. It remained a site of legendary importance in early Welsh tradition: for exx. see G 128, and on the location see K. Jackson, *Modern Philology* xliii (1945), 48–50. Rhŷs suggested (HL 487) that the name of Kilydd's father as here given is corrupt, and that it was originally intended to be 'Cilydd Wledig Celyddon'. *Kyledon* is one of the five men in CO who are given the title of *Gwledig* (see index). GPC 1682 lists other exx. and defines *gwledig* as originally denoting one of 'a number of early British rulers and princes who were prominent in the defence of Britain about the time of the Roman withdrawal'; see further TYP 451–4 (n. on *Maxen Wledic*). Subsequently *gwledig* came to be employed more widely by the Gogynfeirdd, both for temporal rulers and for God. Note here the lenition of a noun in apposition after a personal name (irregularly shown in this text); cf. GMW 15.

Kilyd . . . a uynnei wreic: note the order: subject + a + verb, one of the types of Abnormal order which are commonly found in MW: exx. abound in this text; GMW 179–80.

2. **a uynnwys**: note the ending -*wys* for the pret. sing 3 of the vb.; cf. GMW 123. By the ModW period -*awd*, -*odd* had superseded the various endings found in MW.

Goleudyt: 'Light of the Day'. The earliest occurrence of this personal name is found in the list of the daughters of Brychan Brycheiniog, as given in J 20 (EWGT 43). According to Melville Richards 'Gwŷr, Gwragedd a Gwehelyth', THSC (1965), 40, *Goleuddydd* was not at all a common name in the Middle Ages. Only two instances are listed by Bartrum in *Welsh Genealogies 300–1400* among women born in the period before 1215, and very few in the following period – though 'Goleuddydd' was known to the poets as the name of the girl loved by Gruffudd Gryg (GDG 20, 20; DGG 75, 38).

merch: usually a noun in apposition after a personal name undergoes lenition, but this is rare in both texts of CO; see GMW 15, n. to ll.168–9 below, and introduction p. xxxix.

Anlawd Wledic: A.O.H. Jarman has suggested *Anlawd<an* (intensive) with *blawdd* 'tumult, commotion"; as adj. 'swift, nimble; LlC ii (1952), 127; see also HGVK cxvi and n.; TYP 366 and n. The 12th.-cent. *Vita Iltuti* (based on older materials) preserves this name in the form *Anblaud Britanniae regis* as that of the father of the saint's mother *Rieingulid* (VSB 194; cf. LWS 124). This appears to be the oldest occurrence of the name, and the OW spelling *Anblaud* is closer to the form in CO than are the other forms of the name which occur: *Amlawd Wledic (sic)* BD 136,15 is the father of *Eigyr*, Arthur's mother. (No corresponding name is given as the father of *I(n)gerna* in HRB viii,19.) *Amlawt Wledic* is named also in the 13th-cent. ByS, and BGG (EWGT 61(43), 73(13)). The relationship of first cousins which is postulated between Culhwch and Arthur (and later, by implication, between Culhwch, Arthur, and Goreu fab Custennin (see n. to l.811)), and again between Arthur and Illtud in the *Vita Iltuti* (VSB 196), depends on the kinship of their four mothers as four daughters of *Anlawd/Amlawd Wledic*. (A fifth daughter is named in BGG no. 13 and ByS no. 43 (see n. to *Goreu mab Custenhin*, l.811.).) Outside these sources *Anlawd/Amlawd* is almost unknown. He is not named in TYP, nor anywhere in the Welsh tales except in CO, nor is he ever alluded to by the poets (for a few later refs. see index to EWGT). It is fair to conclude that *Anlawd/Amlawd* derives from the ecclesiastical tradition of the genealogies and Lives of the saints, and that his name was borrowed from these (perhaps independently) by the redactors of CO and of the *Brut*. On *Amlawd Wledic* see also B. F.

Roberts, B xxv, 284, and TWS 109. For *Gwledic* see n. above on *Kyledon Wledic*.

3. **y west**: *gwest* is found in *cywestach* 'copulation, wedded partner', and in *dirwest* 'abstinence, fasting'. It is to be equated with Ir. *feiss*; see DIL: F-fochraic 67–8. This is the vn. of *foaid* 'spends the night', and may be different from *feis* 'feast'. In the use of *gwest* here the idea of spending the night is uppermost, an idea more usually expressed by *kyscu gan* 'sleep with', as in ll.620–1, 989, 1242. Whether *gwest* 'feast' is a different word is not easy to determine: cf. B, ii (1923), 41–4; and l.306 etc. below.

mynet y wlat y gwedi: 'the country went into prayer'. The second *y* here is a form of the prep. *yn* 'into', and *g* in *gwedi* represents *ng*. Note that this is an ex. of a very common construction in MW prose: the use of a vn. instead of a finite vb., especially in the past. Cf. GMW 161.

malkawn: 'if, whether', followed by the interr. prt. *a*. Cf. l. 24 below: these are the only attested exx. of *malkawn*, which seems to consist of *mal* 'as, so that' + *kawn*, 1 sing. imperf. of *cael* 'get, obtain' (GPC 2327). There are other cases in which personal forms have developed an impersonal meaning. Cf. *ot gwnn* PKM 8,16, which literally means 'if I know', but has come to mean 'indeed, surely'; also *uchot, issot* (2 pers. sing.) which have come to mean 'above, below'.

4. **a chaffael mab ohonu**: 'and they obtained a son'. Cf. *mynet y wlat y gwedi* (l.3 above. *Ohonu* is 3 pl. of the prep. *o*. The form ended formerly in *-ud*, then as a result of the tendency to drop *-dd* (which is a marked feature of some dialects) the ending assumed the form *-u*. It later became *-unt/-ynt* under the influence of the 3 pl. of the vb.

5. **o'r awr y delis beichogi**: 'from the hour she became pregnant': *delis beichogi* 'she caught pregnancy': *delis* is pret. sing. 3 of *daly*; cf. GMW 10, 122–3. *Beichogi* means 'conception, pregnancy'; cf. *a'r lleian a gauas beichogi* WLSD 2,19. The pret. sing. 3 here is not followed by lenition of the object; GMW 18.

yd aeth hitheu ygwylldawc: 'she went mad'. Normally the prt. *yn/y* is followed by lenition, in which case we would have *yn/y wylldawc*. But there are cases where the nasal mutation is used, as here; cf. *ymhell/yn bell* 'far'; *ynghynt/yn gynt* 'earlier, sooner;

ynghyntaf/yn gyntaf 'first'; *yngham/yn gam* 'bent'; cf. *yd aeth Kyledyr yg gwyllt* l.996; see TC 245.

6. **tymp**: (Lat. *tempus*) means 'appointed time' for delivery or birth of a child. Cf. *naw mis tymp* in 'Y Trioedd Arbennig', B xxiv (1972), 441.

7. **Sef y**: adv., with meanings such as 'thus, now, then'; cf. GMW 52–3, and 18, 908, 1029; *ysef yd* 908.

myn: means 'place (where)', and is followed by an improper rel. clause: *myn yd* 'where'; GMW 67.

meichad: 'swineherd' consists of *moch* 'swine' and *-(i)ad* denoting the agent. The consonantal *i* causes affection of the preceding vowel (*o>ei*), but here, as often in MW prose, it drops; cf. GMW 6 and p. xv above.

kenuein: appears to be a learned borrowing from Lat. *conventio*, and means 'herd, host, family, community'. Note the loss of *-t*, from earlier *kenueint/cenfaint*; cf. GMW 120. It came to be used of a herd of pigs, as here; and in l.356 below; also of a herd of cattle, LlB 94,6; Ll.Ior. 22,20 below.

8. **enghi a oruc y urenhines**: 'the queen was delivered'. Cf. p. xxv above.

10. **a gyrru Kulhwch arnaw**: 'and he was named Kulwch'. On the use of *gyrru/dodi/rodi ar* cf. GMW 186. Note how baptizing and naming are closely associated, here as in PKM 23,14–16: Peri a wnaethont *bedydyaw* y mab, o'r *bedyd* a wneit yna. Sef *enw* a dodet arnaw, Gwri Wallt Euryn; 77,21–3 mi a baraf *uedydyaw* hwn . . . Sef *enw* a baraf, Dylan.

Kulhwch: to the redactor of the story it is evident that the hero's name meant 'pigsty' (*cul* + *hwch*; cf. Foster, ALMA 33 'burrow of swine'). But *cul* with this meaning is a borrowing from E. *kil(n)*, and is not attested in GPC before Dafydd ap Gwilym in the 14th cent. (=a doubtful ex: O'r *kul* i'r felin o'r sach i'r hopran, GDG 421,5; GPC 629); that is, it cannot be shown to be earlier than the approximate date of the text of CO in WM and RM. But *cul* with the meaning 'lean, slender' is attested in the *Beddau* stanzas, and in three other instances in LlDC. Its Ir. equivalent *cael* 'thin' is found in the 12th-cent. *Dindshenchas* where *Caelcheis* is the name of one of three women who were enchanted into swine of the opposite sex (*Met. Din.* iii, 388, 438; RC xv (1894), 471–2; cf. DIL 'C' col. 10 *cael* 'thin'; ibid. 104 *ceis* 'a young pig'). Idris Foster noted the equivalence between the name *Culhwch* and the semi-cognate Ir. *Caelcheis* (CO(1) lxix–lxx and n. 178), and this equivalence was independently pointed out by P. Ní Chatháin ('Swineherds, Seers and Druids', SC xiv/xv (1979–80), 202). Foster believed that the story of Culhwch's birth reflected an original (perhaps only dimly perceived by the narrator) in which Culhwch was conceived to be a king's son transformed into a boar (as is said in ll. 1075–6 to have been the origin of the Twrch Trwyth; see introduction p. lxvii). This belief is not inconsistent with E. P. Hamp's interpretation of *cul* as 'a North-European substratum term' (that is, one which is pre-Indo-European), denoting a pig, which he believes to underlie the prominence of boars in pagan Celtic culture (ZCP 41 (1986), 257–8). However this may be, the element *hwch* in the hero's name would in itself have been sufficient to account for the pig-associations of Culhwch''s birth-tale. Cf. Lhuyd, *Arch. Brit.*, 236b '*huch, a swine, whether Boar or sow*'. *Hwch* 'pig' is an element which appears also in the personal name *Unhwch*, CLlH iii, 1a; PT xi, 6; *Unhu* LL 143, 23. P. K. Ford has seen in the story of Culhwch's birth a memory of the swine-god *Moccus (The Mabinogi,* 14–16). See further introduction p. xxx.

10–12. **dy wrth y gaffael**: 'because he was found'. On **dy wrth** and **dy Arthur** (l. 12) see introduction p. xxx above.

11. **hagen**: conj. 'however, but, for'. It never occurs first in the sentence, GMW 233. A number of examples occur in this text, but it is not found in ModW. Cf. Ir. *immurgu.*

12–13. **ar ueithrin**: 'to be nurtured'. There are other references in Welsh tales to the placing of children in the care of foster-parents, for example PKM 37,18. It was clearly a feature of Welsh and Irish life in the early period. Fosterage ended for boys at seventeen, and for girls at fourteen, then they returned home. But the bonds remained close, and there are many references to foster-brothers, sisters, and parents, cf. PKM 19,20 and n. In HGVK 10,28 a certain man named *Cerit* is described as Gruffudd's foster-father, and in 1,6 there is a ref. to his foster-mother (*mamvaeth*). Cf. also Peryf ap

Cedifor's *marwnad* for his foster-brother Hywel ab Owain
Gwynedd, H 332.

14. **Goleudyt; merch**: see nn. to l.2 above.

15. **Sef a oruc hi galw**: on *sef* see introduction p. xxv above.

16. **amkawd**: cf. pp. xii, xvi above.

17. **a uynny**: in MW-*y* forms the ending of the pres. sing. 2; GMW
115–16.

ynt: on the use of a pl. vb. before a pl. subject, cf. GMW 179, also n.
to l.37 below.

recdouyd: cf. introduction p. xvii above. On *dofydd*, -*ofydd* 'lord,
master of', etc. see n. to l.176 below; TYP no. 19 *Tri Galouyd Enys
Prydein*, and refs. there cited; cf. B xv, 199.

18. **Sef y**: the *y* here is probably a conflation of the prt. *y+y*, the
infixed pron. obj. sing. 3; and it is the pron. which accounts for the *h*
in *harchaf.* Cf. GMW 23.

20. **athro**: the meaning of this word is not easy to define in detail.
Generally it denotes a man in religious orders, higher in status than
the *yscolheic* or scholar. The pl. *athraon*, occurs in HGVK 13,21: *a'r
escop a'e athraon a holl clas er argluyd Dewi*. In BD 297 *athraon*
translates *doctores, phylosophorum, pontifices, clericos*; cf. also PKM 21,
19, where Rhiannon summons *athrawon a doethon* to advise her. In
Rhigyfarch's Life of St David we find *scriba* corresponding to *athro*
in the Welsh version. On the *scriba* or *sui* in Ireland see K. Hughes,
The Church in Early Irish Society (London, 1966), 136: 'His presence
indicates a school of Latin learning, and his prestige was analogous
to that of the *fili* who professed secular learning.'

22. **marw y urenhines**: 'the queen died'. Cf. *mynet y wlat y gwedi*,
l.3 above and n.

24. **malkawn**: see n. to l.3 above.

gwallocau: 'to neglect', a denominative vb. consisting of
gwallog+ha+u; cf. GMW 117.

25. **y seith ulwydyn**: this ought to be *y seith mlyned* as in R, or *y
seithuet ulwydyn* 'the seventh year'.

y ryn: that is, *yr hyn* 'that which'.

26. **diwarnawd**: 'one day'. Here a n. is used adverbially without a prep. Cf. PKM 78,3 Ual yd oed Wydyon *diwarnawt* yn y wely. See further GMW 226–7.

yn hyly yr brenhin: 'as the king was hunting'. Note that the subject of the vn. follows immediately without a prep. Cf. n. on l.22 above.

corfflan: 'graveyard', from *corff* 'body, corpse', and *llan* 'enclosure', as in *gwinllan, perllan, corlan*.

27. **trw yt**: on the prt. *yt* cf. p. xx above. *Trw* may be a phonetic development and variant of *trwy*, or the -*y* may have been lost through proximity with the *y* of *yt*. We may well have here a survival of an old construction in which the prep. occurs before a rel. clause, a construction which appears to be attested also in Irish; cf. GOI 312 f. Here it means something like 'whereby'.

28–9. **yg kyghor**: 'into counsel', that is, 'he sought counsel' or 'advice'. In MW *yn* (here *yg*) can mean 'into' as well as 'in'; GMW 215.

30. **sef**: here used substantivally, as nominal pred.; cf. GMW 52, and ll.732, 1049 below.

31. **Doget urenhin**: *Doget vrenhin ap Cedic ap Cunedha Wledic* is listed in a late addition to ByS in the hand of Thomas Wiliems, Trefriw, *c.* 1550–1622 (EWGT 67, no. 95, also *Achau'r Saint*, ibid. 70, no. 30). Llanddoged in the commote of Uwch Dulas is the only church in Wales which bears his name: it is a place of easy access from Trefriw and from Llanrwst. *Ffynnon Ddoged* is to be found about sixty yards north of the church; see Francis Jones, *The Holy Wells of Wales* (University of Wales Press, 1954), 173 and refs. there cited. An *awdl* to 'St Doged Frenin' composed by Ieuan Llwyd Brydydd (*c.* 1460–90) is found in two manuscripts: (P 225,160, and J 15,497), both of which are in the hand of Thomas Wiliems, and which thus demonstrate the latter's particular interest and dedication to his local saint, whose fame seems to have been in the main restricted to the Llanrwst area of Denbigh. See LBS ii, 347–9; iv, 393–5; TWS 10, 250.

kyghor uu ganthunt: 'they decided'. On the use of *gan* with nouns and adjectives to denote activity or attitude of mind, see GMW 190.

34. **gorymdeith**: 'travel, take a walk'. It consists of *gor+ymdeith* (Ir. *imthecht*); cf. GMW 156.

y deuth: seldom do we find the affirmative prt. *y* before the vb. at the beginning of a sentence, but examples do occur; cf. ll. 114, 139, 246 etc.; GMW 171.

37. **kwt ynt plant**: lenition of the subject would be expected after a pl. vb., but is here absent; see on *ynt* n. 17 above.

rydyallas: 'has seized'. It consists of the prt. *ry* (see introduction p. xxi) + *dyallas (dy + gallu)*, pret. sing 3 of *dyallu* 'to apprehend, seize'. Later it came to mean 'grasp with the mind, comprehend, understand'; ModW *dyall*, *deall*.

gordwy: here means '(to abduct by) violence'. It is a precise legal term which recurs in the Laws in various contexts; see WLW 63, and p. xvii above.

41. **yt gaffo kanys ry gaffo**: subj. pres. sing. 3 of *ca(ff)el* 'to get, obtain'. In the first ex. the pres. subj. is used to denote future meaning, in the second, with *ry-* it denotes the perfect; see GMW 112–13.

44. **pwy ystyr**: 'what reason?' Cf. also ll. 89, 772 below. *Pwy* is here used adjectivally, as it is still in the spoken language of south Wales. See further GMW 74–5.

46. **kennatau**: 'to send for'; a denominative vb. from *kennat* 'messenger' + *ha* + *u*; cf. GMW 117.

47. **a mab**: the vocative prt. is usually followed by lenition, *a uab*; GMW 15.

50. **tyghaf tyghet**: 'I will swear a destiny'. The same phrase appears in PKM 79,3; 81,7; 83,12, where Aranrhod swears her three destinies on Lleu. But in CLlH ii,21 *tynghet* appears as a blind impersonal force, and one which is not imposed by a human agent. Both usages are paralleled by *geis* in Irish.

llatho: subj. pres. sing. 3 of *llad*, here used with the meaning 'to strike', with *wrth* 'against'. The *đ* of *llad* has become [θ] = *th* under the influence of *h* which originally formed part of the ending of the subjunctive; cf. GMW 128. Note here that the pres. subj. is used with future meaning, as in *yt gaffo* l.41.

51. **Olwen merch Yspadaden Penkawr**: for Olwen see n. to l. 498 below. For the lack of lenition in *merch* see n. on l.2 and cf. l.14 above.

Yspadaden Penkawr: 'Hawthorn Head Giant' according to Rhŷs, CF 487. *Ysbaddad(en)* is the name for hawthorn or whitethorn. *Gorwyn blaen ysbydat* is the opening line of one verse in a series of *englynion* which lists the names of trees and plants, RP 1034,11. Cf. also *ysbydat* in the tree-list in the poem *Cad Goddau*, BT 25,5, ed. M. Haycock in M. J. Ball *et al.* (eds.), *Celtic Linguistics: Festschrift for A. T. Watkins* (Amsterdam, 1990), 297–331. In spite of its traditional associations with Mayday festivities, the hawthorn has slightly sinister connotations in folklore: 'Above most plants in the far west of Europe (it is) a supernatural tree' according to Geoffrey Grigson, *The Englishman's Flora* (St Alban's, 1975), 180. *Ysbyddaden* is found in place-names: *dirispidatenn* LL 202, 2–3; *Waun Yspyddaden* and *Bryn Yspyddaden* are recorded in and near the parish of Llandybie by Gomer M. Roberts, *Hanes Plwyf Llandybie* (Gwasg Prifysgol Cymru, 1939), 248. *Ton Yspyddaden* is the name of a farm in the Vale of Neath, D. Rhys Phillips, *History of the Vale of Neath* (Swansea, 1925), 28; on this name see also Ifor Williams, *Enwau Lleoedd*, 68. Dr J. C. Grooms, 'Giants in Welsh Folklore and Tradition' (Ph.D. thesis, University of Wales, 1988) has recorded that local folklore associates the story of a giant with this locality. Yet both here and elsewhere the name of the plant may have attracted to it a literary (or popular) recollection of the story of Ysbaddaden Pencawr. An obscure allusion by Y Prydydd Bychan (H 245,16) to *Yspadaden Ddinbych* in a *marwnad* to Maredudd ab Owain (d. 1265) appears to associate the Giant with Dinbych y Pysgod (Tenby), according to the interpretation of the poem by Vendryes, EC iii (1938), 316–17. In HRB ii,8 *Spaden* is given as the name of one of the sons of Ebraucus = *Yspladen* BD 24,27; *Spadaden* in Ll. i (see B. F. Roberts, B xxv, 280).

It is easy to believe that Ysbaddaden's very name could inspire terror in Arthur's warriors, not least because of the Giant's later claim concerning Arthur *dan uy llaw i y mae ef* l.733—whatever the exact implication of these words may be. (With this phrase cf. *nyd asswynwys eiroet yn llaw arglwyd* ll.212–13 below.)

52. mynet a oruc serch y uorwyn: love for a man or woman who has never been seen is paralleled in the *Mabinogi* in Rhiannon's love for Pwyll, and in Irish there is a technical term for it – *gradh/sercc ecmaise* – 'absent love, love of someone absent', DIL 'E' 43.

57. Arthur: for the portrayal of Arthur in the story see the introduction pp. xxvii–ix. For general accounts of Arthur in early Welsh sources see T. Jones, 'The Early Evolution of the Legend of Arthur', *Nottingham Medieval Studies* viii (1964), 3–21 (=B xvii (1958), 235–52); K. Jackson, ALMA chs. 1 and 2; R. Bromwich, TYP 274–7; AoW *passim*. For Arthur's relation to Culhwch see n. 2 above on *Anlawd Wledic*.

58. keuynderw: 'cousin'; ModW *cefnder*. On the loss of non-syllabic *-w* cf. GMW 11, and l.407 below.

ar Arthur: *ar* 'to' is usual at an early period before names of persons; cf. GMW 187, and l.246 below.

diwyn dy wallt: the stem of *diwyn* is *diwyg-*; cf. G 380. Other verbs with similar formations are *gorllwyn* 'to watch' (indic. pres. sing. 3 *gorllwc*), *dwyn* 'bring' (*dyg-*). The cutting of hair was a symbolic act indicative of the acceptance of consanguinity, cf. l.163 and see n. on l.164 below.

59. erchych: subj. pres. sing. 2 of *erchi* 'to seek, request', here used with imperative meaning; GMW 113.

yn gyuarws it: *cyfarws* or *cyfarwys* meant a gift, bounty, or boon. According to J. Lloyd-Jones (B ii (1923), 5–6) it derives from **kom-are-wid-to*; cf. **wid-to* > *gwys* 'is known'. A variant is **weid* > *gwydd*; cf. *gwyddost*, also *arwydd* 'sign, token' < **are-weid*. A sign or token seems to be the basic meaning of *cyfarws*, indicating a recognition by the donor of the nobility, respect, or honour of the recipient, and at the same time indicating that he was of a lower status than the donor. *Cyfarws* was given by a king, and paid to all according to their status. The different kinds of gifts which it would be natural for a king to give as a *cyfarws* are listed in BD 129, 6–10, where Emrys Wledig makes gifts at his Whitsuntide feast: to some he gives lands, to some gold and silver, to some horses and rich garments: *yna y gelwit ar bawb y dalu eu kyuarws udunt herwyd eu hanryded.* Cf. WM 174,15–16, *(Peredur) a'r dwy iarllaeth a rodaf it y'th gyfarws* 'and the two earldoms I will give to thee as thy *cyfarws.* Cf. D. *cyvarwysog: cui terra a principe donata est.* The *cyfarws* that Culhwch demanded from Arthur, his lord and kinsman, in recognition of their relationship, was that he should obtain Olwen for him; Arthur's acceptance of his obligation was symbolized by his act in cutting Culhwch's hair. On *cyfarws* see B xxvi (1975), 147–8; GPC 684; HGVK 66–7; TYP 183–4, and refs. there cited.

60–81. The rhetorical passage which follows, describing Culhwch riding to Arthur's court, should be compared with the description of Olwen, ll.487–98 below. Both are composed in the style characteristic of the medieval *araith* ('oration', see introduction pp. lxxiii–iv). Much use is made of elaborate and fanciful compd. nouns and adjectives, and there is a fondness for nominal constructions. The description of Culhwch is static: the only movement is that of his hounds who circle about him.

61–2. yn y penn: the art. is sometimes used instead of a poss. pron., which may explain the absence of lenition here. **Y** could, however, be explained as the poss. pron. sing. 3 masc. with the lenition not formally represented, as is occasionally the case in MW; cf. GMW 14,25, and n. on *ar y penn* l.87 below.

63. gleif: is a gloss on *ennillec.* as was shown by T. Jones, B xiii (1950), 75–7. It derives from ME and OF *glaive* (probably through Anglo-Norman, acc. M. E. Surridge, EC xxi (1984), 247–8, 251), and appears to be a unique occurrence in *Culhwch* of a word of French derivation. Cf. the list of Arthur's regalia BD 148,27–8: *gleif a rodet yn y lav, yr hon a elwit Ron (=lancea* HRB ix, 4). *Bwyall ennillec* 'battle-axe' is attested in *Brut y Tywysogyon* (P 20 version) 150,10–11, and appears to be the equivalent of *bvall deuvinavc* in BD 22,18, as pointed out by B. F. Roberts (B xxiii, 121–2); cf. Lhuyd, AB, 216 *enilheg* 'a hatchet'. Since a lance is not the same thing as a hatchet, *gleif* is clearly an inappropriate rendering of *ennillec*; also since *gleif* is masc. *yndi* in l.64 is also inappropriate, and has perhaps supplanted some such word as *bwyell* (fem.). The form *gleif penntirec*, common to W and R, was explained by T. Jones as due to miscopying an original archetype, in which 'p' was a sign in the MS denoting a gloss (a sign used similarly in *Brut y Tywysogyon*).

64. **kyuelin dogyn gwr yndi o drum hyt awch**: '(having) the length of a full-grown man's forearm in it from ridge to edge'. Cf. GER, *dogyn kyuelin uawr yndaw o'r paladyr*, WM 419,36–8.

68. **lloring elifeint**: *lloring* was explained by Idris Foster and Thomas Jones as derived from OE. *laerig* 'shield-boss, shield', with confusion of *o* and *e* as in W's *as redwn* for *as rodwn* l.486 below (see B viii, 21–3; xiii, 75). R has misread the word as *llugorn* 'lantern', cf. introduction p. xii. *elifeint* < Lat. *eliphantus* (eliphant), 'ivory'; cf. *ysgwyt eliphant* (Cynddelw), H 89,29.

69. **deu uilgi uronwynyon urychyon**: 'two greyhounds, whitebreasted, brindled'. The same collocation of words is found in *Peredur*, WM 157,22–3. Note the lenition of the adjectives after the noun preceded by the numeral 'two'; cf. GMW 34; note also the pl. forms of the adjectives, GMW 36.

71. **yr hwn**:=*yr un* 'the one', also *a'r hwnn* l.72. Cf. GMW 69.

77. **can mu**: 'a hundred cows'; *mu* represents the nasal mutation of *bu*. In primitive society values were originally calculated in cattle, Lat. *pecunia* < *pecus*. In *Vita Cadoci* ch. 62 a sword is named *Hopiclour, quod habuit precium lxx uaccarum* 'which had the worth of seventy cows' (VSB 130).

79. **a'e warthafleu (sangharwy)**: *gwarthafl* is well attested with the meaning 'stirrup, upper part of the boot', GPC 1587. *Sangharwy* is unknown, but Thomas Jones showed (B xiii, 17–19) that *sang* = the 'tread' or metal part of a stirrup. W and R both read *sangnarwy*, in which the second *a* is redundant and *ngn* = -*ng* or -*ngh*, for both of which he cites analogies, and interprets the cmpd. *sang(h)rwy* as 'stirrup-leather' or 'stirrup-strap'; that is, a strap which stretched from Culhwch's thigh to his toe. Owing to uncertainty as to the precise meaning of these words, it is difficult to decide whether *gwarthafleu* is to be interpreted as a gloss on *sangharwy* or the reverse. Cf. introduction p. xi above.

80. **ulaen**: note the lenition of the subject after the sing. 3 imperf. in MW, and cf. also ll.304, 386.

84. **pob dyw kalan Ionawr**: 'every first day of January'. Note the adv. form *dwy* 'day", and cf. l.370 *pob dyw kalan Mei*, GMW 33.

86. **Huandaw**: 'good hearer (-ing)'; *andaw* with the affirmative prt. *hu-*, *hy-*, as in *huawdl*, *hygar* etc.; cf. GPC 1945.

Gogigwr: lit. 'little meat-man', perhaps 'meat-eater' or 'butcher'. This form of the name is supported by l.1120 below.

Llaeskemyn: '?slow step'; *cam* 'step', cf. Ir. *ceimm*.

a Ffenpingyon: cf. *Pen Pingon* ll. 1120–3 (where the three servants of Glewlwyd (see l.111 and n.) are slain together, Llaesgemyn alone escaping). Cf. WM 386,2–4: *A phen pighon. A llays gymyn. A gogyuwlch* (GER).

89. **pwy ystyr**: *pwy* could here be explained as consisting of *py/pa* 'what?'' and *wy/yw* 'is', that is, 'What is the meaning/reason that you do not open it?' Or *pwy* could be taken as adjectival 'what', cf. GMW 75, and l.44 above, l.772 below.

89, 90. **ymwyt, ymual**: both forms contain *yn* 'into' and *bwyt*, *bual*; cf. also ll.772 and 773.

91. **teithiawc**: (Ir. *techtae*) 'one possessing legal claims, lawful, rightful, as prescribed by law', DIL 'T', col.100. Cf. CA 1095 where *Gorthyn Hir* (a descendant of *Kilyd*, see n. to l.1 above) is described as *mab brenhin teithiauc*; also *y urenhin teithiawc* l.586 below.

94. **yspytty**: 'hospice', consisting of *esbyd* (pl. of *osb* 'guest'), in the form *ysbyd*+ *ty* 'house'. Cf. EL 43.

98. **pryt anterth**: < Lat. *ante tertiam* 'before the third hour', that is nine o'clock.

100. **gwnelych**: a clear example of the pres. subj. used to denote the meanings of the imperative and optative; cf. GMW 113, and l.501 below.

105. **diaspat**: as P. K. Ford has pointed out (B xxvi (1975), 147), Culhwch's *diaspad* was intended to be no ordinary shout: it recalls the *diaspad uwch Annwfn* which is cited in an obscure passage in the Laws as a formal means for seeking legal redress; Ll. Ior. §85; trans. HDdL 104 (see n.).

106. **Penn Pengwaed yg Kernyw**: *Penn Pengwaed* corresponds to Penwith, that is Land's End, the furthest extremity of the Cornish peninsula. In LlC xiii (1980–1), 278–81, B. F. Roberts has drawn

attention to the corresponding Cornish form *Pen penwyth* in Exeter Cathedral Library MS 3514, ff.58–60; cf. TYP (2) 542. The conventional measurement of Britain as estimated in *Enweu Ynys Prydein* (TYP 228) was 900 miles from *Penryn Penwaed yng Ngherniw* to *Penryn Blathaon* (Dunnet Head?) in Scotland (see notes to *Celli Wic yGherniw* and to *Penryn Blathaon*, 261–2 below). Cf. Ll.Ior. §90 (Dyfnwal Moelmut) *a uessurus er enys hon o Penryn Blathaon em Pryden hyt em Penryn Penwaed eg Kernyu: sef yu henne, nau can mylltyr, a henne yu hyt er enys hon* (= HDdL 120); *Brut y Tywysogyon* (P 20 version) 59, ann. 1111–14: *ef a gynnullawd henri vrenhin lu dros holl ynys brydein. o bennryn penngwaed yghernyw hyd ymhenryn blathaon ymhrydein.* The evidence cited in n. to l.261 below suggests that Culhwch was at Celliwig when he threatened to give his great shout, and that Celliwig was in fact situated at Penwith or *Pen Pengwaed*.

Dinsol yn y Gogled: each time 'Y Gogled' is alluded to in *Culhwch* (see index) the meaning is *yr Hen Ogledd*, the 'Old North', that is, the lost Brittonic territories in Cumbria and in southern Scotland. The *Vita Cadoci* gives *Dinsol* as the Cornish name for St Michael's Mount: *mons sancti Michaelis . . . qui in regione Cornubiensium esse dinoscitur, atque illius prouincie Dinsol appellatur* (VSB 94). The identification of *Dinsol* with St Michael's Mount was rejected by Idris Foster, B viii (1937), 23–5, and by J. Lloyd-Jones, G 359. Foster's opinion was that *o:e* had been confused in the original of the White Book text of the tale (cf. n. to *lloring*, l.68 above), and that the original form of this name was *Dinsel* – modern Denzell, in the parish of Padstow, where there is an ancient ruined chapel (now a farm) dedicated to St Cadoc. We are indebted to Oliver Padel for the information that this *capella sancti Cadoci* is recorded as late as 1339. Since the name *Dinsol* is unknown outside these two allusions in *Culhwch* and the *Vita Cadoci*, the conclusion seems inevitable that there has been mutual influence between them, and that one of the two has derived the name from the other. But in his threat to give *teir diaspat* Culhwch is claiming that his shout would be so loud and penetrating that it would be heard in places regarded as being at a great distance from each other. It would be natural for him to compare *Penn Pengwaedd*, the furthest extremity of Cornwall, with some place which represented one of the furthest extremities of the island, such as *Penryn Blathaon ym Prydein* (= *Prydyn*, Pictland); see previous note, and cf. n. to l.262 below. If *Dinsol* really represents a Cornish place-name, either Denzell or St Michael's Mount, it could be explained as a name superimposed upon one of the old and nearly forgotten place-names at Britain's northern extremity, such as *Pen(ryn) Blathaon* or *Pentir Gafran*, both of which were places known to Welsh poets, and both are named in EYP. The Exeter Cathedral MS, mentioned above, gives the measurement of 800 miles from St Michael's Mount to *Pentir Gafran* in Caithness – evidently therefore this was another traditional measurement. E. Anwyl in fact corroborated the above view, when he concluded rightly that *Dinsol* represents 'one of the more northerly points of Caithness' (RC xxxiv (1913), 412).

107. **Eskeir Oeruel yn Iwerdon**: 'The Ridge of Coldness in Ireland'. This Welsh name for a place in Ireland is quite unknown outside *Culhwch*, and therefore it is uncertain whether or not it can have been a traditional name. Kuno Meyer (THSC 1895–6, 73) interpreted it as a semi-phonetic rendering of Ir. *Sescenn Uairbeoil*, the name of a place in Leinster, in which *sescenn* means 'unproductive ground, swamp, bog' (DIL 'S' col. 196), and *uarbel* 'cold mouth', is used figuratively for a mountain pass or gap. Meyer's identification was followed by Rhŷs, CF 510n., and by Thurneysen, *Heldensage* 654n. According to G. Murphy, DF iii, 406 *Sescenn Uairbeoil* denoted 'the great marsh near Newcastle, Co. Wicklow'. For Hogan (*Onomasticon Goedelicon* 577) *Sescend Uarbeoil* 'seems near Boherbreena and between it and the sea'. E. Gwynn (*Met. Din.* iii, 499) equates it with *Tonn Uairbeoil*, named in one text of TBDD as the place on the shore near Dublin where the pirates landed before attacking Da Derga's Hostel (which was situated somewhere on the River Dodder). Whether or not there are adequate grounds for equating the Irish and the Welsh names, all the indications show that *Eskeir Oeruel* denoted some place visible from the sea on the east coast of Ireland. Giraldus Cambrensis (*Itin. Cam.* ii, i) observes that on a clear day 'the mountains of Ireland' (that is, the Wicklow mountains) can be seen from St David's. After a discussion of the geography of all the Irish allusions to *Sescenn Uairbeoil,* P. Sims-Williams makes the suggestion 'that *Uarbel* was the Irish name for the gap between the Little Sugar Loaf and Bray Head, the only coastal high ground between Howth and Wicklow' ('The Irish Geography of Culhwch and Olwen', 413–14). Lying south of

Dublin, this identification fits well with the indications given in the *Dindshenchas* and in TBDD. But for the redactor of *Culhwch*, *Eskeir Oeruel*, even if it was a landmark well known to Welsh mariners, is likely to have meant little more than an unidentified place on the Irish coast, to be juxtaposed with *Dinsol* (by which some place in the far north was originally intended) and *Penn Pengwaed* on the western extremity of the Cornish peninsula.

107–8. **yssyd o wreic ueichawc**: 'as many pregnant women as there are'; cf. GMW 68.

111. **Glewlwyt Gauaeluawr**: 'Bold Grey Mighty Grasp'. In *Culhwch ac Olwen* Glewlwyt Gafaelfawr figures as Arthur's gate-keeper, if only on special occasions (see ll.84–6 above). But in *Pa Gur* he is presented as the guardian of a hostile fortress, into which Arthur and his men are seeking to gain admittance. It is suggested in TYP 361–2 that the situation depicted in *Culhwch* is a burlesque reversal of that in the poem, where Glewlwyt appears as *porthawr* of the fortress of *Awarnach* (=Wrnach Gawr ? see n. to l.747). Here in *Culhwch*, instead of presenting his credentials for admission to Arthur's Court, as he was required to do, Culhwch threatens Glewlwyd, and it is Glewlwyd himself who in his address to Arthur enlarges on the young hero's qualifications for admittance (cf. B. F. Roberts, Ast.H. 298–9). Under the influence of *Culhwch*, Glewlwyd figures again as Arthur's gate-keeper both in *Owein* and in GER: WM 223,17–18 and WM 385,35–6 = *Mab* 135,229) – though his status is not very clear in either tale. The duties and privileges of the king's *porthawr* are specified in the Laws; LlB 7,18; 24,21; HDdL 35, etc.

115. **Chwedleu porth genhyt?**: 'Have you news from the gate?' cf. ll.778–9 *Dywawt Wrnach Gawr, 'Whedleu porth y genhyt?'* and Matholwch's words to his swineherds *'Duw a rodo da ywch . . . a chwedleu genhwch?'* (PKM 39,19). Cf. the corresponding Irish phrase *Scéla lib?* 'Have you news?'

116–28. The rhetorical and bombastic speech in which Glewlwyd introduces Culhwch to Arthur's Court has earlier precedents, and may be regarded as formulaic; cf. the series of *englynion* beginning *Mi a wum* 'I have been', LlDC 34,43–63. Marged Haycock has shown (CMCS 13 (1987), 13, 27) that Glewlwyd's speech is closely paralleled in the poem BT 51,10–17, which lists the conquests of

Alexander, and makes a similar use of exotic and alliterating names
for unknown and far-away places: E. Anwyl did in fact suggest that
the *Culhwch* passage incorporates a memory of the Alexander story
(RC 34 (1913), 413). Idris Foster noted what may be an even earlier
precedent in a parallel formulaic speech made by Curoí mac Dairi in
the Old Irish tale *Fled Bricrend* 'Bricriu's Feast', in which Curoí lists
his foreign travels (see ALMA 35, 38; text and trans, in G.
Henderson (ed.) *Bricriu's Feast* ITS vol. 2 (London 1899) 118; LU
ll.9201–5; trans. AIT 277). Like Glewlwyd, Curoí has visited
Europe, Africa, and Greece, as well as Asia, Scithia, and the
columns of Hercules. Glewlwyd's speech has been the subject of a
detailed analysis by B. F. Roberts, 'Yr India Fawr a'r India Fechan',
LlC xiii (1980–1), 281–3. He shows that its purpose was to create a
feeling of wonder by citing a list of strange and unfamiliar names
which served to enhance the speaker's boastful recital of his exploits
in far-off unknown places. Rhyming pairs of names such as **Caer Se
ac Asse**, **Sach a Salach**, **Lotor a Fotor** are resounding but
meaningless invented names, and similar doubts arise concerning
Caer Brythwch a Brythach a Nerthach (l. 122) – all of them
names which are otherwise unknown. But **Caer Oeth ac Anoeth** is
found in a triad (TYP no. 52), and *teulu Oeth ac Anoeth* is known
from the *Beddau* stanzas, LlDC 18, 90: this name may therefore be
assumed to have some traditional background. The same is
probably true of **ymlad deu Ynyr** (ll. 119–20), since *ynyr wystlon*
are named in BT 42,2. **Caer Neuenhyr naw Nawt** (l. 126) has been
discussed by J. Lloyd-Jones, B xiv, 35–7; he shows that *Nawt*
should be emended to *nant* on the authority of Prydydd y Moch's
allusion to *newenhyr naw nant* (H 276,30), where *nant* ('nine streams')
is proved by the rhyme. In *Cad Goddau* (BT 24, 1) the Taliesin
persona boasts *bum yg kaer nefenhir* and the word *naw* has been deleted
in the text after *nefenhir*. *Egrop* in l. 120 is here an obvious mistake for
'Europ(a)': the three continents *affrica, europa, asicia* (Asia) are listed
in BT 5,3–4; 80, 2–3 – although Glewlwyd here only names the first
two of these. India (l. 118) was a land of magic and enchantment in the
Middle Ages, as also were Greece and **Llychlyn** (l. 120), an early
borrowing from Ir. *Lochlann* (Norway). The source for the hear-say
knowledge of these countries lay in the works of Isidore and Orosius,
which are reflected in the *Imago Mundi*, translated into Welsh in the
thirteenth century as *Delw y Byd*. Though Corsica is named in this
work, a lack of exact knowledge is probably the reason for

Glewlwyd's **ynyssoed Corsica** (l. 121). For a note on geographical knowledge in medieval Wales see N. Lloyd and M. E. Owen, *Drych yr Oesoedd Canol* (Gwasg Prifysgol Cymru, 1986), 116–18.

123–4. **Gleis mab Merin**. In RC 34, 413–14, Anwyl prefers R's reading *cleis* for *Gleis*, comparing *Porth Cleis* (l. 1098 below). *Merin* < *Marinus* (a name found in *Bodferin*, Gwynedd).

Mil Du mab Ducum. *Mil Du* 'the Black Animal'. In the early life of St Malo (RC 6, 384; LBS iii, 417) a giant named *Mildu* is resuscitated by the saint from his burial in a cairn. See further *Histoire Litteraire et culturelle de la Bretagne* ed. J. Balcou and Y. Le Gallo (Paris, 1987), 132, where the name in a Breton lay *Mildumarec* (*Mil du* + *marchog*) is compared.

127. **eirmoet**: 'ever, during my time': With the infixed pron. sing. 3 the form is *e(i)ryoet* in MW. Later this form becomes general, and it developed as an impers. adv. with the meaning 'ever'. Under the influence of *y* [i] *er-* became *eir*, which spread by analogy to *eirmoet*, a form which disappeared during the MW period; see GMW 222, and ll. 314, 448, 907 below.

kymryt consists of *kym*+*pryt* 'appearance, form' and means 'of like form, as fair'. Such formations are attested in Welsh, where *ky(f)-*, *kym-* are prefixed to nouns: *kyfliw, kyuurd, kymoned, kyfret, kyfryw, kyhyt, kyflet, kymeint, kyniuer*. See GMW 38 also ll. 395, 448 below.

132–4. **Ys dyhed a beth gadu . . . y kyfryw dyn a dywedy di**: 'It is a shameful thing to leave such a man as you speak of'. On the use of *ys* initially before a nominal pred. see p. xxiii above.

134. **Kei** and 136. **Kei wynn**: ('Fair Kei'). *Cei* is derived from Lat. *Caius*; see Vendryes, EC v, 34; M. Richards 'Arthurian Onomastics', THSC 1969, 257. For a collection of early allusions to *Kei/Cei* see TYP 303–7, and for a suggestion as to an alternative derivation for the name see R. M. Jones, B xiv, 119–23. Cei is Arthur's foremost warrior in *Culhwch ac Olwen*, as he is in the poem *Pa Gur* (see pp. xxxv-vi above). In the poem Cei receives the epithet *Kei guin*, as in l. 136, also (*y*) *gur hir* 'the tall man'. These two epithets are constantly attached to Cei in the Three Romances, cf. TYP 304n. In HRB ix, 11 *Kaius* is described as Arthur's *senescallus* 'seneschal, steward' (= *pen swydwr* BD 156,30); cf. ll. 272–3 below *ny byd gwasanaythur na swydvr mal ef.* Cei is portrayed for the most part in a

favourable light in Welsh tradition, as is manifest from the allusions to him by the poets. In *Culhwch* he is distinguished for his miraculous *cyneddfau* (ll.266–73): his great natural heat and his ability to go without sleep recall the similar attributes possessed by Cú Chulainn (see C. O'Rahilly, *Táin Bó Cúailnge from the Book of Leinster*, 40–1, 179). He is distinguished for his valour and cunning in slaying Wrnach Gawr and Dillus Farfawg, and for riding on the 'two shoulders' of the salmon on his journey up the Severn to free Mabon fab Modron from his prison at Gloucester. But having taken offence at the satirical *englyn* Arthur addressed to him (ll. 978–80), Cei disappears from the story, and plays no part in the final adventures. Nevertheless, Arthur is said to have avenged Cei's death (l.284). The nucleus of the later adverse and contentious portrayal of Cei is indicated already in *Culhwch*, and is further developed in the Three Romances. In TYP no.21, as in l.264 below (see n.), Cei's father is named *Kenyr Keinuaruavc*, but some uncertainty nevertheless exists as to his parentage, and there are suggestions of an unknown story relating to the ambiguous circumstances of his birth. The epithet *gwyn* which is already attached to Cei in *Pa Gur* is evidently a term of endearment: it belongs exclusively to Cei and is never given to any other of Arthur's companions.

134. **myn llaw uyghyueillt**: 'by the hand of my friend'; an asseveration introduced by the prep. *myn* 'by', as in l.957 below; cf. GMW 245.

kyueillt: note that *-llt* has not here been reduced to ll. Cf. BWP 28–9.

136. **Ydym wyrda hyt tra yn dygyrcher**: these words from Arthur are significant as an anticipation of the chivalrous monarch of later Arthurian romance. (On this see B. F. Roberts, AoW 73–4.)

137. **cyfarws**: see n. to l.59 above.

139. **Glewlwyd**: see n. to l.111 above.

agori. an ex. of a vn. used instead of a finite vb. in narrative, with a finite vb. preceding it. Cf. GMW 161, CFG 47; also l.1017 below.

140. **a goryw pawb**: 'what everyone did'; pret. sing. 3 of *goruot*, cf. GMW 147, n. 3. For a rel. clause without an expressed antecedent, cf. GMW 72.

141. **ar y gorwyd y doeth y mywn**: an audacious and disrespectful act. M. L. Sjoestedt has compared the entry of the boy Cú Chulainn into the court of his uncle king Conchobar in the same violent way; (*Gods and Heroes of the Celts*, trans. Dillon (London, 1949), 61–3. P. L. Henry points out (SC iii (1968), 33n.) that Suailtaim, Cú Chulainn's father, also makes a violent entry into the court of King Conchobar (O'Rahilly, *Táin Bó Cúailnge from the Book of Leinster* l.4009, trans. p. 246). There are suggestions that Peredur entered Arthur's court in a similar fashion (though the burlesque parallel is more clear in the French version of the story, where Perceval actually rides into the court, and up to Arthur, so that his horse knocks the cap from the king's head). Peredur's uncouth dress and accoutrements are no doubt in intentional contrast to those of Culhwch (WM 122,20 = Mab. 186–7).

142. **henpych gwell**: 'Hail, may you fare the better'. Here we have an ex. of the pres. subj. used to express a wish, cf. GMW 113; also l. 148 below. The vb. here is *hanuot* a compd. of *bot* 'to be'. The first element is *han* 'from', and the vb. means 'to be from'. But it can mean simply 'to be", as is the case here. (With *han* cf. *ohanaf* 'from me' in MW, also the vb. *gwahanu* 'to separate').

143. **gwaelawt ty**: 'the lower part of the house'. This may well have yielded *glowty* (from *gwalowty*) a form used in parts of south Wales (Pembroke and Glamorgan) for 'cow-house'; TC 25, cf. also LlC ii (1953), 189.

147. **gwir Dyw**: (also ll.162 and 172). *Gwir Duw* 'truth of God'. This oath is explained by T. M. Charles-Edwards (THSC 1970, 284) as corresponding to Ir. *fir nDé* 'truth of God' 'a solemn binding oath . . .' The *fir nDé* was a method of deciding a legal case when all else failed. Thurneysen translates it as 'divine verdict' or 'ordeal'. It involved an oath on relics or on an altar. This, no doubt, replaced other solemn forms of oath which were used in the pre-Christian period'. Cf. DIL 'F' 147 'a religious ordeal or attestation'; HGVK 14, 19, 75.

149. **breint edling (gwrthrychyat teyrnas) arnat** (R: *breint teyrn*) 'the dignity of an *edling* (R: 'of a prince') for you, the one who expects a kingdom'. Both texts incorporate separate glosses on the archaic term *gwrthrychyat* 'one who expects' or 'looks forward', an old term for the heir-apparent, cf. Ir. *tánaise ríg*. It was already

displaced in the Welsh Laws by *edling* (<O.E. *aetheling*). Acc. LlB 4,16–20 *Gwrthrychyat, nyt amgen, yr etlig, y neb a dylyo gwledychu gwedy ef, a dylyir y enrydedu ymlaen pawb yny llys eithyr y brenhin a'r urenhines*. In this place R cannot be copying W, since *teyrn* 'prince' is not the equivalent of *edling*; see introduction p. xi and on the significance of the difference between the two texts here see further T. M. Charles-Edwards, 'The Heir-Apparent in Irish and Welsh Law', *Celtica* ix (1971), 185–6, and D. A. Binchy, 'Some Celtic Legal Terms', *Celtica* iii (1956), 221–31. The *edling* was normally a son, nephew, or first cousin of the king; see D. Jenkins, HDdL 6–7.

151. **bythawd**: an old formation whereby an archaic independent ending -(*h*)*awd* (with future meaning) is added to the form *byd*, fut. sing. 3 of the vb. 'to be'; cf. GMW 119.

pan y: here *pan* means 'that' (conjunct.) and is preceded by *o* 'from'. This occurs elsewhere in MW: *ae o bysgotta pan deuy di* YCM 81,5–6. Cf. GMW 79, also l. 189 below *o vrthdir Uffern pan hanoed y gwyr*. The *y* in *pan y* probably consists of the pers. pron. obj. sing. 3 'that I will begin it'.

153. **uyghyuarws**: on *cyfarws* see n. on l. 59 above.

154. **dwyn dy vyneb**: (R: *dwyn dy agclot*). *Wyneb* 'face' denoted honour; cf. *wynebwerth* 'honour-price', and its Ir. equivalent *log n-enech*. Cf. T. M. Charles-Edwards (THSC 1970, 277), 'in the WB text Culhwch threatens to take away Arthur's honour, in other words to dishonour him as far as the furthest corners of the earth. In the RB text, however, Culhwch threatens to carry Arthur's "dispraise", in other words, to satirize him'. On Ir. *enech* cf. D. Binchy, *Críth Gablach* (DIAS 1941), 84–6.

157. **a'th tauawd**: note how *th*+*d*- (representing the lenition of *t* after -*th* (GMW 16) becomes -*tht*-, cf. GMW 17. Otherwise *a'th dauawt*, as in l. 171.

157–9. **hyt y sych gwynt** etc: for a similar hyperbole see GDG 7, 28 *Hyd y try hwyl hy haul haf* etc. P. L. Henry cites a number of Irish parallels to the citation of the elements as guarantors of an oath, *Ériu* xx (1969), 233–6.

158. **hyt yr etil heul**: (R: *hyt y treigyl heul*). The text is not satisfactory as it stands, and the two texts differ. It would appear

that the original drawn on by both was not very clear: here the vb. *etil*, pres. sing. 3 'reaches' is from *eddylaf* (GPC 1169).

159. **uy llong a'm llen**: *Prydwen* was the name of Arthur's ship; see n. on *Prytwenn* l.938 below. Arthur's *llen* or mantle is not named in *Culhwch*, but is called *Gwenn* in BR 11,19. It is described, though without being named, in 'The Thirteen Treasures of the Island of Britain': *Llen Arthur yng Ngherniw, pwy bynnag a fai deni, efe a welai bawb, ac ni welai neb ef* 'Arthur's Mantle in Cornwall, whoever might be under it could see everyone, and no one was able to see him', LlC v (1958), 36, 53–4; cf. EC x (1963), 442, 461; TYP 241, 247–8. In B xxx (1983), 268–73, P. K. Ford comments on the possibly magical connotations of the element *gwyn/gwen* in the names of Arthur's possessions – *Prydwen, Gwenn* (= his mantle), *Ehangwen* (= his hall), *Carnwennan* (= his dagger), and even in *Gwenhwyfar*, his wife. *Gwyn/Gwen* can mean not only 'white', but also 'pure, sacred'. This leads Ford to advocate the mythical Otherworld origin of Arthur's *regalia*, though this is nowhere expressly stated.

a Chaletuwlch uyg cledyf: *Caletfwlch* is a compd. of *caled*, as adj. 'hard' or as n. 'battle' + *bwlch* 'breach, gap, notch' (GPC 352). Taking *caled* to be the n., meaning 'battle' (GPC 392) as in LlDC 18,76 *ny kilieu o caled*, 'Battle-breach' or 'Breach of Battle' thus appears preferable to 'Hard notch (gap)' or the like, as the meaning of this name. In BD 148 *Caletuvlch* translates *Caliburnus*, the name for Arthur's sword in HRB ix, 4 etc. – a form which Geoffrey of Monmouth must have derived from a written text earlier than any which has survived, since it must have been one in which *bwlch* was as yet unlenited. It thus appears that the *Brut* gives the earliest written appearance of the name *Caledfwlch*. For a number of years *Caledfwlch* was looked upon as a borrowing from the cognate Ir. *Caladbolg (calad* 'hard', as noun 'hardship'; DIL, 'C' 58 + *bolg* 'gap' DIL 'B' 139, on which see O'Rahilly, *Ériu* xiii, 163–4). But this now seems unlikely, in spite of the superficial correspondence between the two names. In the *Táin Bó Cúailnge from the Book of Leinster* (ed. O'Rahilly, (DIAS 1967), l.4720 *Caladbolg* is the name of a sword which Fergus mac Róig inherited from Fergus mac Leite; elsewhere in the same manuscript (LL l. 32517) *caladbuilg* (pl.) appears in the tale *Togail Troi* as a general and unspecific name for swords (cf. EIHM 68n.). Vendryes has argued convincingly (EC v (1940), 15) that in Irish *Caladbolg* was originally a generic name for a sword, rather than the name for any one sword in particular. The editors of the Book of Leinster, R. I. Best, Osborn Bergin, and M. A. O'Brien (DIAS 1954–67) state that the manuscript is the work of one hand written over a long period in the second half of the 12th cent. (see further W. S. O'Sullivan, 'Notes on the Script and Make-up of the Book of Leinster', *Celtica* vii (1966) 1–31, esp. 26–8). Since Geoffrey of Monmouth's HRB first appeared *c.* 1136–8, Geoffrey's *Caliburnus* is older than the date now accepted for the Book of Leinster: if *Caliburnus* is accepted as the Lat. rendering of *Caledfwlch*, the Welsh name must predate 1138. With respect to the occurrence of *Caletfwlch* in *Culhwch*, it must remain uncertain whether the name is a borrowing from the early 13th-cent. *Brut,* or whether it can go back to an earlier redaction of the tale. In favour of its antiquity, however, is the very early occurrence of the name of Arthur's ship *Prydwen* (see n. to l.938): *Caledfwlch*, as the name of Arthur's sword, may well be equally ancient and traditional. In his *Heldensage* 114–15, Thurneysen took it for granted that *Caliburnus* is a borrowing from Ir. *Caladbolg,* and this led him to believe that the Book of Leinster predates HRB. Since modern palaeographical scholarship does not concur with so early a dating for the Book of Leinster, Thurneysen's view can now be discounted. As there is no means of knowing how much older the names *Caladbolg* and *Caledfwlch* may be than the manuscripts in which they first appear – whether in written or in oral sources – the question of the relationship between the two remains incapable of final solution: both may have similarly arisen at a very early date as generic names for a sword. With *Caladbolg* the name of Cú Chulainn's spear the *Gai Bolga,* may also be compared. See further EIHM 68–71, and P. K. Ford, B xxx, 271.

Caledfwlch occurs as a place-name between Llangadog and Llandeilo, Dyfed: here *bwlch* may denote a mountain-gap or pass, that is, 'Pass of Battle'. The names *Kledyf Kyuwlch, Cledyf Diuwlch* in l.334 below, may also be compared, see n.

160. **Rongomynyat uyg gvayw**: both W and R read *rongomyant,* which should plainly be emended to *Rongomynyat* (as indicated Mab 100, 279) from *rhon* 'spear' and *gomyniad* 'striker, slayer' a word attested in the *Gododdin*, CA 345, 1378. Cf. BD 148,27–8 (= HRB ix,4) *Gleif . . . yr hon a elwit Ron.*

Vyneb Gwrthucher: 'Evening Face' – an unlikely name for a shield; cf. P. K. Ford, B xxx, 270. *Gwrthucher* 'evening' is a word which occurs in BT 47,24, and Old Cornish *gurthuher* glosses *vespera*, GPC 1735.

160–1. **uy yscwyt**: R replaces this archaic word for a shield by *taryan*, a borrowing from OE *targe*, cf. K. Meyer, THSC 1895–6; CA 353.

161. **a Charnwenhan uyg kyllell**: 'Little White Haft'. One meaning of *carn* is the hilt or haft of a sword or knife, here found with an affectionate diminutive ending. On *(g)wen*, *(g)wyn* in the names of Arthur's weapons see on l. 159 above.

161–2. **a Gwenhvyuar uyg gwreic**: Arthur's queen is named in l. 358 below as *Penn Rianed yr Ynys honn*. She makes no subsequent appearance in the tale. In BD 153 her origin is given as follows: *y kymerth y brenhin (Arthur) wreic a hanoed o dyledogyon Ruuein, a Guenhvyuar oed y henw, ac yn llys Cadvr yarll Kernyv y magadoed. A phryt a thegvch y wreic honno a orchyuygei holl wraged enys Prydein.* This is the earliest written appearance of the name *Guenhvyuar*, and it renders *Guenhumara, Guenhuuara* etc. in HRB. (On the variant Lat. spellings of this name see HRB ed. Neil Wright, lii and n.; 156.) In EC v (1949), 34 J. Vendryes explained the form *Guenhumara* as a written misinterpretation of OW *Guenhuiuar*, indicating that Geoffrey of Monmouth derived the name from a written Welsh source. (With this cf. n. on *Caletuwlch* l. 159 above.) The Ir. cognate of Gwenhwyfar is *Findabair* 'white fairy, enchantress', the name of the daughter of Queen Medb in the *Táin Bó Cúailnge*; see M. Richards 'Arthurian Onomastics', THSC 1969, 257. For early allusions to Gwenhwyfar see TYP 380–5. She is named in the Triads and in the Three Romances as Arthur's wife and queen but it should be noted that her name does not appear anywhere in the early version of TYP, only in that of W and R. She appears as *Guennuvar* in the Life of Gildas by Caradog of Llancarfan (*Gildas*, ed. Hugh Williams, 408–10; TWS 137; on this allusion see further TYP(2) 553). But she is unknown in all of the other Lives of the Saints. In TYP, as in *Culhwch*, she has a sister *Gwenhwy(f)ach* (TYP 380; see n. on l. 359 below). Gwenhwyfar's father is named in TYP no. 56 as *Gogfran Gawr* 'G. the Giant'. (On the possibility of influence from the *Brut* see introduction p. lxxxii.)

162. **Gwir Dyw**: see n. on l. 147 above.

164–5. **crip eur ... a gwelliu a doleu aryant**: with the symbolic significance of Arthur's cutting and trimming Culhwch's hair cf. the parallel incident quoted from HB in the introduction pp. xxxi–ii above.

167. **Mi a wn dy hanuot om gwaet**: Arthur's words indicate intuitive recognition of Culhwch as his kinsman; cf. Llywarch's words to his son: *Neut atwen ar vy awen/Yn hanuot o un achen* (CLlH I, 2).

168–9. **mab ... merch**: these words form close compds. with preceding personal names, and are normally lenited in MW (GMW 15), but only very rarely in either of the two texts of *Culhwch*, so that the following instances are exceptional: Gwythyr *uab* Greidawl (l.176), Brys *uab* Bryssethach (l.332), Mabon *uab* Modron... Eidoel *uab* Aer (ll.828–9), Gwyn *uab* Nud (l.1133).

170. **keuynderw vyt**: see n.2 above on *Anlawd Wledic*.

171. **Not a nottych**: 'Name what you will'. This ritualistic formula recurs in the words used by Ysbaddaden, ll.568–9 below.

172. **gvir dy deyrnas**: 'truth of thy kingdom' is paralleled in the Ir. term *fír do flátha* (DIL 'F' 146). Cf. n. on *Gwir Dyw*, l.147 above.

173. **Olwen merch Yspadaden Penkawr**: see n. on l.498 below.

175. **asswynaw**: a borrowing from late Lat. *assegno (assigno)*, with the meaning influenced by *swyn* 'charm", and meaning 'to beseech, invoke' with *ar* = 'on' or 'in the name of'. Culhwch invokes from Arthur his boon (that is, that he obtain Olwen for him) in the name of all the men and women present in his court: all are made his witnesses and his sureties that the king will fulfil his obligation. By invoking them, Culhwch places an additional sanction upon the king. The best analogy for this use of *asswynaw* is Cynddelw's poem of *dadolwch* to Rhys ap Gruffudd (LlDC no. 23) *Assuynaw naut duv . . . ar dy guir . . . ar dy gulad*; though in this case the boon invoked by the poet is that of reconciliation with his patron. The legal force of *aswyno* as a binding compulsion is discussed by P. K. Ford, 'Welsh *asswynaw* and Celtic Legal Idiom', B xxvi (1975), 147–53). In l.212 below its meaning is more like 'to submit', and yet another meaning is 'to create by magic', as in PKM 83,24.

Kei a Bedwyr: in the earliest sources these are Arthur's two inseparable companions: in the poem *Pa Gur*, in the *Vita Cadoci*, in the Triads, in HRB and in *Brut y Brenhinedd*. Their names head Arthur's Court List, and they are also the first to be appointed of the hero's Six Helpers (ll.381–411), where it is said that Bedwyr never held back from any enterprise undertaken by Cei. For Cei see on l.134 above. In *Culhwch* Bedwyr receives no patronymic, but in TYP no. 21 he is *mab Bedravc/Pedrawt;=Bedwyr uab bedrawt* in GER (WM 411,41); *Beduir bedrydant* in *Pa Gur* (see p. xxxvi above). Acc. BD 156 *y rodes Arthur y uedwyr y ben trullyat (=butler) yarllaeth Normandi.*

176. **Greidawl Galldouyd**: cf. BR 19,27 *Greidyal Galldofyd*. The meaning of *greid(i)ol* is 'hot, passionate, fierce'; cf. CLIH 115. On the various meanings of *ofydd* and *dofydd* in compds. see J. Lloyd-Jones, B xv, 198–200; GPC 1375, G 519. A triad TYP no. 19 *Tri Galouyd Enys Prydein* ('Three Enemy-Subduers') includes *Greidyawl Galouyd mab Envael Adrann*. The forms in *Culhwch* and in BR attest that medial *d = dd* should be restored in *Galouyd* in the triad, and that the second element is *douyd* 'lord'. Cf. *recdouyd* l.17 above, and introduction p. xvii.

Gwythyr uab Greidawl: *Gwythyr* comes from an oblique case of Lat. *Victor-*, (G 754). Cf. *Withur, Uuithur*; Chr. Br. 101,176; TYP 403–4 and n. to triad 56. Gwythyr's descent from *Greidyawl Galouyd mab Envael Adrann* (triad 19) receives some late corroboration from an entry in *Bonedd yr Arwyr* EWGT 89,22) which adds further names connecting father and son with northern genealogies in BGG. Gwythyr figures later in the tale as hero in the episode of the Lame Ant (ll.942–52), and in his fight with Gwyn ap Nudd for Creiddylad (ll.989–1004). Cf. also LlDC 18,133 *bet y guythur*.

176–7. **Greit mab Eri**: *graid* 'passion, ferocity, valour etc.: (as in *Greid(y)awl* above). Cf. Ir. *greit* 'champion', DIL 'G', 152. *Greit vab Hoywgi* CA 266; *greit confessoris* LL 3,24–5. Cynddelw compares Rhys ap Gruffudd (d.1197) to this hero: *gwr greidyawl ual greid uab ery,* H 110, 2 = RP 1438, 17 *val greidyawl uab greit uab ery*. The rhyme proves that *Ery* is the correct form of the patronymic: perhaps = *er(h)y* 'brave, daring, courageous', CA 135, GPC 1239. *Greit mab Eri* is later listed in a triad of unhappy prisoners (l.916), and later again is imprisoned by Gwyn ap Nudd l.992..

177. **Cyndelic Kyuarwyd**: 'C. the Guide' is later appointed by Arthur as one of the hero's Six Helpers to go with him on his search

for Olwen (l. 399). *Kindilic Corknud* is named in *Englynion y Beddau* as an *alltud* or foreigner, LlDC 18,126. But there is no special reason to identify the two. *Cindilic* was also the name of a son of Llywarch Hen, CLlH vii,9c, and of one of the Gododdin warriors, CA 824 (see n.).

Tathal Twyll Goleu: 'T. of Evident Treachery' or 'Frank Deceit'. Cf. *Tethel* HGVK 54, and *Caer Tathal* 204 below; *Kaer Dathyl yn Arfon* PKM 67,10. Idris Foster ('Irish Influence',34) compares the Irish name *Tuathal Techtmar* EIHM 154 ff. and *Rex quidam hibernie . . . nomine Tathalius*, VSB 270. In B xxix, 614 P. Sims-Williams doubts the Irish derivation of this name, citing Ifor Williams's note PKM 251-2, and the OB forms *Taital, Tatal*, Chr. Br. 166.

178. **Maylwys mab Baedan**: *mael* 'prince'; Ir. *mál*. Baedan could be a diminutive of *baedd* 'boar'. An alternative explanation which has much to recommend it was first proposed by J. Rhŷs in *The Arthurian Legend* (1891), 344, and has recently been revived by P. Mac Cana, *Y Gwareiddiad Celtaidd* (ed. G. Bowen, Llandysul, 1987), 160-1. This would equate the name with *Máel Umai mac Baitán*, an early historical figure belonging to one of the northern Irish dynasties, who is said in the Annals of Tigernach to have slain the brother of the English king Aethelfrith at the battle of Degsastan in AD 603, when it appears he was fighting as an ally of the Scottish ruler Aedán mac Gabráin. Subsequently he became the subject of a lost saga *Echtra Mailuma maic Baitáin* which told of his career (see Mac Cana, *Learned Tales of Medieval Ireland*, 45). This surmise is made the more plausible by the fact that Aedán of Dál Riada has himself entered Welsh tradition as Aed(d)an *Fradawc* 'the Wily' (see TYP 264-6). If correct, this would place *Maylwys/Máel Umai* as the first in the group of Irish saga heroes whose names fill lines 178-180. It is a more acceptable identification than that of E. K. Chambers in his *Arthur of Britain* (London, 1927), 85, where he equates Maylwys with *Melwas*, the abductor of Gwenhwyfar. On *Mael Umai* see further F. J. Byrne, *Irish Kings and High Kings* (London, 1973), 111, 259-60. Like the name which here follows, *Maylwys* can hardly be explained in any other way than as an oral borrowing.

178-80. **Cnychwr mab Nes**: = Ir. *Conchobar mac Nessa*, king of Ulster in the *Táin Bó Cúailnge* and elsewhere in the Ulster Cycle of tales. On this and the following four names see especially P. Sims-

Williams, 'The Significance of the Irish Personal Names in *Culhwch and Olwen*', B xxix (1982), 607–10; HGVK cxiv-cxvii. (Earlier discussions are by Idris Foster, 'Irish Influence', 28–35; ibid. ALMA 34; C. O'Rahilly, *Ireland and Wales*, 114). Not one of these Irish characters appears subsequently in the tale. **Cnychwr mab Nes** may represent a relatively late oral borrowing; the other names reflect corruption at the hand of a series of scribes who are unlikely to have understood the names they were copying, and very little – if anything – of the tales to which they belonged. A corrupt written borrowing can be the only explanation for *Fercos m. Poch* with 'p' for the Insular long 'r' and of **Conul Bernach** = Ir. *Conall Kernach* ('C. the Triumphant'). This form in the text represents Foster's revised reading of the two manuscripts: the letters *n/u* and *r/n* are at times difficult, if not impossible to distinguish, in both W and R (the *varia lecta* give the reading of Gwenogvryn Evans in WM and RM). Cf. the n. to *Llawurodet Uaruawc* l.223, and to *Gliui* ll.831–2 below. **Lluber Beuthach**: < Ir. *Laegaire Buadach* ('L. the Victorious') looks like a mixed oral and written borrowing. **Cubert m. Daere**: < *Curoi mac Dairi* is of particular interest, since the early poem BT 66–7 *Marwnad Corroi m. Dayry* seems to reflect an indistinct memory of the 8th-cent. Irish tale *Aided Conroi maic Dairi (Ériu* ii, 18–35), which tells how Cú Chulainn slew the Munster hero Cú Roí. (For a discussion and trans. of the BT poem see P. Sims-Williams 'Evidence for Irish Literary Influence', 248–57.)

181–2. On the triad of men called **Gwyn(n)** see introduction p. xxxviii. In HL 179 J. Rhŷs identifies *Gwynn m. Nwywre* with the more famous *Gwyn(n) m. Nud(d)*, the only one of the three who is of mythical and legendary fame elsewhere; see on ll.713–14 below. Gwyn ap Nudd is prominent later in the tale in his fight with Gwythyr ap Greidawl, ll.988–1004. The name of *Gwynn mab Nwywre* is duplicated later in the Court-List, l.218 below. *Nwyfre* 'firmament, sky' is compared by Rhŷs with *Cumall*, the patronymic of the Irish *Fionn*, whom he relates to Gwyn ap Nudd. For additional references to *Nwyfre* see TYP 423.

182. **Edern mab Nud**: < *Aeternus* son of *Nodons*, a mythical figure, but one far less prominent in Welsh sources than his brother Gwyn ap Nudd. In HRB x,iv he appears as *Hiderus filius Nu/Nucii* (corrupted in BD 172 as *Hedyr uab Mut*. His name appears also in the *Isdernus* of the Modena archivolt (ALMA 61), and as *Yder fiz Nut* in

Chrétien de Troyes' poem *Erec et Enide*, while in William of Malmesbury's *De Antiq. Glast.* he is *Ider* son of *Nuth*, and *Yder* son of *Nuc* in the 13th-cent. French romance of *Yder* (ALMA 375–6). He is therefore far more widely known in continental than in Welsh sources. Yet he is one of the rare instances in which the combined names of father and son have been transferred together from Welsh (or Breton) into French. Edern mab Nud is unknown in TYP; in GER he plays an unfavourable role parallel to that of his counterpart *Yder* in Chrétien's poem (WM 405, 34). He is also listed in BR 10,1, and was known to Gruffudd ap Maredudd; for refs. see G 438.

182. a **Cadwy m. Gereint**: both MSS read *ac adwy m. gereint*. In B xiii (1950), 136, M. Richards showed that the first name has been wrongly divided, since *Cadw(y)/Cado mab Gereint* is the form of this name attested in ByS, and in the genealogies and triads; see EWGT index 175; TYP 297. BR 19,20, however, retains the misreading *ac adwy* (=RM 159,27; cf. Mab. 151), thus proving the close dependence of BR's Court-List on a text of *Culhwch* (see introduction p. xli) Cadwy's background is that of the Lives of the Saints: his name is Latinized as *Cato* in the *Vita prima S. Carantoci* (VSB 144), where he is a contemporary of Arthur, and as *Catovius rex Britannici* in the Life of St Winwaloeus (EWGT 23). Cf. S. M. Pearce 'Traditions of the Royal King-List of Dumnonia', THSC (1971), 128–139, and see further on *Gereint mab Erbin*, n.219 below.

182–3. **Fflewdwr Flam Wledic**: TYP no. 9 *Tri Vnben Llys Arthur* lists *Ffleudur Flam* (WR adds *ap Godo*). With *Flam* 'flame' cf. *Fflam mab Nwyfre* l.218 below, and the name *Fflamdwyn* PT vi,18. For the title *Gwledic* see on *Kyledon Wledic* n.1 above. The evidence of TYP no.3 (see following n.) suggests that *(G)wledic* has been wrongly borrowed from Dewrarth (R: Dorath) *Wledic*, the patronymic of *Ruawn Pebyr*, whose name follows in the CO list. *Ffleudur Fflam* is cited also in the list in BR 19,27 (=RM 160,2). This suggests miscopying from an earlier text; see introduction p. xlii.

183. **Ruawn Pebyr m. Dorath**: TYP no.3: *Tri Gwyndeyrn Enys Prydein ... Ruuavn Beuyr mab Dewrarth (Dorath R) Wledic*. *Ru(v)awn* < *Romanus,* OW *Rumaun* (the name of one of the sons of Cunedda, from whom *Rhufoniog* is named, EWGT 13). *Pebyr* – *pefr* 'shining, brilliant'. *Dorath/Dewrarth* 'Brave Bear'. Cf. *Rwawn Bybyr uab*

Deorthach Wledic BR 6,4 (= RM 148,17–18), and for further refs. see TYP 500.

183–4. **Bratwen m. Moren Mynawc a Moren Mynawc e hun**: *Brad* in this name has a positive rather than a pejorative meaning: 'cunning, wily'. Cf. *Bratwen m. Iaen a Moren m. Iaen* l.203 below, and the epithet of Aedan *Fradawc* 'A, the Wily', TYP 264. The names of both *Bratwen* and *Mor(y)en* are found in the *Gododdin*, CA 465, 468, 495 (where *Moren* is attested by the rhyme, see n.); also in *Englynion y Beddau* (Stanzas of the Graves), LlDC 18,6, 190. *Mynawc* means 'noble, courteous'; as a noun 'lord, prince' (see CA p. 171 where Ifor Williams compares Breton *Morgen-munuc*, Chr. Br. 152). *Mynawc Gododin* as a proper name occurs in CA 949 (if this is not an error for *Mynydawc*, see n.). In a late genealogy in the hand of Gruffudd Hiraethog, *Moren Mynac* is named as a son of *March ap Meirchion* (*NLW Journal* xx, 373).

184–5. **Dalldaf eil Kimin Cof**: *Cunin Cof* is named as son to one of the daughters of Brychan Brycheiniog, EWGT 15,4. *Cunin* 'splendid, royal' is found in the early inscriptions CVNIGNI (ECMW 142) and CVNEGNI (ibid. 172); on these names see LHEB 182, 191 etc. *Cof* 'mind, memory, memorial'. For *Cunin Cof* see TYP 313–14. *Dalldaf eil Cvnyn Kof* is named in TYP no.73 as one of the 'Three Peers of Arthur's Court', and his horse *Ferlas* is listed among the Triads of Horses, TYP no.41. *Eil* corresponds to Lat. *alter*, Ir. *eile*; it can sometimes mean 'heir, son' (PKM 213; TYP 497; *Celtica* ix, 182).

185. **a mab Alun Dyuet**: the son of Alun Dyfed is not named in *Culhwch*, but in BR and GER he is named *Dyuyr* (BR 19,25 = RM 159,30); WM 411,39; *Run mab Alun Diwed/Alun Dywed...mab Meigen* LlDC 18,74–7. *Mab Alun Dyuet* is named a second time among the *anoethau*, 725 below. There are two possible refs. to this hero by Gr. ap Maredudd: *alun gryfder* RP 1211,11; *llit mab alun* RP 1327,28.

a mab Saidi: cf. *Cas mab Saidi* l.293 below. The Triads list *Kadyrieith* (Fine Speech) (*ap Seidi* in WR only) among *Tri Unben Llys Arthur*, TYP no.9.

a mab Gwryon: cf. *Huabwy/Hunabwy mab Gwryon* l.288 below.

186. **Vchdryt Ardwyat Kat**: *Uchtrit* occurs as a personal name in

LL 279,12; *tref meibion Uch(t)rit* LL 43,24-5. Cf. *Uchdryt m. Erim* l.233 below, and *Vchdryt Uaryf Draws* l.327. *Ardwyat* 'defender, protector, guardian', with *kat* 'host-sustainer'; cf. *Ardwyat mab Kaw* l.210 below.

Cynwas Curyuagyl: (R: *curuagyl*) 'C. Pointed Staff'?; from *cwr* 'corner, edge, point' and *bagl* (Ir. *bachall*) 'staff'. For *Cynwas* cf. LL 173,27 *Conguas*. On the name cf. P. Sims-Williams, B xxix (1982), 615, and refs. cited. Later in the story this character's cattle are slain by the Twrch Trwyth l.1101 below and n.

186-7. Gwrhyr Gwarthecuras: *gwartheg* 'cattle' + *bras* 'fat, stout'. With Gwrhyr cf. *Gwrhyr Gwalstawd Ieithoed* l.346 below.

187. Isperyr Ewingath: 'I. Cat's Claw'. *Ysperir* is named in *Englynion y Clyweit*, B iii (1927), 12, 27.

187-8. Gallcoit Gouynnyat: both MSS read *gouynnynat*: evidently a miscopying (see introduction p. xi). Idris Foster proposed the emendation *gouynnyat*, that is *gofyniad* 'suppliant', comparing *Llwydawc Gouynnyat* in l.1137 below (see n.). This seems preferable to Mab.'s rendering 'the Hewer', taking the word to be *gomyniad* 'striker, killer' both here and in l.1137. With *Gallcoit* cf. *Gallgoic* in l.274.

189. Gwawrdur Kyruach: with *Gwawrdur* cf. CA 359 and n. In this name *gwawr* 'dawn' is used fig. for a warrior, as also in BT 48,6, *a march gwa(w)rdur*. *Kyruach* is 'hunchback' or 'wizened', GPC 807. Cf. the doublet *Gwaredur Kyruach*, l.363. The *-ach* termination appended to the names of Gwawrdur's three sons *Duach, Brathach, Nerthach* 'Black, Wily, Strong', is likely to have a pejorative nuance. On *-ach* see P. Sims-Williams, B xxix, 616. He cites the name *Duach*, however, from the Ir. Life of St Maedoc.

o vrthdir Uffern: 'from the uplands of Hell'. For the same phrase see l.653 and n., also l.1207 below and cf. introduction p. lxxviii and n.99. With *pan* cf. GMW 80, and cf.n. on l.151 above.

190. Cilyd Cannhastyr: for *Cilyd* see n. on l.1 above. *Cannhastyr* 'Hundred Holds' from *can(t)* + *astyr* 'hand, hold' (GPC 408). The epithet seems to imply that its bearer was a thief, since in the Laws a *cyhyryn canastr* was a receiver of stolen goods; see HDdL 160; LlB 114,23: *Tri cheheryn canhastyr yssyd*... Similarly derogatory epithets are attached to his two companions, *Canhastyr Canllaw* 'C. Hundred Hands', and *Cors Cant Ewin* 'C. Hundred Claws'. *Cors* 'bog, swamp'.

191. **Eskeir Gulhwch Gonyn Cawn**: *Eskeir* is either 'leg' or 'mountain ridge', as in l. 107 above. *Conyn Cawn* 'Reed-Stalk', but *conyn* 'grumbler' is attested in Dyfed dialect. Alternatively *Gouyn Cawn* 'reed-cutter' through confusion of *n* and *u*. This name defies explanation.

191–2. **Drustwrn Hayarn**: 'Drust Iron-Fist' (*dwrn* + *haearn*). *Drust* and its dim. *Drosten*, the cognate of Welsh *Drystan* < *Drustanos* are names which recur in the Pictish regnal lists. See TYP 329, and M. O. Anderson, *Kings and Kingship in Early Scotland* (Edinburgh, 1973), 90, 271–3, etc. The form here is evidently a scribal corruption of the name *Drystan* (Tristan), more particularly in view of the fact that *Drystan/Dyrstan mab Talluch* is found in two of the three lists derived from *Culhwch* (see introduction, p. xl): BR 19,21 (=RM 159,27); *Englynion y Clyweit* (B iii, 15 no. 67). The name *Esyllt* (Isolt) is found in l. 372 below. For the story of Tristan in Welsh sources see now AoW ch. 10.

192. **Glewlwyt Gauaeluawr**: See n. on l. 111 above.

Lloch Llawwynnyawc: 'Ll. of the Striking Hand', also *Llwch Llawwynnyawc* l. 291 below. Identifiable with *Lluch Llauynnauc* in *Pa Gur* (p. xxxv l. 14 above). In ALMA 34, Idris Foster compared Ir. *lonnbemnach* 'of the Fierce Blows' – one of the epithets of the god *Lugus* (=*Lugh, Lleu*). *Lonnbemnach* is partly cognate with *llawwynnyawc*, since the second element in both derives from the root *ben-* 'hew, cut' (cf. Thurneysen, *A Grammar of Old Irish*, DIAS 1946, 356). The hand or arm of the god *Lugus/Lugh* is a common element in this tradition; cf. Lleu *Llawgyffes*.

193. **Anwas Edeinawc**: 'A. the Winged'. This name appears in OW spelling in *Pa Gur* (p. xxxv l. 14 above). *An-* (neg. + *gwas* 'dwelling, home'; hence *anwas* 'restless, turbulent' (Ir. *anfoss*). Cf. GPC 164; *edeinawc* < *adain* 'winged'. For *Edenawc* as a personal name cf. TYP no. 22.

There follow the names of five sons of **Seithuet** 'seventh': the name suggests that two more may have dropped from the list. Cf. *Llewei verch Seitwed* TYP no. 58.

194–5. **Gwenwynwyn mab Naw mab Seithuet**: the name is repeated as *Gwenwynwyn mab Naf* in l.250, described as *cysseuin rysswr Arthur* 'Arthur's foremost champion'. In TYP no.14 *Gwenwynwyn mab Naf* (see n.) is one of the *Tri Llyghessawc* or 'Seafarers'. *Naf* 'lord' has replaced *naw* 'nine', unless the latter represents an older spelling of *Naf*.

195. **Gobrwy mab Echel Uordvyt Twll**: *Gobrwy* is a var. of *gwobr*, *gwobrwy* 'reward, gift'. *Gobrwy/Govrowy mab Echel Vordwytwll* is one of the *Tri Vnben Llys Arthur*, TYP no.9.

Echel Uordvyt Twll: evidently the name of a native hero (TYP 335–6), though *Echel* in BD 158 corresponds to *Aschill(us)* (Achilles) in HRB ix,12. Idris Foster's early suggestion of influence from Ir. *Eccel* ('Irish Influence' 33) can now be rejected in view of the evidence of BD and HRB; see on this B. F. Roberts, B xxv, 276; P. Sims-Williams, B xxix, 615. The name *Echel* is used several times by the Gogynfeirdd for purposes of eulogistic comparison, and an earlier instance occurs in the seventh(?) cent. *Moliant Cadwallon*, B vii, 24,10 (ed. R. G. Gruffudd, Ast.H. 28,30). The epithet *Morddwyd Twll* 'Mighty Thigh' was discussed by Ifor Williams, CLlH 70. Since it is not combined with *Echel* in any of the poetic citations of this name, it is uncertain in each one of them whether the allusion is to the native hero or to the classical Achilles.

197. **Datweir Dallpenn**: 'D. Blind Head'. Cf. *Dallwyr Dallpen*, TYP no.26, the owner of the sow Henwen at Glyn Dallwyr in Cornwall (cf. introduction p. lxvii). Two MSS of the early version of the triad give the form *Datweir* for *Dallwyr* (P 47 and C 18). With the name cf. *Dallmor Dallme* in Llywelyn Siôn's version of the *Hanes Taliesin*, EC xiv, 452.

197.8. **Garwyli eil Gwythawc Gwyr**: cf. *Arwyli eil Gwydawc Gwyr* l.1155 below. On *eil* see n. to *Dalldaf eil Kimin Cof* l.184 above.

198. **Gormant mab Ricca**. This name is repeated in the list, l.221 below; see n.

199. **Menw mab Teirgwaed**: 'Little, son of Three Cries (?)'. Cf. Ir. *menb* 'little'. This name, as Rhŷs pointed out (CF 510n.) may have suggested to the narrator the bird-form assumed by Menw in l. 1031 below. Menw is a magician both in *Culhwch* and in TYP nos. 27 *Tri*

Lleturithavc and 28 *Teir Prif Hut Enys Prydein*; see n. TYP 457–8. In l.408 below Menw is appointed by Arthur as one of Culhwch's Six Helpers: he possesses the especial gift of invisibility, ll.408–11.

Digon mab Alar: 'Enough son of Surfeit'.

199–200. **Selyf mab Sinoit**: in BD 193 *Selyf* renders *Solomon* HRB xii, 1. But the occurrence of *Selim* (Sclyf) for the son of Cynan Garwyn in the Harleian Gens. (EWGT 12, 22) indicates that the Lat. name had already been borrowed into Welsh at a date prior to that of the *Brut*; see B. F. Roberts, B xxv, 276; TYP 507.

200. **Nerth mab Kadarn**: 'Might son of Strong'.

200–1. **Drutwas mab Tryffin**: this name appears in a triad first recorded in P 47 (= TYP 46A), but it is not found in either of the two main collections. An anecdote in M 146 (17th. cent.) describes an encounter between Arthur and Drudwas, in which Drudwas was slain by his own *adar llwch gwin* or 'griffins'; see TYP 327–8; RWM i, 168. His sister *Erduduyl merch Tryffin* is listed in l.364 below.

201. **Twrch mab Perif a Thwrch mab Anwas**: two boars, incongruously listed here, whose names would seem to belong more properly to the story of the great boar-hunt. *Peryf* 'lord'. With *Anwas* cf. *Anwas Edeinawc* l.193 above. Under the influence of this list *Twrch mab Perif* appears as one of Arthur's 'counsellors' in BR 19,18 (= RM 159,25). Neither recurs in the story.

202. **Sel mab Selgi**: 'Watch son of Watchdog' (*sel*).

203. **Sulyen mab Iaen**: *Sulien* ('Sunday-born') was the name of the famous 11th.-cent. abbot of Llanbadarn Fawr, and later bishop of St David's; see WLSD xxi–xxix. It was also the name given to an abbot of Nantcarfan in two charters appended to the Life of St Cadoc; VSB 130,134. BD 64,28 gives *Sulyen* for Geoffrey's *Sulgentius/Fulgentius*, HRB v,2 (cf. B xxv, 277). A genealogy in J 20 renders the same name by OW *Ssulgen* (EWGT 50). *Sulien* is otherwise extremely rare. *Iaen* 'ice'.

Bratwen mab Iaen a Moren mab Iaen: cf. *Bratwen m. Moren Mynawc*. ll.183–4 above, and n. *Iaen* 'Ice'.

204–5. **Siawn mab Iaen a Chradawc mab Iaen**: *Siaun* and *Kyradawg* are listed in *Bonedd yr Arwyr* among the six sons and daughters of 'Iaen' (EWGT 85,2). The daughter, *Eleirch*, is described as *mam Kyduan ap Arthur*. If this late corroboration of ll. 203–5 in *Culhwch* has any significance, it means that Arthur's supposed relationship to the family of Iaen was through the daughter Eleirch, and that *kenetyl y Arthur o pleit y tat* (l.205) means that the sons of Iaen were 'Arthur's kinsmen on *their* (not "his") father's side' – they were, in fact, his 'in-laws'.

gwyr Kaer Tathal: *Caer Dathyl yn Arfon* was the chief *llys* of Math fab Mathonwy, PKM 67, 10; 251. Ifor Williams favoured as the site the remote Iron Age settlement of Tre'r Ceiri, difficult of access, on the summit of the mountain Yr Eifl above Clynnog Fawr, west of Caernarfon; similarly W. J. Gruffydd, *Math fab Mathonwy*, 343–4. Cynddelw alludes to *ardal caer dathal* in his *marwnad* to Owain Gwynedd, H 89,21. For the name *Tathal* see n. on *Tathal Twyll Goleu* l.177 above.

206–13. **meibion Kaw**: on *Kaw* (of Prydein=*Prydyn*) see n. to l. 647 below, and TYP 301–3. Nineteen sons are listed in this passage, and one more is added – *Gwarthegyt*, in l.1107. Some of the names given here correspond to the names of the twenty sons and one daughter listed as *Plant Kaw o Dwrkelyn* in *Bonedd yr Arwyr* (EWGT 85). In some instances better forms of the names are preserved in the latter text; see also B xviii (1960), 242. Some of the names are obviously farcical: with **Dirmyc** 'Slander' l.206, (cf. *Dirmig* (*corneu*) in EWGT 85, lists 2 and 3); **Etmic** 'fame' l.206; **ac Ouan** l.207 should perhaps be emended to *a Gouan* (as emended Mab. 101); **Connyn** 'Stalk'; **Mabsant** 'saint's son' l.208; **Llwybyr** 'Path'; **Coch** 'Red' l.209; **Ardwyat** 'Protector, Sustainer' l.210 (cf. l.186 above). With **Angawd** l.207 cf. *Bangar mab Kaw* in *Englynion y Clyweit*, B iii, 13 (39). Others of the names are slightly more identifiable: according to the 12th.-cent. Life of Gildas by Caradoc of Llancarfan, the saint's father *Nau* (*leg. Cau*) *rex Scotiae* had twenty-four sons, but only two of these, *Gildas* and *Hueil*, are named. The earlier 9th.-cent. Breton Life by Vitalis of Ruys gives *Mailocus* as one of the brothers of Gildas, and this name evidently corresponds to **Meilic mab Kaw**, l.209–10, as does *Egreas* to **Ergyryat** in line (see edn. in Hugh Williams (ed.) *Gildas*, 326). For *Caw* as the progenitor of a family of saints cf. TYP nos. 81, 96.

211. **Gildas mab Kaw**: the most famous of the sons of Caw (see above) is Gildas, the 6th.-cent. Welsh/Breton saint and historian, of

whom two *Vitae* have been preserved: Vita I by Vitalis, and Vita II by Caradoc of Llancarfan. According to Vita I: *Beatus Gildas Arecluta fertilissima regione oriundus patre Cauno nobilissimo et catholico viro genitus* (ed. Hugh Williams, *Gildas*, 322). The Lives of Cadoc and of David also name *Gildas Cau filius*, (VSB 84–6, 152, etc.; cf. TWS 135–40).

212. **Calcas mab Kaw**: this appears to be a borrowing of the name *Kalchas* in the Iliad (strangely, however, this name is not included in the Welsh version of *Dares Phrygius* or in HRB). Alternatively, the name may be independent: it appears as *Kalchaw* in *Englynion y Clyweit* (B iii, 15), a form corroborated by the rhyme, and further corroborated by *Galchaw* in the list of the sons of Caw in EWGT 85 (3), 14.

Hueil mab Kaw: the oldest son and heir of Caw, according to both the Lives of Gildas (he is named *Cuillus* in Vita I). Evidently the author of *Culhwch* had inherited parallel traditions about Hueil to those which are found in the two Lives of Gildas, especially Vita II. The phrase *nyd asswynwys eiroet yn llaw arglwyd* 'he never submitted to a lord's hand' ll.212–13, is closely paralleled by Caradoc's words *nulli regi obedivit, nec etiam Arthuro* (Hugh Williams, *Gildas*, 402). But if indebted to Caradoc's Vita, the phrase must post-date *c*.1130. For the meaning of *asswyno* see on l.175 above. Lines 259–60 below refer to the enmity between Hueil and Arthur, and in Caradoc's Life (op. cit, 402) it is claimed that Arthur killed Hueil in the island of *Minau* (that is, the Isle of Man, unless this means in *Manau Gododdin*). Giraldus Cambrensis also knew of the story (*Descr. Cam.* ii, 2, trans. Thorpe, 259), and states that Gildas denounced his fellow-Britons in the way he did because of his anger at Arthur's having killed Hueil. He adds that Gildas threw into the sea many books in which he praised the Britons, and told of Arthur's achievements. Hueil mab Caw is included in TYP no.21, *Tri thaleithyawc Cat* (in the Early Version only). For further refs. see TYP 408–10, and Thomas Jones, 'Chwedl Hueil fab Caw ac Arthur' in *Astudiaethau Amrywiol a gyflwynir i Syr Thomas Parry-Williams*, ed. Thomas Jones (Gwasg Prifysgol Cymru, 1968), 48–66. The author concludes that a story about Hueil and Arthur was in circulation at least by the 11th. cent.

214. **Samson Uinsych**: 'S. Dry-Lip'. Samson is listed as one of the

sons of Kaw in EWGT 85(3)8, and this suggests that his name may have been misplaced, and inadvertently omitted from the list of Kaw's sons in *Culhwch*. Yet the name of St Samson would have been well known as that of the early founder of the cathedral of Dol in Brittany, and St Samson was a saint who had no original connection with Kaw or his family. His *Vita* may be as old as the 7th cent. (a later version is preserved in LL 6–24). Samson also figures in the *Vita Iltuti*, VSB 214–16, and the name Samson occurs among the witnesses to a charter affixed to the *Vita Cadoci*, VSB 132,12. On Samson cf. TWS 115–20.

Teliessin Penn Beird: from an early date the poet Taliesin was presented as a fictional character, as in PKM 44,26. For discussion see Ifor Williams, *Chwedl Taliesin*, and M. Haycock 'Preiddeu Annwn and the Figure of Taliesin', SC xviii/xix, 53. Taliesin is the only one of the Cynfeirdd to be named in *Culhwch*.

215. **Manawedan (R: *Mamawydan*) mab Llyr**: Manawydan is a mythical character, familiar from the *Mabinogi*, who is named also in *Pa Gur* (p. xxxv l.10 above), and in TYP nos.8 and 67. Manawydan has frequently been associated with the Ir. *Manannán mac Lir*, a god connected with the sea. The relation between them is far from clear, however, and a recent view expressed by J. T. Koch (CMCS 14 (1987), 20) is that the figure of Manawydan derives from a long and independent British tradition, and one which has merely been 'assimilated' to that of Manannán mac Lir. On the form of the name see Ifor Williams, B iii, 49; TYP 441–3.

Llary mab Casnar Wledic: *Llary* 'generous'; *casnar* 'hero, lord'; for *Gwledic* see n. to *Kyledon Wledic*, l.1 above. *Casnar Wledic*, father of *Gloyw Walltlydan* (an eponym of Gloucester) is named in PKM 27, 25. Cf. also *Llara m. Kasnar Wledic m. Gloyw gwlat lydan*, EWGT 39,3 (in the genealogy of Madog ap Maredudd); *Llara uab Kasnar Wledic* BR 19,26 (= RM 160,2).

216. **Sberin (R: *Ysperin*) mab Flergant brenhin Llydaw**: *Flergant* was identified by Loth (Mab. 1, 29 and 209n) with *Alan Fyrgan*, or Alan IV, Duke of Brittany, an enemy and subsequently an ally of William the Conqueror (whose daughter he married) and of Henry 1. He died in 1119 (see TYP 270–1). He was therefore an important contemporary figure, who appears also in TYP no.30 and in ByS (EWGT 63, no. 58). L. Fleuriot explained the epithet *Fergant* as

a compd. of *ffer* 'strong, brave' and *cant* 'circle', used figuratively to denote 'complete, perfect' (EC xi, 139). He notes also that Alan Fergant is the last Breton ruler to have borne a Breton epithet. See further TYP cxii–cxv, 270–1; TYP(2) 528; Tatlock, *Legendary History*, 195. Idris Foster suggested that Alan's son *(Y)sperin* could possibly be identified with *Brian fitz Count*, Lord of Abergavenny in 1119 (HW 443), and a prominent figure in the reign of Stephen (see F. M. Stenton, *First Century of English Feudalism* (Oxford, 1932), 28n.). He is the *Brianus filius comitis* of LL 93,8. According to the *Anglo-Saxon Chronicle* (E Text, ed. Whitelock *et al.*, 193) in the year 1127, Brian son of Alan Fergant accompanied Henry I's daughter Maud on her journey to Normandy for her wedding to the Count of Anjou's son.

216–17. **Saranhon mab Glythwyr**: with the patronymic cf. *glithuir (glythfyr)* 'hell, abyss'; attested elsewhere only in LlDC 5,71,140, GPC 1414. Cf. *Glythmyr Ledewic* 1009.

217. **Llawr eil Erw**: *Llawr* 'single, pre-eminent'; as a n. it denotes a champion who fought alone in the front of the army, CA 107. Cf. TYP no.15 *Teir llyghes Gynniweir* ('Three Roving Fleets;) . . . *Lly(n)ghes Llawr mab Eiryf*, and n. TYP 419. *Erw* 'acre': possible emendations are *Eiryf*, as in the triad, and *Erim* (as in ll.233–5 below). For *eil* see on *Dalldaf eil Kimin Cof*, ll.184–5 above.

Anynnawc: (R: *Annyannawc*) from *anian*(?) 'nature, disposition'.

Menw mab Teirgwaed: see n. on l.199 above.

218. **Gwynn mab Nwywre**: a repetition of the name, see n. on l. 181 above.

Fflam mab Nwywre: *fflam* 'flame'; Lat. *flamma*.

219. **Gereint mab Erbin**: a hero of south-west Britain in the late 6th cent.; better known from the romance which bears his name *Chwedl Gereint fab Erbin* (WM 385–451 = GER). This tale is more closely related to *Culhwch ac Olwen* than either of its companion tales *Owein* and *Peredur*: see introduction, p. xl. But the hero *Gereint* was commemorated at an earlier date than this story in the poem LlDC no. 21 (ed. B. F. Roberts, Ast.H. 286–96), which describes Gereint's prowess at the battle of *Llongborth* (?Langport in Somerset), where Gereint was supported by Arthur's followers.

Thus Gereint is shown to have been brought into the orbit of Arthur at an early date. (On the poem see P. Sims-Williams, AoW 46–9, and Thomas Jones, 'Early Evolution', 15–16). The poem and the romance together indicate that in the medieval tradition known in south Wales, Gereint was regarded as having been a hero of Devon-Cornwall: more than one of the early rulers of Dumnonia did in fact bear the name of *Gerent*. In TYP no. 14 *Gereint ab Erbin* is described as one of the *Tri Llynghesawg* 'Fleet-owners' or 'Seafarers' of Britain. For further refs. to Gereint see TYP 355–60. *Erbin* appears in early genealogies (EWGT 45, 10 and 11) as ancestor of 'at least one branch of the ruling dynasty of Dyfed', as R. G. Gruffydd has shown (SC xiv/xv, 96), and it is perhaps significant that in ByS Erbin's father is named as *Custennin Gorneu*, a name apparently remembered in *Custennin (heusawr)* (l. 435 below) and in the name of his son *Goreu* (l. 811). In GER Geraint's father Erbin ap Custennin is portrayed as Arthur's uncle (WM 409, 34–5) which implies a similar pedigree to that in ByS, and one in which Erbin and Uthyr were brothers, both sons of Custennin. *Din Gereint* was the original name for the town and castle of Cardigan (see M. Williams, EC ii (1937), 219–22).

Ermit mab Erbin: unknown; see n. on l. 220.

Dyuel mab Erbin: *Dyuel/Dywel ab erbin* is referred to twice in LlDC 1, 19–20 and ibid. 18, 81, where his grave is said to be at Caeo, Dyfed. A. O. H. Jarman has argued (Ym. M. Th. 18, 33 etc.) that the *Erbin* here referred to was a ruler of Dyfed, and cannot be identified with the *Erbin* who was father of Gereint, and who belonged to Devon (see n.). This Erbin was a son of Aircol Lawhir, EWGT 45, 12; cf. the 'head of Erbin's line' referred to in the poem *Etmic Dinbych* (THSC 1940, 66–83; BWP 163). Even if such a distinction can be made, it was clearly unknown to the author of *Culhwch*, who presents the three sons of Erbin in l. 219 as though they were brothers.

220. **Gwynn mab Ermit a Chyndrwyn mab Ermit**: *Ermid* 'honourable, famed'. It seems to be implied by l. 219 that these too are descendants of Erbin. But *Cyndrwyn* is known elsewhere as the father of Cynddylan of Powys; see CLlH xi. In B xxix, 526–7, and in her *Early Welsh Saga Poetry*, 125–6, Jenny Rowland has ingeniously compared this entry with Harl. Gen. 24 (EWGT 12, 24)

which relates to a royal line of Powys (see Bartrum's note, ibid. 128): *Selim m. Iouab m. Guitgen m. Bodug m. Carantinail (= Caranfael?) m. Cerennior m. Ermic* – where *Ermic* = *Ermit* reflects the common confusion of *c* and *t* in Insular script. *Cyndrwyn mab Ermit* may thus provide a further link in the lost genealogy of this Powysian dynasty. For another link cf. *Gviavn ap Kyndrvyn* TYP 60.

220. Hyueid Unllenn: 'H. One-Mantle'. The name is repeated in BR 19,2 (= RM 159,11). The name *Hyueid* occurs several times elsewhere; *Hyueid Hir* CA 56; *Heueid Hen* PKM 12,23; *Hyueid ap Bleidic* TYP no.68. The latter may be equated with king *Hemeid*, a 9th-cent. ruler of Dyfed, referred to by Asser, who oppressed St David's, and died in 892 (HW 262, 327–30). With *Unllen(n)* cf. the epithet *Unbais* 'one robe' cited B iii, 43.

221. Eidon Uawrurydic: 'E the Magnanimous' is elsewhere unknown.

221–2. Gormant mab Ricca: the name is repeated, see l. 198 above. If *gor* + *mant* = 'Great Mouth(?)' or *gormant* 'excess, superfluity, splendid' (GPC 1491). Cf. the name *Gorlois* 'Great Warrior', husband of *Eigr/Igerna*, the mother of Arthur (HRB viii,19 = BD 136; *Gwrlois* RBB 162). *Gorlois* is a Cornish name; see B. F. Roberts, B xxv, 278, and – on the formation – T. Jones, B xiii, 74–5 (n. on *anorles*). *Gormant* could equally well be Cornish (with the same prefix appearing in the names of father and son). This relationship seems to be implied by the words *brawd y Arthur o barth y uam*.

222–3. Pennhynef Kernyw y tat: Gorlois was *dux Cornubiae/yarll kernyw* in HRB and BD: hence Gormant would have been half-brother to Arthur through *Igerna/Eigr*, the wife of Gorlois and mother of both. These words could therefore possibly reflect a genuine Cornish tradition, drawn upon independently by Geoffrey and the author of *Culhwch*, even though both W and R state unequivocally that Gormant was *mab Ricca*. *Ricca* occurs as a var. of the name of *Rita Gawr* (Cy 27,126; cf. CF 478 n.). But it may be more relevant – if wholly conjectural – to quote the name on the 10th-cent. inscribed stone at Penzance in Cornwall, which Macalister read as *Regis ricati crux* 'The Cross of King Ricatus' (CIIC ii, 181).

Pennhynef Kernyw: according to the triad TYP no.1 *Tri Lleithiclwyth Ynys Prydein*, there was a *Pen Hyne(i)f* at each of the 'Tribal Thrones' at which Arthur was *Penteyrned* – at Mynyw, Penn Ryoned, and Celliwig in Cornwall. For *hynaf, henyf* 'elder, lord, forebear' etc. see TYP 2–3, GPC 1974. In spite of uncertainty as to its status, it seems not unreasonable to equate *Pennhynef Kernyw* with *dux Cornubiae/yarll Kernyw*. Ifor Williams's emendation of *eineuyd* in PT ii,3 to *heneuyd* (PT 29n.; TYP(2)530) indicates that this title could be used of a ruler of the status of Urien Rheged himself. Cf. n. to l.235 below.

223. **Llawurodet Uaruawc**: 'Ll. the Bearded'. Either *llaw* 'hand' or *llaw* 'small' + *brodedd* < *brawd* as in *cymrodedd* 'concord, agreement'; see CA 286, GPC 770. This form is corroborated by other occurrences of the name: *Llauuroded uaruauc* EWGT 62 (54); ibid. 66 (85), 118 (10,b); *buwch Llawuroded Varvawc* TYP 46; *Kyllell Llawfrodedd farfawc* in Y XIII Thlws (TYP 240, EC x, 447; LlC v, 57–8). The letters *n* and *u* are often barely distinguishable in both W and R; cf. the n. on *Gliui/Glini* l.831 below. In the texts of Y XIII Thlws the forms of the epithet vary between *varchawc/varvawc* (cf. on *Dillus Varvawc/Varchawc* l.700 below). With the popularity of *barf* 'beard' in epithets cf. *Kynyr Keinuarvawc* l.264, *Vchdryt Uaryf Draws* l.327, and the name in the following line.

223–4. **Nodawl Uaryf Trwch**: 'N. Cut-Beard'. W and R both read *Uaryf twrch* 'boar-beard', which is paralleled by *Gurgant Varyftvrch* BD 39 (cf. B xxv, 284). The older form of this epithet is G. *Barmbtruch* in Harl. Gen 18 (EWGT 11, 18) and this indicates that *trwch* should be restored as the correct form of the epithet in both cases (as pointed out in Mab. 276).

224. **Berth mab Kado**: *Berth* 'fair, rich, valuable' (as in l.430 below). *Cado* occurs as a var. of *Cadwy* mab Gereint; see n. on l.182 above, and cf. n. to *Kaw o Prydein* l.647 below.

Reidwn mab Beli: cf. *Reidwn uab Eli atuer* l.1114–15 below. *Beli* is a name of frequent occurrence in the genealogies (see EWGT index); ex. *Beli Mawr*, a mythical ancestor-deity claimed by many royal dynasties in Wales and the 'Old North' (TYP 281–3).

224–5. **Iscouan Hael** (also l.1115 below). With *Hael* 'Generous' cf. *Morgant Hael* l.256 below, and n.

225. **Yscawin mab Panon**: (also *Iscawin uab P*, l.1118 below). *Ysgafn* 'light'. Cf. *Kysceint mab Banon* in the poem *Pa Gur* (p. xxxv l.8 above) and G 266 on Kysceint; cf AoW 64, n.31. The form, *Yscawin/Iscawin* in CO is evidence against emending *Kysceint* in the poem to *Kysteint* < *Constantius* (as proposed Ast.H. 300 and 304 n.).

Moruran eil Tegit: *Morfran* 'Great Raven'. The name of his father, *Tegit Voel*, derives from the name of Llyn Tegid, or Bala lake, as told in the mythical tale *Hanes Taliesin*, first recorded in the 16th cent. by Elis Gruffydd. A version similar to his is the basis of the translation by Lady Charlotte Guest, Mab. 263–85. Text and translation (from another version) by P. K. Ford, EC xiv (1974–5), 451–9. For general discussion of the story see Ifor Williams, *Chwedl Taliesin*; LEWP 60–1; TYP 463–4; P. K. Ford, *The Mabinogi*, 159–64. The ref. here to Morfran, together with those in TYP nos. 24 and 41, prove that he was known to tradition as a warrior at a considerably earlier date than that which is assigned to the *Hanes Taliesin*. On *eil* see n. on ll.184–5 above.

226. **y araf**: *araf* 'weapon'. The basic form is *arf*, but between *r* and *f* an epenthetic vowel developed, as it did in other groups of consonants; cf. GMW 12–13. This indistinct vowel in MW took the form *y*, but there was throughout a tendency for it to become assimilated to the preceding vowel, as has happened in this instance. In ModW the vowel is not represented in the written language, but it can usually be detected in the spoken form. Cf. *haraf* below.

228. **yGhamlan**: the triad of the three men who escaped from the battle of Camlan looks like a farcical invention, rather than a traditional triad, see TYP xcii. It does not appear in either of the two main collections, although the battle of Camlan does receive mention elsewhere in TYP. The allusion here to the battle reflects an underlying tradition, which persisted among the poets, of Camlan as a ferocious, tragic, and ill-fated contest which had been brought about for frivolous or insufficient reasons – a view which persisted under various forms throughout Arthurian romance. The earliest allusion to Camlan is found in *Ann. Cam.* 537: *Gueith cam lann in qua arthur et medraut corruerunt*. (On this ref. see T. Jones, 'Early Evolution', 6 = B xvii (1958), 238.) The traditional site of the battle is impossible to determine: *Camlan* may be derived from

Camboglanna 'crooked bank' and it has been frequently located at the site of the Roman fort of this name at Birdoswald on Hadrian's Wall, near a double bend of the River Irthing (see K. Jackson, ALMA 5, and refs. cited). But OW *Camglann* is nowhere attested as a name for Birdoswald, and *Camlann* in *Ann Cam* suggests that the second element is equally likely to be *lann* 'enclosure' as *glan* 'bank'. There are many other 'crooked banks' to be found throughout Britain, and Geoffrey of Monmouth had no hesitation in locating the battle on the river *Camel* or *Camblanus* in Cornwall (HRB xi, 2 = BD 184). However, there can be no certainty that this identification antedates the HRB. See further O. J. Padel, 'Geoffrey of Monmouth and Cornwall', CMCS 8 (1984), 13–14. A tradition that there were ᐧ ry few survivors (three or seven) from this disastrous battle has come down under various forms. With the seven escapers cf. the refrain in *Preiddeu Annwn: Namyn seith ny dyrreith o Gaer Sidi*, and the variants of this motif cited by M. Haycock, SC xviii–xix (1983–4), 68; TWS 201–3.

rac y haccred: 'because he was so ugly'; *rac* with the equative has causal meaning; cf. GMW 42–3, also l.229 below *rac y decket* 'because he was so fair'.

228. **Sande Pryt Angel**: 'S. Angel's Form'. With the name *Sandef* cf. LL 279,7. Elsewhere this name is found among the sons of Llywarch Hen, CLlH i,37c, and in a number of instances in early genealogies (see EWGT index). Tudur Aled recalls *Sandde . . . Bryd angel, byrr i dynged* (GTA i, 355, 63–4).

230. **engyl**: this form is usually pl. of *angel* 'angel', but here it is clearly meant to be sing.

canhorthwy: 'help', a var. of *cynhorthwy*. Note that *a* alternates with *y* before a nasal in an unaccented syllable; GMW 2.

Cynwyl Sant: the patron saint of *Cynwyl Gaeo* and *Cynwyl Elfed*, Dyfed; see O. Jones, *Cymru* i, 260, 367. Lewys Glyn Cothi makes several allusions to the saint (for refs. see G 263). It is somewhat surprising to find St Cynwyl listed among the Giants of Wales by Siôn Dafydd Rhys, Cy 27 (1917), 134. Yet something of his sanctity survives in the allusion: *Ac yghwlad Caer Bhyrdhin yn Cynwil Gayo ydh oedh Cawr a elwid Cynwil Gawr, a dyna yr achaws, agatbhydh paham y gelwir y lhe eto Cynwil, a gwr dwywawl ydoedh hwnnw.*

Cynwyl's name is preserved also in *Lann cinuil*, LL 275, 17–18. Otherwise little is known of him. The influence of Iolo Morganwg is evident in the allusions to Cynwyl in LBS ii, 275–7.

y trydygwr: for *y trydyd gwr* 'the third man', or rather 'one of the three men'. Note the loss of *-d* [đ] in *trydy*; it is frequently lost in final position, GMW 10. Cf. l.545 *trydydyt*, and OW *triti* in the Computus, B iii (1927), 261–2.

232. **Hengroen**: 'Old Skin'.

233. **Uchdryt mab Erim**: with *Uchdryt* cf. l.186 above; on *Erim* see on l.235 below.

234. **Henbedestyr**: 'Old Walker'.

234–5. **Scilti Scawntroet**: (R: *Yscawntroet*), **Yscawntroet** 239. 'S. Lightfoot'. With prosthetic Y- cf. *Yscawin* l.225 above, and GMW 10–12. This name corresponds to that of the Irish hero *Caoilte* in the cycle of tales relating to Fionn mac Cumhaill. His epithet *ysgafntroed* is a half-translation of Ir. *cos-luath* 'swift-footed'. Both name and epithet can be traced back to the 10th-cent. tale 'Finn and Gráinne', ed. and trans. ZCP i, 458. Cf. G. Murphy, *Duanaire Finn* iii,lix; Idris Foster, 'Irish Influence', 34; P. Sims-Williams, B xxix (1982), 610–14.

235. **Erim**: this patronymic has no counterpart in Irish, where *Caoilte* is on all occasions *mac Ronáin*. As Sims-Williams points out (loc. cit., 611) this name does not appear to be Irish, in spite of Kuno Meyer's attempt to associate it with Ir. *erimm* 'course, career' (THSC (1895–6), 73). Sims-Williams suggests the possibility of miscopying, either of the rare name *Eiryf*, TYP 341, or of *he(i)nyf/henyf* 'Elder', etc. (see n. to *Pennhynef* l. 222 above), with confusion of *n* and *r*. Cf. as in *Enim* for *Heinif* in several instances in LL, as is pointed out in Wendy Davies (ed.), *The Llandaff Charters*, 163.

trywyr: 'Three men', consisting of *try* 'three' + *gwyr* 'men'; cf. also l.761. Note the lenition of the n. in a compd. after a numeral which is not normally followed by lenition; similarly in *pumwyr, seithwyr, nawwyr*; cf. TC 133. Note also in these instances the pl. form of the nn., whereas the sing. is usual with numerals. (For some similar instances of the pl. with numerals see GMW 47.)

236. **ny chauas eiroet a'e kyfrettei o dyn**: 'he never found any man who could keep up with him'; cf. GMW 68.

239. **anoethach a uei bellach no hynny**: 'not to mention (anything) that would be further than that'; *anoethach* is comparative of *anoeth* 'strange, difficult'; GMW 39–40. Cf. l.420 below.

241. **am gwypei**: as it stands, this reading is not satisfactory: one would expect the prt. *y* between *am* and *gwypei*.

241–2. **tra uei**: in MW, unlike ModW, *tra* 'while' is followed by lenition, as here; cf. l.276 *uei*; l.249 hyt tra *uu*.

244. **anoethach torri rac y yskafned**: 'let alone break, because he was so light'. Cf. l.239 above, and l.420 below.

245–50. **Teithi Hen mab Gwynhan a weryskynnwys mor y kyuoeth**: this is one of several allusions in medieval Welsh sources to the inundation of low-lying parts of the coastal areas, from the Conwy estuary to Cardigan bay. The best known of these are the allusions in *Mabinogi Branwen*, PKM 39,12 (= Mab 33) where a phrase closely corresponding to this is used *pan oreskynnwys y weilgi y tyrnassoed* 'when the ocean conquered the kingdoms' cf. also ByS (EWGT 60), no. 40 *Seithennin vrenhin o Vaes Gwydno a oresgynwys mor eu tir*, and the poem on the submersion of Cantref y Gwaelod, LlDC no. 39 (see n. on l.618 below on *Gwydneu Garanhir*). Thomas Jones discovered yet another allusion to the inundations in a Lat. triad, evidently translated from Welsh, which is found as a gloss on the 13th-cent. *Cronica de Wallia* in Exeter Cathedral MS 3514, 522; see his 'Triawd Lladin ar y Gorlifiadau', B xii (1948), 79–83. One of the three kingdoms which were inundated was *Regnum Thewthy hen mab Guinnan (sic) brenin kaerrihog. Istud regnum uocabatur tunc Heneys Teithy hen, que fuit inter Meneuiam et Hyberniam. Nullus ex ea hominum siue iumentonum euasit nisi Theithy Hen solus cum equo suo, postea cunctis diebus uite sue infirmus fuit pro timore.* For discussion and trans. see TYP xc–xci, and on the legends in general F. J. North, *Sunken Cities* (University of Wales Press, 1957), esp. 148. This passage therefore constitutes independent evidence for the tradition alluded to in *Culhwch*, since there can hardly be any direct connection between the two. Thomas Jones rejects any direct connection between the names of *Teithi Hen* and *Seithennin*, as was proposed by W. J. Gruffydd, *Math fab Mathonwy*, 147n. With the epithet *Hen* cf. *Gouynyon Hen* 250, and n. on *Gwrbothu Hen* l.252 below.

248–9. y tyuwys heint yndaw a nychdawt hyt tra uu uyw: cf. *postea cunctis diebus uite sue infirmus fuit pro timore* in the passage quoted in n. to ll.245–50 above.

250. Gwenwynwyn mab Naf: (*in R only; W omits*). A repetition of this name; see n. on l.194 above.

251. gysseuin rysswr Arthur: 'A's foremost champion'.

Llygatrud Emys: 'Red-eyed Stallion'. *Emys* < Lat. *amissus*, < *admissus*, GPC 1211. An old sing. form which came to be used as a pl., and a new sing. *amws* was formed. This is either a farcical name, or *emys* may be a misreading of *emyr* 'lord', as was proposed by Wade-Evans, *Welsh Christian Origins* (Oxford, 1934), 102.

252. Gwrbothu Hen: 'G. the Old'. In some instances *Hen* appears to denote 'ancestor', ex. *Priaf hen vrenhin Tro*, TYP 494. For further exx. see EWGT 226, TYP 432, and cf. *Teithi Hen* l.245 above, *Gouynyon Hen* l.250. In OW orthography *Gwrbothu* represents *Gwrfoddw* (cf. CA 179, n. on *mab Bodw*). His name derives from *Gurvodius (Guruodu, Guoruodu) rex ercy(n)g* LL 161,2; 162,1. According to the reckoning made by Wendy Davies, Gwrfoddw ruled *c.* 610–15, though he was not a member of the main line of the rulers of Ergyng (as was *Peibyaw*, see n. on l.599 below); Wendy Davies, *The Llandaff Charters* 39, 75, 103, 172; ibid. *An Early Welsh Microcosm* (London, 1978), 17–18.

Later in the tale these two alleged 'uncles' of Arthur are slain by the Twrch Trwyth, l.1164.

253. Kuluanawyt mab Goryon: for *cul* 'lean, slender' see n. on *Kulhwch*, l.10 above. *Manawyt* occurs as a variant of *Manaw (Gododdin)*, CA l.35, and as an abbreviation of *Manawydan*, BT 34, 9–10; LlDC 31, 21. But the alternative *manawyd* 'awl' is also possible here. According to a late triad, TYP no.80, *Kulvanawyt Prydein* was the father of *Essyllt Fyngwen* (see n. on l.372 below). The name is traditional, since the 12th-cent. Cynddelw alludes to *Kynon vab kulvanawyd* (H 148,10). See TYP 311–12.

Llennl(l)eawc Vydel: (repeated l.293 below). *Gwyddel* = 'Irishman', but there is no possibility of interpreting *Llenlleawc* as an Ir. name. Alternative derivations are from *llen* 'mantle', and *llên* 'literature' or 'cleric(s)', GPC 2152. Hence *llen(n)lleawc* 'one who reads literature', or else *lleawc* 'death-dealing' – if the word is to be connected with the *lle* in *dileaf, dileu*. This difficult name is discussed by M. Haycock (SC xviii-xix, 70) in connection with the ref. to *cledyf lluchlleawc* in *Preiddeu Annwn*. If there is a connection between these two similar forms, as seems likely, it would be possible for *lleawc*, the element common to both, to have caused the substitution of *llen* in *Culhwch* for the earlier element *lluch* 'flashing'. *Llenllyawc gwydel* (sic) is named in *Englynion y Clyweit* (B iii, 13 (47)), in the group of names taken from *Culhwch*; see introduction p. xl.

253–4. **o Bentir Gamon**: that is Loch Garman in Co. Wexford, the south-western tip of Ireland. Like *Esgeir Oervel* (see n. to l.107) this headland is likely to have been a well-known landmark for seafarers coming from Wales (see Sims-Williams, 'Irish Geography', 417). *Llwch Garmawn en Ywerdon* is cited in HGVK 11,13; *Llwch Garman* in B. y Tywys. (P 20 version), ann. 1168. Wexford was a Scandinavian settlement since the 9th cent.

254. **Dyuynwal Moel**: 'D. the Bald'. *Harl. Gen.* no. 10 (EWGT 10,10) lists *Dumngual moilmut map Garbaniaun* as ancestor of *Morcant map Coledauc*, one of the 'Men of the North'. In the corresponding genealogy in J 20 (EWGT 48 (37)) he appears as *Dyuynwawl m. Carbaniaun.* The name was borrowed from the *Harl. Gen.* (or its equivalent) by Geoffrey of Monmouth, who claims that the 'Molmutine Laws' were established by *Dunuallo molmutius filius clotenis regis Cornubiae* (HRB ii,17). BD 32,11 renders this name as *Dyuynwal Moel Mut* 'D. Bald and Silent' (cf. B xxv, 277). A different tradition is found in some versions of the Welsh Laws, which claims that Dyfnwal Moelmut was responsible for measuring Britain from *Pen Pengwaed* in Cornwall to *Penryn Blathaon* in the North; HDdL 120; D. Jenkins, *Llyfr Colan* (University of Wales Press, 1963), 38–9. On the places mentioned see nn. on ll.106 above and 262 below. BD 35 (= HRB iii,5) substitutes Belinus son of Dyfnwal as the ruler who engineered the chief highways across the length and breadth of Britain.

Dunart brenhin y Gogled: *y Gogled* in *Culhwch* always means the 'Old North' and *Dunart* is the Brittonic equivalent of *Domangart* in

Ir., the name of the grandfather of *Aedán mac Gabráin*, as pointed out by K. Jackson, YB xii, 21. Domangart, with his son Gabrán and his grandson *Aedán* were among the early rulers of Scottish Dál Riada, and Aedán entered early into Welsh tradition as *Aedan Vradawc* 'A. the Wily' (TYP 264–6). Cf. *Ann. Cam.* 558: *Gabran filius Dungart moritur.*

255. Teyrnon Twr Bliant: (R: *T. twryf bliant*). One of the group of twelve characters in *Culhwch* whose names are found in the Four Branches (pp. xxxvii–viii and n.23 above): *Teirnon Twryf Uliant* PKM 22,2. *Teyrnon* < *Tigernonos* 'Great Prince'. His epithet is found here in a more archaic form than in PKM, but appears to have been misunderstood and wrongly divided in both W and R: Ifor Williams explained it as composed of *twrb* (OW form of *twrf*) + *lliant* 'flood, current, sea'; hence 'Roar(Noise) of the Flood-tide', taking the allusion to be to the great inrush of the sea into the Severn estuary, known as the Severn 'bore' (PKM 145–7). With the name cf. the poem *Kadeir Teyr (non)* (BT 34).

a Thecuan Glof: *Cloff* 'Lame'.

256. Gwrdiual mab Ebrei: *diual* = *dyfal* 'diligent, assiduous', etc. + *gor* = intensive prefix. (Ebrew (*-iw*, *-yw*) 'Hebrew' does not appear before the 14th cent.: if this is the meaning intended, it can only be an addition to the text.)

Morgant Hael: 'M. the Generous'. *Morgant* is a very common name in the genealogies (see EWGT index). This prohibits any certain identification: the epithet *Hael* suggests possible confusion with Mordaf *Hael*, one of the *Tri Hael* (TYP no.2). More than one *Morcant* is given among the descendants of *Dumngual Moilmut*, associated with the 'Old North' (see n. on l.254 above). More probably in this context, he may be Morgan ap Athrwys, or *Morgan Mwynfawr*, eponymous founder of Morgannwg in the latter half of the 7th cent. (HW 274; see also Wendy Davies, *The Llandaff Charters*, 76, she suggests he lived *c.* 635–710). *Morgant Mwynfawr* is included (with Arthur) in the triad *Tri Ruduoawc* or 'Red Ravagers', TYP no.20. The same name is given to a brother of Rhydderch Hael, EWGT 89(18). See n. TYP 465–6.

256–7. Gwystyl mab Nwython: *gwystl* 'hostage'. Cf. *Gweir m. Nwython*, TYP 378. For *Nwython* see n. on l.994 below.

257. Run mab Nwython: BD 158,18 *Run uab Noython (= Run map Neton* HRB ix, 12). For *Run map Neithon* see *Harl. Gen.* 4 (= *Run m. Neidaon* in J 20, no. 19) and *Harl. Gen.* 16. From some version of the genealogy Geoffrey of Monmouth adopted this name, and BD in turn derived it from HRB. But it is interesting to find that in these sources *Run mab Nwython/Neithon* appears in a list of the attendants at Arthur's Court, in part based on the Harleian Genealogies, but including names of foreign kings and names of the earls of British cities. This is the only instance in which one of these names corresponds to a name in the Arthurian Court-List in *Culhwch*.

257-8. Lluydeu mab Nwython a Gwydre mab Lluydeu o Wenabwy merch Kaw: with *Gwydre* cf. *Gwydre mab Arthur* l. 1116 below. With *Gwenabwy merch Kaw* cf. *Gwenawy* in the list of *Plant Kaw o Dwrkelyn*, EWGT 85, 3(21).

258-60: On *Kaw* and *Hueil mab Kaw* see nn. on ll. 206, 212, 647.

261. Drem mab Dremidyd: 'Sight son of Seer'. The first in the group of farcical invented names among Arthur's followers; cf. *Clust mab Clustfeinat* (see n.), *Medyr mab Methredydd* etc. and introduction pp. xxxviii, xli. The first two are named together in a poem by Gruffudd Llwyd (1380–1410) – presumably being derived from a written text of *Culhwch*.

a welei: 'who could see'. Note that the imperf. in Welsh can denote possibility; cf. GMW 110, also l. 410 below *gwelei, gwelynt*; l. 41 *gwelynt*.

Celli Wic yGherniw: *celli* 'grove' + *gwig* 'forest'. *Celliwig* 'forest grove' is the name of Arthur's court in Cornwall both in *Culhwch* and in the Triads, as well as in the tradition known to the poets from the 12th. cent. onwards; see TYP 3–4; G 128. There have been a number of suggestions as to the location of Celliwig. Killibury hill-fort or 'Kelly Rounds' in the parish of Egloshayle has been the most popular of these until recently, when Oliver Padel drew attention to the name *Thomas de Kellewik* in an entry in an Assize Roll relating to the hundred of Penwith for the year 1302 (*Cornish Archaeology* 16, 115–21, and see now AoW 236–7). Though this is not conclusive, it nevertheless constitutes substantial evidence in favour of equating Celliwig with *Penn Pengwaed* (= Penwith, see n. to l. 106) at any rate in the mind of the narrator of the tale. It would mean that Culhwch was in fact speaking from Arthur's court at Celliwig, when he threatened to give the great shout which would be heard from the furthest extremity of Cornwall to a point in the extreme north and to 'Eskeir Oeruel' in western Ireland. This might well be deduced from ll. 104–7 above, yet the location of Arthur's court to which Culhwch came is nowhere actually stated. Probably the exact location of Celliwig was as nebulous in the minds of Welsh poets and storytellers as were the places in Ireland and in the north of Scotland which are cited in the same passage. There is a marked contrast between the detailed localization of the places in south and west Wales through which the hunt for the Twrch Trwyth passed, and the total absence of directions when the Twrch crossed over to Cornwall. Under the influence of HRB and of the *Brut*, Celliwig was displaced by Caerleon-on-Usk in BR and in the three romances. For another and different Celliwig, in Gwynedd, see M. Richards 'Arthurian Onomastics', THSC (1969), 265.

262. **Penn Blathaon ym Predein**: (R: *Prydein*). A promontory in the far north of Scotland, perhaps John O'Groats, or Dunnet Head in Caithness; see TYP 228, 233–4. The tract *Enweu Ynys Prydein* states that the length of Britain from *Pen(ryn) Blathaon ym Brydein* to *Pen(ry)n Penwaed* in Cornwall (cf. l.106) is 900 miles. *Predein/Prydein* in these instances stands for *Prydyn* < *Priteni*, that is Pictland, the north of Scotland. The two forms *Prydyn/Prydein* are constantly confused in medieval Welsh texts; see AP 21–2; K. Jackson, 'Prydein : Prydyn', *Scottish Historical Review* xxxiii (1954), 16–18, and E. P. Hamp, B xxx (1983), 289–90. See further n. to *Kaw o Brydein* (= *Prydyn*) on l.647 below.

263. **Eidoel mab Ner**: (R: *Eidyol m. Ner*). Presumably he is to be identified with *Eidoel mab Aer* (l.694), though his presence in the Court-List is hardly consistent with the fact that Eiddoel appears among the *anoethau* as a prisoner yet to be released (ll.825–37 below). *Ner* could however represent the name *Ynyr* (as in *y deu Ynyr*, l.119), since in TYP no. 69 *Idon ap Ner* is to be equated with *Idon mab Ynyr Gwent* (ibid. no. 42); see n. TYP p. 412. *Idon rex filius Ynyr Gwent* is named in LL 121,7, etc. On the refs. to him see Wendy Davies, *The Llandaff Charters*, 40,174, where it is suggested that the son of Ynyr was ruler of Gwent Uwchcoed in the years *c.* 595–600, and that he was a contemporary of Gwrfoddw of Erging (see n. to *Gwrbothw Hen*, l.252 above).

Gluydyn Saer: 'G. the Craftsman'. Cf. ll. 1124–5 *Gwlydyn saer, pensaer y Arthur*.

264. **Ehangwen**: 'Fair and Spacious'. There is no other reference to the name of Arthur's hall, but cf. ll. 328–9 below. On *gwyn/gwen* in the names of Arthur's royal possessions, see n. on l. 159 above.

Kynyr Keinuaruawc: 'K. fair-Bearded'. On the name see TYP 307; THSC (1969), 257; and cf. n. on *Kei* l. 134 above. *Kynyr* < *Cunorix*, a name found on an inscription at Wroxeter, (B xxiv, 420n.), The name *Cynyr* is listed in LL 232,13. Kei's father is named here and in TYP no. 21, but elsewhere is almost unknown, and the epithet *Keinuaruawc* seems to be limited to *Culhwch* and to the early version of TYP. Cynddelw couples the names of *Cynyr* and *Cei*, H 95,5.

269. **na mawr na bychan uo**: 'be it large or small'; GMW 232.

270. **na rac vyneb na thra'e geuyn**: 'neither in front nor behind him'; *tra'e geuyn* consists of the old prep. *tra* 'over, beyond' + infixed pron. sing. 3 masc. + the n. *keuyn (= cefn* 'back'). Later, an impersonal form *tracheuyn* developed, and was employed as an adv. with the meaning 'again'; GMW 210.

271. **ny feit neb dwuyr a than**: 'no one suffers water and fire'; *peit* is indic. pres. sing. 3 of *peidyaw*, and means 'suffers'; cf. GMW 165n. It comes from Lat. *patior*. Later it came to mean 'to stop, cease', and in ModW it is commonly employed to express a negative meaning with the vn: *peidio â mynd* 'not to go'; cf. CFG 60–3. The ability here attributed to Cei, of enduring extremities of heat and cold, is one of the magical attributes pertaining to one of the Helpers or 'Extraordinary Companions' in the folk-tale type to which the 'Giant's Daughter' belongs; see introduction p. xxvi. and Stith Thompson, *The Folktale* 54. Cei's remarkable heat is again listed among his *cyneddfau* in ll. 389–93 below.

272–3. **ny byd gwasanaythur na swydvr mal ef**: the *swydwr llys* was one of the officers of the King's Court, according to the Law of Hywel Dda. His function was to carry food to the court and to distribute it. With ref. to this passage see n. on *Kei*, l. 134 above.

274. **Henwas**: Cf. *Henwas Edeinawc*, ll. 233–4 above.

Gallgoic: (R: *Gwallgoyc*). Cf. *Gallcoit Gouynnyat* ll. 187–8 above.

274–5. un arall: 'another companion'(?).

275. trychant tei: 'three hundred houses'. The sing. of the n. is usually found with the numeral, but there are exx. in MW where the pl. is used, as here. Cf. GMW 47.

or: 'if', consisting of *o* (GMW 240–1) + *ry* (ibid. 166–70). This is the explanation usually offered and accepted, but it is hardly satisfactory: *ry* is usually followed by lenition, as is -*r* when it is part of a compd. such as *neur* (*neu* + *ry*) as in *neur gauas ef enw* 'he has got a name', PKM 80, 23. *Or*, however, is never followed by lenition, which leads one to suspect that -*r* should be explained in some other way.

277. Berwynn mab Kyrenyr: cf. *Barrivendi* in an inscription at Llandawke, Carms, cited by D. Ellis Evans (EC xiii (1972), 178; also the mountain name *Berwyn*. With *Kyrenyr* cf. LL 240,11 *cerennhir* (name of a bishop).

278. y gelwir: 'it is called'; *y* probably consists of the prt. *y* + the infixed pron. 3 sing. masc. *y*; GMW 55.

Osla Gyllelluawr: 'O. Great Knife'. In BR 8,25 (= RM 150, 24) this character is transposed to become Arthur's Saxon enemy. M. Richards suggests (BR 46) that this is owing to a recollection of the name of Offa, 8th-cent. King of Mercia, and builder of the dyke between England and Wales which bears his name. The name appears as *Offa Kyllellvawr vrenin Lloegr* in ByS no.71 (EWGT 64).

279. Bronllauyn Uerllydan: 'Breast-Blade Short Broad' – his dagger. (For its ultimate fate see ll. 1194–6 below.)

282. Teir ynys Prydein a'e Their Rac Ynys: 'The Three Islands of Britain and her Three Adjacent Islands'. This formula, which recurs in l.368 (= R: *teir ynys y Kedyrn*) and in l.1057, derives ultimately from a phrase which is first recorded in HB ch. 9 (ed. Dumville 63; ed. Loth, 151–2): *tres magnas insulas (Britannia) habet ... insula Gueith ... Eubonia uel Manau ... Orch. Sic in proverbio dicitur antiquo, quando de iudicibus et regibus sermo fit 'iudicavit Brittaniam cum tribus insulis'.* In *Enweu Ynys Prydein* (TYP 228) this is rendered as *Ynys Brydein ... teir prif Rac ynys yssyd idi ... Mon a Manaw ac Ynys Weir* (R. Vaughan emends the last to *Ynys Weith*). Prydydd y Moch addresses Rhodri ab Owain as *o ynys brydein briawd* *ureint/ ae their rac ynys rec hofeint* (H 271,7–8). In *Culhwch* we find that *Ynys Prydein* is triplicated, just as it is in the praise-poem to Hywel ap Goronwy (LIDC 22,20) *Teir racynis ar teir inis*, and again in the P 50 version of EYP, which has *Teir ynys Prydein: Lloegyr a Chymry a'r Alban*. This division goes back to Geoffrey of Monmouth's division of Britain between the three sons of Brutus – Locrinus, Camber, and Albanactus, HRB ii,1. Thomas Jones showed in B xvii (1958), 268–9 that *ynys* can mean 'land, kingdom', and he quoted examples in which *ynys* renders Lat. *regnum* and Eng. 'realme', as in the passage quoted in n. to ll. 245–50 above, where *Regnum Thewthy Hen* and *Heneys Teithy Hen* are used interchangeably. According to this interpretation *Teir Ynys Prydein* would mean 'The Three Realms of Britain', and Geoffrey may have had in mind the phrase *tres magnas insulas habet* in HB, when he detailed Brutus's division of the island between his three sons. But the earliest examples show that the original formula was 'The Island of Britain and her Three Adjacent Islands', though it seems that the *teir racynys* had the effect of causing *Ynys Prydein* to be similarly triplicated, following a process which is very familiar in Celtic mythology and early literature (cf. TYP 155, and introduction p. xxxviii). As P. Mac Cana has phrased it 'triplication may have had an intensifying force, and it may also convey the concept of totality' (*Celtic Mythology*, 48–9). In *Culhwch* the phrase *Teir ynys Prydein* probably means simply 'Britain' as in HB: with Geoffrey of Monmouth the original mythical concept of the sovereign unity of the Island of Britain has become obscured, and the ancient phrase comes to be given a contemporary geo-political interpretation.

283. **Gwydawc mab Menester:** *Menester* = *mynystr* < Lat. *ministra*, which gave OF *menstre* 'cupbearer' (found in *Hirlas Owein*, RP 1434,1, for the servant who poured out drink for the warriors). In discussing *uch med menestri* in the *Gododdin* (CA 372), Ifor Williams argued that *menestri* derives from the pl. of Lat. *ministra*, and that there is no need to conclude that its occurrence in the poem is an indication of a derivation from French. Owing to the ambiguity of *e* in both CA and CO, the same argument applies here to the sing. form *Menester*. On *Kei* see n. on l. 134 above.

285. **Garanwyn mab Kei:** *Garanwyn* 'White Crane' or, alternatively, 'White Shank'; cf. *Gwydneu Garanhir* 'G. Long Shank', l. 618 below.

Amren mab Bedwyr: *Ambren uab Bedwyr* in GER, WM 388, 2. For *Bedwyr* see n. on l.175 above.

285–6. **Ely a Myr ... ac Eli a Thrachmyr:** the first of these pairs may be a miscopying, since *Eli a Thrachmyr* recurs in l.1159. For *Eli* as a personal name cf. *Ellinus*, the name of a disciple of St Cadoc (VSB 56). Rhŷs refers to a Garth *Eli* in the parish of Llanddewibrefi, CF 537. There is a River *Meheli* in Powys; CLlH 208, EANC 162–3. R. J. Thomas cites also the river name *Elei* in Glamorgan, LL 10, 43, 204; EANC 141–2 and compares the ref. in *Pa Gur* (p. xxxv, l.6 above).

Reu Rwyddyrys: 'R. Easy-Difficult'(?). For *Reu* as a personal name cf. LL 169,7; 201,4.

Run Rudwern: 'R. Red Alder'.

287. **penkynydyon Arthur:** the king's *penkynyd* or Chief Huntsman is listed among the Officers of the Court; HDdL 21–3; LIB 2,18 etc. Cf. *Garselit Wydel, penkynyd Iwerdon,* l.697 below.

287. **Lluydeu mab Kelcoet:** cf. PKM 64,5–6, *Llwyt uab Kil Coet,* and n. ibid. 247, where it is suggested that the name survives in *Cil coed* in the parish of Ludchurch, Pembs.; see *Pem.* i, 906, n. 2. In ll.1055–6 below, Lluydeu's home is at *Porth Kerdin yn Dyuet.* The derivation from the Ir. *Líath mac Celtchair,* suggested by J. Rhŷs and W. J. Gruffydd, has little to recommend it; see P. Sims-Williams, B xxix, 615. With *Lluydeu* cf. *Lluydeu mab Nwython* l.257 above. For the group of names in *Culhwch* which correspond to names in PKM see introduction p. xxxviii, n.23 and cf. *Teyrnon Twr Bliant* l.255 above.

288. **Hu[n]abwy mab Gwryon:** (R: *Hunabwy*). In GER this name recurs as *Kadwry uab Gwryon,* WM 411,41 (RM 265,18 *Hadwry uab Gwryon*).

Gwynn Gotyuron: *Guin Godybrion* is found in *Pa Gur* (above p. xxxv l.8). In a corrupt form it recurs as *Gwyn Goluthon* among the sons of *Iaen* (EWGT 85,2). On *Iaen* see n. on l.204 above.

288–90. Four men all with the name of *Gweir* 'Arthur's uncles, his mother's brothers'. They do not reappear in the story, though TYP 377–8 lists four others named *Gweir.* In *Preiddeu Annwn, Gweir* is the name of the prisoner in *Caer Sidi,* see edn. M. Haycock, SC xviii/xix, 65 (perhaps identical with *Gweir ap Geirioed* of TYP no.52).

Gweir Dathar Wenidawc: 'G. Bird-Servant' appears to correspond to *Gueiryd Adar Wenydyawc* BD 55 (the epithet signifies that he fed birds with corpses on the field of battle). BD evidently has the better form, and it suggests that *Dathar* here should be emended to *Adar*. The corresponding name in HRB is *Arviragus*. As B. F. Roberts points out (B xxv (1973), 283), this is clearly an instance in which the Welsh translator has used the name of a traditional hero called Gweir in place of the classical name used by Geoffrey of Monmouth. Prydydd y Moch employs *adar weinidawc* as a complimentary epithet for a patron, H 273,23.

Tal Aryant: 'Silver Brow'. *Kadellin* is unknown.

Gweir Gwrhyd Enwir: 'G. of False Valour'. Cf. TYP no.19 *Gueir Gwrhytvavr* 'G. of Great Valour', GER: *Gweir gwrhyt uawr* WM 411,35.

Gweir Gwyn Paladyr: (R: *G.baladyr hir*). 'G. White Spear'.

290–1. ywythred y Arthur, brodyr y uam: the phrase is repeated from l.252 above where others of Arthur's 'uncles' are named. The line implies that Llwch was father of Eigr, Arthur's mother.

291. Llwch Llawwynnyawc: the name is repeated; cf. *Lloch Llawwynnyawc* l.192 above, and n.

291–2. o'r tu draw y Uor Terwyn: 'from beyond the Tyrrhene Sea' (*Mab*), that is, the western Mediterranean between Sicily and Sardinia. There are var. spellings of this name: *y Mor Tiren* BD 15,5; *Mor Teryn* RBB 53,25 (= *Tyrrenum Equor* HRB i,12); *y Mor Tyren* HGVK 4,3 and n. Cf. OI *Muir Torrian* DIL 'M' col. 193 and A. Bruford in *Bealoideas* xxxiv (1966), 21. *Mor Terwyn* 'the Tyrrhene Sea' is the most probable meaning here, taking it to be an exotic place-name comparable with the list of remote or unknown places in Glewlwyd's speech to Arthur, ll.116–27 above. Nevertheless *terruin* occurs in collocation with *mor* in LlDC 39,6 *finaun wenestir mor terruin*, where *terruin* is an adj. 'savage' – which is a possible (though less likely) meaning in the present instance. In the line quoted from the above poem, the rhyme *terruin/morvin/cvin* precludes equating *terruin* with *terfyn* < Lat. *terminus*, as advocated by J. T. Koch, B xxx (1983), 299. See P. Sims-Williams, 'The Irish Geography of *Culhwch and Olwen*', 419 and n. 79.

293. **Llenlleawc Vydel:** a repetition of this name; see l.253 above, and n.

ac ardyrchawc Prydein: *ardderchog* 'famous, excellent'. With *Prydein* it should perhaps be understood as an epithet belonging to a name which has been inadvertently dropped from the text, rather than as an epithet belonging to *Llenlleawc* (*Prydein* seems illogical, since he was an Irishman). On *Prydein/Prydyn* in medieval texts see n. on l.262 above. Arthur is described as *arderchawc luydawc lyw* in *Englynion yr Eryr* (B ii, 276,34), and Cadwallon as *lluydawc Prydein* in *Moliant Cadwallon* (B vii, 25,29); on *llwyddawg* see n. on l.1137 below. Or *Ardyrchawc* could itself be a personal name.

Cas mab Saidi: cf. *mab Saidi* l.185 above. For *Cadrieith mab Seidi* see TYP no. 9, and idem pp. 291–2 and refs. cited.

294. **Gwruan Gwallt Auwyn:** *afwyn* means 'bridle-rein', but here it is more likely to be an error for *add(f)wyn* 'fair, beautiful'. Cf. *Gwarae Gwallt Eurin* l.315 below and p. xxxii above (with n. 18).

Gwilenhen brenhin Freinc: (R: *Gwyllennhin*). This name very probably stands for William the Conqueror, though there can be no absolute certainty as to this. *Guilenhin* (sic) *brenhin Freinc* is listed again among the *anoethau* in l.720, and in l.1130 he is slain by the Twrch Trwyth (see n.). *Gwilim uab rwyf Freinc* is listed in both BR and GER (see introduction p. xli). In HGVK 4,16 the Conqueror is described as *Guilim vrenhin*.

295. **Gwittart mab Aed brenhin Iwerdon:** in spite of its apparent irrelevance in the present context, *Gwittart* may perhaps derive from OF *Withard*, as suggested by P. Sims-Williams, B xxix, 606. With his patronymic cf. *Odgar mab Aed brenhin Iwerdon*, see l.635 below.

Garselit Vydel: another Irishman. In l.697 Garselit is described as 'chief huntsman of Ireland', and in l.1117 he is one of the huntsmen slain by the Twrch Trwyth. Kuno Meyer derived his name from Ir. *gearr + selut* 'a short while', though this seems an improbable meaning for a personal name. Sims-Williams (B xxix, 614) rejects any Ir. derivation and proposes *gar* 'leg' as the first element, as in *Garanwyn*, l.285, *Garanhir*, l.618 (see n.).

296. **Panawr Penbagat:** 'P. Head of the Host'.

Atleudor mab Naf: (R: *a fflendor*). This name may represent *(a)Fleudor*, as suggested by Idris Foster (cf. TYP 352), thus connecting it with *Flewdwr Flam (Wledic)*, l.182 above (see n.). *Atleudor* is a completely unknown character, and the fact that *Flewdwr Flam* has already appeared in the Court-List is no obstacle to the identification, since several other names are twice repeated in the List (see introduction p. xxxvii). With *Naf* cf. *Gwenwynwyn mab Naf*, l.250.

Gwyn Hyuar: 'G. the Irascible'. *Hyuar* < *hy* + *bar* 'anger, wrath'.

296. **maer:** < Lat. *maior*. The *maer* was a royal official who shared with the *canghellor* (who ranked above him), the local administration of land which was occupied by self-employed husbandmen; cf. HDdL 122–4.

297. **nawuet a estoues:** 'one of the nine'; cf. GMW 48. with the idiom cf. BR 5,11 (=RM 147,28) *o hynny yd ystovet y Gatgamlan*. (*Ystof* is the thread used as the weaver's warp.) For allusions to the battle of Camlan see n. on ll.226–32 above, and refs. cited.

297–8. **Kelli a Chuel:** two names which are certainly derived from the poem *Pa Gur*, LlDC 31, 33–4 (see pp. xxxiv–v l.18 above), although they are here presented as personal names, and in the poem they appear to be place-names. *Celli* could be derived from *call* 'wise, sensible' (cf. *dall*, *delli*) as suggested by B. F. Roberts, Ast. H. 305n. If they are place-names, it is tempting to connect the first with *Celliwig* see n. on l.261 above. *Cuelli* 'fury, ferocity' is paralleled in a single ex. by Prydydd y Moch, (H 263,10).

298. **Gilla Goeshyd:** 'G. Stag-Leg'. The epithet suits his description. Cf. Ir. *gilla* 'boy, servant'.

299. **pen llemidit Iwerdon:** 'Chief leaper of Ireland'. In HGVK 5,7 *Mathgauyn* is described as *llemhidyd anryved* 'a wonderful leaper', unequalled among the Irish.

300. **Sol a Gwadyn Ossol a Gwadyn Odeith:** (R: *odyeith*). *Sol* and *Gosol* both represent *sawdl* 'heel', *gwadn* 'sole', and *goddaith* 'bonfire'.

304–5. **ef a arllwyssei ford y Arthur yn lluydd:** 'he would clear the way for Arthur in (his) hosts' (that is 'on the march').

305. **Hir Erwm a Hir Atrwm:** these names recur in corrupt form

in *Englynion y Clyweit* (B iii, 13(40)): *A glyweist di a gant lluerwm (sic)/wrth y gyfeillt hirattrwm.*

312. **Huarwar mab Halwn:** (R: *Aflawn*). On *hy-, hu-* as an intensive prefix usually with adjs, as in *hygar, hyglyw* etc. see GPC 1945. *Huarwar = hu + arwar* 'delight, pleasure'; cf. n. to *Gwynn Hyuar (hy + bar* 'anger') l.296 above. Alternatively, R's *aflawn* (= *aflawen*) 'unhappy' would give a contrasting pair with *Huarwar.* For a late triad composed by Moses Williams on the basis of this passage in *Culhwch* see TYP no.93. Like the last two names *Huarwar* has been introduced into *Englynion y Clyweit* (B iii, 14(57)).

313. **yn y gyuarws:** on *cyfarws* see n. on l.59 above.

315. **Gwarae Gwallt Eurin:** 'G. Golden-Hair'. To be equated with *Gwri Wallt Euryn* PKM 26,15, as pointed out by W. J. Gruffydd, *Rhiannon* 91. Cf. *Gwruan Gwallt Auwyn* l.294 above.

315–16. **deu geneu Gast Rymhi:** 'the two pups of the bitch Rymhi' – named in l.316 as *Gwydrut a Gwyden Astrus.* With *Gwyden* cf. *Guidgen* LL 149,27, *Guitgen* EWGT 12 (24). *Astrus* 'crafty, cunning'. It is clear from the account given in ll.930–40 below that the *deu geneu* have been inadvertently omitted from the list of *anoethau* specified by Ysbaddaden; see introduction p. xlviii and n.42. As with *Gwilenhen brenhin Freinc* (l.294) their appearance both in the Court-List and then again among the *anoethau* appears illogical.

317. **Sucgyn mab Sucnedut:** 'Suck son of Sucker'.

318. **bron llech rud:** 'a red breast-fever' (Mab.); *llech* 'rickets, mumps' etc. (GPC).

318–19. **Caccymuri gwas Arthur:** brother to *Hygwyd gwas Arthur*, l.1048, etc.

322. **yr yscubawr:** R adds *yn y ueiscawn. Beisgawn* 'stack, heap of corn-sheaves'. This is the only ex. recorded before the 17th. cent. but *y wisgon* has come down in Ceredigion dialect, with *w* in place of *f*, through false association with *gwasgu*; see B iv (1929), 304, 343–4.

Llwng a Dygyflwng: *llwng* 'gullet'; *cyflwng* 'a swallowing' (? with neg. *di-*)

322–3. **Anoeth Ueidawc:** *annoeth* 'foolish'; *beiddiog* 'daring, bold'.

323. **Hir Eidyl a Hir Amren:** 'Long E. and Long A'. *Eiddyl* 'weak'.

324. **Gweuyl mab Gwastat:** *gwefl* 'lip'; *Gwastad* 'level, constant'.

327. **Vchdryt Uaryf Draws:** 'U. Cross-Beard'. With this name cf. *Vchdryt Ardwyat Kat* l.186; *Uchdryt mab Erim* l.233.

329. **neuad Arthur**: named *Ehangwen* 'Fair and Spacious' l.264 above.

Elidir Gyuarwyd: 'E. the Guide'. Cf. *Cyndelic Gyuarwyd* ll.177, 399.

Yskyrdaf ac Yscudyd: the first may be connected with *ysgryd* 'shiver'; with the second cf. *ysgud* 'swift'.

330. On *Gwenhwyuar* see n. on ll.161–2 above.

332. **Brys uab Bryssethach:** in a list of the ancestors of St Cadog (VSB 118, ch. 46) *Briscethach*, father of *Brusc*, is described as ancestor of *Gladus*, the daughter of *Brachanus* (Brychan Brycheiniog) *de optimis prosapiis regum Hibernensium*. This name appears to correspond with the Irish *dux* named *Briscus* (VSB 142) in the *Vita Prima Sancti Carantoci*, and with *Brosc*, father of *Aed*, one of the progenitors of the Irish tribe of the *Deisi* who settled in Dyfed and founded the ruling dynasty there, perhaps as early as the third century (Kuno Meyer (ed.) 'The Expulsion of the Deisi', Cy 14 (1901), 104–35; EWGT 4 and n.124). In B xxix (1982), 619 P. Sims-Williams concludes from this that 'a text about the Irish settlements of Wales was circulating between Ireland and Wales as early as the 12th. cent., and (that) the list of names in *Culhwch* drew on this lost text, directly or indirectly'. *Brys uab Bryssethach* must however be set beside the other names in *Culhwch* which demonstrably derive from *Vita S. Cadoci* (see nn. to *Dinsol* l.106, *Sawyl Penuchel* l.344, *Kaw o Prydein* l.647, *Mynyd Bannawc* l.597, and introduction p. lxxx). This suggests that *Brys uab Bryssethach* derives either from the Brychan documents which underlie the saint's genealogy as given in the *Vita*, or from a text of the *Vita* (not necessarily the earliest) in which the saint's genealogy had become incorporated. Cf. H. D. Emmanuel, 'An Analysis of the Composition of the *Vita Cadoci*', NLW Journal vii (1952), 220. With *Bryssethach* cf. *Caer Brythach* l.122 above, and on *-ach* in proper names see Sims-Williams, loc.cit. 615–16.

y Rydynawc Du o Brydein: 'The Black Fernbrake in Prydein; (*rhedyn* 'fern'). No specific place of this name has been identified: it is a name of so general a character that it could be almost anywhere. On the ambiguity of *Prydein/Prydyn* see n. on l.262 above.

333. **Grudlwyn Gorr:** 'G. the Dwarf'. (*grudd* 'cheek' + *llwm*? 'bare'). Cf. *Gwdolwyn Gorr* l.364; *Guidolwyn Gorr* l.657 (see n.), and TYP no.28: *Teir Prif Hut . . . Hut Gwythelin Gorr/Rudlwm Gorr (R) a dysgawd y Goll uab Collurewy y nei.* *Cor* glosses *nanus* in the *Vocabularium Cornicum*, and is rendered into OE as *dweorh* 'dwarf' (B xi,3). Another early ex. of *cor* in Welsh is found in LlDC 35,22. On dwarves in early Welsh sources see SC xiv/xv (1979–80), 61.

Bwlch: 'gap, breach'. *Cyfwlch* 'complete, perfect'; cf. *cywlauan gyuulch* LlDC 18,105. As a personal name cf. *Kyuwlch* l.341 below; also CA ll.137, 1312, and *Cimulch* as the name of a witness in the Book of St Chad, LL xlvi.

334. **Kledyf Kyuwlch:** 'Perfect Sword'. This name, and those of his three sons listed previously, seem more appropriate as names for swords than for men. In l.736 below, this name is given as *Kilyd Kyuwlch*. Cf. *Caletuwlch*, the name of Arthur's sword, l.159 above.

Cledyf Diuwlch: 'Unbroken (Gapless) Sword'.

336–7. **Glas, Glesic, Gleissat:** 'Grey, (?), Salmon'. Cf. BT 22,19: *bum glas gleissat.* **Call** 'Sharp, Wily'; **Kuall** 'Speedy'; **Kauall** < *caballus* 'horse'. *Kauall* is given as the name of Arthur's hound, l.1015 below (see n.).

337. **Hwyr Dydwc a Drwc Dydwc a Llwyr Dydwc:** 'Late-Bearer and Ill-Bearer and Full-Bearer' (Mab.).

338. **Och a Garym a Diaspat:** 'Alas and Scream and Shriek'.

339. **teir vyryon . . . teir merched:** for a pl. n. with a numeral cf. *trywyr* l.235 above (GMW 47). But the sing. occurs in *teir morwyn* l.340 below.

Drwc a Gwaeth a Gwaethaf Oll: 'Bad and Worse and Worst of All'. This whole passage, ll.333–40, recurs in the list of *anoethau* ll.736–43 below (see n.).

341–2. *Merch* in place of *Mab* in all three of the names given here, is a mistake which is common to both W and R. Clearly some copyist mistook *m* in his original as an abbreviation for *merch* instead of for *mab* (probably through anticipation of ll.359–72 (see T. Jones, B xiii (1950), 13–14). The correction is corroborated by *Englynion y Clyweit* (B iii, 15 (66)): *A glyweisti a gant eheubryt/mab Kyuwlch* (see introduction p. xi).

Gorascwrn mab Nerth: 'Big-Bone son of Strength'.

342. **Gwaedan:** '(?)Shouter'. According to the Life of St Teilo (LL 116, 6) a certain *regulus Guaidan nomine* violated the sanctuary of St Teilo's church at Llanteilo Fechan, and consequently became demented. Dafydd ap Gwilym also appears to have known a story about some man called *Gwaeddan* (GDG 84,19), though the allusion is obscure. For some further instances of the name see G 601.

342. **Kynuelyn Keudawc, Pwyll Hanner Dyn:** W's form of the epithet *keudawc* is favoured by its adjectival ending (cf. *baruawc, beidawc*, etc), but since no adj. *keudawc* is anywhere attested, R's *keudawt* 'thought, mind, heart' is a possible alternative. Jones and Jones (Mab 106) take *keudawt pwyll hanner dyn* as together constituting Kynuelyn's epithet, and render it 'Half-Wit', understanding *pwyll* 'sense, wisdom' to be a gloss on *keudawt hanner dyn* which subsequently became incorporated into the text in an earlier manuscript (see n. to Mab 276). This interpretation followed that of J. Lloyd-Jones, Cy xl (1929), 260–1, '*hanner dyn* is most certainly descriptive of Kynuelyn, and not of an imaginary Pwyll'. In arguing against this interpretation we would urge that Pwyll was a well-known traditional character, and one among eleven or twelve names from the *Mabinogi* which are incorporated in the Court-List and elsewhere in the tale (see introduction p. xxxviii, n.23), and that *hanner dyn* ('half-man') would be apt as an ironic allusion to Pwyll's lack of sense and foresight which incurred Rhiannon's taunt at the wedding-feast *ni bu uuscrellach gwr ar y synnwyr e hun nog ry uuost ti* (PKM 14,14). Cf. Loth, *Les Mabinogion* i,281, for a similar interpretation. But the epithet *keudawc/keudawt* is not as yet satisfactorily explained.

343. **Dwnn Diessic Unben:** 'D. Vigorous Chieftain' (*di* + *ysig*) cf. LlDC 18,66; 18,143, *Bed mor mauridic diessic unben ... mab peredur penwetic.*

Penn Llarcan: the Ir. name *Lorccan* has been compared by P. Sims-Williams, B xxix, 615.

344. Kynedyr Wyllt mab Hettwn Tal Aryant: 'K. the Wild son of H. Silver Brow'. This name recurs among the *anoethau* as *Kynedyr Wyllt mab Hettwn Clauyryawc* l. 708. A saint *Kynedyr* is commemorated in *lanncinitir* LL 277, 9. On the significance of *gwyllt* 'Wild, mad, deranged' see GPC 1766, and cf. Ir. *geilt*. This was the term used in the early literatures of both Wales and Ireland to denote wild and deranged men living in the wilderness and evading human contacts: the most famous Welsh ex. being Myrddin *Wyllt* (TYP 469–74, and refs. cited). Cf. also *Cyledyr Wyllt* l.994 below. With Kynedyr's patronymic cf. *Kadellin Tal Aryant* l. 289 above.

344–5. Sawyl Penn Uchel: 'S. High Head'. One of the *Tri Thrahawc* or 'Three Arrogant Men' of Britain, acc. TYP no.23 (see n. idem p. 506). In the Harl. Gen. (EWGT 12 (19)) *Samuil Pennissel* 'S. Low Head' appears as a descendant of Coel Hen, one of the 'Men of the North'. In HRB iii,19 this name has been borrowed from the Harl. Gen. (or a similar genealogy), but divided into two successive kings, *Samuil* and *Penissel* . (These are correctly united again as *Sawyl Ben Yssel*, BD 44.) The source for this name in *Culhwch*, however, is probably the Life of St Cadog (VSB 58), where a certain *dux* named *Sauuil Pennuchel* is punished for his high-handed behaviour towards the saint. Possible influence from the triad cannot however be excluded. See also ByS (EWGT 56,13) *Sawyl bennuchel m. Pabo Post Prydein*. OW *Samuil* > MW *Sawyl*.

345. Gwalchmei mab Gwyar: the Black Book of Carmarthen lists *Keincaled m(arch) Gualchmei* among the Triads of Horses (LlDC 6,12), and *Englynion y Beddau* (Stanzas of the Graves) give *bet Gwalchmei ym Peryton* (ibid. 18,24). But as Gwalchmei *mab Gwyar* he first appears in a triad (TYP no.4), and in the *Brut* (BD 171,175), where his name renders *Gualguainus, Gwalgwinus* etc. in HRB (x, 4, 6 etc.); *Gwalchmei uab Gwyar nei y brenhin* BD 183. According to HRB ix,9 the father of *Gualguanus* was Loth of Lodonesia (= *Lleu ap Cynfarch* BD 152), who married Arthur's sister Anna. After a single allusion to *Anna* as Gwalchmei's mother in BD 152 (= HRB ix, ix), elsewhere throughout the *Brut* Gwalchmei is designated *mab Gwyar*, and in Welsh texts *Gwyar* came to be regarded as the name of Arthur's sister. Hence in ll.406 below, Gwalchmei is *Nei y Arthur, uab y chwaer*. For a fuller discussion see TYP civ, 369–75, and on the confusion as to Gwalchmei's parentage see B. F. Roberts, B xxv, 287–8. In a late text of ByS Gwyar is made a daughter of *Amlawd*

Wledic, (EWGT 65 (76)), as are the mothers of Arthur and of Culhwch in other sources (see n. on l.2 above). On the derivation of the name *Gwalchmei* < *Ualcos Magesos* 'Hawk of the Plain' see LHEB 449n. and TYP (2), 552. Gwalchmei's traditional distinction is commemorated in *By Tywys*. (P 20 version) where the annal for 1189 describes Maelgwn son of the Lord Rhys as 'the best Knight, a second Gwalchmei'. *Gwalchmei* is an exceptional instance in the Court-List in which a hero is given an apparent matronymic instead of a patronymic: *Mabon mab Modron* appears to be the only other example.

Gwalhauet mab Gwyar: the names of the two brothers share a common first element *gwal(c)h*, but elsewhere the name *Gwalhauet* is almost unknown. He is cited once in a complimentary epithet by the poet Llygad Gwr in a *marwnad* to Hywel ap Madawg (d. 1268): *gwalch gwrawl gwrhyd gwalhafed* 'a valiant hawk of the might of Gwalhafed' (H 60,23) which indicates that he may be a traditional, rather than an invented character. But any association of his name with that of Sir Galahad (proposed in G 610) is certainly to be rejected.

346. **Gwrhyr Gwalstawd Ieithoed:** 'G. Interpreter of Languages'. This is the earliest occurrence of the word *gwalstawd* < OE *wealhstod* 'interpreter' (GPC 1567). Since he was familiar with the languages of birds and of animals as well as those of humans, Gwrhyr was an essential member of the Six Helpers who accompany Culhwch on his quest for Olwen; cf. l.402 below. He is able to speak on behalf of the others with the Oldest Animals (ll.842–3), and to negotiate on Arthur's behalf with the Twrch Trwyth and his retinue of pigs (ll.1077–82). C. Bullock-Davies has made an interesting comparison between Gwrhyr's activities and the functions expected of the *latimarii* or interpreters on the Welsh marches in the 12th. cent. in her *Professional Interpreters and the Matter of Britain* (University of Wales Press, 1966), 25–6. Gwrhyr's name was borrowed from *Culhwch* into each one of the three 'Derived Lists' (see introduction p. xl) GER (WM 411,41 = RM 265,7); BR 19,25 = RM 160,1); *Englynion y Clyweit* (B iii, 11 (20)).

347. **Kethtrwm Offeirad:** 'K. the Priest'. It is significant that two clerics are introduced into the Court-List – though neither plays any further part in the story. Cf. *Bitwini Escob* l.356 below.

Clust mab Clustueinat: 'Ear son of Hearer'. Neither Clust, nor any other of the group of men similarly described below (ll. 349–53) as possessing extraordinary powers, are named ever again in the story (see introduction p. xliv). Much later the poet Gruffudd Llwyd (*c*. 1380–1410) names *Clust fab Clustfeinydd* with *Drem fab Dremhidydd* (l. 261 above) in a poem of abuse directed against the alert sight and hearing of a Jealous Husband (IGE (2) xlv, 25–30). Both names are also cited in GER (WM 386, 6–7).

348. **seith vrhyt:** *Gwrhyd* here has the meaning of 'fathom': cf. CA l. 2.

349. **Medyr mab Methredyd:** 'Aim son of Aimer'. The feat ascribed to him is similar to that ascribed to Lleu Llaw Gyffes in shooting a wren with a needle *y rwg giewyn y esgeir a'r ascwrn* at Caer Aranrhod, PKM 80.

kychwhynnei: imperf. sing. 3 'he rose'; vn. *kychwynnu/kywhynnu*. Here we have a combination of *chw* and *hw/wh*. The latter prevails in MW prose, as well as in the spoken language of south Wales (as opposed to that of north Wales). They seem to represent the original form. See introduction p. xix.

350. **Eskeir Oeruel yn Iwerdon:** see n. on l. 114 above.

351. **yn gythrymhet:** 'directly, exactly'; equative of *cythrwm* < *kom + *trumbos. OW *cithremmet* gloss *libra*. Cf. OI *cutrumme* 'equal'. The basic adj. is *trwm* 'heavy'.

Celli Wic: see n. on l. 261 above.

351–2. **Gwiawn Llygat Cath:** 'G. Cat's Eye'. For other occurrences of the name *Gwiawn/Gwion* see G 676.

353. **Ol mab Olwyd:** 'Track son of Tracker'(?). This is the last in the group referred to in l. 347 above, of men with peculiar attributes. Some of these – such as *Gwiawn Llygat Cath* – are paralleled by characters possessing similar attributes in other versions of the tale-type AT 513A 'Six Go Through the World' (see IPT 72–5; Stith Thompson, *The Folktale* 53–5). In the event, none of these characters play any further part in the tale, and it is obvious that they are farcical inventions, and not traditional figures, and that they have been purposely created to conform with the tale-type to which *Culhwch* belongs. Their role as the hero's Helpers is taken

over by the Six Helpers who are appointed by Arthur and are named in ll. 381–410 below. See introduction p. xliv.

353–4. **kyn no'e eni:** 'before he was born'. On *kyn(n)* 'before' see D. S. Evans, SC xiv/xv (1979–80), 74–80.

356. **Bitwini Escob:** 'B. the Bishop'. In a triad (TYP no. 1) *Bytwini Esgob* is named as *Pen Esgyb* at Celliwig in Cornwall, Dewi Sant as *Pen Esgob* in *Mynyw* (St David's), and *Cyndeyrn Garthwys* (St Kentigern) as *Pen Esgob* at *Pen Ryoned* in the North (see n. to the triad, and TYP 289). Bytwini's reappearance in *Culhwch* is interesting, since TYP no. 1 is a rare triad which is absent from nearly all texts of TYP (see introduction p. xli). In BR 6, 10–12 (RM 148, 24) *Betwin escob* is one of Arthur's counsellors, and is placed to sit beside him. He appears also in *Englynion y Clyweit* (B iii, 12 (33): *A glyweisti a gant bedwi? oed escob donyawc difri*. Elsewhere he is unknown, though there may be faint memories of his name in the 'Bishop Bawdewyn' who figures in some medieval romances, such as *Sir Gawain and the Green Knight* (ed. Norman Davis (Oxford, 1968) 78n.).

357. **eurtyrchogyon:** 'golden torqued', that is, wearing gold collars as a mark of their nobility. The form is pl. of *eurtyrchog* (*eur + tyrch*, pl. of *torch* 'collar') with adjectival ending -*og*.

357–72. Few of the names of the ladies of Arthur's Court are known from any other source: some appear to be corrupt, and others to be invented names, created to designate the daughters of men already listed as present at the Court. They are said to be the daughters of these heroes: none, except for Gwenhwyfar, are described as their wives. *Merch* in these names is for the most part unlenited, like *mab* (see n. on ll. 168–9 above). The patronymics following *merch* are more frequently unlenited than lenited: cf. TYP no. 56 and n.; TC 100, i, and n. to l. 2 above.

358. **Gwenhwyuar:** See n. on l. 161 above. With *Penn Rianed* 'Chief of Queens' cf. Arthur as *Penn Teyrned yr Ynys honn* (l. 142), and TYP no. 56 *Teir Prif Riein Arthur* 'Arthur's Three Great Queens' – where all three are given the name Gwenhwyfar, each with a different patronymic. (On triplication cf. l. 282 above, and n.) Cf. also Branwen as *tryded prif rieni (= riein ?)* PKM 31, 1.

359. **Gwenhwyach y chwaer:** cf. TYP no. 53: *Teir Gvith Baluavt*

('Three Harmful Blows . . . ') of which one was the blow struck by *Gwenhvyuach* on *Gwenhvyuar*, which is said to have brought about the battle of Camlan. The same episode is recalled in TYP no.84, where Camlan is described as one of the *Tri Ouergat* or 'Frivolous Battles' because it was brought about as the result of a quarrel between Gwenhwyfar and Gwenhwyfach. But there is no other allusion to *Gwenhwy(f)ach* outside *Culhwch* and TYP. On the battle of Camlan see n. on ll.226–31 above.

360. **Kelemon merch Kei:** On *Kei* see n. on l.134 above. His daughter is quite unknown.

360–1. **Tangwen merch Weir Dathar Wenidawc:** unknown. For *Gweir Dathar Wenidawc* see ll.288–90 above, and n.

361–2. **Eurneit merch Clydno Eidin:** *Eur-* is used figuratively in this name; cf. *eurneit* 'llam neu dro gwych', G 498. Cf. *Euronwy* (var. *Creirwy*) *ferch Clydno Eidyn* in ByS (EWGT 57(15)). Clydno Eidyn is known from BGG (TYP 309; EWGT 178) as one of the rulers of the 'Men of the North'. His more famous son *Cynon* was a leader of the Gododdin army; see TYP 323–4, Ast. H. 151–64. *Clydno* derives from *clod* 'fame' and *gno(u)* 'famous, conspicuous' (CA 176,235). For *Cynon fab Clydno* see n. on l.366 below.

362. **Eneuawc merch Bedwyr:** unknown. For *Bedwyr* see n. on l.175 above.

362–3. **Enrydrec merch Tutuathar:** unknown. With the patronymic cf. *tud* 'tribe, people', as in *Tudyr* and *Tudri* < *Toutorix* 'lord of the tribe' (found on an amphora in Gaul, EC xiii (1972), 177–8).

Gwenwledyr merch Waredur Kyruach: Cf. *Gwawrdur Kyruach*, l.189.

364. **Erduduyl merch Tryffin:** cf. *Drutwas mab Tryffin* l.200. The name *Erduduyl* is found in one other instance, in a version of the triad *Tri Gwyn Dorllwyth* (TYP no.70), found among the genealogies in J 20 (EWGT 43,3(5)). Here it is evidently copied from a text much older than the 14th.-cent. MS of the genealogy. In the note to the triad it is suggested that *Erduduyl* may be an error for *Efrddyl* (sister of Urien Rheged); see TYP 186.

364. **Eurolvyn (R: *Eurolwen*) merch Wdolwyn Gorr:** 'Golden

Wheel'. With *Eurolvyn* cf. *Goroluyn* TYP no.66 and n. to *Olwen* l.498 below. With *Gwdolwyn Gorr* ('Dwarf') cf. *Grudlwyn Gorr* l.333; *Guidolwyn Gorr* l.657 and n.

365. **Indec merch Arwy Hir:** One of Arthur's *Tair Karedicwreic,* TYP no.57. Gruffudd ap Maredudd alludes to Arthur's love for *Indeg* RP 1326,16–18, and Dafydd ap Gwilym frequently makes use of her name as a standard of comparison for beauty; see TYP 354–5; 412–13.

366. **Moruyd merch Uryen Reget:** according to the triad *Tri Gwyndorllwyth* 'Three Fair Womb Burdens', TYP no.70 (P 47), Moruyd was a twin with her more famous brother Owein ab Urien Rheged; in TYP no.71 her lover Cynon ap Clydno is named as one of the *Tri Serchawc.* In contrast, *Culhwch* makes no allusion to Urien Rheged or to his son Owein.

Gwenlliant Tec: 'G. the Fair'. Nothing is known of her or her alleged nobility. *Gwenllian* was one of the most popular medieval womens' names; see THSC (1965), 59; EWGT 192.

367. **Creidylat merch Llud Llaw Ereint:** for *Creidylat* see n. on l.988 below, and for *Llud Llaw Ereint* see n. on l.916 below.

368. **Teir Ynys Prydein a'e Their Rac Ynys:** (R: *teir ynys y kedyrn*); cf. PKM 30,21; 41,13). For this recurrent phrase see n. on l.282 above.

369. **Gwythyr mab Greidawl:** see n. on l.176 above.

370. **Gwynn mab Nud:** See n. on ll.181–2 above.

pob dyw kalan Mei: 'every May-Day'. *Dyw* 'day' is used adverbially with names of days and feasts, cf. GMW 33, and ll.480–1 below *pob dyw Sadwrn. kalan* < Lat. *calandae, calendae*. It means the first day of the year, and also the first day of each month. For the contest here referred to, see ll.988–1004 below.

371. **Ellylw merch Neol Kyn Croc:** 'N. Hang-cock' (*Mab.*). Nothing is known of Ellylw, her father, or her longevity. *Ellylw* is however a popular name in genealogies; exx. EWGT 48 (32 and 33).

372. **Essyllt Vynwen ac Essyllt Uyngul:** (R: *vinwen/vingul*). 'E. White/Fair Neck and E. Slender Neck' (cf. *myn* in *mynwgl, mwnwgl* 'neck'). R's 'Slender Fair' *minwen* and *mingul* for *meinwen, meingul*

would be equally acceptable as suitable poetic epithets for a girl. *Es(s)yllt* is attested from the 10th. cent. both in the Cornish place-name *hryt eselt* 'E's Ford' (see O. Padel, CMCS i (1981), 66), and in the var. form *Et(t)hil, Ethellt*, the name of a daughter of Cynan Tindaethwy from whom the second Gwynedd dynasty descended (see EWGT 9 (i); 36 (i); 47 (22), etc.; HGVK ccviii). This name is reproduced as *Esyllt* EWGT 90 (27a), and in refs. by the poets. *Esyllt* is the Welsh name which corresponds to *Isolt, Iseut* in the French 'Tristan' romances, and it is fair to deduce that the allusion here is to the Welsh heroine who later became famous in the continental romances, although the appearance of the name *Esyllt* in duplicate raises certain problems, in comparison with other alliterating pairs of names in *Culhwch* (see introduction p. xxxviii). If *Drustwrn hayarn* l. 191 above (see n.) represents a misreading (or duplicate form) of the name *Drystan*, then *Culhwch* presents the names of both the protagonists in the medieval 'Tristan' romances (as also does the early version of TYP, no. 26). With the exception of Gwenlliant Tec (l. 366), the two Esyllts are the only ones among Arthur's ladies who receive no patronymic. This suggests that their names, coming at the end of the Court-List, may be an addition to it. (Nor do their names appear in any one of the three derived lists, BR, GER, and *Eng.* see introduction p. xl.) In a late triad (TYP no. 80) Esyllt is given as father *Kulvanawyt Prydein*, and this rare name should probably be equated with *Kuluanawyt mab Goryon*, l. 253 above (see n.). Esyllt's name was popular among the *cywyddwyr* as a standard of perfect beauty. See further TYP 349–50; SC xiv/xv (1979–80), 54–65, and refs. cited; 'The Tristan of the Welsh', AoW ch. 10, 209–28.

373. **y gyuarws:** for *cyuarws* see n. on l. 59 above.

374. **kiglef:** pret. sing. 1 of *clybot* 'to hear'. This is an ex. of forming the pret. by reduplication of the initial *k*. (An old formation, found in the classical and Celtic languages.) Cf. GMW 124–5; GOI 624–5.

376. **o'e cheissaw:** 'to seek her'; cf. GMW 53, n. 2; also l. 405 below.

378. **hyny uyd kenhadeu Arthur heb gaffel dim:** 'the messengers of Arthur had not obtained anything'; *hyny* 'until, in order that, that' is here employed as an affirmative preverbal prt.; cf. GMW 245n., also l. 412 below. *uyd* is here a dramatic present with a past meaning; cf. GMW 109; also ll. 412–13 below.

379. **Pawb ry gauas y gyuarws:** 'everyone has obtained his *cyfarws*'. This is a clear ex. of the prt. *ry-* giving a perfect meaning to the pret. 'obtained, got'; GMW 166–7.

380. **wyneb:** 'face'. Often used in the sense of 'honour', see n. on l.154 above, and PKM 33,19–19; 175–6; HDdL 392.

Kei: see n. on l.134 above.

382–3. **nat oes hi yn y byt:** 'that she is not in the world'; *oes* is used with an indef. noun or pron. as subject, but there are a few exx. in OW and MW where the subject is a definite noun or pron., as here; cf. GMW 144.

383. **yscarhawr:** pres. impers. passive. Here we have the independent ending *-hawr* used with future meaning; GMW 121.

384. **angerd:** the meaning varies; cf. GPC 50. Here (as in l. 397) it seems to denote 'special attribute, feature, peculiarity'; in l. 390 it is 'heat'. Kei's magical attributes are described in ll. 266–73 above.

386. **dieu:** pl. of *dyd* 'day', used with numerals; GMW 33.

hyd: a form of the affirmative preverbal prt. *yt*, found at an early period; cf. GMW 171 n., and l.389 below.

ny allei uedyc: (*medyc*). The subject frequently undergoes lenition after the imperf. sing. 3; GMW 17.

391. **kedymdeithon:** 'fellows, companions', pl. of *kydymdeith*, which consists of *kyd-* 'with' and *ymdeith* (GMW 156); cf. *y ymdeith* 'to travel' but later as adv. 'away', also *ymdeith* and *ymeith* (GMW 222–3). In ModW the form is *cymdeithion*, sing. *cydymaith*.

Bedwyr: see n. on l.175 above.

394. **Sef a:** here *sef* is used substantivally, followed by *a*, rel. pron. subj.; cf. GMW 52, and n. to l.800 below, where the full form *yssef a* occurs.

395–6. **Drych eil Kibdar:** *Drych* 'aspect, reflection, example'. It is difficult to estimate its meaning as a personal name. On *eil* see n. to l.184 above. This triad is not included in any of the collections, but TYP no.27 (found only in the early version) lists *Drych eil Kibdar* as one of the *Tri Lleturithavc* or 'Enchanters'.

396. **unllofyawc:** 'one-handed'. It consists of the adjectival ending -*yawc* following *unllof-*: *un* 'one' + *llof* with vowel mut. from *llawf* 'hand'. The -*f* ultimately disappeared leaving *llaw*; cf. *praw*, GMW 9. But when *llaw* forms part of a compd. the -*f* is restored in the form *llof*, as here; cf. *llofrudd* 'murderer', *llofnod* 'signature'.

397. **aeruawc:** consists of *aerfa* 'battle, slaughter, army' + -*awc* (adjectival ending). Here it is a substantive meaning 'warrior'.

398. **gwrthwan:** 'counter-thrust' (*gwrth* 'counter' + *gwan* 'thrust'). The only other ex. of the word is by Cynddelw, H 137,17; see also Lhuyd, AB 235c *gwrthvan* 'a stab'.

399. **Cyndylic Kyuarwyd:** see n. on l.177 above, and cf. *Elidir Gyuarwyd* l.329. Both names indicate the importance of pathfinders in untracked country. See introduction p. xliii and n.36.

402. **Gwrhyr Gwalstawt Ieithoed:** see n. on l.346 above.

404. **Gwalchmei mab Gwyar:** see n. on l.345 above. Neither Gwalchmei nor Cyndylic play any further part in the story.

408. **Menw mab Teirgwaed:** see n. on l.199 above.

412. **deuuant:** 'they come', also *deuant* l.415. Both are exx. of the dramatic present. By bringing the event out of the past into the present, the intention is to make the account more real and vivid. It is a device often employed in MW narrative; cf. GMW 109; also l.378 above; and ll.441, 468, 536, 550, 761 below.

412–13. **hyny uyd kaer a welynt:** 'they could see a fort'. Cf. l.378 above, and l.416 below. *yny* introduces an independent affirmative clause in which there is an element of wonder or surprise; GMW 245n.

415. **eisswys:** 'nevertheless, however' (ModW 'already'). The more common form is *eissoes*; on *wy*/*oe* see GMW 4, n. 4 on *moe*/*mwy* 'more', etc.

416. **han ny uyd dauates uawr a welynt:** 'They could see a great flock of sheep'. Cf. l.412 above.

heb or a heb eithaf iti: 'without end or limit to it'. Cf. CA 416–17 *canaf yty ior*/*clot heb or heb eithaf.*

418. **ach y law:** 'by, near' (*llaw* 'hand'). Cf. GMW 182.

419. **amws naw gayaf:** 'a horse of nine winters'; that is, 'nine winters old'. On *amws* see n. to l.251 above.

420. **anoethach:** that is, 'much less' or 'let alone'. On the formation see GMW 40.

421. **eiroet:** 'ever'. Cf. *eirmoet* l.127 above. Note the loss of *i* in the final syllable, a feature of MW prose and some modern south Wales dialects; cf. GMW 222.

422. **y sawl:** 'such, as many'; GMW 95.

423. **dilis:** here with *prid* 'soil' it apparently means 'genuine, real, very'. In the form as here found we have a case of assimilation, the original form seems to have been *dilys*, from *di* (neg.) + *llys* 'objection, bar'. As an adj. it means basically 'someone or something which cannot be rejected'. See further WLW 209–10.

425. **racco:** here it is an adv. based on *rac*, with the meaning 'yonder'; GMW 60n.

427. **amgeled:** 'care, anxiety': *a* and *y* alternate before a nasal, hence *ymgeled* is a variant form. With the prep. *gan* it means 'to feel desire or anxiety'; that is, 'Do not be anxious about going there'.

430. **Berth yd ytwyt:** 'It is fine you are'. As a form of greeting, the phrase here is quite unique. *Berth* as an adj. is found in CA and LlDC, but this is the only instance in prose in which it has been recorded.

432. **Pieu** consists of *pi* (a form of *pwy*) and *eu* 'is'. Originally *pieu* is interrog. in meaning, as here; 'to whom is? whose is? who owns?'. Later it developed into a rel. cf. GMW 80, also ll.433, 763 below.

433. **Meredic a wyr:** 'Fools of men'. Note the constr. adj. + *a* 'of' + n. = n. + adj. Cf. ll.763–4 below, and *dyhed a beth* l.133 'a shameful thing'; *drwc a serch* l.465 'a bad (kind of) love'.

434. **pan yw:** 'that it is', GMW 80; *bieu* here is rel. 'who owns'.

Yspydaden Penkawr: see n. on l.51 above.

435. **Custenhin Amhynwyedic:** (R: *uab dyfnedic*). R's reading strengthens the case for believing that we have a patronymic rather than an epithet; Mab. 109 renders it *ap Mynwyedig*. But in favour of taking it as an epithet is the analogy with CLlH xi, 78a, *heled hwyedic*

y'm gelwir. Ifor Williams's note to this line points out that in the case of Heledd an adj. seems to be required, and that *hwyedig* as a var. of the n. *hwyedydd* 'hawk, falcon' (GPC 1936–7) can hardly be relevant. The one feature shared in common by Custennin and Heledd, however, was their dispossessed status (cf. TYP 405–6), and some word implying 'expelled from home, exiled' would be acceptable, (see now J. Rowland, *Early Welsh Saga Poetry* 601–2). *Custennin* derives from *Constantinus*, the name of the first Christian emperor in the 3rd. cent. Under his influence the name spread in Britain, and several instances are recorded, including the 6th.-cent. Devon ruler *Constantinus tyrannicus Damnoniae*, who was the subject of a diatribe by Gildas. In Welsh tradition, *Custennin* became the ancestor of the Dyfed dynasty by his alleged marriage with *Elen Luyddog* (Harl. Gen. ii; EWGT 10). Geoffrey of Monmouth employed the name for three separate Constantines (see TYP 314–15), one of whom was said to be the father of Uthyr Pendragon, and hence the grandfather of Arthur (=*Custennyn Uendigeit*, BD 86,19). Rhigyfarch's Life of St David names a certain *Constantinus Cornubiensium rex* who submitted to the saint and was baptized by him (Rhigyfarch's Life of St David, ed. James, ch. 32; VSB 159; cf. Ann. Cam 589 *Conversio Constantini ad Dominum*). This Cornish king could well be the same as *Custennin Gorneu* ('C. of Cornwall'), who is alluded to several times in ByS, where he is father of *Erbin* (EWGT 58, nos. 26, 27; 65, nos. 73, 76). The name Constantine survives in that of a village near Helston in Cornwall, and in Wales it is attested in *Lan Custenhin garthbenni in ercicg*, LL 72,1. See also nn. to *Gereint mab Erbin* l. 219 above, and to *Goreu mab Custenhin* l.811 below.

435–6. am uym priawt: 'because of my wife Ysbaddaden has despoiled me (wrought my ruin)'. Note the significant var. in R: 'because of my wife my brother Ysbaddaden has ruined me'.

438. Olwenn: See n. on ll.487–98 below.

444. y kymhar: if *y* is to be understood as a poss. pron. 3 sing., one would expect lenition to indicate 'his mate'. But *y* could be explained as the def. art. used instead of a poss. pron., as it is occasionally; cf. GMW 25.

445. Pan: is usually interrog., meaning 'whence'; as in *Pan doeth yti y peir a rodeist y mi?* 'Whence came to thee the cauldron thou hast given me?' PKM 35,2. See further GMW 79, and cf. l.762 below.

vr: from *gwr* 'man'. A vocative is lenited, with or without a vocative prt.; GMW 15.

446. **douot:** also *dyuot* and *dyouot* means 'a find, prize, treasure-trove'. Cf. WLW 194–5 'casual acquisitions'; that is, things found by chance. Among these were objects thrown up by the sea. Further instances are cited, WLSD 19–20.

447. **ertrei:** *er* + *trei* 'ebb' means the breaking or surging of waves, the first ebb after high water.

451. **pieu:** is rel. here, and means 'who owns', as in ll. 434, 764, 765.

gwelho: subj. pres. sing. 3 of *gwelet* 'to see'. We have here an ex. of the pres. subj. used with a fut. meaning; see GMW 113. As to its form, notice the retention of *-h-* in the ending of the subj.; GMW 128.

454–5. **llawen a oed genthi:** 'she was glad'. On the use of *gan* with nouns and adjectives to express an attitude of mind or feeling see GMW 190. *a* is unusual and unexpected here between the nominal predicate *llawen* and *oed*, as this is not a rel. construction; cf. *a thrist oed* later in this line.

455. **y nei uab y chwayr:** see n. on *Anlawd Wledic*, l.2 above, and on *Goreu mab Custenhin*, l.811 below. Allusions scattered through the tale indicate that the mothers of Arthur, Culhwch, and Goreu were all sisters, and all were daughters of *Anlawd Wledic* (as also was the mother of St Illtud, VSB 194) see n. to l.2 above. But Goreu's mother is never given a name (nor is Goreu himself on his first introduction into the tale, ll.469–70). It is tempting to connect her with *Dywanw merch Anlawd Wledic* of BGG 13, who was 'married' to *Tutuwlch Corneu*.

456. **eneit:** here means simply 'life', not 'soul', as is usual in MW; cf. l.484 below.

461–2. **mynet dwylaw mynwgyl:** an expression consisting of *mynet* 'to go' + *dwylaw* '(two) hands' + *mynwgyl* 'neck', and meaning 'to embrace'. It is not infrequent in MW texts; ex. GDG 53,7–8.

464–5. **pei mi ry wascut uelly:** 'were it me you had squeezed thus'. Here *pei* is subj. imperf. sing. 3 of the vb 'to be', which later developed as a conditional conjunction, usually in the form of *pe* in ModW. Note that *ry-* with the imperf., as in *ry wascut*, conveys the sense of a pluperfect.

465. **ny oruydei ar arall uyth rodi serch im:** 'no one else would ever have to make love to me'. *goruydei* is imperf. sing. 3 of *goruot* 'to overcome, oblige, compel' (*gor* + *bot* 'to be over', GMW 146–7). The subject is usually a vn.; here *rodi (serch im)* lit, 'to make love to me would not overcome another'.

drwc a serch hwnnw: 'that was an evil love'. Cf. *dyhed a beth* l. 133 above.

468. **pan at pawb eu damsathyr:** lit. 'when all allow(ed) themselves to be busied': *gat* is indic. sing. 3 of *gadu* 'to let, allow', and is an ex. of the dramatic present; cf. *deuuant* l. 412 above. This is the only recorded ex. of *damsathyr*, but cf. *amsathyr* 'trampling, thronging, etc.' ll. 90, 773, (GPC 102).

472. **ys gohilion hwnn:** 'he is what remains'. *Gohilion* = *gwehilion* 'remnant'. Note the order of the words in this nominal sentence; copula (*ys*) + pred. (*gohilion*) + subject (*hwnn*). Cf. GMW 139n. 3.

488–9. **y mynwgyl y uorwyn:** 'the maiden's neck'. The *y* before *mynwgyl* may be the def. art. or the poss. pron. 3 sing. fem.; either 'the neck' or 'her neck'. In any event, neither is usual before a definitive genit., but a few exx. do occur in MW; see GMW 25 (d).

487–98. This rhythmical and rhetorical passage describing **Olwen** (see n. on l. 498) and her beauty may be compared with the parallel rhetorical description of Culhwch riding to Arthur's court, ll. 60–81 above. Each is elaborately constructed in balanced periods embodying formulaic phrases or fanciful similes: the whole being reminiscent of the device of 'runs' in Gaelic folk-tales (see introduction p. lxxiv). The comparison of Olwen's beauty with the beauty of running water finds many parallels in the poetry of the Gogynfeirdd and the Cywyddwyr. The colour-comparisons are conventional: the comparison with the whiteness of the swan is familiar (and cf. Gwen *Alarch* l. 361 above); so is that of Olwen's hair as more yellow than the broom (**banadyl**) l. 490), and that of her cheeks as more red than the rose or the foxglove (**fion**), l. 496. *Fion* is cognate with Ir. *sian*, which is similarly used in a famous OI description of the heroine Deirdre (*Longes mac n-Uislenn*, ed.

Vernam Hull, (New York, 1979), l.34). **Canawon godrwyth**
(l.492) 'the shoots of the marsh-trefoil' (Mab. cf. GPC 1424), 'wood
anemone', (Guest). *Cenawon coed* means 'buds, catkins'. But cf. Ir.
ceann(a)bhán 'bog cotton, cotton-grass' (Dinneen, *Irish-English Dic-
tionary*); with **godrwyth** < *go* + *trwytho*) 'moist, steeped, damp',
that is, 'moist cotton grass'. The comparison of Olwen's eye
to that of a **hebawc mut** (l.493) or 'mewed hawk' (ll.393–4), though
it is unparalleled elsewhere, has been explained by ref. to the Laws of
Hywel Dda (see B. Lewis-Jones, B xxiii, 327–8): the falcon was kept
in a *mut* 'cage', it was 'mewed' or kept quiet while it moulted.
According to the Laws it was more valuable after this, that is, when it
had moulted and lost its feathers. *Mut* < Lat. *mūto*; cf. LlB 54–5;
HDdL 183. The significance of this comparison seems to be that no
falcon thrice moulted (**trimut**), that is, a falcon in its prime, and with
freshly-grown feathers, had eyes more fair than were Olwen's. Cf.
Culhwch's horse *pedwar gayaf* (l.60): evidently it was a young horse in
its prime. With **golwc** 'eye' cf. *golygon orwyllt* PKM 42,16.

497. **Pedeir meillonen gwynnyon:** 'Four white trefoils'. Cf. the
pedeir tywarchen or 'four sods' cast up by the hooves of Culhwch's
horse, l.74 above. With the use of a pl. adj. after a sing. n. preceded
by a numeral, cf. *deu uilgi uronnwynyon urychyon* l.69 above, and
GMW 36n.

a dyuei: note that the vb. here is sing. with a pl. subject in the
Abnormal Order, whereas it is usually pl., though exx. of the sing.
are found in sentences of this type; cf. GMW 180; SC vi (1971),
45–6.

498. **y gelwit hi Olwen:** with the fanciful explanation of Olwen's
name, as deriving from *ôl* 'track' and the fem. of *gwyn* 'white', cf.
the fanciful explanation given for the name of Culhwch *vrth y gaffel
yn retkyr hwch* (l.11 above), and of Goreu – *Goreu dyn yw* (l.810), and
that of Pryderi (PKM 26). There are many exx. in Irish of such
fanciful etymologies, and the text of *Cóir Anmann* 'True
Explanation of Names' (ed. Stokes, *Irische Texte* (Leipzig, 1897),
285–444) gives a series of such interpretations of the names of Irish
legendary and historical figures. To the redactor (or author) of the
tale, Olwen's name meant 'White Track', yet this is not necessarily
its original meaning. In EIHM 304 T. F. O'Rahilly compared *Olwen*
with the girl's name *Eurolvyn* 'Golden Wheel' in l.364 above, and

compares this name with *Ar(y)anrot* 'Silver Wheel' (PKM 269–70; TYP 277–8). O'Rahilly rejects *Olwen* in favour of *Olwyn* 'wheel' (with the older spelling of *e* for *y*) as the original form of this name, and adds abstruse mythological speculations. However that may be, there is no doubt as to the meaning of Olwen's name for the writer of the tale: the 'four white trefoils' which grew miraculously in her footsteps are a folklore motif (ST 'A' 262.1 and 'F' 971.6) associated in some sources with the Virgin Mary and with saints – according to TWS 230 this same miracle was associated in Glamorgan with St Dwynwen. The secondary meaning of *gwyn/gwen* 'holy' may have given a semi-religious connotation to Olwen's name, even if its primitive meaning lay elsewhere.

The name of *Olwen* was unknown to the poets before the 15th. cent. exx. GDE p. 33,13; LGC 372,69, etc.

500. **y gwelas:** the *y* here consists of the affirmative verbal prt. *y* + the infixed pron. obj. *y* which has coalesced with it 'he saw her'.

501. **ti a gereis:** a clear ex. of the Mixed Order, with the emphasis on the initial element: 'It is you whom I have loved'. Originally this element was preceded by a form of the copula; see GMW 140–1.

gwnelych: subj. pres. sing. 2; an ex. of the pres. subj. denoting command or wish 'Will you come with me?' Cf. GMW 113.

503. **elwyf:** subj. pres. sing. 1. Here the pres. subj. denotes future meaning; cf. GMW 113. Also *gwelwyf* l.518 below. This use is common in early poetry, but is more rare in prose.

510. **y hystauell:** 'to her chamber', consisting of the prep. *y* and the poss. pron. *y*, followed by *h*-; cf. GMW 23.

ystauell: according to the Laws of Hywel Dda the *ystauell* 'chamber' was normally occupied by women. The king had his own *ystafell*, which contained his bed. It was the duty of the *gwas ystafell* or 'chamberlain' to look after the king's bed, and to carry messages between the hall and the chamber. No doubt he came to know many secrets, as is implied in PKM 3,11; also see n. idem, 138.

511. **porthawr:** the reading departs from that of G. Evans in WM, who reads *keithawr*. Thomas Jones deciphered the reading of W as *porthawr* (not *keithawr*), corresponding to R's *porthawr* (see B xii, 85).

513. **neuad:** in contrast to the *ystauell*, the *neuad* was a scene of great activity, and a focal point of the court, where the war-band would be gathered around the chief, and there would be carousing and drinking. Arthur's *neuad* was called *Ehangwen*, l.264 above, see n.

513–14. **Henpych gwell ... o Duw ac o dyn:** the same form of greeting 'from God and from man' is employed by Prydydd y Moch to Llywelyn ab Iorwerth, H 282,26.

516. **Mae:** this can be employed in MW (and by some later classical poets, such as Goronwy Owen) at the beginning of a sentence with the meaning 'Where is/are ... ? Cf. GMW 143; also 547, 561, 987 below.

517. **Drycheuwch y fyrch:** The forks needed to lift Ysbaddaden's eye-lids have a striking and unique parallel in the OI tale 'The Battle of Moytura', where the giant Balor has a similar characteristic; see AIT 44; E. Gray (ed. and trans) *Cath Maige Tuired* 60–1; CO (1) xciii–xciv. The giant's injunction is repeated in l.547 below.

518. **defnyt uyn daw:** 'the substance (that is, the future shape) of my son-in-law'. On this use of *defnydd* 'material, substance' see GPC 914 D. A. Binchy, *Celtica* iii (1956), 225, and n. on *deifnyawc*, TYP no. 4. Cf. also l.549 below.

522. **tri llechwayw gwenhwynic:** 'three poisoned stone spears'. Cf. the *llechwayw gwenwynic* cast by the *addanc* in the tale of *Peredur*, WM 156,30. The ref. to *hayarn* in l.527 suggests that the spear-point alone was of stone (flint?). *Lluchwayw* 'flashing/lightning spear', is an alternative favoured by Jackson (*A Celtic Miscellany* 316) and this word is in fact attested in GIG xx,112 (see n.). There are no other exx. of either word; unless there has been mutual influence between the two texts in WM, the occurrence of the word in *Peredur* is evidence against the possibility of the substitution of *lluchwayw* as the correct word here.

524–5. **yn gythrymhet:** cf. l.351 above.

529. **Gwest a orugant vy y nos honno:** 'they spent the night'; cf. *gwest* n. on l.2 above.

532. **egweti:** also *agwedi*, a legal term meaning 'dowry'. It was the bride's property, handed over by her father to the bridegroom on her marriage. It could be recovered by her, if before the end of seven

years she was separated from her husband. Cf. HDdL xxix, 310; WLW 117–18.

amwabyr: (var. *amwobr, amobr*) the fee payable by the girl's father to his overlord on the occasion of her marriage. See HDdL 311.

534. **Hi a'y ffedeir gorhenuam a'e fedwar gorhendat:** 'She and her four great-grandmothers and her four great-grandfathers'. This was the basic family unit of four generations, which shared both privileges and responsibilities, according to the primitive Celtic social structure. The necessity to obtain their permission for Olwen's marriage was therefore raised by her father in order (purposely) to present a legal obstacle to it. The same unit of relationship was known in Irish as the *derbfine* ('certain kindred'), and it had similar connotations; see DIL 'D' 32; and cf. WLW 199. The Welsh unit of the *gwely* was broadly similar in meaning, though etymologically unrelated.

538. **mab Teirgveth:** elsewhere *mab Teirgwaed* (see n. on l.199). The name is here preserved in OW spelling.

560. **yssyt:** this is the only regular rel. form of the vb. in Welsh, consisting of *ys(s)* 'is' + *yt* [iđ]. The meaning is 'who/which is'; cf. GMW 63.

562. **mi a'e heirch:** 'it is I who seek her'; an ex. of the Mixed Order, with emphasis on the initial element, as in l.566 below *ys mi a'e heirch*. Originally it was preceded by a form of the copula; cf. GMW 140–1.

563. **Dos yma:** 'Come here' – whereas *dos* usually means 'Go'; GMW 136.

567–8. **a nottwyf arnat ti:** 'that which I shall name to thee'. This is an ex. of a rel. clause without an expressed antecedent; cf. *nod a nottych* l.171 above, and ll.568–9 below, 'Name what you will'; GMW 72–3.

There follows the long list of the *anoethau* or tasks stipulated by Ysbaddaden, of which barely a quarter are actually fulfilled; see introduction pp. xlvii–viii, li.

570–1. **y diwreidyaw o'r dayar:** the text as printed here is based on the reading of the manuscript by Thomas Jones, and discussed by him, B xii (1948), 85. It includes *losci* for WM's *loski*. The reading of the MS was unclear to Gwenogvryn Evans, who reproduced this passage differently. R's reading is again differently phrased, and is slightly confused.

574–5. **a merch:** 'and (my) daughter' for *a'm merch*. Occasionally the form of certain combinations, such as *a'm* – here for *a'm m* – suggests that the copyist wrote what he heard, rather than what he read; in other words, somebody was dictating to him. (See introduction p. xiii.) Also ll.710–11, 752. Cf. ll.756–7 *y merch i*.

578. **yssit ny cheffych:** 'there is that which thou wilt not get' – a neg. rel. clause without an expressed antecedent, as in l.584 below. Cf. also ll.567–8 above.

579. **Amaethon mab Dôn:** that is, 'Great/Divine Ploughman' (*amaeth* < Gaul. *ambactus* 'ploughman, husbandman', GPC 80). In this name it is possible that there may be a recollection of the name of the pagan Celtic god of agriculture. *Don* is the equivalent of Ir. *Donu, Danu*, the mother of the gods or *Tuatha Dé Danann*, the 'tribes of the goddess Danu'. In Wales the family of Don are associated with magic and enchantment, and play a large part in the *Mabinogi* – in *Math fab Mathonwy*, Gwydion (the supreme magician) and Aranrhod are children of Don. (See PKM 252–3, Mac Cana, *Celtic Mythology* 75–6; and cf. EWGT 90.) Only two allusions, other than the present one, survive to *Amaethon mab Don*: the poem *Echrys Ynys* (BT 68,16, discussion BWP 172–80) and a prose fragment from P 98B referring to a dispute between *Amaethaon* (sic) and Gwydion sons of Don, which brought about the battle of *Goddau* (see CLlH l–li; RWM i,613).

580–1. **ny elly ditheu treis arnaw ef:** 'you cannot force him' also ll.586–7, 591, 615, 629–30, 664–5, 748–9. But *ny elly titheu y dreissaw ef* ll.621–2, also ll.625, 659–60.

584–5. **Gouannon mab Don:** 'Great/Divine Smith' (W. *gof*, Ir. *goba* 'smith'). The Gaulish *Gobannonos* was evidently a smith-god; see previous note, and refs. Like his brother *Amaethon*, *Gofannon* is a shadowy figure, obliquely alluded to in *Math fab Mathonwy* as the slayer of his nephew *Dylan eil Ton*, the son of *Aranrhod*, which is described as *trydyd anuat ergyt* 'one of the Three Ill-Fated Blows' (PKM 78; the triad is not found in TYP). *Gouannon* is also named in a poem belonging to the story of Taliesin (RP 1054,35–7): *neu bum* *gan wyr keluydon/gan uath hen gan gouannon* ... *blwydyn ykaer gofannon* (= BT 3,2: *yg kaer ofanhon*). Gofannon's cognate figure in Ir. is *Goibniu*, the skilled craftsman-god in *Cath Maige Tuired* (ed. Gray, 125; AIT 42–3; cf. EIHM 314–17), and in *Lebor Gabála Érenn*, the 'Book of Invasions of Ireland' (ed. Macalister, ITS vol. 41 (Dublin, 1941) 164–5, etc.). In Ir. folklore he appears as *Gobban Saer* 'G. the Craftsman'. The Gaul. personal name *Gobannitio* may be compared, and also the British place-name *Gobannio*, now *(Aber)gavenny*; see D. E. Evans, *Gaulish Personal Names* (Oxford, 1967), 350–1, and G 545. For Llyn Gofannon in the commote of Uwch Gwyrfai, Gwynedd, see B xxi, 147–9; YB xiii, 33n.

585. **y waret:** 'repair, renew, mend', cf. l.387 above. Here it means to 'set' the plough; that is, to turn it at the head of the 'selion' or furrow.

586. **y urenhin teithiawc:** 'for a lawful/rightful king'. Cf. *mab brenhin gvlat teithiawc* l.91 above; CA 1095 *mab brenhin teithiauc*; ibid. 1072 *mab teyrn teithiawc*; LlDC 34,56 *mab goholheth teithiawc* (see Ast. H. 318); *teithi* 'innate characteristics'; Ir. *techte* 'fitting, rightful'.

589. **deu ychen:** 'two oxen'; *ychen* could be explained as a survival of the old dual, but it could also be the ordinary pl., which in MW is sometimes used with numerals; GMW 34,47.

Gwlwlyd Wineu: this is a var., if not a corruption, of a very early triad (TYP no.45): *Tri Phryf Ychen Enys Prydein: Melyn Gwaianhwyn, a Gwineu Ych Gwylwylyd, a'r Ych Brych* (see n. to triad). *Gwineu* ('Chestnut'), the name of the ox, has here been converted into an epithet for *Gwlwlyd*, the owner of the other two oxen named in the triad, as in l.593 below. This *anoeth* is duplicated, as is clear from the repetition of *yn deu gytbreinhawc* 'both yoked together' in l.594 below. If *Gwlwlyd* is a compd. of *gwlf/gwlw* 'notch' (cf. GPC 1684), and *llwyd* 'grey', then 'Grey-Notched' is an epithet more suited to an ox than the name of a man, and it should perhaps be understood as such, both here and in the triad. *Gwylwylyd* 'meek and gentle' (GPC 1764) in the triad would then be a corruption of *gwlwlwyd*, the older form preserved in CO and also in the P 47 text of the triad (see *v.l.* to triad). Elsewhere *Gwineu* is given as the name of Cei's horse, TYP no.42.

593. **Y Melyn Gwanhwyn:** 'Yellow Spring' (?), the first of the

three oxen named also in triad no.45. The oldest version of the triad in P 16 reads *Melyn Gwaianhwyn* (see also the *v.l.* to the triad), rather than *gwanhwyn/gwannwyn*, the forms given in the two MSS of *Culhwch*. *Gwaeanwyn* (OW *guiannuin*) is the older form of *gwanwyn* 'spring', a form attested as tri-syllabic by the metre in GDG 14,31 (see n., and GPC 1575–6), indicating that 'Yellow Spring' is the name here intended, rather than a colour compd. of *gwan* 'pale, weak' and *gwyn*, giving 'Yellow Pale-White' (as wrongly translated both in TYP and in Mab. 114n.).

Yr Ych Brych: 'the Speckled (brindled) Ox' – the third name also given in the triad. The antiquity of this name is proved by the entry in *Preiddeu Annwn* (BT 21,2) *yr ych brych bras y penrwy* 'the brindled ox, stout the collar' (see M. Haycock's note, SC xviii/xix, 74).

593–4. yn deu gytbreinhawc: the same phrase is employed by Gwynfardd Brycheiniog in his *awdl* to St David, when he describes the saint's oxen as *deu ychen . . . deu gar a gertynt yn gydpreinyawc* 'two kinsmen who strode yoked together', H 198,23–4. St David's oxen have been conflated in folklore with the *ychen bannawg* (see following note). It is tempting to see here an ironic allusion to the traditional asceticism of David's monks: *Boum nulla ad arandum cura introducitur, quisque sibi et fratribus diuitie, quisque et bos* 'There is no bringing in of oxen to have ploughing done, rather is everyone both riches and ox unto himself and the brethren' *Rhigyfarch's Life of St David*, ed. James, ch.22.

596. deu ychen bannawc: *bannawc* means 'high, conspicuous', but in ref. to oxen it means 'horned'.

597. Mynyd Bannawc: 'horned' or 'peaked' mountain, an ancient Welsh name for a mountain in Scotland, one of the nearly-forgotten place-names in the 'Old North'. It survives today only in the name of the 'Bannock' Burn. According to K. Jackson '*Bannog* is a range of uplands . . . which almost entirely blocks the narrow neck-land of Scotland between Stirling and Dumbarton . . . the Bannock Burn . . . flows out into the Forth near Stirling . . . Strategically (it is) one of the most significant mountain barriers in Scotland, forming the southern boundary of Pictland in the west' (OSPG 5–6, 78–9; cf. W. J. Watson, *Celtic Place-Names of Scotland* (Edinburgh, 1926), 195–6). References in early poetry always refer to *tra* Bannawc 'beyond B.', apparently in every instance denoting the land of the Picts (*Prydyn*): *un maban e gian o dra bannawc* CA 255; *Yssydd Lanfawr tra Bannawg* CLlH v,7a: *clywed y gyma yd tra bannawc* H 3,8 (Meilyr Brydydd). More significant in the present context, however, are the allusions in the *Vita Cadoci* (VSB 82,100) which preserve the same opposition between *ultra/citra montem Bannauc* as is found here in *y parth hwnt* and *y parth hwnn* (*i'r Mynydd Bannawg*), since these are strikingly suggestive of a textual relation between CO and the *Vita Cadoci* (see further n. to *Kaw o Brydein* l.647 below). In folklore the *dau ychen bannog* are associated with the building of Llanddewibrefi (see TWS 66–7). The story of these famous oxen appears to be recalled in the place-name *Cwys yr Ychen Bannog* 'the furrow of the Y. B.' – a mountain dyke which divides the parishes of Caron-uwch-Clawdd and Caron-is-Clawdd, north-east of Tregaron in Dyfed. Certain of the Cywyddwyr recall the story of the *ychen bannawg*: see GDG 130,15–16, and especially GLM xci,5–8, xlii,75–6, GTA 338,43.

598. **Ys hwy yr rei hynny:** 'They are those/Those are the ones'. An early form of the nominal sentence, consisting of copula + pred. + subject. Later the pl. form *hwy*, which anticipates *Nynnyaw a Pheibyaw* was replaced in all cases by the sing. *ef, ys ef* becoming *sef*. Cf. *sef* in the glossary, and GMW 52–3. Note the form *yr* of the art., where *y* would be normal; cf. GMW 24.

599. **Nynhyaw a Pheibyaw:** these are the only instances of incontrovertibly historical figures among the *anoethau* (although the Court-List offers a number of others). *Nynhyaw* and *Peibyaw* were two sons of *Erb*, traditionally a king of *Erging* or Archenfield in the 6th. cent. Wendy Davies conjectures that *Erb* ruled from *c.* 525–55 (*The Llandaff Charters* 75; *An Early Welsh Microcosm* 66). On Erging see HW 280. The genealogy of the two brothers is given in J 20 (EWGT 45 (9) and (10). *Peibyaw < Pab* (Lat. *papa + iaw (io)*, acc. M. Richards, B xix, 113. In the genealogy *Peibyaw* is named *Pibiawn glawrawc*, that is, *claforog, clafyr(i)og* 'drivelling'', or alternatively 'scorbutic, leprous' (GPC 488). (Cf. *Hettwn Clauyryawc* ll.708–9 below.) In the life of St Dubricius (LL 78) the saint's grandfather is described as *Quidam rex fuit ercychi (sic) regionis, Pepiau nomine clauorauc uocatus britannice Latine uero spususus*. His name is Latinized as *Proprius* in Rhigyfarch's Life of St David (ed. James, ch.13, from Digby MS) = *Pepiau* VSB 154 (Vespasian MS). WLSD 39 gives the

name as *Pebiawc*: in all these versions St David is said to have cured
the king of his 'blindness'. Cf. TWS 99–100.

a rithwys Duw yn ychen am eu pechawd: cf. the similar
explanation given for the Twrch Trwyth's transformation into a
boar in ll. 1075–6 below: *Brenhin uu, ac am y bechawt y rithwys Duw ef
yn hwch.*

607–8. **hyt pan vo ef a uo pennlliein guynn am penn vym
merch:** 'so that it may be a white veil for my daughter's head'. Here
we have an ex. of the mixed construction in a subordinate clause,
where the emphasized part (*ef* 'it') is brought forward to the
beginning of the sentence or clause, preceded by a form of the
copula (*vo*) corresponding in tense and mood to that of the main vb.
(*uo*). The latter is rel., preceded by the rel. pron. *a*. See GMW 140–1.

vym merch: similarly l. 757, but cf. *a merch* ll. 574–5 and n.

611. **bragodi:** 'to make bragget'. MW *bragawt* was a drink made of
honey and ale fermented together; later it was made from sugar and
spice and ale. Cf. Meilir Brydydd in his elegy to Gruffydd ap Cynan
(d. 1137): *kyn myned mab kynan ydan dywawd/keffid yny gyntet uet a
bragawd* (H 2,1–2) 'Before the son of Kynan went under the earth,
there were obtained in his hall mead and bragget'.

613. **Llwyr mab Llwyron:** 'Complete son of Complete' *llwyr*, pl.
llwyr(i)on; cf. *Llwyr Dydwc* (l. 338): both fabricated names. *Llwyr's
kib* is the first in a series of vessels of plenty, some of which have
specific parallels in the 'Thirteen Treasures of the Island of Britain'
(see introduction pp. xlix–l); others, such as this, are absent from
the list, but bear a general resemblance to items in it.

pennllat: from penn 'chief' and *llat* 'ale, beer'; fig. 'gift, virtue'
(GPG 2076). Cf. *llawen gwyr odywch llat* 'Happy are men over beer'
(CLlH vi,26b). *Pennllat* here means 'the choicest drink'.

618. **Mwys Gwydneu Garanhir:** *mwys* 'basket, hamper' < Lat.
mensa; cf. CLlH 129. One of the Vessels of Plenty listed among the
'Thirteen Treasures' is *Mwys Gwyddno Garanir: bwyd i un gwr a roid
ynddo, a bwyd i ganwr a gaid ynddo pan agorwyd* (TYP 240: LlC v, 55;
EC x, 463). *Gwydneu Garanhir* 'G. Long Shank' was a legendary (and
possibly historical) character of the 'Old North' who became a
figure in Welsh traditional stories, in particular in the legendary

Taliesin story, and in that of the submersion of 'Cantref y Gwaelod' in Cardigan Bay, commemorated in the poem 'Boddi Maes Gwyddneu' (LlDC no. 39), and in a dialogue poem with Gwyn ap Nudd (see n. on ll.713–14 below). See further B. F. Roberts, Ast.H. 311–18; TYP 397–400; and cf. n. on *Teithi Hen* ll.245–50 above.

pob tri nawyr: 'every three nine men'. For *nawyr* 'nine men' cf. *trywyr* l.235 above. On the construction cf. TC 145–6 on *pob* + numeral; here 'three nines at a time'. Cf. *bob un bob deu* l.941 below.

624. Gwlgawt Gododin: the name corresponds to that of *Gwlyget Gododin*, CA 369–70, the steward of Mynyddawg Mwynfawr: *ancwyn mynydawc enwawc e gwnaeth* 'he made the feast of Mynyddawg famous'. The ref. shows that the redactor of *Culhwch* must have known not only the name, but also the function of Mynyddawg's steward. The form here is nearer to the original than that of the scribe of CA: as Ifor Williams has pointed out (n. CA p. 166), it would have been easy for a scribe to miscopy an original *Gwlgot* (later written as *Gwlgaut*) as *Gwlget*. For other names in the tale which are paralleled in the *Gododdin* see n. on *Kilyd*, l.1 above, and introduction p. xxxvii n.22.

627. Telyn Teirtu: this item is not included in the list of the 'Thirteen Treasures of the Island of Britain', though it seems quite probable that it may have originally belonged to the list, as is indicated by P. C. Bartrum, EC x, 460. The only other known allusion to it is by Dafydd ab Edmwnd, who claims that *telyn Deirtud* (sic) is silenced because of the death of Siôn Eos (meaning that poetry is silenced) *Oxford Book of Welsh Verse* ed. T. Parry, 140,18. Since *Castell Teirtut* is named in LL 134,8 *Teirtud* ('three peoples') is most probably the correct form of the name.

628. Pan uo da gan dyn: for the requirement that an early Ir. harper should be able to play *golltraige, gentraige, suantraige* 'a sorrow-strain, a joy-strain, and a sleep-strain' see K. Meyer (ed.) *The Triads of Ireland* (Dublin, 1906), no.122, and DIL 'S' col.402.

632. Adar Rianhon: on the Birds of Rhiannon (three in number) who enchanted the followers of Bendigeidfran with their singing during their stay at Harlech, see PKM 45, 3; Mab. 38–9; and for a similar description of magic birds see *Owein* (ed. R. L. Thomson, Dublin, 1968) ll.180–2, 268–9; Mab. 160–1, 163. Irish parallels are cited by Anne Ross, 'Sacred and Magic Birds', PCB ch. vi. This task has been omitted from the text of the Red Book, and neither text refers to its completion.

635. **Peir Diwrnach Wydel:** 'The Cauldron of D. the Irishman'. This item unmistakably corresponds to another of the 'Thirteen Treasures': *Pair Dyrnwch Gawr (var. Dyrnog, Tyrnog, Dyrn(f)wch etc.), pe rhoid iddo gig i wr llwfyr i ferwi, ni ferwai fyth; o rhoid iddo gig i wr dewr, berwi a wnai yn ebrwydd* (TYP 240, LlC v, 60, EC x, 467–8). The similarity between the names of the giants *Diwrnach* and *Wrnach* was noted by Idris Foster, CO(1) lxii, who advocated an Ir. derivation for *Diwrnach*, comparing Ir. *Diugurnach, Digornaig*, etc. ('Irish Influence' 32). P. Sims-Williams (B xxix, 603–4) shows that this can hardly be assumed. Cf. the Gaul. name *Durnācos*, recorded by Holder, *Alt celtische Sprachschatz* (Leipzig, 1898–1913), i, 1382, and by J. Whatmough, *Dialects of Ancient Gaul* (Michigan, 1983), item 78. Sims-Williams prefers some variant of *Dyrnawc/Dyrnog* as the original form of this name. Both *Dyrnawg Gawr* and *Diwrnach Wydel* possessed a magic *peir* or cauldron, and there is good reason to identify the two. The epithet *Gwydel* here is certainly the equivalent of *Gawr*. Cf. *Dyrnbhwch Gawr yghwlad Euas* (Ewyas) listed by Siôn Dafydd Rhys among the Welsh Giants in Cy 27, 144. It is also relevant to compare *peir pen annwfn ... ni beirw bwyt llwfyr* in *Preiddeu Annwn* (BT 55,2–3), and M. Haycock's note, SC xviii/xix (1983–4), 69. Cf. introduction pp. lviii–lix. For the completion of this task see ll.1036–56 below.

635–6. **Odgar mab Aed brenhin Iwerdon:** P. Sims-Williams has shown (B xxix, 605–6) that this name corresponds to Fr. *Og(i)er* < *Audagari*. Cf. *Odyar franc* in GER (WM 385,26). *Odgar* (later *Odyar*) may be a fairly early French borrowing into Welsh, not least because *ffranc* is attested as early as the 9th. cent. in the Juvencus *englynion*, B vi, 102; BWP 90–2). Sims-Williams comments that 'the most likely explanation is the author of the story was unable to distinguish one foreign name from another, and used Irish and Frankish names interchangeably'. Yet there may have been a native hero of a similar name, since Prydydd y Moch describes Llywelyn ab Iorwerth as *rwysc odyar* (H 271,24) and as *gymrawd gotyar* (H 297,7), and Gruffudd ap Maredudd refers to *lluryc Otar* (R 1206,32). The Ir. name *Aed* occurs too frequently to allow it to be associated with any particular king. It was early adopted into Welsh as *Aed(d)*;

see EWGT 168; B xxix, 604n.7, and TYP 263–4 for *Aed* and its dim. *Aedan*. Cf. *Gwittard mab Aed brenhin Iwerdon* l.295 above.

639. Yskithyrwyn Penn Beid: 'White Tusk Chief of Boars'. In ll.1018–20 this boar's head is cloven in two by Kaw of Prydein, who abstracts the *ysgithr* (tusk) from his head. For the *ysgithr* see further n. on l.1090 *y grib a'r ellyn a'r gwelleu* below.

643. a'e tynho o'e penn: 'who may draw it (that is, the *ysgithr*) from his head'. Here it is stipulated that Odgar mab Aed is to perform this act, but in the event (ll.1018–20) it is Kaw of Prydein who accomplishes it. It looks as though the name of Odgar (in 1036–9 a hostile king of Ireland) has been substituted for that of Kaw of Prydein because the redactor of the tale could not refrain from making his pun on the name of *Caw/Cadw* in ll.646–7.

o'e penn: one would expect lenition of *penn* here, as also in *o'e teyrnas* l.648 below.

647. y Kaw o Prydein: (*y kadw o Prydein* W; *y gado* R). This name should certainly be restored here as *Kaw* (*pace* the readings of both W and R), and this is corroborated by the fact that it is Kaw of Prydein/Prydyn, not Odgar mab Aed, who obtains the tusk of Ysgithrwyn (l.1020). He is *Kaw o Prydein* in all subsequent appearances in the tale (although we must depend on the text of R alone for these). The occurrence of the names *Hueil, Gildas*, and other identifiable names in the list of the sons of Kaw in ll.206–13 above (see notes) confirms the identity of their father with *Kaw o Prydein*. *Cado* occurs in the genealogies as a variant of *Cadwy* (EWGT 174–5), and cf. also *Berth mab Kado* l.224 above. But *Kadw/Kado* here is an instance of word-play on the name of Kaw, who is required to 'keep' (*o gadw*) the tusk of Ysgithrwyn Ben Beid. (A similar collocation of *Kaw/cadw* is found in ll.1228–9 below, and cf. n. on l.700 for a similar jocular play on words.) *Caw o Prydein/ Prydyn* is a legendary figure known from the Lives of Cadoc and of Gildas and from ByS as the father of the saint. According to one version of TYP nos. 81, 96, his family was one of the *Tair Gwelygordd Saint* ('Families of Saints') of Britain. The two *Lives* of Gildas (ed. Hugh Williams, *Gildas* 322–413) agree that the saint's father *Caunus (Cawus)* ruled somewhere in Scotland: this was at *Arecluta* 'the Rock of the Clyde' (Dumbarton) according to the 9th. cent. Breton *Vita*; or (less precisely) in *Scotia* according to the 12th.

cent. *Vita* by Caradog of Llancarfan. The *Vita Cadoci* (VSB 82–4) tells how on a visit to Scotland the saint and his followers exhumed the bones of an enormous giant, whom St Cadog miraculously resuscitated, and by doing so won for the giant a temporary respite from hell. The giant names himself as *Cau Pritdin seu Caur*, and tells how he had ruled formerly *ultra montem Bannauc* (see n. on l. 597), that is, in *Prydyn* or Pictland. There, no doubt, were to be found the *trugein cantref Prydein* over which he ruled. *Prydein* 'Britain' and *Prydyn* 'Pictland' (Ir. *Cruithne*) were constantly confused in medieval texts, as was pointed out by Ifor Williams, AP 21–2. (On the confusion of the two see further K. Jackson, *Scottish Historical Review* 33 (1954), 16–18.) In the *Vita Cadoci* Caw is portrayed as an oppressive ruler who has much to answer for, whereas in *Culhwch* he is a leading hero who accomplishes two of the *anoethau* single-handed: winning Ysgithrwyn's tusk, collecting the blood of the *Gwiddon Orddu* for the Giant's shaving, and finally shaving Ysbaddaden with the tusk. In accordance with the frequent transference to Wales of the traditions of northern heroes, Caw is described as *o Dwrkelyn* (a commote in Anglesey) in *Bonedd yr Arwyr* (EWGT 85(3)). One version of this genealogy (Ll 187) adds further that Caw was *arglwydd Cwm Cowlwyd: Caw oedd yn trigo yn edeirnon yn amser Arthur* (see variants listed in B xviii, 242). See further TYP 301–3; TWS 135–7; OSPG 79.

652–3. **Y Widon Ordu merch y Widon Orwen:** 'the Very Black Witch daughter of the Very White Witch'. With the latter cf. the Breton woman's name *Orven, Orguen*, Chr. Br. 223. Witches are familiar and sinister figures in the popular literature of all countries: together with the Nine Witches of Gloucester who gave instruction to Peredur in the use of arms, cf. the nine witches, all sisters, who attacked St Samson during his journey from Wales to Brittany (CO (1) lxxiii–v; and refs. cited TWS 117). Like the 'Very Black Witch' these too had a mother who was a witch. But the episode of the witches has its closest parallel in the poem *Pa Gur* (LlDC no. 31; see introduction pp. xxxv–vi, ll. 21,44) which refers to Arthur's contest with a witch, and also to Cei's having slain nine witches.

653. **Pennant Gouut yg gwrthtir Uffern:** 'The Valley of Grief in the Uplands of Hell'. *Gouut = gofid* 'grief, distress'; for *gwrthtir Uffern* see also ll. 189, 1207–8. *Uffern* the 'Otherworld' is evidently synonymous in the tale with *Annw(f)n*, cf. the *dievyl Annwuyn* l. 714

below), as it is also in *Preiddeu Annwn* cf. (l.20) *rac drws porth vffern llugyrn lloscit* (see M. Haycock's note in her edition of the poem, SC xviii/xix (1983–4), 71). In the present instance the 'Otherworld' appears to be located in north Britain: Arthur travels *parth a'r Gogled* (l.1208) to reach the witches' cave. Yet the place-names *Foel Wyddon, Padell Nant Wyddon* etc. in the area of Pumlumon appear to indicate a secondary localization of the story in Ceredigion (cf. CO(1) lxxv n. and n. on *Dillus Varchawc* l.700 below).

655–6. **y keffir:** the *y* here is a conflation of the pre-verbal prt. *y* + the infixed pron. obj. 3 sing. *y*. Cf. GMW 23.

657. **Guidolwyn Gorr:** 'G. the Dwarf'. Cf. *Eurolvyn merch Wdolwyn Gorr* l.364 (R), and *Grudlwyn Gorr* l.333 (see n.). A similar (and perhaps identical) name in TYP no.28 is *Gwythelin Gorr*: this suggests that an original *Gwyddelyn* 'little Irishman' may lie behind this name, especially in view of Dafydd ap Gwilym's version of the triad (GDG 84,40) which has *Eiddilig Gor, Wyddel call* (see notes, TYP pp.55 and 403). But *olwyn* 'wheel' is the second element in this name, as in those of the father and daughter in l.364; cf. also *Goroluyn* TYP no.66.

a gatwant: 'which keep'. Here we have an affirmative rel. clause, in which the rel. is subject. In such a clause the vb. is usually sing. but sometimes, as here, it is pl.; cf. GMW 61, and further SC vi (1971), 42–56.

662. **aruaeth:** 'manner, way'. R's reading here is undoubtedly correct, as was pointed out by T. Jones, B xiii, 77.

663. **Rinnon Rin Baruawc:** 'R. Stiff Beard' (*rhyn* 'stiff'). *Bar(y)f* and *baruawc* 'beard, bearded' are prominent epithets in *Culhwch* (see introduction p. xxxii, n. 18).

667. **crib a guelleu:** 'the comb and scissors'. In l.1090 a razor (*ellyn*) is added to them, to take the place of Ysgithrwyn's *ysgithr* or tusk, which was undoubtedly originally intended as the implement with which the Giant was to be shaved. Cf l.164 above, and n.

668. **rac y rynhet:** 'because of its stiffness'; cf. GMW 43.

669. **deu yskyuarn:** 'the two ears'. Cf. *ysgyfarnog* 'hare' (Cornish *scovarn*). On the prosthetic *y* see GMW 11–12.

669–70. **Twrch Trwyth mab Tared Wledic:** 'The Boar Trwyth'. Refs. in poetry from the *Gwarchan Cynfelyn* onwards (see introduction p. lxv) provide secure evidence that *trwyd* was the original form of this name, and *trwyd* is cognate with Ir. *triath* 'king/boar' (see DIL 'T' 307–8). The *Torc Triath* or Twrch Trwyth was thus a mythical giant boar known from the earliest sources in both Irish and Welsh. To account for the form *trwyth* in both W and R it must be supposed that an earlier copyist of the story misread *t* = *d* in his prototype for *t* = *th* – an easy enough mistake to make when the name *trwyd* no longer held meaning for him. (For a similar error see n. to *Gwrbothu (= Gwrfoddw) Hen*, l.252 above.) The earliest refs. in Welsh poetry suggest that the tradition of the giant boar was at one time known independently of both *Culhwch* and HB, whether or not it existed independently of the story of Arthur. The unique citation here of *Tared Wledic* as the name of the Twrch's father indicates that the boar was regarded as a king transformed, and this supposition is borne out by ll.1075–6 below *Brenhin uu, ac am y bechawt y rithwys Duw ef yn hwch*. Though unparalleled elsewhere in Welsh sources, it has been pointed out that the names of both the Twrch Trwyth and his father have been transmitted in slightly var. forms in two 12th.-cent. French romances; see Idris Foster in ALMA 39, and R. Roberts, 'Tors fils Ares, Tortain', BBIAS xiv (1962), 91–8, and cf. AOW p. 280.

673. **Drutwyn keneu Greit mab Eri:** *Drutwyn* 'Fierce/Brave White'. There is some confusion over the purpose for which Drudwyn the 'whelp' or pup of Greit mab Eri was required, since in l.701 below Drudwyn has become *deu geneu*, probably by confusion with *deu geneu gast Rhymhi*, said to have been captured in ll.930–40 below (see nn. on ll.315, 930–1). Later Drudwyn participates in both of the great boar-hunts (ll.1014, 1106). On *Greit mab Eri* see on l.176 above.

676–81. **Cors Cant Ewin, Canhastyr Canllaw, Kilyd Canhastyr:** all three have been previously named as members of Arthur's Court (ll.190–1). Their inclusion here seems redundant, and appears to be an inept borrowing from the Court-List, especially since in l.984 it is stated that the *cynllyuan* or leash to hold Drudwyn must be made from the beard of Dillus Farfog. But this is duplicated by the statement in ll.1005–6 that Arthur obtained the leash of Cors Cant Ewin.

681. **y daly:** note the form with the consonantal -*y*, deriving from an original *g*. In ModW the form of the vn. is *dala/dal*; cf. GMW 10. The stem is *dal(h)y*, as in *dalhyo* ll.675, 678, 701, 707.

685. **Mabon mab Modron:** < *Maponos* son of *Mátrona* 'the Youth God son of the Mother Goddess'. Evidence for the cult of the god *Maponos* comes mainly from North Britain, where dedications to him were made by high Roman officials garrisoning the Wall: on four of these *Maponos* is equated with Apollo. His name survives in that of the village of Lochmaben in Dumfriesshire, and in that of the 'Clochmabenstane' near Gretna on the Solway estuary. One or other of these places may well be the *locus Maponi* listed in the Ravenna Cosmography. Anne Ross shows that this area of southern Scotland was the centre of the cult of *Mabon/Maponos*, PCB 368–70. See further P. Mac Cana, *Celtic Mythology* 32–3; TYP 433–5, and introduction p. lx above. Traces of the cult of *Maponos* have also been found in Gaul, and his mother *Modron* < *Mátrona* is the tutelary goddess of the River Marne. *Mabon am Mydron* (sic) is named in *Pa Gur* (p. xxxv, l.7 above), and in the additional *Beddau* stanzas in P 98B, where his grave is located in Nantlle, Gwynedd (see T. Jones, PBA liii (1967), 136 (16).

689. **Guyn Mygtwn, march Gwedw:** 'White Dark Mane' (< *mwng* 'mane' + *dwn* 'dark, dun'). A var. of this name occurs among some additions to *Trioedd y Meirch* in P 47 (TYP no. 46A, see TYP xxx) which lists *Myngrwn* ('round/curved mane') *march Gwedw* as one of the *tri rodedicvarch* or 'three bestowed horses'. It is stated briefly below that Arthur obtained Mygdwn (l.1006), and that Mabon rode Mygdwn into the Severn in pursuit of the Twrch Trwyth (l.1177). With Mygdwn's name cf. the list of horses by their colour made by the poet Gwalchmai: *lliaws du a dwn a mygdwn melyn*, H 28,17.

kyfret: *kyf-* + *ret*, ModW *rhed*, meaning 'as swift as, of equal pace with'. As regards the formation, cf. *kyfoet, kyfryw, kyniuer*, etc. See GMW 38, and l.728 below.

690. **hela:** 'to hunt', also l. 735. We also find *hely* in l.731 (< *selg), a consonantal stem as in *daly* above. There were two separate developments in these forms: *y* was vocalized as *a*, or it was dropped to produce forms such as *dal, hel*, etc. Cf. GMW 10.

694. **Eidoel ... mab Aer:** (*Aer* 'slaughter, battle'). *Eidoel mab Ner* is named in the Court-List, l.263 above. Presumably the two are identical, and either patronymic could have arisen as a miscopying of the other. The medial -*d*- in *Eidoel* is ambiguous, since it may stand for either -*d*- or -*dd*-. J. Lloyd-Jones interpreted the first name as *Eiddoel* (G455), and suggested it is the same name as is found in LlDC 3, 15 *gur oet eitoel gorvy reol*. (But it is possible that *eito(e)l* here is a common noun 'praise'; see Jarman LlDC 87, and refs. cited.) In CO (1) xlvii–ix Idris Foster discussed Geoffrey of Monmouth's forms *Eldad* and *Eldol*, *Eidol* which are translated in the *Brut* respectively as *Eidal esgob Caerloyw* (BD 123) and *Eidol yarll Caer Gloev* (BD 99); see introduction pp. lxi–ii. Foster concluded that the same name, transmitted either orally or in writing, underlies all the var. forms in HRB and BD, as well as *Eidoel* in *Culhwch*, who was said to be imprisoned in the fortress of *Gliui*, that is, in Gloucester (see nn. to ll.831, 923 below), and released from there, in the episode recounted in ll.825–38 below. R's variant form of this name is *Eidyol* in l.263, and this form may be compared with an allusion by Casnodyn to *eil eidyol y lit* (RP 1246, 33), which adds to the evidence that the name derives from an older tradition. To these forms may be added that of *Eltat* (*Eldad*), son of *Eldoc*, in the direct line of descent from *Gloyw*, the eponym of Gloucester, in the genealogy of Gwrtheyrn as given in the *Historia Brittonum* (EWGT 7–8; HB ed. Dumville, 102; ed. F. Lot, 189). Cf. also Prydydd y Moch, H267,11, *Eidol*.

697. **Garselit Wydel, penkynyd Iwerdon:** a character previously named in the Court-List, l.295 above (see n.). Though there is no story of the achievement of this task, it is evident that it was accomplished, since *Garselit Wydel* is slain by the Twrch Trwyth in l.1117. His name is one of the names borrowed from *Culhwch* in *Englynion y Clyweit* (B iii, 14 (59)). The *penkynyd* or Chief Huntsman was one of the twenty-four officers of the king's court, LlB 2,16 etc., see HDdL 10,14.

700. **Dillus Varchawc:** (*dissull varchawc* in W and R) 'D the Horseman'. Elsewhere *Dillus Uar(r)uawg* 'D. the Bearded' in the story of the completion of this task, ll.953–84 (where the text of R is alone available), but *Dillus uab Eurei* in Arthur's satirical *englyn* (l.979). This latter patronymic is attested by Cynddelw's allusion in his *marwnad* to Owain Gwynedd (d.1170): *Grym dillut dullus uab eurei*, H 95,4. A similar variation between *farchawc/farfawc* is found

in the name *Llawfrodedd Farchog/Farfog* in the different texts of the 'Thirteen Treasures of the Island of Britain' as listed by E. Rowlands, LlC v (1958), 58. In spite of the concurrence of the two MSS in giving this epithet, it seems likely that in this instance *varchawc* is a jocular word-play upon an original epithet *varuawc* 'the Bearded', since it is with the victim's beard that this task is concerned. (This is comparable with the jocular word-play upon the name of *Caw/cadw* in l.647 (see n.).) The idea of a giant's strength as embodied in his hair is a widespread folk-tale motif (ST 'D' 1831, and 'F' 531.1.6.13). Evidently the story of Dillus was localized in the Pumlumon area by the time that *Culhwch* took shape (see CO (1), lviii, n.137). Variants from other parts of Wales are cited in the introduction pp. lvii–viii.

701. **y deu geneu hynny:** presumably the 'two pups of the bitch Rymhi' (ll.315, 930–1) are here meant. They have been omitted from the list of the *anoethau*, though they should clearly have been included in it: see n. on ll.930–1 below. There is additional confusion, since according to l.964 the leash from the beard of Dillus was needed to hold *Drutwyn keneu Greit mab Eri* (l.673).

702. **ac ef yn vyw:** 'and he being alive, while he is alive'; cf. Arthur's words *a mi yn uyw* (l.1170), and GMW 231.

703. **o'e vywyt:** 'of his life, in his life, while he lives'. Cf. *ac ef yn vyw* l.702 above.

708–9. **Kynedyr Wyllt mab Hettwn Clauyryawc:** 'K. the Wild, son of H. the Leprous'. (On *clafyr(i)og* see n. to *Nynhyaw a Pheibyaw* l.599 above.) *Kynedyr Wyllt* receives a different patronymic in l.344; see n. There may be a further confusion with *Cyledyr Wyllt mab Nwython*; see n. to l.994 below.

713–14. **Guynn mab Nud:** a mythical figure, associated in origin with *Uindos* son of *Nodons*. Both *Nudd* and *Nodons* are the Brittonic equivalents of the Irish deity *Nuadu*; see TYP 428; CMT 130–1. *Gwynn mab Nudd* was identified by Rhŷs (HL 179) with the Ir. *Fionn mac Cumhaill*, though it is difficult to determine how far the identification can be maintained on the basis of existing sources (see G. Murphy, *The Ossianic Lore and Romantic Tales of Medieval Ireland* 8; ibid. *Duanaire Finn* iii,lxxxi–ii, and note by Idris Foster, ibid. 198–204). That *Culhwch* may perpetuate an original concept of

Gwyn ap Nudd as a divine huntsman gains some support from the continuity of his portrayal in folklore as a mythical huntsman, and as the leader of the *cwn Annwn* or 'hell-hounds'. Dafydd ap Gwilym makes a number of allusions to Gwyn ap Nudd, and these always portray Gwyn in a sinister light: the Mist is a deception caused by Gwyn (GDG 68), the Owl is the bird of Gwyn (GDG 26), and the bog-hole is Gwyn's fish-pond (GDG 127), etc. See E. I. Rowlands, LlC v (1959), 122–35, and for a comprehensive discussion of all the allusions to Gwyn ap Nudd in medieval Welsh prose and poetry, see B. F. Roberts, LlC xiii (1980–1), 283–9; ibid. Ast. H. 311–18, for an edition and discussion of the dialogue poem between Gwyn ap Nudd and Gwyddno Garanhir (LlDC no. 34). The fulfilment of the task of capturing Gwyn ap Nudd in compliance with the Giant's demand is implied though not narrated in *Culhwch*: it seems to have been superseded by the episode in which Arthur arbitrates between Gwyn and Gwythyr ap Greidawl (ll. 988–1003).

714. **ar:** the form is a combination of the rel. prt. *a* and the pre-verbal perfective prt. *ry-* (preserved in R). Cf. GMW 62–3.

dieuyl Annwuyn: *Annw(f)n* is a name for the Celtic Otherworld. In PKM 99–101 Ifor Williams explained the name as composed from *dwfn* 'world' and a prefix *an-* meaning 'in'. Hence *Annwfn* was frequently regarded as 'in' or 'under' the earth, the 'In-world' or 'Otherworld'. Under Christian influence *Annwfn* came to be regarded as synonymous with hell, as is evident in the present instance: conversely *Uffern* 'hell' is used in the tale in a context where it plainly designates the pagan Otherworld (see n. to l.653 above.) Gwyn's partaking of the 'nature of the devils of Annwfn' indicates a recognition on the part of the redactor of the tale that Gwyn ap Nudd belonged to a sinister and forbidden mythology. In *Buchedd Collen*, the 'Life of St Collen', Gwyn is described as *Brenin Annwn*, and is defeated by the superior powers of the saint. In one text he is entitled *brenin Annwn a'r tylwyth teg*, which suggests that *dieuyl Annwuyn* here is synonymous with the *tylwyth teg* or fairy people. (For *Buchedd Collen* see T. H. Parry-Williams (ed.) *Rhyddiaith Gymraeg I* (Gwasg Prifysgol Cymru, 1954), 36–41, and refs. in TWS 224–5.)

718. **Du march Moro Oeruedawc:** Cf. BT 48,10–11 *Du moroed enwawc/march brvyn bro(n) bradawc*, and TYP no.44: *Tri Meirch a*

dugant y Tri Marchlwyth: Du Moro (R: *Du y Moroed) march Elidir Mwynvavr* ... *Du* 'Black' is the name of the horse in each of these three instances: in *Culhwch Du* 'Black' belongs to an otherwise unknown *Moro Oeruedawc* (? = *aeruedawc* 'leading in battle'; see G 12; TYP no.25 and n.), but in the triad *Moro/Moroed* is a part of the horse's name, and his owner Elidir Mwynfawr is a character famous in other contexts (TYP 344). In the line quoted from BT the meaning of *moroed* is uncertain: it may be an exclamation '*Du*, how famous (he was), the horse of B'. This celebrated horse was known to the poets: see GGl xxii, 41–6; GTA 392,75–6; 400,59–60. (An additional note in TYP(2) 536–7 cites Lat. *morellus*, F. *morelle* as a name for a black or dark chestnut horse, and cites *morellus de cornubia* as a description given to King Edward I's horse.) Neither *Du* nor his owner play any further part in the tale.

720. **Guilenhin brenhin Ffreinc:** 'William king of France'. This name is generally believed to denote William the Conqueror, who lived from 1027–87, and ruled from 1066 over England and Normandy together. (Note, however, that France is distinguished from Normandy in ll. 1058–9 below.) *Gwilenhen (sic) brenhin Freinc* has already been included in the Court-List (l.294 above); later in the tale he is slain by the Twrch Trwyth (l.1130). The Conqueror's visit to St David's in 1081 is considered to be an important date in relation to the composition of *Culhwch*; see introduction p. lxxxii, ALMA 38–9, WLSD xxx. *Gwilim uab rwyf ffreinc* appears in both of the two lists of names derived from *Culhwch* in BR 19,15 (= RM 159,23) and GER (WM 411,31 = RM 265,13) – though it is possible that these latter allusions could be to the Conqueror's son William Rufus (1087–1100).

725. **mab Alun Dyuet:** though previously included in the Court-List (l.185) this character receives no name throughout *Culhwch*, though in the lists in BR and GER he is named *Dyuyr mab Alun Dyuet* (WM 411,39 = RM 265,17; BR 19,25 = RM 159,30–160,1). The *Beddau* stanzas name *Run mab Alun Diwed* (LlDC 18,74), also *Bet alun dywet ... mab Meigen*, (ibid. 75–7) = PBA LIII,122; 24,25.

ellygywr da: 'a good unleasher', from *ellwng* 'to loose, unleash'. There are various forms of this vb.: *gellwng, gillwng, gollwng, dillwng,* and *ellwng,* as here.

728. **Anet ac Aethlem:** with *Aethlem* cf. *Aethlon,* Chr. Br. 105.

Evidently these two swift hounds were obtained, though they are not referred to again until at the end of the tale when they disappear into the sea in pursuit of the Twrch Trwyth.

732. **kyuoethawc:** an adj. formed from *kyuoeth* 'territory, dominion, power, wealth'.

733. **dan uy llaw i y mae ef:** 'he is under my hand'. These significant words are found only in the text of W. Cf. the corresponding Ir. phrase *teit fó laimh* 'submit to' (DIL 'L' 39–40,F171), and 212–13 above (of Hueil mab Kaw) *nyd asswynwys eiroet yn llaw arglwyd*. Clearly some form of subjection to an overlord is implied in both cases, though this need not be a feudal act of homage (see P. Ford, B xxvi, 152). Yet they fail to clarify the relationship between Ysbaddaden and Arthur: more particularly since in ll.374–5 Arthur declares that he has never even heard of Olwen or her father.

736–43. A repetition of ll.333–40 above, see n. In l.736 **Syuwlch** appears in the place of *Seuwlch* in l.333, and **Kilyd Kyuwlch** in place of *Kledyf Kyuwlch* in l.334; in l.741 **eu teir gureichon** 'their three witches' replace *eu teir vyryon* (with *teir* for *tri*) 'their three grandsons' in l.739. No more is heard in the tale of this interesting family. On the use here of the pl. with numerals see GMW 47, and cf. n. on *trywyr* l.235 above.

745. **pei dygwydei y nef ar y dayar:** 'though the sky should fall on the earth'. *Dygwydei* consists of *dy-* + *cwydei*, imperf. sing. 3 of *cwydaw* 'to fall'. *Dygwydaw* later came to mean 'befall, happen'. In ModW the form of the vn. is *digwydd*, and the meaning is invariably 'to happen'. Other prefixes are employed with *cwydaw*, in forms such as *gogwydaw, tramgwydaw*. The fear that the sky should fall was the ultimate disaster feared alike by the Gauls and the early Irish. Cf. Cynddelw's words in his *marwnad* to Rhirid Flaidd, *Gwr am gwnaeth hiraeth hir ysgar ac ef/yny del llu nef ar llu daear* (RP 1429,29–30, also LlDC 17,215 *Kyn duguitei awir y lavr a llyr en lli*). Cf. C. O'Rahilly, *Táin Bó Cúailnge* (Recension I, 4043–4, trans. 234); K. Jackson, *The Oldest Irish Tradition: A Window on the Iron Age*, 13, 31. P. L. Henry points out the existence of Ir. and Gaul. parallels to these words of Ysbaddaden, SC iii (1968), 35n.

747. **Wrnach Gawr:** 'W. the Giant'. The syntax in l.765 below

establishes beyond any doubt that *Wrnach* is the radical form of the name, not **Gwrnach* as was previously supposed by J. Rhŷs and T. F. O'Rahilly (CF 565; *Ériu* xvi (1952), 12); see n. by Thomas Jones, LlC i (1950), 129. In the list of the *civitates* of Britain in HB (ed. F. Lot, 211) there is an unidentified city named *Cair Urnarc* (var: *Urnahc, urnach, urnath*, etc.); see B v (1931), 19–21 for Ifor Williams's study of the names of the *civitates*, comparing the forms given in Mommsen's edition of HB with those in RM p. 309. The names of *Wrnach Gawr* and *Diwrnach Wydel/Gawr* should be compared (see n. to l.635 above): Sir Idris Foster in ALMA (38n.) considered the *-ach* termination in *Wrnach* as indicative of Ir. influence, following O'Rahilly's view. But this need not necessarily be the case, as was shown subsequently by P. Sims-Williams, B xxix, 615–16. He proposes that the Welsh termination *-ach* 'is suggestive of various shades of uncouthness, brute vigour, and primitive heroism'. More significant in the present instance is a comparison of *Wrnach* with the form *Awarnach* in the poem *Pa Gur* (above p. xxxv l.21), where Arthur is said to have fought with a witch *in neuat awarnach*. It is not difficult to believe that *Awarnach* here conceals the name of *Wrnach*, as has been proposed by B. F. Roberts in a note to his edn. of the poem, Ast. H. 305. The completion of this task follows immediately: the last of the *anoethau* is thus the first to be accomplished.

747. **Ny ledir:** these words are slightly ambiguous: we would expect *Ny ledir ef* or *Nys lledir*, if the ref. were to the Twrch Trwyth, as might be expected. But it is *Wrnach* himself who in the event is slain by his own sword, and the purpose of hunting the Twrch Trwyth was not, in any case, to slay him, but to obtain the treasures from between his ears.

752. **a merch:** cf. on ll.574–5 above.

763–4. **Meredic a wyr ywchi:** 'Fools of men that you are'. Cf. l.433 above.

768. **kerd:** 'craft, occupation'; OI *cerd* 'craft'; also ll.774, 775, 781, 785, 798, 803.

771. **pyr:** consists of *py* 'what?' and the prep. *yr* 'for', and means 'Why, for what?'. It exemplifies an old constr. in which the prep. is placed after the interr. pron.; GMW 77. But there is here a further

semantic development, in that *pyr* seems to mean 'that' rather than 'why?' Cf. the development in the meaning of *pan*, which is first interrogative, and then a conjunction meaning 'that'; cf. GMW 79–80.

772–3. ym mwyt ... ymual ... yn neuad: the practice regarding the separation or coalescing of the prep. seems to vary. This may be indicative of a copy made by dictation rather than by the copyist's direct vision; cf. nn. on ll. 574–5, and 89, 90, 608.

783. Oed reit y mi wrth hwnnw: 'I had need of him' (that is, 'need would be to me of him') – an archaic constr. with the copula in the form *oed* coming first; cf. ll. 490–1, 496 above, 795 below, and GMW 139–40.

783–4. Ys gwers yd wyf yn keissaw a olchei vyg cledyf: 'For a while I have been seeking (one) who would polish my sword'. In *ys gwers ys* 'is' is used with nouns of time to denote a period of time 'it is a while, for a while'; cf. Fr. *il y a*. In *yd wyf* the present is used with perfect meaning 'I have been seeking'.

a olchei vyg cledyf: The rel. clause occurs without an expressed antecedent; cf. GMW 72.

787–8. Kadeir a dodet y danaw: 'a chair was placed beneath him', another alternative form of the Abnormal Order: object + *a/yr* + vb.; cf. GMW 180.

792. ae guynseit ae grwmseit: 'white-bladed or dark-bladed'. On *seit* 'blade' see n. by D. Jenkins, B xxxv (1988), 55–61.

793. malpei teu uei: 'as if it were thine'.

y lleill: more usually *y neill* 'the one'; cf. GMW 86.

795. oed well: cf. n. on l. 783 above.

y'm gwlat: 'in my country'; cf. GMW 199.

795–6. bei oll yt uei val hynn: 'were it completely like this'; on *oll* see GMW 98–9.

796. Dyhed a beth: 'a shameful thing'; GMW 37, also ll. 132–3 above.

797. kydymdeith: ModW *cydymaith* 'companion, fellow'. On the loss of *d* cf. (y) *ymdeith* > *ymeith* 'away'; GMW 156, 222–3.

799. **ar arwydon:** 'by means of signs/tokens'.

800. **yssef a dygyrch y guaet y ar y guynt:** 'it is that which will draw', that is, 'it will draw'. Here we have the constr. of the Mixed Sentence, with the copula in the form *ys* coming first; cf. GMW 140–1. Later *yssef* was reduced to *sef*, GMW 52–3.

806. **Custenhin heussawr:** previously named as *Custenhin Amhynwyedic*, l.435 above, and cf. n. to *Goreu mab Custenhin* l.811 below.

809. **amkeudant:** note the agreement between a pl. vb. and a following subject in the pl.

807–8. **mal nat oed vwy no dim ganthunt:** this phrase is absent from R. The variant readings of the two texts and the difficult syntax of the passage in ll.804–12 is the subject of a discussion by J. MacQueen entitled 'Goreu mab Custennin', EC viii (1958), 154–63.

811. **Goreu mab Custenhin:** *Goreu* 'Best'. As in the case of *Kulhwch* (l.10) and *Olwen* (l.497–8) a fanciful onomastic explanation is once more given for a personal name whose composition was either misunderstood by the redactor, or he was making a deliberate pun upon it, as is the case with *Kaw/cadw* in l.647 above. But *Gurou, Guorou* is an attested personal name in LL 172,10; 221,10; 232,20. Alternatively, the name could have originated here from a wrong division of *Custennin Gorneu* 'C. of Cornwall', which is attested in ByS and elsewhere in genealogies (for refs. see EWGT 179). Here OW *Corneu* = MW *Cernyw*, the ref. being to Custennin *Amhynwyedic/heusawr* (see n. to l.435) the father of the boy. It may be significant that the same epithet 'of Cornwall' in OW spelling occurs in BGG no.13 *Tutuwlch Corneu tyuysauc o kernyw* (TYP 239, EWGT 73) – who is said to have married an unnamed daughter of *Amlawt Wledic*. Goreu's name is reproduced in both BR 19,16 (= RM 159,23–4) and GER (WM 411, 34), as well as in TYP no. 52. On the triad, and on Goreu's role in the story see introduction p. xxx–i, lx–lxi above.

812. **heb wybot y'r Cawr:** 'without the Giant's knowing'. An ex. of an early constr. where the subject of a vn. follows the vn. governed by the prep. *i* 'to'; GMW 162, cf. l.26 above *yn hyly yr brenhin*, where *yr* appears to be the form of the article, though it could alternatively be explained as consisting of *y* 'to' + *r*.

813. **daruu:** pret. sing. 3 of *daruot* 'to happen'. It is used as an auxiliary vb. with a vn. as grammatical subject, to convey a passive meaning 'the sword's burnishing was completed'; cf. GMW 163.

814. **a ranghei y uod idaw y weith:** 'whether his workmanship pleased him'. The idiom *rengi bod* (stem *ranc*) means 'to please, satisfy'; cf. GMW 154–5. Also l.815 *a ranc bod yw genhyf* 'and I am pleased with it'.

817. **a chaffwyf inheu gwneuthur:** 'and may I be allowed to make/let me make'. The pres. subj. in a principal clause may denote wish or desire, as it does here; *cael* 'to get, obtain' with vn. as object is used with the meaning 'to be allowed to'. In ModW *a gaffi ddangos y ffordd i chi* 'may I be allowed to show you the way?'

821–2. **dwyn a vynnassant o tlysseu:** '(they) took as many jewels as they wished'. On the constr. here cf. GMW 68, and ll.107–8 above.

822. **yg kyuenw yr un dyd ymphen y vlwydyn:** 'on that same day at the end of a year'. *Kyuenw* consists of *kyu+enw* 'name' and means 'cognomen, epithet'; here the anniversary of that day, cf. GPC 691.

828. **Mabon uab Modron:** see n. on l.685 above.

828–9. **Eidoel uab Aer:** see n. on l.694 above.

831, 832. **Gliui.** The correct form of this name is certainly *Gliui* < *Glevi*, genit. of Lat. *Glevum* < Brit. *Gleuon*, OW *Gloiu* (LHEB 325–6), and *Gliui* is the eponym of Gloucester. *Cair Gloiu* is listed among the cities of Britain in the *Historia Brittonum* (HB ed. Dumville, 62; B v, 19). From this point in the tale the text of RM is alone available, and Gwenogvryn Evans read the form in the MS as *Glini*. But the letters *n* and *u* are continually liable to confusion in the texts of both W and R (cf. nn. to *Conul Bernach* ll.179–80, and to *Llawurodet* l.223 above), and as the name stands in R col.833 it can be as easily interpreted either as the one or as the other, as can be seen from the plate in RM facing p.128 of the Oxford edn. Idris Foster re-examined the Red Book, and concluded that the form is *Gliui*, (see *Y Traddodiad Rhyddiaith yn yr Oesoedd Canol* (ed. G. Bowen), 75. The form *Glini*, since this form had become conventional, owing to its adoption by Jones and Jones in Mab. Lady

Charlotte Guest's translation reads *Glivi* (Everyman edn. 122–3), evidently on the basis of the transcript of the Red Book made for her by Tegid (= J. Jones, 1792–1852). The three 18th.-cent. transcripts from the Red Book made by Moses Williams (see introduction p. ix, n.2) both have *Glini*, but it is clear that the persistence of this misreading has taken no account of the word's etymology, which was first demonstrated by Idris Foster. Var. forms of the Lat. name for Gloucester are *Clevum* (for *Glevum*) in the Antonine Itinerary, and *Glebon Colonia* in the Ravenna Cosmography (LHEB 325; see n. on l.923 below). OW *Gloiu* rapidly became personalized, as can be seen from the descent given in HB to Fernmail, king of Buellt and Gwerthrynion *c*.800: *Gloiu da ... Ipse autem Gloiu da aedificavit urbem magnam super ripam fluminis Sabrinae quae vocatur Brittanico sermone Cair Gloiu, saxonice autem Gleucester* (EWGT 8; HB ed. Dumville, 102; cf. B xi, 44). In HRB iv,15 Geoffrey of Monmouth tells that the emperor Claudius built Gloucester, and he derives the city's name from *Gloius*, son of the emperor Claudius: in BD 55,58 the emperor's name is changed to *Gloev* and it is said that from him the city is called *Caer Gloev*, adding that according to some it is named after the emperor's son *Gloev Gvlat Lydan*. Cf. EWGT 46, 15 (from J 20) *Gloew Gwalltir, y gwr hwnnw a wnaeth ar ymyl Hafren tref ac oe enw ef y gelwir yn Caer Loew*; and PKM 27 *Gloyw Walltlydan uab Cassnar Wledic o dyledogyon yr ynys hon*. For amplification see CO(1) xlvi–xlviii and notes.

841. Gwrhyr Gwalstawt Ieithoed: see n. on l.346 above. The story of the search for the Oldest Animals here begins, see introduction pp. lxii–iii.

845–6. gobeith yw gennyf y neges yd eloch ymdanei y chaffel: 'I am hopeful regarding the mission on which you go that it can be accomplished.' On this use of the prep. *gan* see GMW 190.

847. Mwyalch Gilgwri: 'the Blackbird of C.' *Cilgwri* < *cil* 'corner, retreat' + personal name *Gwri*. *Cilgwri* in the form *Killgury* is first attested as a name for the Wirral peninsula in Camden's *Britannia* (1587). This is confirmed later by Lewis Morris in his *Celtic Remains* (London, 1878), 90. But there is another *Cilgwri* in the parish of Llangar near Corwen, as pointed out by M. Richards, 'Arthurian Onomastics' 256 and n. In B xxi (1966), 30–7 D. Machreth Ellis listed five refs. to *Cilgwri* by medieval poets: the earliest of these is by Seisyll Bryffwrch in his *marwnad* to Owain Gwynedd (d. 1170), MA(2) 236a, 49 (= NLW 4973B 21 v, 22). Both writers conclude that, in default of further evidence, the Wirral *Cilgwri* is the most likely to be the one referred to in *Culhwch*, though this is incapable of final proof. The late triad TYP no.92 gives the Blackbird a different habitat, describing it as *Mwyalchen Gelli Gadarn*.

849. **yn deir nossic:** cf. ll.686, 873–4, 885, 904.

859. **Redynure:** 'Fernhill' or 'Brackenhill' is a name which might be found at a number of different places in Wales. J. Rhŷs identified it with the name of a farm, shortened to 'Dynvra' in the parish of Aberdaron at the extremity of the Llŷn peninsula (HL 555n.). As a possible alternative M. Richards suggests (loc. cit.) that it might be the original name of Farndon in Cheshire (OE *fearn-dun*): this would bring it into the probable neighbourhood of *Cilgwri* (see n.847 above).

867–8. **yr hynny hyt hediw yd wyf i yma:** 'from then until today I have been here'. Note how the present *wyf* has acquired perfect meaning; cf. GMW 109, and n. on ll.783–4 above, also l.889.

871. **Cuan Cwm Kawlwyt:** *Cuan* 'Owl' (Old Breton *couann*). This is the only instance of *cuan* attested before the 18th. cent. (GPC 626): the common word for owl is *tylluan*, and *Tylluan Cwm Cawlwyd* is found in all the folk-tale versions of the 'Oldest Animals' (see T. Jones, NLW Journal vii (1951), 62–6; THSC (1970), 22–4; D. Ifans, B xxiv (1972), 461–4; TYP 220–1). *Llyn Cowlyd* is the name of a small lake between Capel Curig and Llanrwst, Gwynedd. J. Lloyd-Jones suggested that this may be the place which is here intended by the name *Cwm Kawlwyt*, and he draws attention to *ad stagnum Cawlwyd* in a charter of Llywelyn ab Iorwerth to the abbey of Aberconwy (*Enwau Lleoedd Sir Gaernarfon* (Gwasg Prifysgol Cymru 1928), 93). This seems the most probable identification, though M. Richards (loc. cit.) cites two other instances of the name in Radnorshire and Carms.

874. **as:** a syllabic form of the infixed pron. obj. sing. 3; cf. GMW 56.

882. **Gwern Abwy:** *Gwern* 'alder tree' sometimes means 'swamp'. Unlike the other place-names with which the Oldest Animals are

associated, *Guernabui* is attested as a personal name in LL 75,27; *guernapui* 166,4 (see Ifor Williams's note on *Gwe(r)nabwy*, CA 150–1, and the variants cited LHEB 451). Rhŷs identified the name with that of a farm *Bodernabwy* (< *Bod Wernabwy*) near Aberdaron (HL 555n.), and his conjecture was confirmed by J. Lloyd-Jones, *Enwau Lleoedd*, 36, 61.

886. **yr ys pell o amser:** 'a long time past'. On the use of *ys* 'is' before a noun denoting time see GMW 142–3. Later *yr* was combined with *ys*: *yr ys* > *ers* in ModW, but *ys* in the form '*s* still occurs in the spoken language – '*slawer dydd*' 'since many a day, in times past'. Note the use here of *pell* to denote time rather than distance; cf. OW *amgucant pel amtanndi* 'they contended long for it' in the *Surexit* Memorandum, CMCS 7 (1984), 99.

888. **weithon:** 'now'; adverbial use of *gweith* 'time'; *y weith hon* 'this time, now'; cf. GMW 227.

890. **un treigyl:** 'one time, once'; *treigyl* means 'turn, time'. Note the epenthetic vowel *y* (GMW 12); *treigylgweith* (PKM 1,2) is used similarly.

891. **Llynn Llyw:** no doubt the place is the same as *Llyn Lliwan* in l.1179 below (see n.); a pool situated somewhere on the Severn estuary (see map). *Lliw* 'colour, hue, tint', as adj. 'bright, shining'; cf. OI *lí* 'brightness', as in PKM 39,10 *Lli ac Archan*. *Lliw* is a recurring element in place-names; exx. include *Lliwen, Y Iliwedd*, etc. see EANC 121.

893. **wers vawr:** 'for a long time'; *gwers* 'a while' is here used adverbially, which explains the lenition; cf. GMW 15, 227.

895. **carant:** 'kinsmen'; pl. of *car*. Later we have the analogical formation *kereint*, GMW 29.

895–6. **mynet yg gwrys wrthaw:** 'to launch an attack upon it'; *gwrys* 'attack, onslaught'.

896. **kennadau a yrrwys ynteu:** 'he sent emissaries': the Abnormal Order, cf. ll.786–7 above.

904. **y gymeint:** *kymeint* 'as much' is here used with the def. art., and is clearly regarded as fem., hence the lenition. Cf. TC 80, GMW 94–5.

905. **gan bob llanw:** 'with every flood-tide'. The Severn is tidal; cf. n. on l. 1179 below.

906–7. **yno y keueis i ny cheueis eirmoet o drwc y gymeint:** 'I never obtained (before) in my life as much harm as I obtained there'; on *eirmoet* see n. on l. 127 above.

908. **ysef yd:** cf. n. on l. 7 above on *sef y*, where *sef* is employed adverbially. Here we have the full form of the combination of copula + pron. consisting of *ys* + *ef* 'it', later reduced to *sef*, which is commonly employed in both MW and ModW.

910–11. **am y uagwyr a'r karcharawr:** 'on the other side of the wall from the prisoner'. On *am . . . a(c) . . .* cf. GMW 182.

klywynt: imperf. pl. 3 of *klywet* 'to hear'. The imperf. of *klywet* and *gwelet* 'to see' can also denote possibility; cf. GMW 110. Hence 'they could hear'.

914/ **Mabon uab Modron.** See n. on l. 685 above.

914–16. **ny charcharwyt neb kyn dostet . . . a mi.** TYP no. 52 gives a var. form of this triad *Tri Goruchel Garcharavr ynys Prydein*. It is found only in the WR series of Triads (not in the Early Version), and therefore the authority for it is neither less nor more than that for the triad given here: there can be no certainty as to which is anterior to the other (see introduction pp. lx–lxi above). *Mabon uab Modron* is the only name which is common to the two versions of the triad.

916. **Llud Llaw Ereint:** 'Ll. Silver Hand' is named in l. 367 above as the father of *Creidylat*, but is otherwise a name unknown outside this tale. Rhŷs argued (HL 125, CF 447–8) that *Llud(d)* is derived by metathesis from *Nud(d)* (the father of *Gwyn ap Nudd*), originally the Romano-British deity *Nodons*, (to whom the Roman temple at Lydney Park on the Severn was dedicated), and also the Ir. deity *Nuadu*, a protagonist in the tale of *Cath Maige Tuired*, where he bears the epithet *Argat Lamh*, which corresponds to *Llaw Ereint*, and an elaborate myth is told to account for his 'Silver Hand' (see CMT 130–1; AIT 32; PCB 201; TYP 428).

Greit mab Eri: see n. on ll. 176–7 above. Later in the tale (l. 992) he is a prisoner of Gwyn ap Nudd.

917. **ar gaffel dy ellwng:** 'that you may be freed'. Note the use of *ar* with the vn. to denote purpose or intention; cf. GMW 188.

aryant: 'silver' < * *arganto-*. The *-nt-* belongs to the original form, cf. Cornish *arghans*; Breton *arc'hant*. Later it was reduced to *-n(n)*, as happened generally in final unaccented syllables; cf. *ugeint* > ModW *ugain*; also 3rd. pl. of verbs and prepositions.

918. **presennawl:** 'worldly'; an adj. form of *pres(s)en(t)* 'world' (l.715) found in early poetry, especially religious verse; ex. LlDC 7,22; 20,6.

y gymeint: 'as much'; cf. l.904 above.

920. **ymchoelut:** 'to turn, return'. Note the use of a vn. instead of a finite vb., with a following subject governed by the prep. *o*. This vb. assumes a variety of forms: *ymchwelut, ymhwelut, ymhoelut*; cf. GMW 11.

923. **Kaer Loyw.** See n. on ll.831–2 above, where *Gliui* is shown to be derived from *Glevi*, genit. of Lat. *Glevum*. He became in Welsh the eponym of (Cair) Gloiu, MW *Caer Loyw*, OE *Gleucester*. According to LHEB 325–6 'the etymology in relation to W. *gloyw* and Ir. *glé* is obscure'. On the Roman city *Glevum colonia* established in AD 96–8 on the site of the former legionary fortress at Gloucester see P. Salway, *Roman Britain* (Oxford, 1984), 97, 153, 471, etc.; S. Frere, *Britannia* (London, 1987), 189, 229–30.

925. **tra yttoed vilwyr Arthur:** 'while Arthur's soldiers were'. Note the lenition of the subject after the imperf. sing 3: this is common in MW, cf. l.953 below, and GMW 17–18.

927. **atref y doeth Arthur:** 'A. came home': another type of abnormal word-order, with adv. + *y* + vb.; GMW 180.

930–1. **deu geneu Gast Rymhi:** on the 'two pups of the bitch Rymhi' (named *Gwydrut* and *Gwydren Astrus*) see n. on ll.315–16 above. This task appears to have dropped from the list of the *anoethau* as stipulated by the Giant; see introduction p. xlviii, n.42.

931. **a wys:** *gwys* is an old pret. passive (< *wid-to) 'is known'; cf. GMW 127.

932. **Aber Deu Gledyf:** the confluence of the two rivers Cleddau, near to Milford Haven (*cleddyf, cleddau* 'sword') cf. Ifor Williams,

Enwau Lleoedd 57. Hence the commote named *Daugleddau* (*-yf*) in the cantref of Rhos. See n. to l.1101 below.

933. **Tringat:** with this name cf. the name on the 5th.- or 6th-cent. inscribed stone at Llanybydder, Carms., which reads TRENACATUS IC IACIT FILIUS MAGLAGNI, with TRENACCATLO in Ogham lettering on the reverse side; see ECMW 102 and no.127; LHEB 645. *Tren* 'strong' equates with Ir. *trén*, and there are several instances of names ending with *-cat* (*cad* 'battle'), ex. *Gwyngat* mab Caw 208; *Dinogat* CA 1101. In l.1127 below the Twrch Trwyth kills *Gwyn mab Tringat mab Neuet*. A late version of the 'Thirteen Treasures' includes *cwlldr* (the coulter of) *Tringer fab Nuddnot* (see TYP cxxxii n.1.).

934. **rith:** 'form'; Ir. *richt* (**prptu*), cf. LP 27.

936. **ysgrybul:** also *ysgrybyl* HGVK 272; LlB 27,21; WLSD 5,19. A collective term for a full stock of animals, a borrowing from Lat. *scrĭpulum, scrūpulus* (EL 13–14); OW *scribl*; cf. B v (1931), 234–5. See further LlB 177, HGVK 96.

938. **Prytwenn:** Arthur's ship *Prydwen* 'Fair Form' is named three times in *Preiddeu Annwn* in the recurrent refrain *tri lloneit prytwen* 'three full loads of P'; BT 54,23; 55,12; 55,17. See edn. by M. Haycock, SC xviii/xix, 60, 68; and cf. n. on l.159 above. In LL 207,19–20 *messur pritguenn* is recorded as a place-name in the diocese of Llandaff (cf. YB xii, 22–3). Due to a misunderstanding, Geoffrey of Monmouth borrowed *Priduen* as the name of Arthur's shield (HRB ix, 4). On Arthur's *regalia* see P. Ford, B xxx (1983), 268–73.

940. **yn eu rith e hunein:** 'into their own form'. From this statement it must be deduced that the bitch Rymhi and her pups were transformed back into the form of human beings.

941. **bob un bob deu:** 'every one, every two', that is, 'one by one, two by two'.

942. **Gwythyr mab Greidawl:** see n. on l.176 above.

clywei: 'he could hear'. Cf. l.911 *klywynt*.

944. **achub:** a borrowing from Lat. *occupo*. The meaning varies; here it means 'to make for, rush'.

949–50. **naw hestawr llinat:** cf. ll.605–8 above.

952. a'r morgrugyn cloff a doeth: on the international folk-tale of the 'The Grateful Ants' see introduction p. lxiii above, and IPT 79–81. In Cy xlii, 132 W. J. Gruffydd noted that the very rare detail of the Lame Ant is paralleled in a version from Yugoslavia, for which see Wratislaw, *Sixty Folk-tales* (London, 1889), 25–9. Cf. CO(1) lv.

954. Carn Gwylathyr: the name has not survived, and Pumlumon has many heights upon which this incident might have been localized. Since Cei and Bedwyr saw the smoke 'towards the south', the cairn on the top of Drum Peithnant has been suggested as a suitable site; see CO(1) lviii n.

957. Myn llaw vyng kyueillt: 'By my friend's hand' – a frequent expletive in MW. *Kyueillt* < **kom + altio*; cf. BWP 28–9; LHEB 663. Later it became *cyfeill, cyfaill*, with *-llt > ll*. Also l.134 above.

959–60. On *Dillus Uarruawc* and the variations in his epithet between *Var(r)vawc. Varchawc* see n. on l.700 above.

960. llyna: 'behold < *syll yna* 'look there'; GMW 246. Also *llyma* 'look here'. Both are obsolete in ModW, where the forms are *dyma, dyna*.

961. heb y Bedwyr: 'said B'. Cf. also ll.962, 967, 968, *heb y Kei*: the *y* here is not the def. art., which in any event would not be used correctly before the name of a person. It belongs to the vb. *heb* (**sequ*), Ir. *sech-*. This vb. also has the forms *hebyr* (**sequ + re*, which is deponent) and *heby*; the one being used before consonants, the other before vowels: ModW *ebr, ebe, eb*. It is used in reported speech; cf. also MW *hebu* 'to speak'; *ateb, gwrtheb* 'to answer'. Cf. further LP 394; WG 377; GMW 154.

962. A'e hatwaenost di ef?: 'Do you know him?' (2 pers. sing.). Here the infixed pron. *e* is used with the interr. prt. *a*; cf. GMW 55; on the *h-* see ibid. 23.

964. Drutwyn keneu Greit uab Eri: on *Drutwyn* and his owner *Greit uab Eri* see nn. on ll.176, 673 above. There is confusion here, since in l.676 it is said that the leash of Cors Cant Ewin is needed to hold Drutwyn, and here it is the leash of the beard of Dillus that is needed for this purpose: conversely, in l.700 above, the leash from the beard of Dillus is required to hold *y deu geneu hynny* (that is, the pups of the bitch Rymhi – *recte* Drutwyn).

967. **wrth hynny:** 'concerning that'.

969. **kyscu a wna:** 'he will fall asleep'. On the use of *gwneuthur* as an auxiliary vb. cf. l.8 above *enghi a oruc y urenhines*.

977. **y kanei Arthur yr eglyn hwnn:** Arthur's satirical verse implies that if Cei had not caught Dillus at a disadvantage by a trick, it is Dillus who would have been the winner. The verse is a three-lined *englyn milwr*, with seven syllables to the line, end-rhyme and alliteration (see Morris-Jones, *Cerdd Dafod* 319–20). *Englynion* are also attributed to speakers in the tale of Math fab Mathonwy (PKM 89–90), and Ifor Williams gave his opinion that their employment for inset speech-passages in tales (as here) reflected the technique of the oral story-teller (cf. CLlH xxxvii–li). *Englynion* are appropriated elsewhere to Arthur: in TYP no.18 he is said to have composed an *englyn* in honour of his three *Cadfarchog* or 'Battle-Horsemen'. Later, the treatise on Giants by Siôn Dafydd Rhys (Cy 27, 140) quotes an *englyn* in which Arthur gave his reply to a giant named *Cribwr*, whose sisters (witches) Arthur had slain. Since Arthur is listed as one of the *Tri Oferfeirdd* or 'Frivolous Bards' of Britain (TYP no.12), it is the less surprising to find that occasional examples of his *awen* have come down. In this case Cei took such great offence at Arthur's *englyn* that from this point he disappears completely from the tale, and is heard of no more.

979. **Dillus uab Eurei:** See n. on l.700 above.

986. **Drutwyn keneu Greit uab Eri:** See n. on l.673 above. The ensuing incident, concerning the contest for Creiddylad seems to have replaced two of the stories of the achievement of *anoethau*: the obtaining of *Drutwyn* and the obtaining of Gwyn ap Nudd.

988. **Kyn no hynny ychydic:** 'shortly before then': *kyn* 'before' is regularly followed in MW by *no* 'than' before a personal and demonstrative pron.; cf. GMW 44; D. S. Evans, SC xiv/xv (1979–80), 74–80.

Creidylat uerch Lud Law Ereint: the name of *Creidylat* was previously given in the Court-List (l.367), where the contest for her between Gwyn ap Nudd and Gwythyr uab Greidawl was anticipated; Gwyn and Gwythyr have also been previously included among the members of Arthur's Court (ll.176, 181). The dialogue in *englynion* in the Black Book between Gwyn ap Nudd and

Gwyddno Garanhir also names Creiddylad: *hud im gelwir guin mab nud/gorterch creurdilad* (sic) *merch lut* (LlDC 34,17–18; ed. B. F. Roberts, Ast. H. 311–18). The terms of Arthur's arbitration between the two contestants have been compared with Arthur's arbitration between March and Drystan in the *Ystoria Trystan* – that the one shall have Esyllt as wife during the winter, and the other during the summer; see CO(1) lix–lx, TYP 332 and refs. cited. For *Llud Llaw Ereint* see n. on l.916 above, where he is included in the triad of Famous Prisoners. (*Credeilat uerch lud* is named also in the derived list in *Englynion y Clyweit* (B iii, 14 (60)).

990. Gwyn uab Nud: see n. on ll.713–14 above.

a'e dwyn y treis: on the idiom *y treis* 'by force' see B xiii, 3; GMW 201, and cf. TYP 50 on *ae y dwyll ae y dreis*. Lenition would be expected after *y* 'of, from' which derives from OW *di* < *dē* (Lat. *de*).

992. goruot o Wyn: 'Gwyn was the victor'. Another ex. of a vn. used instead of a finite vb. in narrative: cf. *mynet y wlat y gwedi* (l.3 above). On *goruot* 'to overcome' see GMW 146–7.

dala: 'to catch, hold'; again the vn. is used instead of a finite vb. In MW the more common form is *daly* < *dalg*; cf. GMW 10.

Greit mab Eri: see nn. on ll.176, 673 above.

Glinneu eil Taran: 'G. son of Thunder'. One of the group of some ten names in the tale which correspond to names in the *Mabinogi*; see introduction p. xxxviii and n.23 and cf. *Gliuieu Eil Taran*, PKM 44, 26. On *eil* see n. on ll.184–5 above.

993–4. The characters named in these lines all have associations with the 'Old North'. As K. Jackson indicated (YB xii (1982), 20–2) this concentration of northern names suggests that north Britain was the ultimate place of origin for the Creiddylad episode, and that this incident was one of the surviving fragments of tradition emanating from there – however imperfectly this was realized by the redactor of the tale. There are parallels in both Irish and Welsh to the intervention of mortal rulers as arbitrators in quarrels between Otherworld rulers, ex. Pwyll's intervention in the contest between Arawn and Hafgan in the *Mabinogi*, and the similar interventions made by Cú Chulainn and Laeghaire mac Crimthann in OI tales, as pointed out by Jackson, 'Some Popular Motifs in Early Welsh Tradition', EC xi (1964–5), 84–7; cf. AIT 181.

993. Gwrgwst Letlwm: 'G. Half-Bare'. *Gorust Letlwm* is named in BGG (EWGT 73(i)) as a grandson of Coel Hen, and hence as belonging to one of the two main branches of the *Gwyr y Gogledd*; cf. also the older but imperfect version of the same genealogy from Harl. MS 3859 (EWGT 10–1, nos. 8 and 12). With this epithet Jackson compares the *deu Wydel uonllwm* 'two bare-bottomed Irishmen'. PKM 44,18; both epithets being similarly suggestive of some primitive kind of kilt being worn by their possessors.

Dyfnarth y uab: this name does not appear in any Welsh genealogy, but Jackson compares (loc. cit) the name *Dunart brenhin y Gogled* in the Court-List, l.254 above, and suggests that both represent the name of *Domangart*, who was grandfather of the Scottish ruler *Aedán mac Gabráin*, the son of Fergus mac Erca, who founded the kingdom of Dal Riada in Scotland (on *Aedan mac Gabrain* in Welsh tradition see TYP 264–5, and cf. n. to *Maylwys mab Baedan* l.178 above). If correct, this identification would of course preclude any historical connection with *Gwrgwst Letlwm*.

993–4. Penn uab Nethawc: some element appears here to be lacking. *Pen(n)* is by itself an unlikely personal name. *Nethawc* could be a corruption of *Neithon*, the name which developed in Brittonic as *Nwython*, corresponding to *Nechton, Nechtan* in Irish and Pictish; cf. OSPG 48n. If so, it would be a doublet of *Nwython*, which follows immediately in the text. *Pen(n)* would in that case be a possible corruption of *Run*, corresponding to *Run mab Nwython*, l.257 above (see n.).

994. Nwython. See previous note. This name is familiar from the allusion in the *Gododdin* to *wyr Nwyth(y)on* 'the grandson of N.' (CA 967), in the lines which celebrate the victory of the men of Strathclyde over those of Dal Riada in 642, and the slaying of their ruler Domnall Brecc. The royal genealogy of Strathclyde is given in Harl. MS 3859 (EWGT 10, no. 5): in it is named *Eugein map Beli map Neithon*, and Ifor Williams argued that *Eugein* (= *Owein*) is the 'grandson of Nwython' referred to in the poem; see BWP 80–1; OSPG 98.

Cyledyr Wyllt: 'C. the Wild'. With the name cf. CVLIDORI on a

5th.-cent. inscribed stone at Llangefni, CIIC 320; LHEB 597. The epithet *gwyllt* invites comparison with that of *Myrddin Wyllt* and of Suibhne who bears the cognate Ir. epithet *Geilt*: both of them being from stories essentially belonging to north Britain, as Jackson points out. But any such association borne by the epithet *gwyllt* is lost sight of here, and Cyledyr's *dementia* is explained as due to the gruesome compulsion imposed on him of eating his father's heart. The incident here has an Ir. parallel in the story of Labraid Loingsech; see CO(1) lx; RC xx, 429 ff.; and Myles Dillon, *The Cycles of the Kings* (Oxford, 1946), 7–8. Cf. n. to *Kynedyr Wyllt* l. 344 above.

995. **kymhell:** < Lat. *compello*. The meaning in MW is 'to force, compel'. Later it came to mean 'urge, persuade'.

996. **yd aeth Kyledyr yg gwyllt:** cf. *yd aeth hitheu ygwylldawc* l. 5 above.

997. **dyuot hyt y Gogled:** the meaning of *Y Gogled* throughout *Culhwch* is *Yr Hen Ogledd* 'The Old North', that is the lost Brittonic kingdoms in Cumbria and in southern Scotland – Manaw Gododdin, Rheged, and Strathclyde. Cf. l. 106 above, and n.

1002. **bob duw kalan Mei:** 'every May day'. On Celtic May Day customs see A. and B. Rees, *Celtic Heritage* (London, 1961), 285–90.

1006. **Mygdwn march Gwedw:** *Guyn Mygdwn march Gwedw* has been previously listed among the *anoethau*, l. 689 above (see n.). Nothing is known of this horse's owner.

cynllyuan Cors Cant Ewin: another of the *anoethau*; see on l. 676 above.

1007–8. **Mabon uab Mellt:** 'M. son of Lightning': a name which appears in the poem *Pa Gur* (LlDC 31,23), though it is otherwise unknown. In both cases it is tempting to regard him as a doublet of *Mabon uab Modron*, though O'Rahilly inferred his origin from a lightning-god *Meldos* (EIHM 52 and n.). He takes part in the hunt for Ysgithrwyn, l. 1013 below. Ifor Williams compares the name of the Gaulish tribe *Meldi*, B x (1939), 41.

1008. **Gware Gwallt Euryn:** see n. on l. 315 above.

1008–9. **deu gi Glythmyr Ledewic:** (*Glythuyr* 1014). Neither these hounds nor their owner are specified among the *anoethau*, but the ref. here implies that their owner's name has dropped from the list. *Ledewic* 'Breton'; that is, he came from *Llydaw* (Brittany); hence Arthur's expedition thither to obtain the hounds. Later these hounds are led by Gwarthegyt mab Caw on the hunt for the Twrch Trwyth, l. 1107 below. Cf. *Saranhon mab Glythwyr* 216–17.

1010. **Gwrgi Seueri:** a character known only from this reference, and not previously included among the *anoethau*. *Gwrgi* (<*gwr* + *ci*) 'Man Hound' is not uncommon as a personal name; see refs. cited TYP 391; GURCI is found on an inscr. from 7th-9th cents. at Llangors, Brecon (ECMW no. 59). *Seueri* presumably derives from the name of the 3rd.-cent. emperor Severus, known from a number of allusions in HB (see Dumville's edn. 117), in one of which he is associated with the building of Hadrian's Wall (*Guaul*). From this source or from the *Brut* (BD 64), his name became included in Welsh genealogies; for refs. see EWGT 213. The genit. form of the name found here suggests derivation from a written source, see P. Sims-Williams, B xxix (1982), 606.

Odgar uab Aed: see n. on ll. 635–6 above.

1011–12. **yd aeth Arthur y'r Gogled:** evidently the redactor, or a preceding scribe, had forgotten that Arthur had just returned from the North, and from freeing the prisoners held there by Gwyn ap Nudd. Cyledyr Wyllt (see n. on l. 994) appears not to have been included among those freed: hence the second journey to the North. Alternatively there may well be confusion here with *Kynedyr Wyllt*, listed in l. 708 among the *anoethau*.

1013. **Yskithyrwynn Penn Beid:** see n. on l. 639 above.

1014. **Drutwyn geneu Greit mab Eri:** see n. on l. 673 above.

1015. **Cauall ki Arthur:** instances of *cafall* < Lat. *caballus* 'horse' are found in the Hengerdd (CA 1203; CLlH vii, 22a; and cf. PT 38n. on *caffon*). This word in its original meaning 'horse' is found above in ll. 337, 739, where *Call, Kuall,* and *Kauall* are the three horses of Cleddyf Kyuwlch. Since *carn* means both 'hoof' and 'cairn' it seems more probable that *Cabal/Cafall* originally designated Arthur's horse (whether as a common noun or as a personal name) rather than his hound. But the misunderstanding goes back at least as far as the passage describing Arthur's hunt for the Twrch Trwyd (Trwyth) in the *Mirabilia* attached to HB (see introduction p. lxvi and n.75). In GER the mistake – if it is one – of representing *Cauall* as Arthur's hound rather than his horse is perpetuated in the ref. to *annwylgi Arthur, Cavall oed y enw* (WM 402,19–20). On the mountain-name *Corn Cafallt* near Rhaeadr Gwy, see CF 538–40. Two places in Meirionnydd are designated *Carreg Carn March Arthur* acc. Pem. iv, 530.

1016. **Kaw o Brydein:** see n. on l.647 above.

1016–17. **Llamrei kassec Arthur:** this name is given in *Canu'r Meirch* BT 48,15; (TYP c–ci), though Llamrei is not specifically appropriated to Arthur in these lines: *A march Arthur . . . a Llamrei llavn elwic.* G. suggests that *llavn* here is an error for *llam*, which would give 'Llamrei of surpassing leap(?)'. *Llamrei* < *llam* 'Leap' + *grei* 'grey' meaning 'Grey Leap(er)' or alternatively *llam* + *re* 'swift' hence 'Swift Pace(d)', as rendered in GPC 2094.

1017. **achub yr kyuarth:** this seems to mean that Kaw went up to the boar (*achub*) so that it stood at bay, or because it stood at bay. On *yr* cf. GMW 219–20.

1020. **a nottayssei Ysbadaden:** Ysbaddaden had not in fact specified any particular hounds for the hunt of Ysgithrwyn Ben Beid. Cf. ll.1110–11, where it is claimed that the *tri meib Cledyf Divwlch* had won great fame in slaying this boar.

1024. **Kelli Wic yng Kernyw:** see n. on l.261 above.

1025. **Menw mab Teirgwaed:** see n. on l.199 above.

1026. **Twrch Trwyth:** see introduction section VIII and n. on 669–70 above.

salwen: here the MS clearly requires emendation to *salwett*, equative of *salw* 'mean, ugly'. With *rac* a causal meaning is expressed 'because it would be so mean to go to fight with him'; cf. GMW 42–3.

1028. **Neur daroed idaw diffeithaw traean Iwerdon:** 'he had destroyed', lit. 'to destroy had happened to him'. We must here distinguish between the grammatical subject, which is the vn. *diffeithaw*, and the logical subject contained in *idaw* 'to him'. Cf. CFG 34–5; B xvi (1955), 76–87.

neur: < *neu* + *ry*, GMW 170.

daroed: imperf. sing. 3 of *daruot y* 'to happen to' (GMW 145–6); here with pluperfect meaning.

1028–9. traean Iwerdon: 'the third part of Ireland'. This may mean three of the five *coiceda* or 'Fifths' of Ireland; see n. to l. 1069 below.

1029. y ymgeis ac wynt: 'to seek them out'; that is, to search for the Twrch Trwyth and his seven piglings; cf. l. 1067 below.

Esgeir Oeruel yn Iwerdon: see n. on ll. 106–7 above.

1036. Odgar uab Aed: see n. on l. 635 above.

1037. peir Diwrnach Wydel: see introduction pp. lviii–lix and n. on l. 635 above.

1040. kychwynnu: 'to start, rise, set forth'. The meaning 'to rise' survives in dialect (Glam.) > *kywhynnu* > *kywynnnu* > *cwnnu/ cwnni*; cf. LP 19. Here, as elsewhere in MW, it means 'to set forth'; cf. also l. 1095 *Kychwyn*.

1041. ysgawn: (adj.) 'light'; an interesting form which shows the alternation of *w/f*, cf. GMW 9. Whereas the standard literary form is now *ysgafn, ysgawn* is still echoed in *ysgon* in south Wales.

1041–2. Prytwen y long: see n. on l. 938 above.

1043. gwelsant niuer Otgar: 'the host of Otgar saw'. Note here how a subject in the form of a collective noun is preceded by a pl. vb.; cf. GMW 179, also SC vi (1971), 42–56. The vb. is usually sing. in such cases.

1045. pei as rodei: 'if he were able to give it'. *Pei* (later *pe*) 'if' is here a conditional conj., but was originally the subj. imperf. sing. 3 of the vb. 'to be'; cf. GMW 242–3. *As* is a syllabic form of the infix. pron. obj. sing. 3. GMW 56.

1047. keuyn: (noun) 'back', ModW *cefn*. Note that the epenthetic vowel (between *u* and *n*) is here represented by *y*, as is usual in MW; cf. GMW 12.

1051. Llenlleawc Wydel: see n. on l. 253 above.

Kaletvwlch: see n. on l. 159 above.

1054. swllt: < Lat. *solidus*; cf. OCo *sols*, gl. *pecunia*, Br. *saout* 'cattle'. Now it means 'shilling', but formerly it meant 'treasure, wealth': yn y lle yd oed *swllt* y brenhin a'e vrenhinolyon oludoed 'where was the king's treasure and his royal riches', *B. y Tywys.* (J. Rhŷs and J. G. Evans, *The Texts of the Bruts from the Red Book of Hergest* (Oxford, 1890), 406).

1055. **diskynnu:** 'land, disembark'. The vn. is used instead of a finite vb.: with regard to the meaning, cf. ac yn Abermenei e *disgynnassant* 'and in Abermenei they disembarked' HGVK 12,10–11; also ll.1062, 1097 below.

Llwydeu mab Kel Coet: see n. on l.287 above.

1055–6. **Porth Kerdin yn Dyuet:** *cerddin* 'rowan tree'. Unfortunately this place is unknown: Lady Charlotte Guest in her note (*The Mabinogion*, 333) suggested that it is Porth Mawr, near St David's Head, or else Pwll Crochan, five miles west of Fishguard. These suggestions were agreed by Idris Foster, 'Irish Influence', 30–1.

1056. **ac yno y mae messur y peir:** this direction would favour Pwll Crochan ('Pool of the Cauldron') as the place where Diwrnach's cauldron came to land. Cf. *messur pritguenn* (l.938 above, and n.). The latter may well have been a name for the same place.

1057. **a oed o gynifywr:** 'all the warriors there were'. Here we have a rel. construction found in MW, in which a noun or pron. governed by *o* 'of' (forming part of the antecedent) is placed within the rel. clause, or at the end of it. The antecedent may not be formally expressed, in which case the noun governed by the prep. is usually sing., as it is here. The meaning conveyed is 'all the, as many as'. Cf. *a oed o of yn Iwerdon* 'all the smiths that were in Ireland', PKM 36,9.

1057. From this point onwards a number of names of persons are introduced, many of whom have not previously been named in the story (see introduction p. xliv).

1057–8. **Teir Ynys Prydein a'e Their Rac Ynys:** see n. to l.282 above.

1059. **Gwlat yr Haf:** 'the Summer Country'. This came to mean the county of Somerset, but originally it denoted the greater Dumnonia, the whole of the south-western peninsula. (Not to be confused with Iolo Morganwg's equation of *Gwlad yr Haf* with *Deffrobani*, or Ceylon: see THSC (1968), 323–4.)

1059. **a oed o gi gordethol a march clotuawr:** 'all the picked dogs and famous horses that were'. The MS reading *gicwr dethol* indicates miscopying from an earlier prototype. See n. on l.1057 above.

1062–3. **y erchi nawd idaw:** the phrase *erchi nawd* seems here to have superseded the older *asswynaw nawdd*, as employed by Cynddelw in his *englynion* to Rhys ap Gruffydd (LlDC no. 23; H 150–1) see P. Ford, B xxvi (1975), 151–2. Cf. also n. on l.174 above.

1065. **bwyttal:** later known as *dawnbwyd* 'food-gift', the tribute of food (pigs or sheep, butter, bread, vats of bragget) to which the king was entitled twice-yearly from his subjects; LlB 201n.; HDdL 128–9.

1067. **a'e seithlydyn moch:** 'and his seven piglings'; *llydyn* (pl. of *llwdwn*, a word for the young of any animal) is one of the special pl. forms employed only with numerals; see B xxv, 117–18, GMW 47. *Moch* serves as the pl. of *hwch*: the pl. *hychod* is not attested before the late 15th. cent., nor does the sing. *mochyn* appear at an earlier date than DD. Six of the seven piglings are named below: *Grugyn Gwallt Ereint, Llwydawc Gouynnyat, Twrch Llawin, Gwys, Banw,* and *Bennwic* (see ll.1136–65). The seventh (unnamed) is slain in l.1073.

1067–8. **gellwng cwn arnaw:** 'dogs were let loose on him'. Here we have a vn. used instead of a finite vb., with passive meaning; cf. GMW 163. For another ex. of the same use cf. *brathu* Bendigeituran yn y troet 'B. was wounded in the foot', PKM 44,23.

1069. **pymhet ran y Iwerdon:** 'the fifth part of Ireland'. Clearly the narrator knew of the ancient and traditional division of Ireland into five provinces or *coiceda*; Ulster, Munster, Leinster, Connacht, and Meath. See EIHM 171–83; PKM 48; HGVK 38; and cf. *traean Iwerdon* 1028–9 above.

1071. **namyn a gawssant o drwc y gantaw:** 'except for all the ills they got from him'. Cf. l.1057 above.

1073. **naw nieu:** 'nine days'. Note the nasal mutation in *dieu* after *naw*; cf. GMW 22. Also note the pl. form *dieu*, used with numerals; GMW 47.

1074. **ystyr:** 'meaning', here used in the sense of 'history', < Lat. *historia*. See B. F. Roberts, 'Ystorya', B xxvi (1974), 13–20.

1075. **Brenhin uu ... y rithwys Duw ef yn hwch:** the Twrch Trwyth's father was named Tared *Wledic*; see n. on ll.669–70 above, and introduction pp. lxvii–viii.

1078–9. **yn rith ederyn:** the same words are used of Menw in l.1031. *Gwrhyr*, the linguist, adopts a bird's form in order to negotiate with the boars in their lair.

ef a'e seithlydyn moch: see n. on l.1067 above. *Ef a* 'he and' or 'with'. Cf. WG 422, LP 123, TC 150, 348–9, GMW 50–1.

1082. **y harchaf:** on *h-* here cf. GMW 23n.1.

1083. **Grugyn Gwrych Ereint:** 'G. Silver-Bristle'. *Grugyn* is one of the group of names in *Culhwch* which are paralleled by names in the *Gododdin* (see n. to *Kilyd*, l.1 above). Grugyn is the speaker on behalf of the Twrch Trwyth and his retinue of pigs: his words and those of Gwrhyr make it evident that he too had been transformed from a human into a boar. *Grugyn* derives from *grug* 'heather' + dim. suffix. It is cognate in form and meaning with OI *froich*, MI *fráech* (GPC 1536). It is therefore significant that the dim. form *Fráechán* is the name given in the *Dindshenchas* of *Dumae Selgae* to one of three men who were enchanted into swine of whom *Caelcheis* (= *Culhwch*, see introduction p. lxix) is another; see RC xv (1894), 470–2; *Met. Din.* iii, 386–94; CO(1) lxix.

According to Siôn Dafydd Rhys, *Grugyn Gawr* was the name of the giant who occupied *Garth Grugyn* (see n. to l.1160).

1090. **y grib a'r ellyn a'r gwelleu:** 'the comb and the razor and the scissors'. In the Giant's original specification of the treasures to be obtained from between the ears of the Twrch Trwyth (ll.668–90) the *ellyn* (razor) was omitted: this was because the *ysgithr* (tusk) of Ysgithrwyn Ben Beid was intended to be the razor with which Ysbaddaden was to be 'shaved'. Although the tusk was obtained (l.1020), its purpose seems to have been forgotten by the narrator: hence the addition here of a razor to the other implements. In l.1185 the razor is obtained, in l.1187 the scissors (*gwelleu*) are obtained, and in l.1200 the comb (*crib*). Yet, in the event, nothing is said of any of these implements being used for the 'shaving' of Ysbaddaden. It is Caw of Prydein, who had won the tusk of Ysgithrwyn (l.1020) who eventually 'shaves' Ysbaddaden, and it can be assumed that he used Ysgithrwyn's tusk with which to do so.

1095. **parth a Chymry:** *Cymry* < **Combrogi* 'fellow-countrymen' originally denoted the inhabitants of both Wales and of Cumbria, hence the modern name. The earliest use of the term *Cymry* for Wales is found in the praise-poem of the 7th. cent. (?) to Cadwallon ap Cadfan (B vii, 23–32; ed. R. G. Gruffydd, Ast. H. 27–34). In the 10th. cent. *Armes Prydein, Kymry* is employed a number of times (see AP(2) 20–1). In WG 13, J. Morris-Jones pointed out that the mis-spelling *Cymru* came to be used subsequently for 'Wales', and the true form *Cymry* was then retained as the pl. of *Cymro* to mean 'Welshman'. *Brython* – rather than *Cymry* – is used invariably in the poetry of Aneirin and Taliesin to denote all or any of the Brittonic peoples. The present instance is the only occurrence of the name in *Culhwch*; cf. PKM 37,22; 38,4.

1096–7. **a tharaw [l]lygat:** adv. 'and in the twinkling of an eye'. Cf. *yn enkyt y trawyt yr amrant ar y llall* 'the moment one eyelid was struck against the other' WLSD 7, 36–7. The *l* of R must be changed to *ll*.

1096. **Prytwen:** see n. on l.938 above.

1098. **Porth Cleis yn Dyuet:** the harbour at the mouth of the River Alun, five miles south-west of St David's, famous as the place where Gruffudd ap Cynan landed from Ireland in 1081, before joining with Rhys ap Tewdwr and advancing with him to meet with his adversaries at the battle of Mynydd Carn; see HGVK 13–14; CO(1) lxxi, and introduction p. lxxxii.

1099. **Mynyw:** *Menevia*, the old name for St David's. See HW 263–4; HGVK 73, WLSD 55–6.

1101–2. **Kynnwas Kwrryuagyl:** In her edn. of the *Mabinogion* (Everyman, 334) Lady Charlotte Guest identified this personal name with the place-name Canaston Bridge (now on the main A40 road between Narberth and Haverfordwest). However, *Cynwas Curyuagyl* is a character who has been previously named in the Court-List; see n. on l.186 above.

a oed yn Deu Gledyf o dyn a mil: 'all the men and beasts there were in *Dau Gleddyf*' (= Milford Haven, see n. on l.932 above). With the constr. cf. *a oed o gynifywr* l. 1057 above, and GMW 68. The extent of the commote of Deugleddyf is defined by Giraldus Cambrensis (*Descr. Cam.* I, v: 'From the same mountains [Preselau] come the two Cleddau streams. Between them is the region called

Deugleddyf, which is named after them. One runs by Llawhaden Castle and the other through Haverfordwest, and so they join the sea. Deugleddyf means "Two Swords".'

1104. **Presseleu:** the Preselly mountain in Pembs.

1105–6. **Ely a Thrachmyr:** in ll.286–7 the pair are described as *penkynydyon Arthur* 'A.'s chief huntsmen'; see n.

1106. **Drutwyn keneu Greit mab Eri:** cf. l.673 above, and n.

1107. **Gwarthegyt mab Kaw:** *Gwarthegyd* 'cattle-raider'. An addition to the sons of Kaw listed in ll.206–12 above, and a character unknown elsewhere.

1107–8. **deu gi Glythmyr Ledewic:** see n. on ll.1008–9 above.

1108. **Cauall ki Arthur:** see n. on l.1015 above.

1109. **o deu tu Nyuer:** 'on the two banks of the Nyfer'. The River Nyfer (Nevern) divided the cantref of Cemais into two commotes, *Uch Nyfer* and *Is Nyfer*. On the importance of Nanhyfer or Nevern in the Middle Ages see HW 263.

1110. **gwyr a gauas clot mawr:** 'men who obtained great fame'. Notice that the obj. *clot* retains the radical after the pret. sing. 3 *cauas*; cf. GMW 18, TC 216–17. This would be helped by the tendency for -*s* to cause provection; GMW 17, n.2.

1112. **Cwm Kerwyn:** *Foel Cwm Cerwyn* (1760 ft.) is the highest point on the Preselly mountains; it is the source of the River Clydach; see Pem. i. 97. *Cerwyn* 'tub, cask, barrel'; cf. PKM 86,27 and n.

1114. **Tarawc Allt Clwyt:** previously unmentioned. *Allt Clwyt* = *Al(t) Clut* 'the rock of the Clyde'. This was the central stronghold of the kingdom of Strathclyde, now Dumbarton, the 'Fortress of the Britons'.

1114–15. **Reidwn uab Eli Atuer:** cf. *Reidwn mab Beli*, named in the Court-List, l.224 above; see n.

1115. **Iscouan Hael:** also named in the Court-List, ll.224–5 above. With the previous name and *Iscawyn mab Panon* (l.1118 below) these names form a triad, apparently transplanted together in a group from the Court-List.

1116–17. **Gwydre uab Arthur:** a character unknown elsewhere (cf. *Gwydre mab Lluydeu* l.258).

1117. **Garselit Wydel:** also named previously in the Court-List, l.295 above. In l.697 he is described as *penkynyd Iwerdon.*

Glew uab Yscawt: *Yscawt* = *ysgod* 'shadow, ghost', but cf. *Unic Glew Yscwyd* PKM 33,16. On names in *Culhwch* from the *Mabinogi*, see introduction p. xxxviii n. 4.

1118. **Iscawyn uab Panon:** see l.225 above; cf. n. on l.1115.

1120–3. **Huandaw a Gogigwr a Phen Pingon ... Llaesgemyn:** According to l.85 above, these four were *raclouyeit* or 'deputies' to *Glewlwyt Gauaeluawr* (see n. on l.111 above).

tri gweis: 'three servants'; cf. *tri meib* l.1110 above.

1123. **gwr ny hanoed well neb ohonaw:** 'a man because of whom no one was the better'. *Hanoed* is imperf. sing. 3 of *hanuot*, which consists of *han* 'from, of' (cf. *gwahanu, gwahaniaeth, ohanaf* 'of me'), and means 'to be from'. The prep. *o* forms part of its construction, as here. *Hanuot* can also simply mean 'to be'.

1124–5. **Gwlydyn Saer:** cf. *Gluydyn Saer*, the craftsman who built Arthur's hall *Ehangwen* (l.264 above).

1126. **Pelunyawc:** now *Peuliniog*, the easternmost of the eight commotes of Cantref Gwarthaf, which lay between Narberth and Carmarthen, Pem. i, 388. It is explained as 'the land of Paulinus', HW 265, CF 512–13.

1126–7. **Madawc mab Teithyon:** another name new to the story; see n. on l.1057.

1127. **Gwyn mab Tringat mab Neuet:** on *Tringat mab Neuet* see n. on l.933 above. *Gwynn mab Tringat*'s name is reproduced in GER (WM 411,33–4 = RM 265,14). For *Neuet* cf. ll.339, 742.

1128. **Euryawn Pennlloran:** another new name. *Lloran* is perhaps a dim. of *llawr* 'champion'; cf. *Llawr, Lloryen* as personal names, CLlH i, 42c, 43c.

1129. **y rodes kyuarth udunt:** 'he stood at bay against them'. On *rhoi cyfarth* see n. PKM 237. Cf. l.1158 below, which provides another ex. of the non-lenition of the obj. after the pret. sing. 3.

1129–30. **Kynlas mab Kynan:** again, a name not previously introduced. Cf. *Kynlas kynweis* CA 1448; *Cinglas map Eugein dantguin*, EWGT 10(3); HW 133.

1130. **Gwilenhin brenhin Freinc:** see nn. to ll. 294 and 720. If these allusions do indeed refer to William the Conqueror, it is tempting to speculate as to whether there may be here an ironic reference to the Conqueror's death in 1087 – perhaps, for the narrator, an event of the recent past. But it can only be a matter of speculation whether the author would have been more, or less, likely to have permitted William to have been slain by the Twrch Trwyth, if his death had taken place before the time of writing. William I died in France under doubtful circumstances (apparently as the result of an accident with his horse), and he was buried afterwards at Caen in Normandy (DNB xxi, 300; F. M. Stenton, *Anglo-Saxon England*, 620). The introduction into the narrative of the names of contemporary figures of the 11th. and 12th. cents. can be paralleled in the Triads: see TYP cxii–iv on *Alan Fergant*, the Breton ruler who was William's contemporary and ally – the *Flergant brenhin Llydaw* of l. 216 above.

1131. **Glynn Ystu:** the ref. is to a wooded area in Carnwyllion commote along the right bank of the Gwendraeth Fawr river, equidistant at some eight miles from Aber Tywi (l. 1128) and the Llychwr valley (l. 1156) to the east. The extent of the forest is defined thus in a 1609 survey of the lordship of Carnwyllion (part of the duchy of Lancaster): 'the place called Glynystun alias Glynystyn lyeth in the parishes of Llanelly and Llanon from the brook Carwyly [sic] unto Mynidd Mawre alongst the easte syde of the river called Gwendraeth Vawr' (SDLLW 282; cf. 'West Ynis Ystu', idem. 260). This description seems to indicate that the wood ran from Carway up along the Gwendraeth Fawr valley as far as Mynydd Mawr, near Tumble – a distance of some six miles. Rhŷs noted a farm called Clyn Ystyn in the upper reaches of the valley (CF 513, THSC (1894–5), 146–7. Cf. also Pem. iv, 416). A vast wooded area such as this would explain why Arthur's men and dogs should have lost their quarry, as is stated.

1131–2. **yd ymgollassant y gwyr a'r cwn ac ef:** 'the men and dogs lost (sight of) him'. Note once more the use of a pl. vb. before a pl. subject; cf. l. 1043 *gwelsant niuer Otgar*.

1135. **hela:** 'to hunt' < *selg, Ir. *selg*, LP 33. In MW the form *hely* also occurs, with non-syllabic -*y*, along with a var. *hela*. Later -*y* was dropped, yielding *hel*, found mainly in north Wales, whereas -*a* persisted in the south of the country.

1136. **Dyffryn Llychwr:** the valley of the River Llychwr from present-day Ammanford down to Pontarddulais; the river's course, in this area, marks the boundary between the commotes of Carnwyllion and Gŵyr uwch Coed.

1136–7. **Grugyn Gwallt Ereint:** 'G. Silver Hair', clearly an error for *G. Gwrych Ereint* 'G. Silver-Bristle', l. 1083 above.

1137. **Llwydawc Gouynnyat:** one of the Twrch's seven piglings (see on l. 1067 above). For *gofyniad* 'suitor, suppliant' see GPC 1434. But the editors of Mab. render the epithet 'the Hewer', as in the case of *Gallcoit Gouynnyat* (see n. to ll. 187–8 above), taking it to be an error for *gomynyat* 'striker, killer, hewer' (GPC 1459), a word which is elsewhere attested in only two other instances: CA 345 *en trin gomynyat*; ibid. 1378 *gomynyat gelyn*. For a possible onomastic association with Llwydawc's name cf. *Carn Pen Rhiw Llwydog* (see n. to l. 1158 below). Another instance of the personal name occurs in LlDC 18,99 *Llvytauc uab Lliwelit*. Llwyddog 'having an army, warlike, etc.' is also an epithet applied to Arthur in *Englynion yr Eryr* (B ii, 276,34); to Cadwallon, who is *lluyddawg Prydain* in the praise-poem addressed to him (B vii, 25, 29; see n. Ast. H. 33), and to *Helen luicdauc* (sic. EWGT 10), *Elen Luydavc* TYP no. 35). Cf. n. on *ardyrchawc Prydein*, l. 293 above.

1140–1. **a oed o gi ry nodydoed:** 'all the dogs that had been named'. Cf. *a oed o gynifywr* l. 1057 above. At an early period the pre-verbal prt. *ry-* was used without *a* in a proper rel. clause; cf. GMW 62–3, 166–8. *nodydoed*, plup. impers. pass. of *nodi* 'to name'; cf. GMW 127–8.

1143. **dathoedynt:** 'they had come'; an early formation in which the imperf. of *bot* (*oed*, etc.) was added to the pret. stem to form the plup. Such forms had become rare by the late MW period, and have disappeared completely in late lit. ModW. Cf. further GMW 130–6.

nyt ymwelsei ac wynt: 'he had not seen them'. *Ymwelsei* is the plup. sing. 3 of *ymwelet*, which consists of *ym-* + *gwelet* 'to see'. A vb. containing this prefix is usually followed by *a(c)* 'with'; cf.

GMW 181–2. *Ymwelet a* here means 'to see', but it can also mean 'to visit', which is the usual meaning in ModW.

1144. **dygwydaw:** 'to fall, attack', consisting of *dy* + *cwydaw* 'to fall' (Br. *coezaff, di-gouezout*). Later in ModW in the form *digwydd* it developed a different (but not unrelated) meaning: 'to happen, befall'. Cf. also l.745 above, and l.1179 below.

1145. **ymrodi y gerdet ohonaw ynteu:** 'he endeavoured to proceed'. *Ymrodi* consists of *ym* (reflexive) and *rodi* 'to give'. In ModW *ymroi* means 'to do one's best'. *Kerdet* in MW generally meant 'to travel, go'; in ModW it means 'to walk'.

Mynyd Amanw: also *Dyffryn Amanw*, l.1149. The name survives in that of the Aman stream (Ordnance Survey 22/7517), which flows into the Llychwr (see Pem. iv, 416). The mountain may well be near to the source of the stream: cf. the location of the village of Brynaman. It is here associated by folk-etymology with *banw* 'pigling': the first of a series of onomastic allusions which are continued through the next paragraph of the text. Most of the locations mentioned in this section of the text – Dyffryn Llychwr, Mynydd Amanw, Twrch, Gwys, Dyffryn Amanw, Llwch Ewin and Llwch Tawe – can be identified in general terms. But it is difficult to offer a coherent account of the boar's wanderings between the rivers Llychwr and Tawe.

1147. **Twrch Llawin:** the river Twrch flows into the Tawe below Ystradgynlais; cf. *Turch* LL 134,12; *adblain Turc* 42,20. *Llawin* contains the adj. *llaw* 'small'. With these names cf. *Twrch mab Perif* and *Twrch mab Anwas* l.201 above.

1148. **gwys** means 'young pig', more specifically, a sow (GPC 1788). Here it is the name of a rivulet which runs into the River Twrch near Ystradgynlais. Ifor Williams comments on this and the following two names, 'Cydio y mae'r storiwr bob enw lle sy'n cadw enw mochyn â hela'r Twrch Trwyth. Yn Nhrefaldwyn y mae *gwys* yn byw ar fochyn hyd heddiw', *Enwau Lleoedd* 45.

1149. **Dyffryn Amanw:** the valley of the Aman river, between the villages of Ammanford and Brynaman. Cf. the reference to a payment *pro terris vocatis Glyn Amon ii s.* (shillings) (SDLLW 228) in a survey of 1609. The non-syllabic *w* of the ending is not found in later references to the stream: 'Amman' in 1541 (Dynevor MS collection) and 'the river Ammon' in 1609 (SDLLW 296): c. 1584/5 we read of the entrance of the River Aman into the Llychwr at Aberaman (MA 123).

Banw a Bennwic: *Bennwic* is a dim. of *banw* 'young pig' (see n. on l. 1145), and is recorded in GPC 272 in this one instance alone.

1150–1. **Grugyn Gwallt Ereint**. See n. on l. 1136–7 above.

1151. **Llwydawc Gouynnyat:** see n. on l. 1137 above.

1152. **Llwch Ewin:** Rhŷs's identification of Llwch Ewin with a bog mere *Llwch is awel* in Betws parish (CF 515) is unacceptable; the lake *Llyn Llech Owain* (cf. SDLLW 294) deserves consideration, but the boar is unlikely to have re-crossed the Llychwr river. Can there be a connection with the 'castellum Lluchewin' (Llangadog castle) mentioned in *Ann. Cam.* under the years 1205 and 1208? See Pem. iv, 416 and *By Tywys.* 195 (P 20 version). *Castell Luchewein* is said to have been burned in 1205 and again in 1208, acc. Pem. iv, 416. However, Siôn Dafydd Rhys in a note in C18,4 seemingly suggests a location for the lake (and Llwch Tawe) on the Black Mountain: 'Pylher y twrch Trwyth yssydh yn aml ar hyd y mynydh dv yn Swydh Coer Bhyrdin ac yn lheodh eraill'. On the basis of 'rwng Tawy ac Euyas' (l. 1166), one should perhaps look for the lake on the south Wales coast well to the west of the Wye's mouth; cf. 'rwng Llynn Lliwan ac Aber Gwy' (l. 1179).

1153. **rodi kyuarth:** see n. on l. 1129 above.

1154. **Echel Uordwyt Twll:** a stream called *Egel* flows into the Clydach, a tributary of the Tawe; see CF 536. This could have been spuriously identified with the place where *Echel* – evidently a traditional figure (see n. on ll. 195–6 above) – was thought to have been slain by the Twrch Trwyth.

1155. **Arwyli eil Gwydawc Gwyr:** cf. *Garwyli eil Gwythawc Gwyr* l. 197 above.

1156. **Llwch Tawy:** this is the older name for Llyn y Fan Fawr, Brecon (see Pem. iv, 372, 417). It is the place where the boars separate, and Grugyn goes northwards. Cf. Rhys Amheurig *c.* 1584/5 in *Morganiae Archaiographia*; 'TAWE; a river which springeth out of Llyn Llwch Tawe, in Brecon, and issuing there forth in a swift course, runneth to Ystradcallwen and thence to Ystradgynlais about one mile by south. The river called Twrch doth enter Tawe at Aber Twrch' (MA 122).

1158. **Din Tywi:** the location seems uncertain. Acc. Phillimore's note (Pem. iv, 408) 'The present writer does not agree with Rhŷs's suggestion (CF 515) that the *Din Tywi* where Grugyn next went after Llwch Tawy, was possibly Grongar. The old suggestion of Lady C. Guest that *Din Tywi* was the *dinas* above Twm Sion Catti's cave is rendered probable by the fact that on the top of the mountain, a mile or two to the east, there is a *Carn Twrch*, and four or five miles up the (stream) *Pysgottwr* there is a *Carn Pen Rhiw Llwydog*, which may commemorate the boar Llwydog, who seems to have gone with Grugyn from *Din Tywi* to Llanilar' (that is, to Garth Grugyn).

1159. **Eli a Thrachmyr:** see n. on ll.285–6 above.

1160. **Garth Grugyn:** acc. *ByTywys. Kastell Garth Grugyn* was built in 1242 by Maelgwn Fychan, grandson of Rhys ap Gruffudd. The place is now Castle Hill, Llanilar 'on the top of which Robert Vaughan saw a work where a castle had been', Pem. iv, 491 (cf. RWM ii, 848; HW 700n.). In Siôn Dafydd Rhys's account of the Giants (Cy 27,138) *Grygyn gawr o oedh yn trigaw yn Castelh Crygyn obhywn plwybh lhan Hilar.* On *Grugyn* see n. on l.1083 above.

1161. **Ruduyw Rys:** another character introduced for the first time. Rhŷs equated his epithet with *rhysswr* 'champion' (as in l.251, etc.); cf. CF 530n. Alternatively it could be the personal name *R(h)ys. Ruduyw* may derive from *rhudd* 'red' or *grudd* 'cheek' + *byw*.

1162. **Llwytawc:** that is, *Llwydawc Gouynnnyat*, see nn. on l.1137, and on l.1158 for *Carn Pen Rhiw Llwydog*.

Ystrat Yw: the rivulet *Yw* is a branch of the River Rhiangoll, which flows into the Usk. It gave its name to the commote of Ystrat Yw in the south-east of the cantref of Talgarth, which formed the south-east corner of the kingdom of Brycheiniog (HW 272; CF 517–18).

1163–4. **Hir Peissawc:** another name previously unmentioned. *Hir Peissawc* 'Long tunic' is more easily acceptable as an epithet than as a proper name. Cf. *Peisrudd* 'Red Tunic' (*pesrut* EWGT 9 (1)).

1164. **Llygatrud Emys a Gwrbothu (Hen):** Arthur's two 'uncles' were previously named in the Court-List; see n. on ll. 251–2 above.

1165. **vrodyr:** notice the occurrence of lenition in a noun in apposition after a personal name; cf. GMW 15; also TC 22–3.

1166. **Tawy ac Euyas:** the River Tawe (*Tauuy* LL 134, 12) flows into the sea at *Abertawe* (Swansea). *Ewias* (*Euias* LL 32, 22) was the cantref which lay between Talgarth and Erging (HW 279). See W. Rees, *A Historical Atlas of Wales*, plate 28.

1167. **Gwyssyaw Kernyw a Dyfneint:** that is, Arthur mustered all the fighting men from the whole of south-west Britain, (= *Gwlat yr Haf*, l. 1059 above, see n.).

1168. **Aber Hafren:** the mouth of the River Severn. But it is not made clear at what point on the Severn estuary the mustering took place. On *Hafren* < Lat. *Sabrina* see LHEB 519, 591.

1169–70. **myn gwrhyt gwyr:** 'by the valour of men'. An unusual expletive.

1170. **nyt a mi yn uyw yd aho:** 'not while I live (not with me being alive) shall he go to Cornwall'. The independent phrase is an absolute construction, with the meaning of a subordinate clause; cf. GMW 231, also l. 702 above. *Aho* is subj. pres. sing. 3, a formation which conforms to that of the regular vb.: *a-ho*, cf. *car-ho*. *Mynet* 'to go' is an irregular vb., and the usual form of the pres. sing. 3 is *el*, GMW 133. The form here denotes future meaning, but with an affective element.

1174. **a'e ragot:** 'to waylay (ambush) him': another ex. of the vn. used instead of a finite vb.; cf. ooo. It occurs as a noun: *orachot yn luhyn hac dieithyr luhyn* 'as regards ambush in the woods and outside' (*Privilege of Teilo*) LL 120, 15–16. As a vn: *Ac y kerdws y niuer hwnnw yny gawssant lle adas y eu ragot ac ymgudyaw yno* 'and that company proceeded until they found a suitable place to waylay them, and hid there', BD 174, 8–9. It occurs also in the Laws; BD 6, 15, n.

1176–7. **anghen yn anghen:** 'need for need', that is, 'by sheer force', see introduction p. xx. On *Mabon uab Modron* see n. on l. 685 above, and introduction pp. lx–lxi.

1177. **Gwynn Mygdwn march Gwedw:** see n. on l. 689 above.

1178. **Goreu mab Custennin:** see n. on l.811 above, and introduction pp. xxx–xxxi.

Menw mab Teirgwaed: one of the original 'Six Helpers'; see n. on l. 199 above.

1179. **Llyn Lliwan:** named in l.891 above as *Llyn Llyw*, the home of the Salmon. Evidently it was a lake or pool which overflowed into the Severn estuary. Among the *Mirabilia* of Britain described in HB ch. 69 is *Oper* (= *aber*) *Linn Liuan* (see HB ed. Loth 213; text and trans. CF 407). According to this description, where the Severn estuary is tidal and the river meets it in spate, it causes a whirlpool and a very great noise. This phenomenon is known as the Severn 'bore' or 'eagre'. Ifor Williams describes it in his note on the name *Teirnon Twryf Uliant* (PKM 147, see n. on l.255 above), and suggests that the latter's epithet 'Roar of the Flood-Tide' may have reference to it; cf. also Kenneth Jackson, YB xii, 17–18. It is tempting to suggest that there is another ref. to the Severn 'bore' in ll. 1183–4 below, which describes the great commotion caused by the Twrch Trwyth in the Severn estuary. The 'marvel' of *Linn Liuan* was borrowed from HB into HRB ix, 7 (ed. Wright, 106), where it appears as *Linliguum*; BD 151 *Lynn Llywan*. The location of the tidal pool is here given as near the Welsh border *yn emyleu Kymry ar glan Hauren*; similarly in the 16th.-cent. text *Rhyfeddode yr Ynys* 'yn ymyl Kymru ar lan Havren ... llyn Lliwon' (T. H. Parry-Williams, *Rhyddiaith Gymraeg: Y Gyfrol Gyntaf* (Gwasg Prifysgol Cymru (1954), 66). Its border was defined by the course of the River Severn, according to HRB ix,7. Should we then look for the lake on the river's English shoreline in Gloucestershire? Camden does not mention the pool in his *Britannia* (edn. 1695), but describes the Severn bore as 'a Gulph or whirlpool', before adding 'Sometimes it overfloweth its bank, and wanders a great way into the neighbouring Plains (of Gloucestershire), and then returneth back as conqueror of the land'. Further, in view of the ref. to 'Oper Linn Liguan' and 'fluminis illius' in the *Mirabilia*, should we be looking for a river-mouth in this area? However, to judge from the present ref. linking Aber Gwy with *Llyn Lliwan*, the pool was situated on the Welsh side of the Severn estuary. From the testimony of the Salmon we know that the lake lay some way below the town of Gloucester, and in view of the Salmon's assertion that he would regularly swim with each tide as far as the town (ll.905–6), it is interesting to note that Camden depicts the 'daily rage' of the Severn as losing its force 'at the first bridge' – namely at Gloucester itself.

1180–1. **Osla Gyllelluawr:** see nn. on ll.278 above, and 1193–6 below.

1181. **Manawydan uab Llyr:** see n. on l.215 above.

Cacamwri gwas Arthur: see n. on l.318–19 above.

1182. **Gwyngelli:** 'White Grove' – an improbable personal name, hitherto unattested.

1183. **yn y traet:** 'in (= by) his feet'; an ex. of the non-lenition after the poss. pron. sing. 3 masc; or else, as happens sometimes, of the art. used as a poss. pron. Cf. GMW 25, also ll.61–2 above.

1185. **a chael yr ellyn:** see n. on l.1090 above.

1186. **Kyledyr Wyllt:** see n. on l.994 above.

1190. **a gaffat o drwc:** 'all the ill that was got'; cf. GMW 68, also l.1198 below.

1193. **deu uaen ureuan:** 'two quernstones'. Cf. the *mein sugyn* ('load-stones' or 'suction-stones') which hindered Bendigeidfran, PKM 40,20 and n.

1199–1200. **o drwc y gilyd:** 'from (the one) ill to the other'. On the use of *cilyd* 'fellow, companion' cf. GMW 96–7. Here the *y* consists of the prep. *y* 'to' and the poss. pron. infixed sing. 3 *y*. Cf. GMW 53 n.2.

1202. **Anet ac Aethlem:** the two hounds who were specified among the *anoethau*, l.728 above.

1204. **Kelli Wic yg Kernyw:** see n. on l.261 above.

1206–7. **y Widon Ordu merch y Widon Orwen:** see n. on ll.652–3 above.

1207–8. **Pennant Gouut yg gwrthtir Uffern:** see n. on l.653 above. For the parallel phrase *o vrthdir Uffern* cf. l.189 above. In the episode of the Black Witch 'the upland of Hell' is clearly situated in north Britain. The 'Old North' is the meaning of '*Y Gogledd*' here and elsewhere in the tale; cf. l.107, etc. The episode appears to bear some relation to Arthur's fight with a witch in *Pa Gur*, and this poem also appears to have a northern location (see introduction pp. xxxv–vi and n.21).

1209–10. Gwyn uab Nud a Gwythyr uab Greidawl: these characters were both previously associated with an episode located in north Britain (ll.988–1004).

1216. yll deu: ModW *ill dau*. *Yll* is a form of *oll, holl*, and occurs with numerals in apposition after pers. prons. or endings; here it means 'both'. For the 1 and 2 pl. the forms of the poss. pron. are used before the numeral. Cf. GMW 99.

1219. dywedassant: a pl. vb. before a subject which consists of two personal names; cf. l.1043, etc.

1221. Hir Amren a Hir Eidil: previously named as Arthur's servants, l.323 above.

1223. drafferth: in MW lenition is attested of the subject after the pret. *bu*; GMW 18.

1224–5. ell pedwar ar Lamrei kassec Arthur: On *Llamrei* see n. on ll.1016–17 above. This farcically excessive load on a horse's back is reminiscent of the 'Three Horses who carried the Three Horse-Burdens', TYP no.44. Each of the three went on a journey carrying several men on its back. With *ell pedwar* cf. *yll deu* l.1216.

1226. Carnwennan y gyllell: see n. on l.161 above.

1227. yny uu yn deu gelwrn hi: 'until she was as two tubs'. Notice how the pron. *hi* is separated from the copula *uu* by the nominal predicate *yn deu gelwrn*. The more normal construction would be *yny uu hi yn deu gelwrn*. But the order in which the pron. is deferred until the end is also attested. It is found in Irish and in modern spoken Welsh. Cf. GMW 58, n.2.

1234–5. Eillwyt … Meu. These two forms represent affirmative answers to questions, the one introduced by the prt. *a*, and the other by *ae*. Notice that the answer is denoted by repeating the form following *a/ae*, here by *Eillwyt/meu*. Later the form *do* came to be used for the first, and *ie* for the second. Cf. GMW 176–7.

1236. diolwch: 'to thank', consisting of *di = golwch* 'praise', which was later reduced to *diolch*; cf. B ii (1924), 125. In MW *diolwch* has a direct obj., as here (representing the thing for which thanks are due), and an indirect obj., governed by the prep, *y* 'to', which refers to the person(s) to whom the thanks are due.

diolwch y mi hynny: 'to thank me for that'. In ModW *am* came to be used to denote that for which thanks are due: *diolch i mi am hynny*.

1239–40. **gwallt y penn:** 'the hair of the/his head'. On *y penn* cf. *yn y traet* l. 1183 above.

1242. **y kyscwys Kulhwch gan Olwen:** 'C. slept with Olwen'. A more archaic phrase is used in l. 3 above, *gwedy y west genthi* (see n.).

1243. **tra uu vyw:** 'while he lived'. Notice that *tra* 'while' in MW (unlike ModW) is followed by lenition (*uu* < *bu*); cf. GMW 21.

Abbreviations

Languages ModW = Modern Welsh; MW = Middle Welsh; ME = Middle English; OI = Old Irish; OW = Old Welsh; OF = Old French.

Manuscripts C = Cardiff; J = Jesus, Ll. = Llanstephan; M = Mostyn; P = Peniarth; R = Red Book of Hergest (J111); W = White Book of Rhydderch (P4).

AB	Edward Lhuyd, *Archaeologia Britannica* (Oxford, 1907)
AIT	T. P. Cross and C. R. Slover, *Ancient Irish Tales* (London, 1936; repr. with revised bibliography by C. W. Dunn, Dublin, 1969)
ALMA	R. S. Loomis (ed.), *Arthurian Literature in the Middle Ages* (Oxford, 1959)
Ann.Cam	*Annales Cambriae*; *Cy* ix, 141 ff.; ed. J. Morris, *Nennius' British History and the Welsh Annals* (see under HB below)
AoW	R. Bromwich, A. O. H. Jarman, Brynley F. Roberts (eds.), *The Arthur of the Welsh* (University of Wales Press, 1991)
AP	Ifor Williams (ed.), *Armes Prydein* (University of Wales Press, 1955, etc.); English edn. trans. R. Bromwich (DIAS, 1972, 1982)
Ast.H.	R. Bromwich and R. Brinley Jones (eds.), *Astudiaethau ar yr Hengerdd* (University of Wales Press, 1978)
AT	Anti Aarne and Stith Thompson, *The Types of Folktale: A Classification and Bibliography* (Folklore Fellows Communications, no.74, Helsinki 1928, 1961)
B	*Bulletin of the Board of Celtic Studies*
BBC	J. Gwenogvryn Evans (ed.), *The Black Book of Carmarthen* (Pwllheli, 1907)
BBIAS	*Bibliographical Bulletin of the International Arthurian Society*

BD	Henry Lewis (ed.), *Brut Dingestow* (University of Wales Press, 1942)
BGG	*Bonedd Gwŷr y Gogledd* (EWGT 73; TYP 238–9)
BR	Melville Richards (ed.) *Breudwyt Ronabwy* (University of Wales Press, 1948)
BT	J. G. Evans (ed.), *Facsimile and Text of the Book of Taliesin* (Llanbedrog, 1910)
BWP	Ifor Williams (ed. R. Bromwich), *The Beginnings of Welsh Poetry* (University of Wales Press, 1972, 1980, 1990)
ByS	*Bonedd y Saint* (EWGT 54–67; VSB 320–3)
By Tywys.	T. Jones (ed.), *Brut y Tywysogyon* (Peniarth 20 version) (University of Wales Press, 1941)
CA	Ifor Williams (ed.), *Canu Aneirin* (University of Wales Press, 1938, 1970, etc.)
CF	John Rhŷs, *Celtic Folklore* (Oxford, 1891, 1980)
CFG	Melville Richards, *Cystrawen y Frawddeg Gymraeg* (University of Wales Press, 1938)
Chr.Br	J. Loth, *Chrestomathie Bretonne* (Paris, 1890)
CIIC	R. A. S. Macalister, *Corpus Inscriptionum Insularum Celticarum* (2 vols., DIAS 1945, 1949)
CLlH	Ifor Williams (ed.), *Canu Llywarch Hen* (University of Wales Press, 1935, 1953)
CMCS	*Cambridge Medieval Celtic Studies*
CMT	E. A. Gray (ed. and trans.) *Cath Maige Tuired: The Battle of Mag Tuired* (ITS vol. liii, Naas, Kildare, 1982)
CO(1)	*Culhwch ac Olwen* (testun Syr Idris Foster wedi ei olygu a'i orffen gan Rachel Bromwich a D. Simon Evans, University of Wales Press, 1988).
Cy	*Y Cymmrodor*
DD	J. Davies, *Dictionarium Duplex Britannico-Latinarum*, 1632.
DIAS	Dublin Institute for Advanced Studies.
DIL	*Contributions to a Dictionary of the Irish Language* (Dublin, Royal Irish Academy, 1942–1976)
DNB	*Dictionary of National Biography*
EANC	R. J. Thomas, *Enwau Afonydd a Nentydd Cymru* (University of Wales Press, 1938)
EC	*Études celtiques*

ECMW	V. E. Nash Williams, *The Early Christian Monuments of Wales* (University of Wales Press, 1950)
EIHM	T. F. O'Rahilly, *Early Irish History and Mythology* (DIAS, 1946)
EL	Henry Lewis, *Yr Elfen Ladin yn yr Iaith Gymraeg* (University of Wales Press, 1943)
EWGT	P. C. Bartrum (ed.) *Early Welsh Genealogical Tracts* (University of Wales Press, 1946)
EYP	*Enweu Ynys Prydein* (TYP 228–37)
G	J. Lloyd-Jones, *Geirfa Barddoniaeth Gynnar Gymraeg* (University of Wales Press, 1931–63)
GDE	Thomas Roberts, *Gwaith Dafydd ab Edmwnd* (Bangor, 1914).
GDG	Thomas Parry, *Gwaith Dafydd ap Gwilym* (University of Wales Press 1952, 1963, etc.)
GER	*Chwedl Geraint fab Erbin.*
GIG	D. R. Johnston, *Gwaith Iolo Goch* (University of Wales Press, 1988)
GGl	J. Ll. Williams and Ifor Williams (eds.), *Gwaith Guto'r Glyn* (University of Wales Press, 1939, 1961)
GLM	Eurys Rowlands (ed.), *Gwaith Lewys Môn* (University of Wales Press, 1975)
GMW	D. S. Evans, *A Grammar of Middle Welsh* (DIAS, 1964).
GOI	R. Thurneysen (trans. Binchy and Bergin), *A Grammar of Old Irish* (DIAS, 1946)
GPC	*Geiriadur Prifysgol Cymru* (1950–)
GTA	T. Gwynn Jones (ed.), *Gwaith Tudur Aled* (University of Wales Press, 1926)
H	J. Morris-Jones and T. H. Parry-Williams (eds.), *Llawysgrif Hendregadredd*
HB	*Historia Brittonum* ed. (i) T. H. Mommsen, *Monumenta Germanica Historica* xiii, *Chronica minora Saeculi* iv-vii, vol. iii (Berlin, 1888); ed. (ii) F. Lot, *Nennius et l'Historia Brittonum* (Paris, 1934); ed. (iii) D. N. Dumville, *The Historia Brittonum; The Vatican Recension* (D. S. Brewer, Cambridge, 1985); ed. (iv) with trans. J. Morris, *Nennius' British History and the Welsh Annals* (London and Chichester, 1980); trans. A. W. Wade-Evans, *Nennius's History of the Britons* (London, SPCK, 1938).

HDdL   Dafydd Jenkins, *The Law of Hywel Dda* (Llandysul, 1986)

HGCr   Henry Lewis, *Hen Gerddi Crefyddol* (University of Wales Press, 1931)

HGVK   D. Simon Evans (ed.), *Historia Gruffud vab Kenan* (University of Wales Press, 1977)

HL   John Rhŷs, *The Hibbert Lectures on Celtic Heathendom* (London, 1898)

HRB   *Historia Regum Britanniae* ed. (i) A. Griscom (from Camb. Univ. Lib. MS 1706, London, 1929); ed. (ii) J. Faral, *La Légende Arthurienne* (from Trin. Coll. Camb. MS 1126; Paris, 1929); ed. (iii) Neil Wright (from Bern MS 568; Woodbridge, Suffolk, 1985). trans. Lewis Thorpe (Harmondsworth, 1966).

HW   J. E. Lloyd, *A History of Wales* (London, 1911, 1939)

IGE(2)   Henry Lewis, Thomas Roberts and Ifor Williams (eds.) *Cywyddau Iolo Goch ac Eraill* (University of Wales Press, 1937)

IPT   K. H. Jackson, *The International Popular Tale and Early Welsh Tradition* (University of Wales Press, 1961)

ITS   Irish Texts Society

IW   Ifor Williams

LBS   S. Baring-Gould and J. H. Fisher, *Lives of the British Saints* (4 vols., London, 1907–13)

LEWP   Ifor Williams, *Lectures on Early Welsh Poetry* (1944, repr. 1970)

LGC   *Gwaith Lewis Glyn Cothi*, ed. Tegid (2 vols. Oxford, Hon. Soc. Cymmrodorion, 1837)

LHEB   K. H. Jackson, *Language and History in Early Britain* (Edinburgh, 1953)

LL   *The Text of the Book of Llan Dâv* ed. J. Gwenogvryn Evans and J. Rhŷs, (Oxford, 1893)

LlB   S. J. Williams and J. Enoch Powell, *Cyfreithiau Hywel Dda yn ôl Llyfr Blegywryd* (University of Wales Press, 1942)

LlC   *Llên Cymru*

LlDC   A. O. H. Jarman (ed.), *Llyfr Du Caerfyrddin* (University of Wales Press, 1982)

Ll.Ior.	Aled Wiliam (ed.), *Llyfr Iorwerth: The Venedotian Code of the Welsh Laws* (University of Wales Press, 1960)
LP	H. Lewis and H. Pedersen, *A Concise Comparative Celtic Grammar* (Göttingen, 1937)
LU	R. I. Best and O. J. Bergin, *Lebor na h-Uidre; The Book of the Dun Cow* (Dublin; Royal Irish Academy, 1929)
LWS	D. Simon Evans (ed.), *Lives of the Welsh Saints by G. H. Doble* (University of Wales Press, 1971)
MA	L. James (ed.), Rice Meyrick's *Morganiae Archaiographia* (South Wales Record Soc. I, 1983)
Mab	Gwyn Jones and Thomas Jones (trans.) *The Mabinogion* (London, 1949, 1963, 1989)
Met.Din.	E. J. Gwynn, *The Metrical Dindshenchas: Text, Translation, and Commentary* (Dublin, Royal Irish Academy, 1903–35)
NLW Journal	*Journal of the National Library of Wales*
OSPG	K. H. Jackson (trans.) *The Oldest Scottish Poem: The Gododdin* (Edinburgh, 1969)
PBA	Proceedings of the British Academy
PCB	Anne Ross, *Pagan Celtic Britain* (London, 1967)
Pem	Owen's Pembrokeshire ed. Henry Owen (4 pts. London: Cymm. Record Series i) 1892–1936)
PKM	Ifor Williams (ed.), *Pedeir Keinc y Mabinogi* (University of Wales Press, 1930, 1951, etc.)
PT	Ifor Williams (ed.; trans. J. E. Caerwyn Williams) *The Poems of Taliesin* (DIAS, 1968, 1987)
RC	*Revue celtique*
RIA	Royal Irish Academy
RM (R)	J. Rhŷs and J. Gwenogvryn Evans (eds.), *The Mabinogion from the Red Book of Hergest* (Oxford, 1887)
RP	J. Gwenogvryn Evans (ed.), *The Poetry from the Red Book of Hergest* (Llanbedrog, 1911)
RWM	*Report on Manuscripts in the Welsh Language* (Historical MSS Comission, London, 1898)
SC	*Studia Celtica*
SDLLW	William Rees (ed.), *A Survey of the Duchy of Lancaster*

Lordships in Wales, 1609–1613 (University of Wales Press, 1953)

SDR   Henry Lewis (ed.), *Seith Doethon Rufein* (University of Wales Press, 1967)

ST   Stith Thompson, *Motif-Index of Folk Literature* (6 vols., Copenhagen, 1955–8)

TBDD   Togail Bruidne Da Derga ed. i) E. Knott (DIAS, 1963); ii) ed. and trans. W. Stokes (RC xxii; repr. Paris, 1902)

TC   T. J. Morgan, *Y Treigladau a'u Cystrawen* (University of Wales Press, 1952).

THSC   *Transactions of the Honourable Society of Cymmrodorion*

TPC   T. P. Cross, *Motif-Index of Early Irish Literature* (Bloomington, Indiana, 1952)

TWS   E. R. Hencken, *Traditions of the Welsh Saints* (D. S. Brewer, Woodbridge, 1987)

TYP   R. Bromwich (ed. and trans.), *Trioedd Ynys Prydein: The Welsh Triads* (University of Wales Press, 1961; new edition 1978, repr. 1991)

VSB   A. W. Wade-Evans (ed. and trans.), *Vitae Sanctorum Britanniae et Genealogiae* (University of Wales Press, 1944)

WG   J. Morris-Jones, *A Welsh Grammar* (Oxford, 1913)

WLSD   D. Simon Evans, *The Welsh Life of St David* (UWP 1988)

WLW   D. Jenkins and M. E. Owen, *The Welsh Law of Women* (University of Wales Press, 1980)

WM (W)   J. Gwenogvryn Evans (ed.), *The White Book Mabinogion* (Pwllheli, 1907); new edition with introduction by R. M. Jones (University of Wales Press, 1973)

YB   J. E. Caerwyn Williams (ed.), *Ysgrifau Beirniadol* (Denbigh, 1965–)

YCM   S. J. Williams (ed.), *Ystorya de Carolo Magno* (University of Wales Press, 1930)

YmMTh   A. O. H. Jarman (ed.), *Ymddiddan Myrddin a Thaliesin* (University of Wales Press, 1951; new edition 1967)

ZCP   *Zeitschrift für celtische Philologie*

Select Bibliography

(in addition to works cited above under Abbreviations)

Anwyl, E. 'Notes on Kulhwch and Olwen' RC xxxiv (1913), 152–6; 406–17.

Bowen, Geraint (ed.) *Y Traddodiad Rhyddiaith yn yr Oesau Canol* (Llandysul, 1974).

Cowell, E. B. 'The Legend of the Oldest Animals', Cy v (1882), 169–72.

Davies, Wendy, *Wales in the Early Middle Ages* (Leicester, 1982).
— — *The Llandaff Charters* (National Library of Wales, 1979).
Dillon, Myles, *Early Irish Literature* (Chicago, 1948).
— — *The Cycles of the Kings* (Oxford, 1946).
— — (ed.) *Irish Sagas* (Dublin Stationery Office, 1959).

Edel, Doris, *Helden und Freiersfüssen: 'Tochmarc Emire'* und *'Mal y kavas Kulhwch Olwen'* (Amsterdam, 1980)
— — 'The Catalogues in *Culhwch ac Olwen* and Insular Celtic Learning', B xxx (1983), 253–73.
— — 'The Arthur of *Culhwch ac Olwen* as a Figure of Epic Heroic Tradition', *Reading Medieval Studies* ix (1983), 3–15.
Emmanuel, H. D. 'An Analysis of the Composition of the *Vita Cadoci*', NLW Journal vii (1951–2), 217–27.
Evans, D. Ellis, 'A Comparison of the Formation of Some Continental and Early Insular Celtic Personal Names', B xxiv (1972), 415–34 (repr. EC xiii, 171–93).
— — *Gaulish Personal Names* (Oxford, 1967).
Evans, D. Simon, 'Culhwch ac Olwen: Tystiolaeth yr Iaith', YB xiii (1985), 101–13.
— — 'Y Bucheddau' ch. ix in *Y Traddodiad Rhyddiaith yn yr Oesau Canol* ed. Geraint Bowen (Llandysul, 1974).
— — 'Llyfr Du Caerfyrddin', LIC xiv (1983–4), 210–15.
— — See also GMW, HGVK, WLSD, LWS.

Ford, P. K. *The Mabinogi and Other Medieval Welsh Tales* (Berkeley, 1977).

Ford, P. K. 'Welsh *asswynaw* and Celtic Legal Idiom', B xxvi (1975), 147–53.

—— 'On the Significance of Some Arthurian Names in Welsh', B xxx (1983), 268–73.

Foster, I.-Ll. *Astudiaeth o Chwedl Culhwch ac Olwen* (University of Wales MA thesis, Bangor, 1935).

—— 'The Irish Influence on Some Welsh Personal Names', *Feilsghribhínn Eoin Mhic Neill* (Dublin, 1940), 28–36.

—— 'Gwyn ap Nudd' in *Duanaire Finn*, ed. Gerard Murphy (ITS vol. xliii, Dublin, 1953), 198–204.

—— 'Culhwch ac Olwen' and 'Rhonabwy's Dream', ch. iv in ALMA, 31–43.

—— 'Rhagarweiniad: Y Cefndir', ch. i in *Y Traddodiad Rhyddiaith* ed. Geraint Bowen (Llandysul, 1970).

—— Notes on *lloring, Penrhyn Pengwaedd, Dinsol, Porth Clais*, B viii (1937), 21–7.

—— 'Culhwch ac Olwen', ch. iii in Geraint Bowen (ed.) *Y Traddodiad Rhyddiaith yn yr Oesau Canol* (Llandysul, 1974).

Ganz, Jeffrey, (trans.) *The Mabinogion* (Harmondsworth, 1976).

—— (trans.) *Early Irish Myths and Sagas* (Harmondsworth, 1981).

Gray, E. A. (ed. and trans.) *Cath Maige Tuired; The Battle of Mag Tuired* (ITS vol. lii; Naas, Kildare, 1982).

Gruffydd, W. J. 'Mabon fab Modron', RC xxxiii (1912), 452–60.

—— 'Mabon vab Modron' THSC xlii (1930), 129–47.

—— *Math fab Mathonwy* (University of Wales Press, 1928).

—— *Rhiannon* (University of Wales Press, 1953).

Guest, Lady Charlotte, (trans.) *The Mabinogion* (London, 1949; repr. Everyman, 1932). See also Mab.

Gwynn, E. J. *The Metrical Dindshenchas; Text, Translation, and Commentary*, 5 vols. (Dublin, Royal Irish Academy Todd Lectures Series, viii–xii, 1903–35).

van Hamel, A. G. (ed.) *Compert Con Culainn and Other Stories* (Dublin Stationery Office, 1933).

—— 'Aspects of Celtic Mythology', PBA xx (1934), 207–48.

Hamp, E. P., 'Culhwch, the Swine' ZCP 41 (1986), 257–8.

—— 'The Pig in Ancient Northern Europe' (1) *Marija Gimbutas Festschrift* (ed.) S. N. Skomal and E. C. Polome (Washington, 1987).

Haycock, Marged (ed.) 'Preiddeu Annwn', SC xviii/xix (1983–4), 52–78.

Henry, P. L. 'Culhwch ac Olwen; Some Aspects of Style and Structure', SC iii (1968), 30–8.

Hogan, E. *Onomasticon Goedelicum* (Dublin, 1910).

Ifans, Dafydd 'Yr Anifeiliaid Hynaf', B xxiv (1972), 461–4.

—— with Rhiannon Ifans, *Y Mabinogion* (Version in Modern Welsh with an introduction by Professor B. F. Roberts (Llandysul, 1980).

Jackson, Kenneth. 'Some Popular Motifs in Early Welsh Tradition', EC xi (1964–5), 83–99.

—— 'Rhai Sylwadau ar Culhwch ac Olwen', YB xii (1982), 12–23.

—— *The Oldest Irish Tradition: A Window on the Iron Age* (Cambridge, 1964).

—— See also IPT, LHEB, OSPG.

James, J. W. *Rhigyfarch's Life of St. David: Text, Introduction, Translation* (University of Wales Press, 1967).

Jenkins, Dafydd, *Hywel Dda: The Law* (Llandysul, 1986).

—— Notes on *said, gwrmsaid, gwynsaid, yslipanu*; B xxxv (1988), 55–61.

—— with M. E. Owen (eds.) *The Welsh Law of Women* (University of Wales Press, 1980).

Jones, Bedwyr L. note on *na golwc hebawc mut, na golwc gwalch trimut* (=CO lines 493–4) B xxiii (1970), 327–8.

Jones, D. Gwenallt *Yr Areithiau Pros* (University of Wales Press, 1934).

Jones, Thomas 'Chwedl yr Anifeiliaid Hynaf', NLW Journal vii (1951), 62–6.

—— 'Triawd Ladin ar y Gorlifiadau', B. xii (1948), 79–83.

—— 'Nodiadau Testunol ar Lyfr Gwyn Rhydderch,' B xii (1948), 83–6.

—— Notes on *sangnarwy, lloring, Gleif penntirec*, B xiii (1950), 17–19, 75–7.

—— 'Datblygiadau Cynnar Chwedl Arthur,' B xvii (1958), 235–52.

—— 'The Early Evolution of the Legend of Arthur' (=trans. of the above by Gerald Morgan) *Nottingham Medieval Studies* viii (1964), 3–21.

Jones, Thomas 'Teir Ynys Prydein a'e Their Rac Ynys,' B xvii (1958), 268–9.

— — 'Chwedl Huail fab Caw ac Arthur' in Thomas Jones (ed.) *Astudiaethau Amrywiol a gyflwynir i Syr Thomas Parry-Williams* (University of Wales Press, 1968).

— — 'The Black Book of Carmarthen Stanzas of the Graves,' PBA liii (1969), 97–136.

— — See also Mab.

Knight, Stephen *Arthurian Literature and Society* (London, 1983) (with a chapter on 'Culhwch ac Olwen').

Knott, Eleanor (ed.) *Togail Bruidne Da Derga* (Dublin, 1935; 2nd edn DIAS 1963).

Loth, J. (trans.) *Les Mabinogion* (Paris, 1913).

— — 'La date de la composition de Kulhwch et Olwen,' RC 32 (1911), 428–41; repr. in his *Contributions á l'étude des Romans de la Table Ronde* (Paris, 1912), 37–51.

— — See also Chr. Br.

Lloyd-Jones, J. *Enwau Lleoedd Sir Gaernarfon* (University of Wales Press, 1928).

— — See also G.

Mac Cana, Proinsias *Celtic Mythology* (London, 1970).

— — *The Mabinogi* (University of Wales Press, 1977).

— — *The Learned Tales of Medieval Ireland* (DIAS 1980).

— — (with Arwyn Watkins) 'Cystrawennau'r Cyplad mewn Hen Gymraeg', B xviii, 1–25.

MacQueen, John 'Goreu son of Custennin', EC viii (1958), 154–63.

Murphy, Gerard (ed. and trans.) *Duanaire Finn: The Book of the Lays of Finn*; Part iii: Introduction, Notes and Glossary (ITS vol. xliii, Dublin, 1953).

— — *The Ossianic Lore and Romantic Tales of Medieval Ireland* (Dublin, 1955).

Ní Chatháin, P. 'Swineherds, Seers, and Druids', SC xiv/xv (1979–80), 200–11.

Ní Shéaghdha, Nessa, *Tóruigheacht Dhiarmada agus Ghráinne: The Pursuit of Diarmaid and Gráinne* (ITS vol. xlviii, Dublin, 1967).

O'Rahilly, C. *Ireland and Wales: Their Historical and Literary Relations* (London, 1924).

—— *Táin Bó Cúailnge*: Recension I (DIAS 1976).
—— *Táin Bó Cúailnge from the Book of Leinster*: Recension II (DIAS 1967).
O'Rahilly, T. F. 'Buchet the Herdsman' *Ériu* xvi (1952), 7–20.
—— See also EIHM.
Owen, Hugh (ed. and trans.) Siôn Dafydd Rhys's treatise on the Giants from Peniarth MS118, Cy 27 (1917), 115–52.

Padel, Oliver 'Kelliwic in Cornwall', *Cornish Archaeology* 16 (1977), 115–20 (includes note by Peter Moreton on 'Killibury Fort and Kelli Wic').
—— 'Geoffrey of Monmouth and Cornwall', CMCS 8, 1–20.
Pearce, S. M. 'Traditions of the Royal King List of Dumnonia', THSC 1971, 128–39.
—— 'Cornish Elements in the Arthurian Tradition', *Folklore* 85 (1974), 145–63.

Radner, Joan N. 'Interpreting Irony in Medieval Celtic Narrative: the Case of *Culhwch ac Olwen*', CMCS 16, 41–59.
Rees, Alwyn and Brinley, *Celtic Heritage* (London, 1961).
Rhŷs, John, 'Notes on the Hunting of Twrch Trwyth', THSC 1894–5, 1–34; 146–8.
—— See also CF, HL.
Richards, Melville, 'Arthurian Onomastics', THSC 1969, 251–64.
—— See also BR.
Roberts, B. F. 'The Treatment of Personal Names in the Early Welsh Versions of *Historia Regum Britanniae*', B xxv (1973), 274–90.
—— (ed.) 'Ymddiddan Arthur a Glewlwyd Gafaelfawr', Ast. H, 296–309.
—— 'Tales and Romances' ch. ix in A. O. H. Jarman and Gwilym Rees Hughes (eds.) *A Guide to Welsh Literature*, vol. 1 (Swansea, 1976).
—— Notes on *Pen Pengwaedd, Yr India Fawr a'r India Fechan, Gwyn ap Nudd*, LIC xiii (1980), 278–89.
—— 'From Traditional Tale to Literary Story', ch. 7 in L. A. Arrathoon (ed.) *The Craft of Fiction* (Rochester, Michigan, 1984).
Roberts, Ruth 'Tors fils Ares, Tortain', BBIAS xiv (1962), 91–8.
Rowland, Jenny *Early Welsh Saga Poetry* (The Boydell Press, Bury St. Edmunds, 1990).

Sims-Williams, P. 'The Significance of the Irish Personal Names in *Culhwch ac Olwen*,' B xxix (1982), 600–20.

— — 'The Evidence for Irish Literary Influence on Early Medieval Welsh Literature' in *Ireland and Medieval Europe* ed. D. Whitelock *et al.* (Cambridge, 1982), 235–57.

— — 'The Irish Geography of Culhwch and Olwen', *Celtic Studies in Honour of Professor James Carney* ed. Liam Bretnach *et al.* (Maynooth, 1988).

Thompson, Stith *The Folktale* (New York, 1951).

— — See also ST.

Thorpe, Lewis (trans.) *Geoffrey of Monmouth: The History of the Kings of Britain* (Harmondsworth, 1966). See also HRB.

— — (trans.) Gerald of Wales: *The Journey Through Wales/The Description of Wales* (Harmondsworth, 1978).

Thurneysen, R. *Die irische Helden und Königsage* (Halle, 1921).

Watkin, Morgan, *La Civilisation Française dans les Mabinogion* (Paris, 1963).

— — 'Sangnarwy ac oed yn *Culhwch ac Olwen*' y Llyfr Gwyn', B xiii (1950), 132–6.

Whitelock, D. (trans.) *The Anglo-Saxon Chronicle; A Revised Translation* (London, 1961).

Williams, Hugh (ed. and trans.) *Gildas: De Excidio Britanniae* (includes *Vitae Gildae*) (London, 1899).

Williams, Ifor *Chwedl Taliesin* (University of Wales Press, 1957).

— — *Enwau Lleoedd* (Liverpool, 1945; University of Wales Press, 1962).

— — See also CA, CLlH, PKM.

Williams, J. E. Caerwyn, 'Olwen', YB vii (1971), 57–71.

— — *Traddodiad Llenyddol Iwerddon* (University of Wales Press, 1958).

— — *Y Storïwr Gwyddeleg a'i Chwedlau* (University of Wales Press, 1972).

Glossary

The numbers refer to the lines where the word occurs; 'n.' following a number denotes that the word is further explained in the notes; 'n.' used as part of a grammatical description, for example 'nm.' 'nf.' or 'n.pl.' refers to a noun. When a word is referred to in the introduction, the page where this occurs is given in roman numbers.

a pre-verb. affirm. prt. 1, 8, 9, 10, 12, 17 etc.

a interr. prt: direct qu. 36, 82, 479, 483, 570, 602, etc; indirect qu. whether, if 3, 24, 781, 814, 861, 884.

a rel. pron. subj. 30, 32, 35, 37, 71, 72 etc. 657 n.

a rel. pron. obj. 2, 15, 23, 36, 133, 137 etc.

a rel. prt. 245, 354, 606, 813.

a prep. of 133, 465n., 763n., 796n. Cf. GMW 37.

a(c) prep. as 1, 127, 271, 303, 331, 387 etc.

a(c) conj. and 4, 8, 8, 9, 12, 14, 15 etc. but 17, 45, 82, 84, 1032, **a'm** and my **a merch** 574 n., 752; before **eu** 282, 597, 940, 946, 1216, 1217, Cf. GMW 54.

a interj. oh! 47 n.

abreid adv. hardly, with difficulty 894, 981.

ach y law prep. beside him 418, 522–3 (R **geir y law**), 537. Cf. GMW 182.

achaws nm. cause, reason 733.

achlan adv. entirely 1052, 1053.

achub vn. seize, rush forward/ towards, make for 944 n., 1017, 1212, 1218, 1225; imperf, pl. 3 **achubeint** 306.

adaned n.pl. of **adein** wing 1083.

adar n.pl. birds 632, 843.

adaw vn. leave 721; pres. sing. 3 **edeu** 481; imperf. pl. 3. **edewynt** 309.

aduot vn. happen, be: fut. sing. 3. **atuyd** 555, **hatuyd** 542. Cf. GMW 145.

adnabot vn. know, recognize; pres.

sing. 1. **atwen** 962, 2. **atwaenost** 962n.; pret. sing. 3. **adnabu** 500.

adref adv. home 443, 839, **atref** 32, 927n. **atreff** 43, **attref** 355, 404.

adaw vn. promise 20; pres. sing. 1. **adawaf** 508; pret. sing. 1. **edeweis** 425; plup. sing. 3. **adawsei** 25.

adef vn. confess, promise; imper. sing. 2. **adef** 506.

adoet nm. deadly harm, hurt 422, 546, 560: xvii.

ae interr. prt. is it? 565, 788, 1235, **ae ... ae ...** whether ... or 687; **ae ... ae ...** either ... or ... 421, 792, 917–18.

aeduet adj. ripe 573.

ael nf. corner 76, 77; pl. **aeleu** eyelids 548.

aelawt nmf. limb 53.

aeruawc nm. warrior 397n.: – .

aual nm. apple 76, 77; pl. **aualeu** 548, **aual y garr** n. knee-cap 524, **aual y lygat** eye-ball 552.

auon nf. river 905.

auory adv. tomorrow 519, 1092.

affwys nm. depth, abyss 894, 1193, 1196: xvii.

agalen nf. whetstone 791.

agori vn. open 139n., 468, 786, 801; pres. (fut.) sing. 1. **agoraf** 89, 771, 2. **agory** 89, 103, 103, 772, 3. **egyr** 130; impers. **agorar (Ragorer)**: xxi, xxi 98, 100, **agorir** 774; imper. sing. 2. **agor** 88, 771.

angerd nmf. peculiar quality, strength 384, 397; heat 390.

anghen yn anghen adv. by sheer force, need for need 1176: xx.

aghengaeth nm. injunction 130: xvii.

agheu nmf. death 533, **angheu** 980.

anghleuach adj. comp. of **anghleu** inaudible 105: xviii.

anghyfnerth nmf. infirmity, weakness, misfortune 983.

anglot nmf. dishonour, satire 104. See n. on 154.

aghred adj. without faith, pagan 409.

alauon nf. middle, pit of the stomach 539: xviii.

alarch nmf. swan 495.

allan adv. out 34, 129, 540, 553, 799, 804, 1217.

am conj. because 241n; prep. around 70, 488, for 369, 1090, about 112, on 448, 608, 1227, because of 259, 260, 278, 435, 498, 599, 981, 996, 1075; sing. 3. masc. **amdanaw** 418, **ymdanaw** 76; fem. **amdanei** 488, **ymdanei** 533, 846; pl. 3. **amdanunt** 483 **am y ... a(c)** the other side ... from 910–11n., 911–12.

amaeth nm. husbandman 578.

amaethu vn. till, cultivate: subj. pres. sing. 3. **amaetho** 579.

amkawd vb. pret. sing. 3. said 16, 29, 35, 38, 38, 43, 45, 49, 53, 82, 111, 114, 128, 134, 142, 152, 155, 166, 169, 424, 426, 464, 470, 472, 474, 476, 525, 769, 774, 815; pl. 3 **amkeudant** 430, 513, 545, 559, 762, 809n. (R **dywat** 16, **dywaut** 35, **dywawt** 43, 49, 53, 82, 114, 128, 142, 424, 474, 476, 525, 545, 815, **heb** 29, 38, 45, 111, 134, 152, 155, 470, 472, 769, 774, pl. 3 **dywedassant** 430, 559, 762: xvi, xvi, xvi.)

amdiuwynaw vn. destroy, despoil: pret. sing. 3. **amdiuwynwys** 436: xviii, xxi.

amgeled nm. care 427n.

amheu vn. dispute, doubt: pres. sing. 3. **amheu** 507.

amlymu vn. clean, strip 21 (R **amlynu**).

amrant nm. eyelid 518 (R **ael**: xii.)

amsathyr nm. throng 90, 773: xvi, xvii.

amwabyr nm. maiden fee, paid by the bride's father to the lord 532n.: xvii.

amws nm. horse 419n., 1184, 1186: xvii.

an poss. pron. prefix. pl. 1. our 138, 138, 967, 1088; also **yn**.

anadyl nfm. breath 385, 423.

anaf nm. harm, wound 421, 432, 546, 560.

anuab nm. man without offspring, childless 39.

anueitrawl adj. immeasurable, immense 972.

anhed nfm. abode 6.

anhuned nm. wakefulness, sleeplessness 751.

anllawd adj. precious 62: xviii.

an(n)iueil nm. animal, beast 861, 870, 881; pl. **anniueileit** 843.

anoeth nm. wonder, marvel, (thing) difficult to find; pl. **an(n)oetheu** 827, 930, 986, 1205, 1232: xvi, xvii.

anoethach adv. (comp. of **anoeth**) much less, not to speak of 239 (R **yghwaethach**) n., 244n., 420 (R **agwhaethach**) n.: xvii.

anreith nf. spoil, booty; pl. **anreitheu** 283.

anwar adj. cruel, savage, undutiful 525, 540, 553.

anwaydu vn. draw blood: pret. sing. 3. **anwaydwys** 396: xxi.

anwyd nm. cold 391.

ar dem. pron. antecedent to rel. clause those (who) 108.

ar (**a** rel. prt. + **ry** pre-verb. prt.). 714n. R **a ry**.

ar prep. on, upon 19, 24, 60, 67, 68, 87 etc., to 39, 58n., 246, 444; + vn. 917n. at 556, of 413, 760, among 804, by means of 799; sing. 1. **arnaf** 542, 567, 854, **arnaw** 556, 2. **arnat** 54, 150, 173, 547, 561, 568, etc., 3. masc. **arnaw** 10, 22, 80, 227, 267, 269 etc.; fem. **arnei** 248, 422, 528, 852, 853; pl. 1. **arnam** 624, 3. **arnadunt** 110, 373, 410, 1140, (R **at(t)**39, 58, 246, 444: xvi).

ar benn prep. on top of 301, 417, 953.

ar draws prep. across 281.

ar droet adv. on foot 237.

ar dy gam adv. (by) walking 128–9.

ar dy redec adv. (by) running 129.

ar drws prep. at the entrance to, in front of 105; also **yn drws**.

ar eu hol adv. after them 523, 537, 551.

ar uarch adv. on horseback 237.

ar ueithrin adv. to be reared, nursed 12–13n.

ar uor adv. by sea 938.
ar hyt prep. along 905.
ar y helw ynteu adv. in his possession 1122.
ar werth adv. for sale 748.
ar y delw hon(n) adv. in this form 1081, 1086, 1088.
ar y mor adv. by sea 1095; also **ar uor.**
ar y rot adv. in a circle 1051.
ar y tir adv. by land 939.
aradyr nmf. plough 320, 598.
araf nm. weapon 226n.: xix.
arall pron. other subst. 41, 389, 465, 1147; adj. 17, 267, 268, 270, 272 etc.; pl. **ereill** 95, 474, 744, 939.
arch nf. request 439.
archenat nm. foot gear 78.
archoll nfm. wound, thrust 260, 398.
ardyrchawc adj. famous, eminent 293n.
aruaeth nfm. plan, manner 662n.
aruoll vn. take, receive, hold 523, 538, 551; pres. sing. 2. **aruolly** 505.
arglwyd nm. lord 104, 213, 240, 753, 839.
argywed nm. harm 353, 428.
aryal nm. spirit, passion 714.
aryanhyeit adj. silver 63.
aryant nm. silver 917n.; adj. 165, 1084.
arllwyssaw vn. empty, clear; imperf. sing. 3. **arllwyssei** 305n.
arswydaw vn. fear greatly, dread: pret. sing. 3. **arswydwys** 393: xviii, xxi.
arwyd nm. sign, token: pl. **arwydon** 799.
as pers. pron. infix. obj. sing./pl. 3. syllabic form 485, 874n., 1045n. Cf. GMW 56.
asgwrn nm. bone 1233.
asseu adj. left 71, 73.
asswynaw vn. beseech, implore, invoke 174, 175n.; pret. sing. 3. **asswynwys** 212, 373. Cf. B xxvi (1975), 147–53, 154–8: xvi, xvii, xxi.
at prep. to: sing. 1. **attaf** 897, 2. **attat** 94, 860, 884, 902, 3. masc. **attaw** 790, 998, 1062, 1133, fem. **attei** 15, 21, 455.
atref: see **adref** above.

atteb nm. answer 520, 777, 1085.
athro nm. instructor, preceptor 20n., 24.
awch nfm. edge 64.
awel wynt nf. a gust of wind 728.
awr nf. hour, time 5.
awyr nfm. air 75.
ays nf. shield 67. Cf. G 13–14 (R **chroes**): xii, xvii.

bach nf. bend 906.
baed nm. boar 1019, 1021, **baed coet** n. wild boar 960.
banadyl n. coll. broom 490.
bann nm. top, point, peak 832.
bannawc adj. horned 596n.
banw nmf. pigling 1146.
baryf nf. beard 639, 700, 702, 964, 974, 976, 979, 1233, **baraf** 327, 966: xix.
bed nm. grave 20, 21, 24, 27.
bei cond. conj. if 134; also **pei.**
beich nm. burden 269.
beichawc adj. pregnant 108, 109, 110.
beichogi nm. pregnancy 5n., 108.
bellach adv. further, more 546, 1171.
bellaf adv. farthest 155.
bendigaw vn. bless: imperf. sing. 3 **bendigei** 356.
bendyth nf. blessing 947, 1064.
benyn nm. carver 335, 738.
berth adj. fair, prosperous 430n.; comp. **berthach** 430.
berw vn. water 555, **berwi** boil 636; heat imperf. impers. **berwit** 541, **berwid** 556 (R **gweirwyt**).
beth interr. pron. what? 929, 985.
bieu rel. whose is, who owns 434; also **pieu.** Cf. GMW 80–1.
blayn/blaen nm. tip 79, 80n., 242, beginning, start, 556.
bleidast nf. she-wolf 935.
blew n. coll. hair, beard 227, 228, 651; **blewyn** sing. a hair 80.
blodeu npl. flower(s) 490.
blwydyn nf. year 22, 25n., 85, 377, 378, 822; pl. **blynet** (with num.) 353.
bod vn. to be 227, 230, **bot** 265, 414, 796, 892, 970, 1028; indic. pres. sing. 1. **vyf** 379, 435, 776, 783n., 867n., 889, 2.**wyt** 167, 170, 431, 435, 843, **ytwyt** 430, 3. **yw** 18, 30,

40, 44, 103, 170 etc., **ydiw** 158, **y mae** 145, 686, 694, 733, 775, 841 etc., **y may** 369, **mae** 166, 797, **mae?** (GMW 143) 516n., 547, 561, 967, **oes** 38, 82, 82, 382n., 432, 473, 504 etc., **ys** (GMW 141–3) 132n., 472n., 566, 598n, 783n,: xxiii, xxiv, **yssit** [there is] 504, 578n, 584, 913, **osit** [if there is] 266, **yssyd** rel. (GMW 63) 107, 127, 437, 534, 596, 606 etc., **yssyt** 560n., pl. 1. **ydym** 136, 2. **ywch** 433, 437, 869, **ywchi** 764, 3. **ynt** 17n., 37n., **ydynt** 878, **yssydynt** [they are] 115, 779; consuet. pres. fut. sing. 1. **bydaf** 16, 83, 869, 880, 899, 3. **byd** 96, 137, 266, 267, 268, 268, 269, 271, 272, 272, 378, 413n., 416n., **bydhawt** 99, **bythawd** 151n., imperf. sing. 1. **oedwn** 852, 3. **oed** 7, 11, 12, 33, 35, 77 etc.: xxi, xxv, **oet** 165, 419, = **bydei** 470, 783n. (cf. GMW 110–11) **yttoed** 463, 925n., 953, 969, 1183; pl. 3. **oedynt** 205, 252, 324, 728, **oydynt** 415; consuet. past. sing. 3. **bydei** 65, 71, 72, 282, 302, 326, 386, 388, 390, 392, 398, 497, 980; pret. sing. 1. **bum** 117, 118, 119, 120, 121, 122, 124, 125, 3. **bu** 31, 128, 155, 249, 249, 259, etc., pl. 3. **buant** 969; subj. pres. sing. 2. **bych** 150, 3. **bo** 83, 105, 132, 143, 145, 145 etc., pl. 2. **boch** 431, 3. **bwynt** 110 (R **bont**): xiii imperf. sing. 3. **pei** 464n., 980, **bei** 66, 71, 72, 239, 240, 241 etc.; imper. sing. 3. **poet** 144, 147, 527, 541, 556, **boet** 146, **bid** 427.

bod nm. will, pleasure 794.
bodi vn. drown 1192.
bogel nmf. navel 325.
boneu (n. pl. of **bon** root) 878.
bonhedic adj. noble 11.
bore nm. morning 23, 1092, 1119.
botheu n. pl. bottles 657, 663.
bragodi vn. make bragget 611n.
brathu vn. pierce, prick, spur 1184.
brawt nm. brother 222, 1048, 1211; pl. **brodyr** 252, 284, 291, 1165n.
breint nfm. privilege 149n.
brenhin nm. king 23, 26, 28, 32, 33, 45 etc.

brenhin teithiawc nm. rightful king 586n.
brenhines nf. queen 8, 22, 25, 36, 39.
breu adj. brittle 705, 966.
bric nm. top 242.
bron(n) nf. edge 280, breast, bosom 495, **dwy uron** 495, 542, **bron llech** breast-fever 318n.
bronwynyon adj. pl. whitebreasted 69n.
brychyon adj. pl. of **brych** brindled, spotted 69n.
bryt nm. mind, desire, will 619.
bryssyaw vn. hasten 958.
bu nfm. (head of) cattle 77n., 78.
budugawl adj. victorious, clever, able 387, 802.
buelin nm. drinking horn 131: xvii.
bwrw vn. throw, aim at: imperf. sing. 3. **byryei** 327, 1226; **bwrw lludet** get rid of weariness 1203.
bwyt nm. food. meat 89, 94, 132, 153, 309, 356 etc, **bwyd** 544, 574.
bwyellic nf. small axe, hatchet 1018: xviii.
bwyt(t)a vn. eat 476, 620, 1043; pres. sing. 3. **bwyta** 95.
bwyttal nm. tribute of food 1065n.: xviii.
bychan adj. small 269.
byt nm. world 48, 155, 383, 413, 434, 438 etc, **byd** 302.
bydydyaw vn. baptize 10: xix.
byhyt bynnac indef. rel. however long 150.
byn adj. keen 738, **byneu** 336.
bys nm. toe 80, finger 449; pl. **byssed** 492.
byth adv. ever 55, 110, 431, 482, 710; also **uyth**.
byw adj. alive 249, 372, 534, 554, 687, 702n, 1243; n. life 440, 508, 767 (R **bywyt** 440, 508, 767).
bywyt nm. life 703n.

kat nf. army, host, band 1173: xvii.
cadarn adj. strong 614.
kadeir nf. chair 564, 787.
catlys nf. bailey 808, 1241.
cadw vn. keep, tend 7, 417, 646, 1229; pres. sing. 2. **ketwy** 433, pl. 3. **catwant** 657; subj. pres. sing. 3. **cattwo** 656.

catwent nf. battle, assault 918.

cadwyn nf. chain 681.

kaer nf. fort 413, 415, 433, 434, 478, 511 etc. pl. **keyryd** 760, **keyryt** 413.

caeu vn. close, shut: pres. sing. 3. **kae** 130.

caffael vn. get, obtain, be able 4n, **caffel** 11, 40, 57, 173, 378, 446 etc., **cael** 1185n., **cahel;** pres. sing. 1. **kaffaf** 153, 154, 509, 753, 754, 2. **keffy** 156, 162, 171, 172, 507, 507, 533, 567, 568, 710, 711, 751, 752, 752, 758, 838 (R **kehy** 568) **kyffy** 164: xix, 3. **keiff** 620, 754; imperf. sing. 2. **kaffut** 1237, 3. **caffei** 27, 29, 1039; pl. 3. **keffynt** 4, 812; impers. **keffit** 314; pret. sing. 1. **keueis** 449, 784, 906, 907, 3. **cauas** 236, 379, 1005, 1033, 1110, 1188, 1245, pl. 3. **cawssant** 1071, 1071, impers. **cahad** 313, **kaffat** 1190n., 1191, 1199, 1200, **kafat** 1198; subj. pres. 1. **caffwyf** 55, 56, 548, 567, 817n., 2. **keffych** 51, 578, 578, 584, 584, 589 etc., 3. **caffo** 41n., 41n., pl. 1. **caffom** 383, impers. **caffer** 672, 757, 919, 1091.

kalan Ionawr nm. first day of January **kalan Mei** first day of May 84n., 370n., 1002n.

calet nm. something hard, battle 304 (see n. to **Caletuwlch** 159).

calloneu n. pl. of **callon** womb 109, **kallon** heart 166, 995, 996, **calon** 266.

cam nm. fault, wrong, harm 471 (R **drwc**), 485, 835: xii.

camse nm. robe 487: xviii.

can num. + n. hundred 77, 865.

can conj. since, because 431n.

canhorthwy nm. help 227, 230n; see also **engyl**.

canhymdeith vn. accompany, keep up with 238, 1189.

cans conj. since, because 785.

cantref nm. cantred, district 647.

canu vn. sing. play (music) 628; pres. pl. 3. **canant** 743.

canyt conj. (**can** + **ny(t)**) for/since ... not 404, 456, 504, 614, 701, 860.

kanys conj. (**kan** + **ny** + **s** pers. pron. infix. sing./pl. 3 obj.) since ... not ... it 41; (**kan** + **ys** it is) for 408, 694, 704, 869, 966.

canywch conj. (**cany** + **wch** pers. pron. infix. pl. 2. obj.) since ... not ... you 478. (R **canych gwelas**).

car nm. kinsman 694, 753, 829; pl. **carant** 533 (R **cares**), 895n.

carchar nm. prison, captivity 831, 914, 915, 916, 916, 922, 924, 999.

carcharawr nm. prisoner 836, 837, 911, 926.

carcharu vn. imprison: pret. impers. **carcharwyt** 915.

carn nfm. hoof 74, haft 248.

carngragen adj. shell-hoofed 61: xviii.

caru vn. love: pret. sing. 1. **kereis** 501.

cas nm. hatred, enmity 259.

kassec nf. mare 1017n., 1225.

catbritogyon n. pl. leaders of hosts 144.

kawn n. coll. reeds 243; sing. **conyn** 243. Cf. n. **Eskeir Gulhwch Gonyn Cawn** 191.

cawr nm. giant 812, **kawr** 815, 819, 820.

kedymdeith nm. companion, fellow 797n., 797; pl. **kedymdeithon** 807, 809.

keuyn nm. back 898, 926, 1047n.

keuynderw nm. cousin 12, 58n., 170, 695, 844, **kefynderw** 407.

keibedic past partic. hoed, tilled, 602.

keing nf. branch 866.

keirch nfm. oats 321, 834.

keissaw vn. seek 376, 442, 446, 695, 751, 784 etc. try 461, 1218; pres. pl. 2. **keisswch** 898; imperf. impers. **keissit** 280; pret. sing. 3. **keisswys** 241 xxi; subj. pres. sing. 2. **keissych** 834; imper. sing. 2. **keis** 757.

kelein nf. body, corpse 447, 448, 450, 451.

kelu vn. conceal 44, 470; pres. sing. 1. **kelaf** 45.

kelwrn nm. tub 1227n.

kenedlaeth nf. race, kind 857, 876.

kenetyl nf. kindred 205.

keneu nm. cub, whelp, pup 315, 673, 701n., 708, 930n., 935, 940, 964, 986, 1014, 1106; pl. **canawon** shoots 492, or cotton grass (see n. to 492)

kenuein nf. a herd (of swine) 7n., 356.

kennat nfm. messenger, representative 1036, 1040, **kennad** 482; pl. **kenhadeu** 376, 377, 378, 437, **ken(n)adeu** 856, 860, 869, 872, 880, 884, 896n., 902.

kennatau vn. send for 46n., 487; pres. sing. 1. **kennattaaf** 485.

kerd nf. craft 91, 768n., 774, 775, 781, 785, 798, 803, **kerth** 96: xii; pl. **kerdeu** songs 93, 98.

kerdawr nm. craftsman 91, 773.

kerdet vn. go, travel 240, 413, 443, 510, 543, 759, 847, 943, 1145n.; imperf. sing. 3. **kerdei** 242, 243, 1084; pret. pl. 3. **kerdassant** 513, 910; imper. sing. 2. **kerda** 756.

kesseil nf. armpit 791.

ki nm. dog 336, 428, 557, 685, 739, 1008, 1014, 1015, 1021, 1059n., 1107, 1108, 1140, 1189; pl. **kwn(n)** 92, 1020, 1067, 1096, 1132, 1144, 1155, 1173.

kib nfm. coffer 468, cup 613.

kic nm. meat, flesh 968, 1233.

cilyd pron. the other, another, companion; cf. n. to l.1: **o drwc y gilyd** from one mischief to another 1199–1200n. Cf. GMW 96–7.

cladu vn. bury: subj. imperf. impers. **cladhet** 347.

cledyf nm. sword 67, 159n., 336, 738, 747, 784 etc.; pl. **cledyueu** 776, 783, 789.

cleuyt nm. ailment, sickness 16.

cleuydawd nmf. wound (from a sword) 386.

cleheren nf. gadfly 526: xvii, xviii.

cleicaw vn. immerse 1183: xviii.

cleis nm. streak, stripe 791.

clot nmf. fame 155, 1110n.

clotuawr adj. praiseworthy, celebrated 1060.

cloff adj. lame 952.

cludweir nf. wood-pile 461: xviii.

clun nf. thigh 67, 79.

klyuychu vn. fall ill 14: xix.

klywet vn. hear, **clybot** 459, 944, 996; imperf. sing. 3. **clywei** 348, 943n., pl. 3. **klywynt** 911n.; pret. sing. 1. **kiglef** 374n, 879, 889, **kigleu** 854, 868, 2. **klyweist** 934.

cnawd nm. flesh 491.

kneuen nf. nut 854.

knithyaw vn. pluck 703, **knithiaw** 973: xvii.

cnwch ysgwyd nm. shoulder-swell 70: xviii.

coch adj. red 327, 867; comp. **cochach** 496.

coet npl. trees, woods 242, 242, 864, 876, 877, 877, 1084.

congyl nfm. corner, quarter 1107.

collen derwen nf. oak-sapling 865.

colli vn. lose, be lost: pres. sing. 2. **colly** 755; pret. sing. 3. **kolles** 1195, impers. **collet** 420.

conyn nm. stalk 66.

corfflan nf. graveyard 26n. (R **cordlan**) xvii.

corn nm. horn 624; pl. **kyrn** 744.

coys nf. leg 351.

cret nf. faith 138, 147, word, pledge 485, 503, 566 (R **clot** 138), 147: xii.

credu vn. believe, trust: subj. pres. sing. 3. **crettwy** 484 (R **cretto**: xiii); pl. 2. **crettoch** 907.

crib nf. comb 667n, 668, 1090n., 1187, 1187, 1199, 1200, **crip** 164, 530.

cribaw vn. comb 165.

croen nm. skin 1233; pl. **crwyn** 418.

croyw adj. sweet 310.

krwydraw vn. wander 377.

cryuangheu n. pl. **claws** 892: xix.

cuan nf. owl 871: xviii.

cussul nm. advice 505: xvii.

kwt conj. where? 29, 37n., 515 (R **pa le** 29, **ble** 37, **pan** 515: xii, xvi, xvii, xxii.

cwm nm. valley 875.

kwynaw vn. lament 913; pres. sing. 3. **kwyn** 912.

kwynuan nmf. lamentation, mourning 911.

kychwyn(nu) vn. rise, get up, set out 1040n, 1095, 1208; pres. pl. 1. **kychwynnwn** 1093; imperf. sing. 3. **kychwhynnei** 349n.: xix; pret. sing. 3. **kychwynnwys** 1103, 1111, 1230: xxi.

kyt conj. though 275, 319, 396, 578, 582, 584 etc., **kyd** 576.

kytbrein(h)awc adj. yoked together 590, 594n.: xv, xvii.

kydenawc adj. shaggy 418: xix.

kydymdeithas nfm. company 475.

kydymdeithon n. pl. of **kydymdeith** comrade 391n.; also **ked-.**

kyuagos adj. close, near, 414.

kyuarch vn. ask, **kyuarch gwell** greet 787; pres. sing. 2. **kyuerchy** 83, 771; pret. sing. 1. **kyuer(c)heis i well** I greeted 146: xv, xix.

kyuaruot vn. come against, meet: pret. sing. 1. **kyuaruum** 604, 3. **kyuaruu** 1163; subj. imperf. sing. 3. **kyuarfei** 304.

kyfuarth nm. barking, baying 1017n., 1142, **rodi kyuarth** stand at bay 1112, 1116, 1129n., 1153.

kyuarws nm. gift, boon 59n., 137, 153n., 156, 175, 313n., 373, 379.

kyuarwyd nm. guide 399n. 400, 858, 869, 880, 899.

kyueillt nm. friend 134n., 957n.

kyueisted vn. take a seat 100.

kyuelin nf. forearm 64n.

kyuenw nm. anniversary 822n.

kyuereit nm. need 307 (R **kyfueir**).

kyuyeith adj. of the same language 843.

kyflawn adj. complete, full 146, 146, 497.

kyuodi vn. rise 384, 440, 469, 510, 521, 549, 829, 1033, 1046; pres. sing. 3. **kyuyt** 441, pl. 3. **kyuodant** 536, 550.

kyuoeth nm. territory, country 246, 1241.

kyuoethawc adj. having territory, power, authority 732n.

kyfret equat. adj. as swift 689n., 728 (R **kynebrwydet**): xii, xii, xvii.

kyfredec vn. keep pace with: subj. imperf. sing. 3. **kyfrettei** 236.

kyfreitheu n. pl. of **kyfreith** law 112, 135.

kyfrwch vn. meet, converse 425.

kyfrwg prep. between 148, 462, 499, 669 (R **y rwng**) 462, **geyr llaw** 499.

kyfryw adj. such a 133.

kyuyg adj. narrow 280.

kyghor nm. counsel, advice 29n., 31n., 135, 503, 967, 1172.

kynghori vn. advise 1209.

kynghorwyr n.pl. counsellors 29.

kyhyt equat. adj. as long/tall as 387.

cylchynu vn. surround, encircle 939.

kyllagwst nfm. stomach-ache, colic 543: xvii.

kyllell nf. knife, dagger 89, 161n., 247, 281, 772, 794, 1194, 1227.

kyllellprenneu npl. wooden tweezers 703, 966, 970, 974, **kellellprenneu** 817.

kymhar nmf. companion, mate, spouse 444, **kym(m)ar** 15, 44.

kymhell vn. force, compel 995n.

kymibiawc adj. tubular 61: xviii.

kym(m)eint equat. adj. as much 303, 853, **y gymeint** 904n., 907n., 918n. Cf. GMW 94–5.

kymmwyd adj. equal. as well-born (MS **kynmwyd**) 1.

kymot vn. to make peace, reconcile 897, 1005.

kymrwt nm. cement, mortar 760: xviii.

kymryt equat. adj. as handsome, of like form 127n., 395, 448 (R **kyuurd**) 127, **kyfret** 395, **degac no** 448.

kymryt vn. take 9, 164, 444, 536, 550, 790, 818, 926, 1019, 1228; pret. sing. 3. **kymerth** 1017; imper. sing. 3. **kymeret** 1004.

kyn (no) prep. before 353n., 397 (R **yn gynt**), 988n., 1198, **kynn** (without **no**) + n. 952, + vn. 989, 1102, 1187.

kyn (+ equat. adj.) as 915.

kyn ny conj. though ... not 156, 803, 834, **kyny** 797, 1088, **kyn nys** (**ny** + **'s** pers. pron. infix obj. though ... not ... her) 53.

kyndynnyawc adj. tenacious, resolute 268: xvii.

kyndeirawc adj. mad 557.

kynhebrwydet equat. of **ebrwyd** swift 330.

cynifywr nm. warrior 1057n.

kynyon n. pl. of **kyn** stump 878.

kyn(n)edyf nf. quality, peculiarity 235, 247, 268, 270, 272, 388, **kynedef** 267.

kynneu vn. kindle, light 392.

kyn(n)llyuan(n) nm. leash 675, 676, 679, 682, 700, 963, 964, 976, 978, 1006.

kynnullaw vn. gather 990; pret. sing. 3. **kynnullwys** 1057: xxi.

kynt comp. of **kynnar** prompt, quick 65, adj. former 1222, adv. before, formerly 415 (R **nor bore**).

kyntaf superl. of **kynnar** prompt, quick 65.

kynteit nf. first swarm 611.

kynyd nm. huntsman 684, 707; pl. **kyn(n)ydyon** 731 (R **kedymdeithon**), 1135, 1138.

kynydyaeth nf. huntsmanship 685.

kyrchu vn. seek out 31, approach, make for 81, 458, 769.

kyscu vn. sleep 97, 308, 386, 751, 969, 971, 989; pret. sing. 3. **kyscwys** 1242 xxi; subj. pres. sing. 3. **kysco** 620.

kysseuin adj. first 251: xiii, xvi.

kystal equat. of **da** good 144, 271, 796.

kythreul nm. devil 227.

kythrymhet adj. direct, exact, 351n., 525n.: xvii.

kyweithyd nf. troop, company, 421, 780.

'ch pers. pron. infix. obj. pl. 2, 766.

chwaer nf. sister 359, 406, **chwayr** 455.

chwechach comp. adj. sweeter 610: xvii.

chwedleu n. pl. news 115n.

chwennych vn. desire, long for: pres. sing. 3. **wennych** 662.

chwi pers. pron. simple affix. aux. pl. 2. 431, 477, 763, 855, 868, 880, 890, 899.

chwitheu pers. pron. conjunct. indep. pl. 2. 437, 515; affix. aux. 1089.

chwyuyaw vn. stir, move: imperf. sing. 3. **chwyuei** 80 (R **chrymei**).

da n. possessions 150, good 1071; adj. good 47, 103, 388, 507, 628, 725, 792, 815, adv. well 30.

dadleu nm. debate 804.

dauates nf. flock of sheep 416:.

dangos vn. show: imper. sing. 2. **dangos** 450, 3. **dangosset** 319.

dala vn. capture 992n., 993, sting 526, bite 540, 557, **daly** hold 681n.: xix pret. sing. 3. **delis** 5n., 1012; subj. pres. sing. 3. **dal(h)yo** 614, 675, 678, 701, 707, 963; imper. sing. 3. **dalet** 474.

damsathyr nm. throng 468n. (R **y chware**): xii, xviii.

dan prep. under. 133, 243, 302, 690, 733, 791, + vn. while 959; sing. 3 fem. **deni** 1213: xx, **dan eu hub ac eu hob** squealing and squalling 1217.

dant nm. tooth 35.

dar nf. oak tree 865, 866.

daruot vn. happen: imperf. sing 3. **daroed** 973, 1028n.; pret. sing. 3. **daruu** 813n., 825, 1172.

darogan nfm. prediction, prophecy 40.

darparu vn. prepare, intend: plup. sing. 1. **darparysswn** 837.

darware vn. frolic, sport about 73: xviii.

datrithaw vn. transform, restore to original form 940.

daw nm. son-in-law 525, 540, 549, 553.

dayar nf. earth, ground, land 159, 348, 571, 745, 946, 1188.

dechreu vn. begin 151.

deuawt nf. custom, practice 419.

deueit n.pl. sheep 417, 432.

defnyt uyn daw nm. my future son-in-law 518n., 549: xviii.

dec aradyr ar ugeint n. thirty ploughs 319–20.

deng milltir a deugeint n. fifty miles 348.

deg trawst a deugeint n. fifty beams 328.

dec tryuer a deugeint n. fifty tridents 897–8.

degwyr a deugeint n. fifty men 94.

deheu nm. south 956, adj. right 72, 72.

deiuaw vn. singe 960: xvii.

deon n.pl. of **da** nobles 144: xvii.

deu num. masc. two 62, 69, 119, 148, 315, 323 etc., fem. **dwy** 73, 351, 495, 533, 542, 908 etc.

deu peinawc adj. two-headed 19.
deudec num. twelve 119.
deuglust n. (the) two ears 1026, **deu glust** 1090, 1233.
deuparth n. two thirds 116, 116.
dewissaw vn. choose 101; subj. pres. sing. 2. **dewissych** 101.
di pers. pron. simple affix. aux. sing. 2. 36, 83, 134,, 154, 380, 433, 570, 602, 794, 816, 832, 838, 839, 840, 861, 873, 962, 965, 1235, **dy** 771, 957.
dial nm. vengeance 854; vn. avenge 284; pres. impers. **dielir** 471.
dianaf adj. unwounded, unhurt 1035.
dianc vn. escape: pres. sing. 2. **dihengy** 508; pret. sing. 3. **dieng(h)is** 231, 1138, **dihengis** 246.
diaruu vn. disarm 1216.
diaspat nf. shout 105n.
diaspedein vn. shout, cry out 744; subj. pres. sing. 2. **diaspettych** 111.
didan adj. pleasant, entertaining 93, 97, 149.
didanu vn. entertain 627, 633.
didawl adj. without a share 145 (R **didlawt** 714n.): xii.
diednedic vb. adj. twisted 464: xviii.
dieuyl n.pl. of **diafwl** devil, demon 714n.
dieu npl. of **dyd** day (with numerals) 386n., 1073n., Cf. GMW 33, 47.
diua vn. destroy, lay waste: pret. impers. **diuawyt** 877.
diuetha vn. destroy 896.
diuudyawc adj. tireless, vigorous 695.
diuwyn adj. unmolested, untouched 1001.
diffeith adj. desolate, wild 1070.
diffeithaw vn. lay waste, destroy 821, 1028.
diffryt vn. defend 946, 1191; pret. sing. 3. **diffyrth** 1142.
digawn nm. sufficiency, enough 281, 1087.
digoni vn. make, do, prepare: pres. sing. 1. **digonaf** 790; pret. sing. 3. **digones** 528, impers. **digonet** 528; subj. pres. sing. 3. **digonho** 579, 584, 803 **dygo(n)ho** (R **gwypo**) 798.
digribyaw vn. rush into, towards; pret. sing. 3. **digribywys** 1136: xxi.
digrif adj. pleasant, agreeable 834, 1220.

diheu adj. sure, certain, true 970, 1027.
dilis adj. real, true, genuine 423n.
dillat n.pl. clothes 756.
dim pron. anything 22, 24, 102, 276, 378, 502 etc.
diot vn. take out/away 816, 897, 995, 1187, 1238.
diolwch vn. thank 1236n., 1236.
diotta vn. partake of drink 307: xvii.
direidyeit adj. pl. of **diryeit** wicked, villainous 517 (R **direitwyr**).
diskynnu vn. dismount 140, arrive 766, descend 1031, 1079, land, disembark 1055n., 1062, 1097; pres. sing. 3. **diskyn** 801.
disgyrryaw vn. shout, cry out 512.
dispeilaw vn. unsheathe, draw 945.
distrych nm. foam 491: xvii.
ditheu pers. pron. conjunct. affix. aux. sing. 2 17, 116, 506, 586, 591, 834.
diwarnawt nm. day 385, **diwarnawd** adv. one day 26n.: xx.
diwethaf adv. last 231.
diwreidyaw vn. uproot 571n.
diwyn vn. trim 58n., 163.
dodi vn. place, put 443, 1047, 1050, 1240, raise (a shout) 1141; pres. sing. 1. **dodaf** raise 104; imperf. impers. **dodit** 280; pret. sing. 3. **dodes** 226, 228, 714, impers. **dodet** 564, 788, 1141, 1224; subj. pres. impers. **dotter** 656, 658; imperf. sing. 3. **dottei** 820.
douot nm. a find 446n. (R **bud**) xii.
dogyn nmf. (full) measure, fill 64n., 1044.
doleu n.pl. loops 164.
doluryaw vn. hurt, wound 1118.
drannoeth adv. on the morrow 1119.
draw adv. yonder, beyond 292, 570, 590, 602, 607.
drem nf. sight 554.
dros prep. over 328, 433, 808, 943, 1143, in return for 532.
drwc nm. ill, evil, mischief 54, 835, 907, 1071n., 1087, 1094, 1190n., 1198, 1222, 1231; adj. bad, evil 18, 465, 516.
drws nm. door, entrance 1225, 1226.
drwy prep. through, by means of 919.

drychauel vn. rise, raise; imperf.
sing. 3. **drychauei** 262; pret. sing.
3. **drychauwys** 354; imper. pl. 2.
drycheuwch 517, 547 (R **dyr-**).
drygeir nm. ill report 104.
dryssien nf. briar 19, 28: xvii.
du nm. black 605, 761.
duhunaw vn. wake 632.
dur adj. hard 541.
duw adv. day 1002n. Cf. GMW 33.
dwuyr nm. water 271, 280, 385, 1196.
dwy: see **deu**.
dwyuron nf. breast 539.
dwylaw n. dual hands 267, 463.
dwyn vn. bring, bear 32, 598, take
    away 154, 821, 849, 990; pres. sing.
    1. **dygaf** 103, 380, 777; pret. sing.
    3. **duc** 1187, impers. **ducpwyt** 119,
    685, 862, 873, 885, 904, **ducpwyd**
    354; subj. pres. sing. 3. **dycco** 91,
    269, **dyccwy** 768 (R. **dycko**) 768,
    774), 774: xvi; imper. sing. 2. **dwc**
    947.
dwyrein nm. east 125, 658.
dy poss. pron. prefix. sing. 2. + n.
    18, 44, 50, 58, 83, 146, etc., + vn.
    167, 917, 1220.
dyallu vn. catch, capture; pret. sing.
    3. **dyallas** 37n. (R **llathrudawd**)
    xii, xiii, xix.
dyd nm. day 306, 324, 759, 822, 1068,
    1072, 1119, **dyt** 301, 414, 530, 575;
    dyd brawt day of judgment 1002,
    1004, **dyt br.** 370–1.
dydgweith adv. one day 942,
    dytgweith 34.
dydwyn vn. bring 790.
dyuot vn. come 39, 46, 429, 447, 455,
    459 etc., **dyuod** 545; pres. sing. 2.
    doy 762, 3. **daw** 94, 479, 480, 482,
    483, 580 etc., pl. 1. **down** 948, 3.
    deuuant 412 (R **deuthant**) n.,
    deuant 415n., **doant** 744; consuet.
    pres. fut. sing. 3. **dypi** 535; pret.
    sing. 1. **deuthum** 836, 850, 863,
    875, 886, 887, 891, 902, 2. **dyuuost**
    129, 3. **dyuu** 6, 6, 7, 9, 114, 139:
    xvi, xvi, **deuth** 34, 247, 404, 876,
    945, 1103, **doeth** 141, 246, 445, 454,
    605, 805, 927, 1018, 1112, 1142,
    1160, pl. 1. **doetham** 860, 883, 3.
    dyuuant 809, **deuthant** 559, 823,
    910, 1211, **doethant** 531, 949, perf.

sing. 1. **dothwyf** 152, 3. **dothyw**
99, 116 (R **ethyw**), 439, **dodyw**
767; pl. 1. **dodym** 477, 2.
dodywch 477: xvi, xvi, xvi, xvi;
plup. pl. 3. **dathoedynt** 1143n.;
subj. pres. sing. 3. **delwyf** 906, pl.
2. **deloch** 881. impers. **dyffer** 659;
imperf. sing. 3. **delhei** 275, 279,
457, 619, pl. 2. **delewch** 1088, 3.
delhynt 306, 409; imper. sing. 2.
dos 563n., 3. **doet** 908, pl. 1. **down**
426, 2. **dowch** 519.
dyuynnv vn. summon 997, 1133.
dygaboli vn. beat soundly, dress
down 1216: xviii.
dygredu vn. visit 6: xvii.
dygrynnyaw vn. close in 1182.
dygwydaw vn. fall, attack 1144n.:
xxv, 1179; imperf. sing. 3.
dygwydei 745n.; pret. sing. 3.
dygwydwys 866, 1194: xxi.
dygyrchu vn. make for, seek 26, 499
(R **dyuot**), 1042; pres. sing. 3.
dygyrch (draw) 800; imperf. sing.
3. **dygyrchei** (draw) 65; pret. sing.
3. **dygyrchwys** 1186; xxi subj.
pres. impers. **dygyrcher** 136;
imper. sing. 2. **dygyrch** come! 382.
dyhed adj. deplorable, shameful 133,
470, **dyhed a beth** a deplorable
thing 133, 796n. Cf. further GMW
37.
dylyet nfm. duty, obligation 856.
dyn nm. man 127, 133, 226, 236, 276,
425 etc., anyone 1138; pl. **dynyon**
876.
dynessau vn. approach, move towards
558, 1180.
dyrnawt nm. blow 972.
dyrnued nmf. hand breadth 389, 888.
dyrys adj. rough, wild 590.
dyskymon nm. fuel, kindling 391:
xviii.
dyw adv. day 84n. (R **duw**), 370n,
480.
dywedut vn. say, speak, tell 47, 102,
531, 776, 825, 901 etc.; **dywedud**
113; pres. sing. 1. **dywedaf** 168,
519, 799, 905, 1089, 2. **dywedy** 36,
133, 375, pl. 1. **dywedwn** 1087.
impers. **dywedir** 562, 789; imperf.
sing. 1. **dywedwn** 874, impers.
dywedit 265; pret. sing. 3.

dywawt 39, 500, 565, 778, 782, 788, 802, 814, 826, 832, 835, 839, 841, 850, 863, 883, 886, 912, 957, 985, 1038, 1045, 1075, 1184, 1206, 1234, **dywawd** 49, 265, 374, 379, 381, pl. 3. **dywedassant** 947, 1219n.; subj. pres. sing. 2. **dywettych** 382; imper. sing. 2. **dywet** 167, 861.

dy prep. to 12. Cf. GMW 201 (R **y**) 12: xx.

dy urth prep. from, because 10–11. Cf. GMW 200–1: xx.

'e pers. pron. infix. obj. sing. 3. masc. 130, 162, 171, 172, 236, 259, 508, 567, 579, 643, 789, 857, 874, 899, 905, 962n., 1047, fem. 383, 485, 496, 562, 566, 1237.

'e poss. pron. infix. sing. 3. masc. + nn. 79, 279, 284, 440, 456, 572, 640, 643n., 648n., 702, 702 etc.; fem. 101, 375, 482, 492, 497, 532 etc.

'e poss. pron. infix. sing. 3. masc. + vn. 56, 154, 353, 523, 523, 523 etc. fem. 282, 368, 376, 461, 487, 537 etc.

'e poss. pron. infix. pl. 3. + vn. 1216.

ederyn nm. bird 851, 1031, 1079.

edling nm. aetheling, heir-apparent 149n.: xi, xvii.

edrych vn. look at, see 549, 814, 954, 1025; pres. sing. 3. **edrych** 130; also **ydrych.**

educher adv. till evening 759, 1068.

etil vb. pres. sing. 3. reaches, goes Cf. GPC 1169.

ef pers. pron. simple indep. sing. 3. masc. 1, 41, 141, 231, 265, 271 etc.; **ac ef yn vyw** while he is alive 702, Cf. GMW 231.

ef pers. pron. simple affix. aux. 3. masc. 16, 449, 581, 587, 622, 625 etc.

ef a pre-verb. affirm. prt. 6.

egweti nmf. portion, dowry, paid by the bride's father to her husband 532n.

enghi vn. to be delivered 8n.: xvii.

eglyn nm. englyn 977n.

engyl canhorthwy nm. attendant angel 230n.

ehawc nm. salmon 892.

eidi poss. pron. (stressed) sing. 3. fem. hers 495.

eingon nfm. anvil 851, also **einon.**

eil nm. son 184n, 197, 217, 225, 395, 992, 1155, adj. second 529, 537, 877.

eillaw vn. shave 638, 639, 651, 1232; pret. impers. **eillwyt** 1234n., 1234.

einon nmf. anvil 528, also **eingon.**

einym poss. pron. (stressed) pl. 1. ours 948.

eiras nmf. stake 462, 463.

eiryach vn. spare, save 87 (R **arbet**).

eiroet adv. ever 53, 213, 236, 238, 241, 309, 401, 404, 420, 421n., 456, 729, 767, **eiryoet** 961; **eirmoet** 127n., 374, 907n., **eirmoyt** 448, Cf. GMW 222.

eirychu vn. charge, impute 502: xviii.

eisseu nm. need 276, **yn eisseu** lacking 951: xv.

eissoes adv. however, nevertheless 982, **eisswys** 415n.: xx.

eissywet nm. need, lack 380.

eisted vn. sit 499, 953; imper. sing. 2. **eisted** 148.

eithaf nm. end, limit 417.

eithyr prep. apart from, except 159, 951, 1122.

eithyr hynny adv. save then, at other times 85.

ellwng vn. free, release 917, swing 1051.

ellygywr nm. unleasher 725n.

ellyn nmf. razor 1090n., 1185n.

emendigeit adj. cursed 525, 527, 540, 541, 553, 556.

eneit nmf. life, soul 456n., 484, 755, 1091, 1238; **eneit dros eneit** life for life adv. 1146–7, 1171.

ennillec nf. battle-axe (see n. on **gleif**) 63.

enw nm. name 1148.

erbyn prep. by, against 573.

erchi vn. ask, seek, request 21, 437, 439, 454, 457, 477, 505, 515, 562n., 1037, 1038, 1044, 1062n.; pres. sing. 1. **archaf** 18, 1082, 3. **eirch** 562, 565, 566; pret. sing. 3. **erchis** 503; subj. pres. sing. 2. **erchych** 59n., 3. **archo** 506.

eredic vn. plough 572, 590.
ereill pron. pl. subst. others 131.
ergryn nm. trembling, dread 1061.
ergydyaw vn. proffer: subj. pres.
sing. 3. **ergyttyo** 96.
erhyl nf. hunt 1015, 1105: xvii.
ertrei nm. breaking of waves, first
ebb after high water 447n. (R
tonneu): xvii.
erw nf. acre 238.
esgyll n.pl. of **asgell** wing 878.
esgynnu vn. mount: pret. sing. 3.
esgynnwys 1016: xxi.
estofi vn. weave, plan, plot: pret.
sing. 3. **estoues** 297n.
estwng vn. bend down, settle: pres.
sing. 3. **estwg** 652.
estynnu vn. stretch, dress 651.
etiued nm. offspring 4, **ettiuet** 40.
etmic nm. honour, praise 138, 147.
etwa adv. again, yet 49, 478, 606,
ettwa 380, 535, 606.
eu poss. pron. prefix. pl. 3. their + n.
108, 109, 283, 330, 331, 331 etc., **ac
eu** 1217, **y eu** 543, 558, 811; + vn.
414, 1099, 1192, 1218, **ac eu** 597,
940, 946, 1216, 1216. Cf. B xiv,
24–9.
eur nm. gold 78, 917; adj. 61, 62, 67,
164, 441.
eurcrwydyr adj. gold-chased 68.
eurdwrn adj. gold-hilted 67.
eurtyrchogyon npl. gold-torqued
ones 357n.
ewythyr nm. uncle 259; pl.
ewythred 252, 1165, **ywythred**
290n.: xix.

ual conj. as 500, 942, 1192, 1196,
1211, how 1085; **y ual** conj. how
825.
ual kynt adv. still, despite that 927.
ual hynn adv. like this 796.
uelly adv. thus, so, 465, 939, 946,
1005, 1245.
ui pers. pron. simple indep. obj. sing.
1. 893; dep. affix. aux. sing. 1. 113,
484, 502, 754, 776.
uy poss. pron. prefix. sing. 1. 54, 116,
134, 153, 159, 160, 162, 169, 484,
516, 548, 548, 554, 562, 565, 568,
620, 733, 838, 878, 936, **uyg** 135,
159, 160, 161, 161, 166, 547, 668,

784, 853, 892, **uym** 20, 432, 436,
608, 638, 638, 651, 757, 891, 893,
uyn 39, 150, 503, 518, 518, 549,
908.
uyth adv. for ever 266, 370, 1002;
with neg. ever 248, 270, 276, 314,
465, 652 etc; from **byth**.

fion nm. foxglove, rose, 496: xvi,
xvii.
flamgoch adj. flame-red 488.
ffo vn. flee 1053.
foc nf. forge 541, 556: xviii.
ford nf. way, road 241, 305, 1084.
frawdunyaw vn. wheedle 153: xviii.
frwyn nfm. bridle-bit 61.
fust nf. flail 320.
fynhawn nf. spring 493.
fynhonus adj. welling 493.
fyrch n.pl. of **forch** fork 517n., 547.

gadu vn. leave, let, allow 133, 1001;
pres. sing. 2. **gedy** 833, 3. **gat** 449,
468n., 703, impers. **gedir** 767;
imperf. sing. 3. **gadei** 276; subj.
pres. impers. **gatter** 92, 112 (R
ellyngir); 554 imper. sing. 2. **gat**
784, pl. 1. **gadwn** 968.
gauaelgi nm. mastiff 418, 512.
gauylgygwng adj. with well-knit
fork 61.
gal penn nm. headache 555: xviii.
galw vn. call 15, 20, 393, 399, 402,
404, 408; pres. impers. **gelwir** 278;
imperf. impers. **gelwit** 498, 810 .
gallu vn. be able 300, 1224, **gallel**
782 (R gwybot), 789 (R gwdost);
pres. sing. 1. **gallaf** 502, 2. **gelly**
580n., 586, 591, 615, 621, 625, 629,
659, 749, 840, pl. 2. **gellwch** 1081,
impers. **gellir** 648, 664, 701, 735;
imperf. sing. 3. **gallei** 386n., 409;
pret. sing. 3. **gallwys** 237, 1189:
xxi; subj. sing. 3. **gallo** 948, pl. 1.
gallom 1094, impers. **galler** 667.
gan prep. with, by 263, 447, 504, 530,
628, 902 etc. sing. 1. **gennyf** 606,
845n., **genhyf** 381, 501, 557, 576,
582, 588 etc., 2. **gennyt** 44, 97 (R
genthi), 837, 842, 917, 948, **genhyt**
508, 580, 621, 732, 775, 791, 792, 3.
masc. **ganthaw** 388, 420, 440, 456,
767, 785, 1041, 1229, **gantaw** 830,

927, 1008, 1027, 1067, 1150 etc.;
fem. **genthi** 454, 455n., 456, 935,
989, 1040, **genti** 3, pl. 1. **genhym**
115, 382, 1220, 2. **genhwch** 427, 3.
ganthunt 31, 781, 808, **ganthu** 32:
xvi, xxi, **gantunt** 824, 976, 1055,
1173, 1232; **gan anwaeret** adv. up
the slope 526.
garth nmf. thicket 570.
garwson nm. dreadful noise 944.
gast nf. bitch 939.
gawr nfm. shout, clamour 1141.
gayaf nm. winter 419n.
geueil nf. forge 304.
geir nm. word 1045.
gel nfm. leech 540.
geluin nmf. beak 853.
gellwng vn. drop, let loose, send,
unleash, 998, 1067n., 1140, 1210;
pres. sing. 1. **gellynghaf** 375;
imperf. sing. 3. **gellyngei** 325;
pret. impers. **gellwngwyt** 729: xx;
imper. sing. 2. **gellwng** 1221.
gemmeu n.pl. of **gem** gem, jewel
490.
geni vn. be born 354.
gesseuin adv. first 113: xvii.
girat adj. grievous, bitter 943.
glanhau vn. clean 793.
glaw nm. rain 133, 157, 389.
gleif nmf. spear, sword 63n.
glo nm. charcoal, cinders 571.
glwth nm. couch 349.
glynn nm. glen, wooded valley 875.
glynu vn. stick, keep close, remain
faithful/loyal to: pres. sing. 3 **glyn**
807.
gobeith nmf. hope 845, 917.
gochel vn. avoid, flee from: pret.
sing. 3. **gochelawd** 961: xxi.
godrwyth nmf. marsh trefoil (GPC
1424)?, see n. to 492.
gof nm. smith 527, 851.
goueneic nmf. hope 473.
gouyn vn. ask 165, 848, 884, 903,
933, 1080, 1133; pres. sing. 1.
gouynnaf 36, pl. 2. **govynnwch**
855, 868, 879, 890; pret. sing. 1.
gouynneis 782, 2. **gouynneist** 781,
3. **gouynnwys** 1074: xxi.
goglyt vn. snatch 460.
gogof nf. cave 937, 1209, 1211, 1218,
1221, 1226.

gohilion n.pl. residue, remnant 472n.
golchi vn. wash 481, 638.
goleu nm. light 130.
golut nmf. wealth 918.
golwc nmf. eye 493, 494, 494, look,
glimpse 1039: xviii.
golwython n.pl. chops 92, 131.
goranhed nm. ample supply 132 (R
parawt): xviii.
gordethol adj. picked, select 1059.
gordibla nm. mighty plague 313:
xviii.
gordtorch nm. collar, torque 70, 488.
goresgyn vn. conquer, subdue 1241.
goreu superl. of **da** good 405, 406,
776, 810.
goreureit adj. golden 131.
goruot vn. overcome, be answerable
(with **ar**) 992n.; fut. sing. 3.
goruyd 756; consuet. past. sing. 3.
goruydei 465n.; subj. pres. sing. 3.
gorffo 1003. Cf. GMW 146–7.
gorhendat nm. great-grandfather
534n.
gorhenuam nf. great-grandmother
534n.
gorllewin nm. west 659, 1010.
gorsetua nf. mound 417.
goruc defective vb. pret. sing. 3 did
8, 9, 15, 20, 21, 24, 27, 28, 43, 47,
52, 52n., 60, 102, 141, 165, 166,
393, 440, 441, 443, 443, 444, 460,
468, 499, 510, 521, 523, 536, 538,
551, 778, 787, 791, 793, 794, 813,
820, 829, 832, 848, 897, 901, 923,
924, 929, 932, 933, 938, 941, 944,
971, 972, 976, 978, 995, 997, 1020,
1029, 1031, 1033, 1044, 1047, 1064,
1065, 1078, 1080, 1098, 1100, 1105,
1109, 1133, 1139, 1168, 1180, 1208,
1212, 1215, 1217, 1225, 1228, 1241;
pl. 3. **gorugant** 32, 412, 458, 467,
521, 529, 531, 543, 549, 759, 811,
830, 847, 859, 871, 901, 958, 1043,
1095, 1222; impers. **gorucpwyt** 10,
46, 519, 769, 790, **gorucpwyd** 12,
487 (R **gwnaethpwyt**) 10, 12, 519:
xiii, xxv.
gorwen fem. of **gorwynn** bright,
shining, gleaming 334, 737.
gorwyd nm. horse 60, 74, 81, 141n.:
xvii.
gorymdeith vn. walk, stroll 34n.

goryscalawc adj. overflowing 93: xvi, xvii.

goryw defective vb. pret. sing. 3. did 140n.

gossot vn. place 462, 820.

gowan adj. piercing, stabbing, pointed, 335, 738: xvii.

grayan n.coll. gravel 493.

griduan nm. groaning, moaning, 911, **gridua** 943.

grud nfm. cheek 496; slope, tilth 602.

grwmseit nm. dark blade 792. Cf B xxxv (1988), 55–61: xvii.

gwadneu npl. soles of foot 304.

gwae interj. woe! 39.

gwaet nm. blood 64, 167, 652, 655, 800, 1206, 1228.

gwaelawt nm. lower end, bottom, depths, 106, 322, **gwaelawd** 102, **gwaelawt ty** lower half of a house 143n.: xviii.

gwaeth comp. of **drwc** bad 96, 143, 400, 526, 554, 567, 1191, 1222.

gwal nfm. lair 1032, 1079.

gwala nf. enough, plenty, fill 312, 314, 968.

gwalch nmf. falcon 494.

gwallaw vn. serve, deal out, pour 624: xvi.

gwallocau vn. neglect 24n.: xvii.

gwallt nm. hair 58n., 162, 530, 668, 1213, 1214, 1239 (R **gwall**) 530.

gwan nmf. stab, wound, stroke, 335, 738; vn. pierce, stab, 524, 538.

gwanu vn. stab, pierce, 552; pret. sing. 3. **gwant** 259, 557.

gware nm. play 1198.

gwaret vn. move, recover, heal 387, 585n., 948, 949.

gwarthaf superl. of **(gw)ar** as n. upper end 101, **gwarthaf dy** the upper end of the house 143–4.

gwarthafleu n.pl. stirrups 79n: xi.

gwarthau vn. asperse: pres. sing. 2. **gwerthey** 381.

gwarthec ncoll. cattle 1100.

gwas nm. youth, lad 469, 471, 805, 1218, servant 318, 323, 330, 1048, 1049, 1122, 1181; pl. **gweisson** 516, 547, **gweis** (with num.) 1121n.

gwasanaeth nm. service 467.

gwasanaethu vn. serve: imper. sing. 3. **gwasanaethet** 131.

gwasanaythur nm. servant 272n.

gwascaru vn. disperse 811, 941, 1243.

gwascu vn. squeeze, press 463, 973; subj. imperf sing. 2. **gwascut** 464.

gwastat adj. level 302.

gvayw nmf. spear 160n., 228, 335, 398, 738, 799.

gwchi n. coll. drones 611: xviii.

gvden nf. withe 464.

gwedy prep. after 3, 1005, 1009, 1023, 1043, 1046, 1053, 1061, 1101, 1115, **wedy** 1218, **(g)wedy hynny** after that, thereafter 866, 949, 968, 974, 1007, 1036, 1195.

gweti nf. prayer 4.

gwedu vn. suit: imperf. sing. 3. **gwedei** 30.

gweuyl nf. lip 325.

gwegil nmf. nape of the neck 553.

gwein nf. sheath, scabbard 281, 816, 818, 820, 1195, 1195.

gweith nm. work 586, 814n, 815, 852.

gweitheu adv. sometimes 75, 76.

gwelet vn. see 27, 1039, 1217, 1220; pres. sing. 1. **gwelaf** 570, 603, 2. **gwely** 570, 602, 965; pl. 2. **gwelwch** 763, 875, 3. **gwelant** 761, impers. **gwelir** 270; imperf. sing. 3. **gwelei** 261n., 401, 410, 496, pl. 3. **gwelynt** 410, 413n., 416n., impers. **gwelit** 1085; pret. sing. 1. **gweleis** 448, 3. **gwelas** 478, 500, pl. 3. **gwelsant** 1043n., impers. **gwelasit** 760; subj. pres. sing. 1. **gwelwyf** 518, 3. **gwelho** 451n., pl. 1. **gwelhom** 479, impers. **gweler** 480.

gwell comp. of **da** good 321, also 145, but here = greeting from **henpych gwell** in line 142 above; **pwy gwell genhyt** which do you prefer 791, **oed well genhyf** I would prefer 795.

gwelleu nm. shears 667n., 669, 1090n., 1187.

gwelliu nm. shears 164 (R **gwelleu**).

gwen nf. smile 314.

gwen fem. of **gwyn** fair, bright, comely, 334.

gwen(h)wynic adj. poisoned 522n., 527, 550, 558.

gwenith nmf. wheat 834.

gwennawl nf. swallow 75.

gwenwyn nm. poison 1035.

gwenyn n. coll. bees 611.

gwereskyn n. overcome, conquer, overrun 33; pret. sing 2. **gwereskynneist** 124, 3. **gweryskynnwys** 245: xxi.

gwers nf. a (good) while 783n.

gwerth nm. value 77, 78.

gwerthuawr adj. valuable, precious 78, 489.

gwest nmf. stay, (for the night) 3n., 529n., feast 306, 307, 309: xvii.

gwestei nm. guest 767.

gwichaw vn. squeal 512.

gwin nm. wine 93.

gwir adj. true, just, right, 170, 567, 788; n. truth 147n., 162n., 172, 172n.: xi.

gwiscaw vn. dress, put on 442.

gwiw adj. meet 48, 530.

gwlat nf. land, country 3, 91, 401, 409, 795, 1093, 1124, 1244, **gwlad** 4, 401.

gwled nf. feast 611.

gwlith n.coll. dew 66.

gwlithin nm. dewdrop 65.

gwlychu vn. wet: pres. sing. 3 **gwlych** 157.

gwneuthur vn. make, do 467, 575, 817, 835, 856, 970, 971, 999, 1088, **gwneuthyr** 704; pres. sing. 1. **gwnaf** 102, 154, 154, 174, 380, 857, 1172, 3. **gwna** 628, 629, 969n., pl. 1. **gwnawn** 1086, 1094, 3. **gwnant** 555; imperf. sing. 3. **gwnaei** 23; pret. sing. 1. **gwneuthum** 895, 3. **gwnaeth** 264, 806, 945, 1031, 1069, 1077, 1079, 1083, 1086, 1097, 1153, 1156, 1176, pl. 3. **gwnaethant** 33, 808, 825, 955, **gwnaethont** 429 (R **gorugant**), impers. **gwnaethpwyt** 801, 852, 1001, 1118, 1144: xxv; plup. sing. 3. **gwnaethoed** 1087; subj. pres. 2. **gwnelhych** 566, **gwnelych** 100n., 501n., 3. **gwnel** 428, pl. 2. **gwnelhoch** 1172, **gwneloch** 485; imperf. sing. 3. **gwnelei** 421, impers. **gwnelhit** 134, **gwnelit** 574; imper. sing. 2. **gwna** 41, 793, pl. 2. **gwnewch** 439, 1172.

gwr nm. man 64, 354, 445n., 449, 504, 512 etc; pl. **gwyr** 94, 189, 204, 433, 438, 764 etc.

gwrach nf. crone, witch 35, 36, 38, 40, 1209, 1211, 1212, 1220, 1226; pl. **gwreichon** 741.

gwrda nm. nobleman, lord 48, 797; pl. **gwyrda** 136, 998, 1005.

gwrdaaeth nf. nobility 137.

gwreic nf. woman, wife 1, 2, 17, 19, 29, 30 etc.; pl. **gwraged** 17, 338, 741.

gwreicca vn. seek a wife 27, 47, 49.

gwreicda nf. lady 34, 43.

gwres nm. warmth, heat 267, 656, 657.

gwrhyt nm. fathom 348n. (R **cuppyt**); xii; valour 1170n.

gwrteith vn. dress, trim 668, 813.

gwrtheb vn. reply 1083.

gwrthrychyad teyrnas nm. heir to the kingdom 149n.: xi.

gwrthtir nm. highlands, uplands 653n, 1027, **gwrthdir** 189n.: xvii.

gwrthtrwm adj. very heavy, oppressive 109.

gwrthwan nm. counter-thrust 398n.: xvii.

gwrych n.coll. bristles 1033, 1084, 1085.

gwrys nm. attack: **mynet yg gwrys wrthaw** set upon him 895–6n.

gwybot vn. know 812n.; pres. sing. 1. **gwn(n)** 167, 471, 899, 2. **gwdost** 848, 861, 873, 884, 903, pl. 1. **gwdam** 861, impers. **gwys** 434, 686, 693, 931n.; imperf. sing. 1. **gwydwn** 30, 3. **gwydat** 346, 403 **gwydyat** 1122, 1134, 1135; pret. sing. 3. **gwybu** 970, impers. **gwybuwyt** 1201; subj. pres. sing. 1. **gwypwyf** 904, 3. **gwyp(p)o** 764, 899; imperf. sing. 1. **gwypwn** 874, 3. **gwypei** 241, 1223.

gwych adj. fine, well 590.

gwychyr adj. fierce, gallant 1018, **gwychyrda** in full fury 1034.

gwydbedin nm. fly, gnat 262, **gwydbedyn** 352.

gwydlwdyn nm. wild beast 710.

gwyllt adj. wild 996; comp. **guylltach** 709; superl. **guylltaf** 710.

gwyn nm. light, shade, (white) colour 314.

gwyn hwyl (incl. **gwynt**) nm. urge, desire 240.
gwynn adj. fair, white 136, 495, 608; pl. **gwynnyon** 497n.; comp. **gwynnach** 491, 492 (R **tegach**): xii, 495; n. white 605.
gwynseit nm. white-blade 792. Cf. B xxxv (1988), 55–61.
gwynt nm. wind 65, 133, 157, 555, 800, 954, 956.
gwyssyaw vn. summon 923, 1167.
gyd (a) prep. along with 33, **gyt a(c)** 682, 805, 844, 984, 1011, 1159, 1162, 1180, 1231.
gynt adv. formerly 117, 118, 119, 120, 122, 124, 125; earlier (than), before 857, 870.
gyntaf adv. first 100, 826, 851, 863, 875, 887.
gyrru vn. drive 1175, 1216, set 409, 530, send 23, 1036, 1077, 1105, go 938 **gyrru ar** name 10n.; pres. sing. 1. **gyrraf** 428; pret. sing. 1. **gyrreis** 3. **gyrrwys** 896n.: xxi; 1025, impers. **gyrrwyt** 1201.
gys(s)euin adv. first 604, 694; also **gesseuin**.

ha interj. ah! 36, 54, 374, 381, 450, 464, 501, 766, 788.
haccred equat. of **hagyr** ugly 226n.
hagen conj. however 11n., 18, 85, 505, 856, 868, 880, 899, 960, 1027, 1033.
hagyr adj. ugly, unbecoming, improper 721.
hallt adj. salt 311.
han ny see **hyn(n)y**.
hanbwyllaw vn. care, be concerned; imperf. sing. 3. **hanbwyllei** 745 (R **yny debycko**).
hanuot vn. to be (from) 167n.; pres. sing. 1. **hanwyf** (well) I shall fare the better 640; fut. sing. 3. **hanbyd** 526, 554; imperf. sing. 3. **hanoed** 189, 1123, (well)n.; subj. pres. sing. 2. **henpych gwell** hail! 142n., 148, 513–14n.; imperf. sing. 3. **hanffei** (well) 1039 Cf. GMW 147.
hanner nm. half 1019, middle 1227, **hanher** half 793.
hawd adj. easy 56, 576, 577, 582, 583, 588 etc.

hayachen adv. almost 1218.
hayarn nm. iron 527, 541, 558; pl. **heyrn** 585.
heb vb. said 57, 452, 517, 535, 827, 935, 1234, 1235 **heb yr** 931, 932 **heb y** 961n., 962, 967, 968, 1091. Cf. GMW 154.
heb prep. without 5, 35, 352, 378, 386, 405 etc. past. sing. 3. masc. **hebdaw** 421, 698, 721; impers. adv. **heibaw** past, by 1100.
hebawc nmf. hawk 493.
hebcor vn. spare, do without: pres. impers. **hebcorir** 715.
hediw adv. today 99, 853, 866.
heuyt adv. either (with neg.) 42, 965; also 396, 1155, 1160.
heibaw see under **heb** prep.
heint nmf. sickness, disease 249.
hely vn. hunt 731, **hela** 690n., 717, 735, 939, 1135n.: xix; pres. impers. **helir** 672, 698, 713, 721, 724, 727; also **hyly**.
hen adj. old 35.
herwyd prep. by 1213, 1214, 1239.
hestawr nmf. hestor (a measure) 605, 950n.
heu vn. sow 572; pret. impers. **hewyt** 604.
heul nmf. sun 158, 263.
heus(s)awr nm. shepherd 417, 429, 430, 440, 458, 806n.
heyernyn nm. iron 320.
hi pers. pron. simple indep. sing. 3. fem. 15, 16, 33, 43, 382, 416 etc.
hi pers, pron. simple dep. affix. aux. sing. 3. fem. 934, 939, 1237.
hitheu pers. pron. conjunct. indep. sing. 3. fem. 5, 21, 50, 444, 480, 704, 1196, 1215.
hitheu pers. pron. conjunct. dep. affix. aux. sing. 3. fem. 459, 461, 463, 487, 1214.
hoedyl nf. life 504.
holi vn. claim: pres. sing. 2. **holy** 832; chase, pursue: pret. impers. **holet** 1200.
holl adj. all the 346, 402, 842, 895.
hollti vn. split: pret. sing. 3. **holldes** 1019.
hon(n) dem. pron. adj. fem. this 108, 143, 147, 152, 357, 358 etc.

honno dem. pron. subst. sing. 3. fem.
her, she, it 369, 371, 620, 865.
honno dem. pron. adj. sing. fem. that
376, 439, 450, 457, 529, 604, 625,
628, 633, 1099, 1242.
hun nf. sleep 276.
hunaw vn. cause to sleep: pres. sing.
3. **huna** 633.
hwch nfm. pig, swine 11, 1074, 1076.
hwnn dem. pron. subst. sing. 3.
masc. him, he, this, 472, 474, 878.
hwnn dem. pron. adj. sing. 3. masc.
this 16, 105, 145, 471, 761, 881,
913, 977.
hwnnw dem. pron. subst. sing. masc.
him, he, that, it 452, 466, 572, 574,
606, 709 etc.
hwnnw dem. pron. adj. sing. masc.
that 414, 579, 606, 614, 685, 759,
1068, 1075, 1152.
hwy pers. pron. simple indep. pl. 3.
598; dep. affix. aux. pl. 3. 467, 1063,
1093.
hwyntwy pers. pron. reduplic. indep.
pl. 3. they 949.
hyt nmf. length 385, **hyd** 238.
hyt prep. to, as far as 64, 66, 70, 307,
307, 325 etc., **hyd** 101, till 370,
1002, 1143; conj. as far as 155, 157,
157, 158, 158, 158, **hyd** 425.
hyt att prep. to, as far as 847, 1065.
hyt na conj. so that ... not 105, 317,
320, 410, 744, 1138, **hyd na** 22,
428, **hyt nas** (**nas: na + s** infix.
pron. obj. sing/pl. 3) so that ...
not ... it/them 410, 1121, 1223.
hyt pan(n) conj. so that 132, 463 (R
yny) 518, 548, 552, 571, 573, 607n.
etc., until 9, 19, 51, 55, 479, 539
etc., **hyd pan** 382, 412.
hyt tra conj. so long as, while 136,
249, 553.
hyt yg prep. to, as far as 923, 975,
1009–10, 1131, 1158, 1160, 1204 **hyt
yng** 1024.
hyt ym prep. to, as far as 79, 261–2,
1098–9, 1104, 1145, **hyt yn** 831,
859, 891, 933, 1007 etc., **hyt y**
906.
hyd nm. stag 228.
hyly vn. hunt 26n.; also **hely**: xix.
hyn comp. of **hen** old 861; superl.
hynaf 881.

hynn dem. pron. subst. sing. this 396.
hynn dem. pron. adj. pl. these 840.
hynny dem. pron. subst. sing. that 20,
40, 57, 59, 103, 162 etc.
hynny dem. pron. subst. pl. those
(things) 757, 757, 1124 **hynny** dem.
pron. adj. pl. those 236, 598, 701,
708, 754, 804 etc.
hyn(n)y conj. until 113, 504 (R **hyt
pan**), 672.
hyny affirm. prt. 378n., 412n., 759,
han ny 416. Cf. GMW 245.
.
i pers. pron. simple dep. affix. aux.
sing. 1. 16, 45, 102, 127, 135, 146
etc.
y poss. pron. prefix. sing. 3. masc. +
n. 47, 53, 63, 63, 67, 78, etc.; +
equat. adj. 226, 229, 244, 668.
y poss. pron. prefix. sing. 3. fem. + n.
6, 6, 15, 20, 35, 44, etc.
y poss. pron. prefix. sing. 3. masc. +
vn. 3, 11, 153, 227, 229, 238, etc.
y poss. pron. prefix. sing. 3. fem. +
vn. 31, 846.
y poss. pron. prefix. pl. 3. + vn. 1212.
'y poss. pron. infix. sing. 3. masc. 406,
572.
'y poss. pron. infix. sing. 3. fem. 442,
534.
'y infix. pron. obj. sing. 3. 152, 284,
320.
y prep. to, for, of 9, 25, 35, 46, 48, 84
etc.; + vn. 23, 34, 58, 97, 113, 308
etc.; sing. 1. **y mi** 49, 170, 268, 783,
833, 1236, **ymi** 856, **imi** 36, 48, 266,
450, 473, 473, 754, 797, 816, **ym**
638, 640, 651, 652, 887, **im** 55, 172,
173, 399, 465, 503, 535, 833, 834,
835, 846, 894. 2.**y ti** 445, **iti** 18, 40,
47, 502, 506, 532, 535, **itti** 835, 837,
841, 843, 1234, **yt** 585, 777, **it** 18,
30, 36, 50, 56, 58, 59, 96, 446, 505,
507, **itt** 848, 949, 1236, 1237; 3. sing.
masc., **idaw** 21, 59, 130, 132, 314,
325 etc., **itaw** 38, 40, 42, 53, 67,
165, 265, 319, 504, 572, fem. **idi** 6,
20, 33, 275, 394, 629, 768, 848, **iti** 7,
77, 417, 485; pl. 1. **ynni** 1088, **in**
532, 561, 2. **ywch** 869, 900, 1089,
iwch 520, 3. **udunt** 462, 825, 973,
1046, 1063, 1116, 1129, 1137, **utunt**
392.

y prep. to + poss. pron. infix. sing.
3. fem. to her 510n.; masc. to his
1244; + vn. 844, 948.

y prep. in 795n.

y prep. from, with, by: **y ergyt** at a
blow 821.

y am prep. apart from, besides 358.

y ar prep. from 64, 349, 800n., 1226,
from upon 1215, on 231, 1186; 3.
sing. masc. **y arnaw** from upon
821, 887, 1203–4.

y dan prep. under 385, 517, 598, 791;
sing. 3. masc. **y danaw** 62, 81, 564,
648, 788, 1050.

y uynyd adv. up 440, 1192, 1196.

y gan prep. from: sing. 2. **y genhyt**
from you 566, with you 779; 3.
masc. **y gantaw** 894, 998, 1032,
1071, 1185, 1187, 1191, 1200.

e hun reflex. pron. himself 184, 196,
198, 787, 1015, 1021–2, 1072, his
own 401, 471, 1106, **e hunan** 628,
1123; pl. **e hunein** 940.

y treis adv. by force 990n.

y waeret adv. down 325.

y wrth prep. from 686, 862, 874, 885,
904; compared with 1199; of, about
374–5, 848, 855, 861, 873, 884, 890,
903, 1134; sing. 3. fem. **y wrthi**
934; pl. 3. **y wrthunt** 956.

iach adj. well, healthy 980.

iawn adj. right, proper 6, 842, 844,
855; superl. **iawnhaf** 929, 930,
iawnaf 826, 827, 985, 986.

ieithoed n.pl. of **ieith** language 346,
402, 842.

ieuanc adj. young 805, 851.

ell pron. used with num. in
apposition: **ell deu** the two of them
975, **yll deu** 1216n., **ell pedwar**
1223–4, 1224n.

inheu pers. pron. conjunct. affix. aux.
sing. 1. 567, 607, 711, 752, 753,
758, 817, 895, 1238.

ir adj. fresh 311.

y'r llawr adv. to the floor/ground
1213, 1215.

is prep. below, behind: sing. 3. masc.
istaw 76.

is y law adv. behind his hand 389.

issot adv. down, below 936.

llachar adj. bright 304.

llad vn. slay 31, 511, 812, 974, 983,
994, 1023, 1051, 1100, 1101, 1111,
1115, 1218, cut off 820, 945, 1240;
pres. sing. 1. slay **lladaf** 484
impers., slay **lledir** 747, (fut.),
lladawr 475 (R **lledir**); imperf.
sing. 3. cut **lladei** 74, strike 352;
pret. sing. 1. **lledeis** strike 892, 2.
slay **lledeist** 123, 123, 3. slay
lladawd 283, 284, 473, 936, 1021,
1073, 1113, 1116, 1120, 1124, 1126,
1129, 1156, 1161, 1163, 1169; pl.
3. slay **lladassant** 1138; impers.
slay **lladwyt** 1147, **llas** 1146,
1147, 1149, 1161, 1165; subj. pres.
sing. 3. strike **llatho** 50n., (R
kyflado), pl. 3. slay **lladwynt** 729
(R **lledynt**): xiii, xxi, xxi.

llall pron. subst. other 325.

llamm nmf. leap 299.

llammu vn. leap: imperf. sing. 3.
llammei 298.

llanw nm. tide 905n.

llaw nf. hand 63, 63, 134, 151, 213,
390, 733n., etc.

llawen adj. happy 43, 162, 173, 376,
454.

llawer pron. subst. many 1124,
1155, 1161, 1169.

llawn adj. full, sated 315, 1054,
1195.

llawr nm. ground, floor 66, 88.

lle nmf. place 100, 241, 280, 831,
859, 870 etc., cause 913.

llechwayw nm. stone-spear 522n.,
537, 550.

lleuein nm. wailing 943.

lleueryd nmf. speaking, telling (of)
1046.

llefrith nm. milk 662, 663.

llemidit nm. leaper 299n.

llen(n) nf. mantle 76, 159n.

llenwi vn. fill, flood 1184.

llestyr nm. vessel, bowl 481, 614,
656.

lleturith nm. spell 409 **lledrith** 428.

llettyeu npl. of **lletty** lodgings 811.

llettywyr n. (pl. of **llettywr**) those
who lodge 812.

lliaws pron. subst. a multitude 1159.

llidyaw vn. grow angry 1217.

llifdwr nm. torrent 280, 281.

lliueit adj. whetted 63.

llinat n.coll. flax seed 605, 950; sing.
  llinhedyn 952.
llith nm. food (for animals) 92.
llithraw vn. glitter; imperf. sing. 3.
  llithrei 1085.
lliw nm. colour, hue 68.
lliuaw vn. blush 52; pres. sing. 2.
  lliuy 54.
lloer nf. moon 556.
llong nf. ship 159, 938, 1042, 1054.
lloring elifeint nn. ivory boss 68n.
  (R. **llugorn**): xii, xviii.
llosci vn. burn 571; imperf. sing. 3.
  lloskei 423.
llu nm. host 282, 840, 941, 990; pl.
  lluoed 279, 1052, 1053, 1096, 1104,
  1139, 1197, 1243, **lluydd** 305.
lluchet nf. lightning 68: xviii.
lludu nm. ashes 572: xviii.
lludet nm. weariness 1203.
llusgaw vn. drag 1240.
llwdwn nm. animal, beast 420: xviii.
llygat nm. eye 130, 352, 353, **llegat**
  276; pl. **llygeit** 548, 554.
llygru vn. afflict, damage 18, 432;
  pret. sing. 3. **llygrwys** 816: xxi.
llyn(n) nmf. drink, liquid 90, 132,
  153, 574, 614, 656, 664, 772.
llyna interj. lo there! behold! 960n.,
  962.
llys nmf. court 9, 46, 81, 88, 96, 97,
  112, 135, 152, 458, 545, 559, 823,
  1232; fem. 108.
llysuam nf. step-mother 47, 55.
llysuwyd nm. lack of appetite, nausea
  543: xviii.

'm pers. pron. infix. obj. sing. 1. 37,
  436, 484, 527, 540, 553, 833.
'm poss. pron. infix. sing. 1. + n. 84,
  159, 167, 505, 517, 753 etc.
'm poss. pron. infix. sing. 1. + vn.
  432, 505, 627, 633.
mab nm. son, boy 1, 4, 9, 10, 12, 14,
  etc., **uab**, 176, 332, 829, 849, 862,
  873 etc., **m** 178, 179, 181, 181,
  182, 183, 183; pl. **meib** 1110,
  mabyon 95, **meibon** 188, 291,
  meibion 333, **meibyon** 736.
maen nm. stone 760, 887, **deu uaen**
  ureuan two quernstones 1193n,
  maen treigyl rolling stone 88.
maendy nm. house of stone 913.

maer nm. overseer 296n., 635, 1037.
maes nm. field, meadow 397, 416,
  1084, **mays** 423.
maestir nm. plain 412.
magwyr nf. wall 910, 912, 926.
mal prep. like 73, 74, 88, 228, 273,
  526, 540, 557, 1083.
mal(y) conj. as 28, 145, 415, 441,
  536, 549, 552, 557, 945, 1224, so
  that 409, 812, 907, **mal na** so
  that . . . not 110, as if . . . not
  807.
malkawn conj. whether, if 3n., 24:
  xviii.
malpei conj. as if 793n., **malphei**
  819, **y malphei** 814, **mal pei nat**
  as if . . . . not 308–9.
mam nf. mother 14, 169, 222, 252,
  259, 291, 453, 604, 686, 850, 863,
  874, 885, 904, 1165.
man adj. small, fine, petty 321,
  493, 840.
manec nf. glove 443, 444, 445.
march nm. horse, steed 92, 232,
  689, 718, 1006, 1059, 1177, 1189;
  pl. **meirch** 337, 740, 1096,
  meirych 753.
marchawc nm. rider, horseman 406;
  pl. **marchogyon** 1173.
marchogaeth vn. ride 753.
marw adj. dead 16, 250, 422, 487,
  704; n. **death** 547; vn. die 22n.
marw dlws nm. the jewel of a
  dead man 450.
mas nf. metal 303.
mawr adj. great, big 269, 412, 416,
  420, 570, 804, 875, 1061, 1110.
mawred nm. grandeur, majesty 368,
  530.
mawruredic adj. magnanimous 367.
medru vn. hit; imperf. sing. 3.
  medrei 350.
medwl nm. mind 331.
medyc nm. doctor 386.
meglyt vn. snatch, seize 521 (R
  ymauael), 1050.
meichad nm. swineherd 7n., 9.
meillonen nf. trefoil 497.
mein gefyn nm. small of the back
  539.
meint nmf. force, strength, amount
  390, 972, 1043, 1093.
mel nm. honey 610, 610.

melyn adj. yellow 470; comp.
melynach 490.

merch nf. daughter 2, 14, 32, 48,
51, 56 etc.; **m.** 360, 361; **a merch
inheu** and my daughter 711, 752,
y merch i for my daughter 757;
pl. **merched** 339n., **merchet** 357,
742.

meredic adj. foolish, stupid 433n.,
763n.

mererit nm. pearl(s) 489.

merthrolyaeth nf. martyrdom 560.

messur nm. measure 606, 1056.

messuredic past. partic. passive.
measured 951, **yn uessuredic oll**
in full measure.

methu vn. fail: pres (fut.) sing. 3.
methawd 108: xxi.

meu poss. pron. sing. 1. mine,
possession 1235n, 1235.

mi pers. pron. simple indep. sing. 1.
30, 83, 103, 104, 116, 118 etc.

miui pers. pron. redup. indep. sing.
1. 868.

mil nm. animal, creature 237, 729 (R
lwdyn), 1102; pl. **mileit** 857.

milgi nm. greyhound 69n.

milwyr n.pl. (sing. **milwr**) warriors
148, 174, 829, 922, 925, 981, 1109,
1168, 1175.

milltir nf. mile 348.

min(h)eu pers. pron. conj. indep.
sing. 1. 39, 45, 431, 502, 1235,
minneu 851, 878.

mis nm. month 66.

moch n.pl. swine, pigs 8, 8, 354, 355,
1073, 1135, 1146, 1148, 1150.

modrwy nf. ring 441, 442, 444, 445,
449; pl. **modrwyeu** 482.

moes nf. usage, custom, practice 765.

moli vn. praise 154.

mor adv. so 528, 840.

mor nm. sea 158, 245, 446, 450, 1143,
1201, **morawl** 317.

moruwyt nm. sea-food 447.

morgrugyn nm. ant 349, 952n.

morwennawl nf. sea-swallow 73.

morwyn nm. maiden 52, 266, 340,
366, 367, 375, 479, 489, 501, 604,
743, 1001, 1004.

mut adj. mewed 494: xvii.

mur nm. wall 906.

mwc nm. smoke 955, 958.

mwy comp. of **mawr** great, big
419, 474, 561, 761, 807, **mwyuwy**
all the more 137.

mwy(h)af superl. of **mawr** great,
big 66, 137, 302, 368, 389, 391,
413 (R **teckaf o**).

mwynhau vn. be of use, be
effective: pres. sing. 3. **mwynha**
655, 704, **mwynhaa** 965.

mwynyant nm. use 702.

mwys nf. hamper 618n.

myn prep. (in oaths) by 134n., 431,
957n., 1085, 1169n., **myn llaw
uyghyueillt** by the hand of my
friend 134, **m. ll. uyng kyueillt**
957n.

myn (yd) n. place (where) 7n., 429,
498, 563 (R **lle ydd**): xvii.

mynet vn. go 3n., 28, 43, 52, 60,
380 etc. pres. sing. 1. **af** 776, 858,
905; imperf. sing. 3. **aei** 442; pret.
sing. 1. **euthum** 446, 890, 3.
edyw 89, 772, **aeth** 5, 34, 553,
909, 988, 996 etc., pl. 3. **aethant**
975, 1152, 1156, impers. **aethpwyt**
1146; subj. pres. sing. 1. **elwyf**
113, 503n., 504, 542, 554, 3. **aho**
1170n, pl. 2. **eloch** 845; imperf.
sing. 2. **elhut** 426, 3. **elei** 241,
elhei 394, 405, 440, 498 pl. 3.
elhynt 308, 309; imper. sing. 2.
dos 58, 129, 399, 424, 505, 839, 3.
aet 798, pl. 1. **awn** 536, 1093, 2.
ewch 846.

mynet dwylaw mynwgyl vn.
throw arms around neck, embrace,
greet 461–2n.

mynnu vn. wish, desire; pres. sing.
1. **myn(n)af** 163, 575, 607, 620,
639, **mynhaf** 566, 572, 594, 633,
2. **mynny** 17n., **mynhy** 561;
imperf. sing. 3. **mynnei** 1, 27, pl.
3. **mynnynt** 780; pret. sing. 3.
mynnwys 2: xxi, pl. 3.
mynnassant 821; subj. pres. sing.
2. **mynnych** 19, 3. **mynho** 619,
impers. **mynher** 628; imper. sing.
2. **myn** 546, 560.

mynwgyl nm. neck 70, 462, 488.

mynych adj. frequent, often 446,
543, 936.

mynyd nm. mountain 242, 302, 710,
943.

'n pers. pron. infix. obj. pl. 1. 383, 475, 1086.

'n poss. pron. infix pl. 1. + nn. 536.

na(c) conj. (n)or 272, 375, 579, 687, (n)either 915, **na(c) ... na(c)** (n)either ... (n)or 236–7, 270, 310, 310, 310–11 etc. whether ... or 269, **na(c) ... na(c) ... na(c)** 1189.

na(c) neg. prt. + imper. 41, 427, 438, 546, 546, 559, 560; + answer 88, 771.

na(t) pre-verb. neg. prt. 19, 50, 55, 382, 479, 483 etc. + nn. 471.

na wir interj. no indeed! 135.

nachaf interj. lo! behold! 447, 761.

nac nm. nay, refusal 1040, 1046.

namyn prep. (with neg.) except, but 90, 317, 395, 432, 615 etc.; conj. but 141, 153, 241, 314, 425, 475 etc.

nas (na neg. + 's infix. pron. obj. sing.) 89, 772, 1039, 1135.

naw num. nine 384, 384, 385, 385, 398, 419 etc.

naw mod adv. nine times 610, 709.

nawd nm. protection 438, 1063, 1063.

nawuet ord. ninth, one of the nine 297n.

nawn nm. noon 307.

neb pron. (with neg) anyone 145, 228, 271, 394, 410, 428 etc. (with cond. conj.) 1045; adj. any 767, **y neb** he (who) 868. Cf. GMW 105–6.

nef nf. heaven 68, 745.

neges nf. message, quest 240, 331, 394, 400, 405, 457 etc.

nei nm. nephew 406, 455.

neillparth nm. one side 1185.

neithawr nf. wedding feast 608.

neithawrwyr n.pl. wedding-guests 574, 636.

nerth nm. strength, help 838, 1018.

nes comp. of **agos** near 415; prep. (with vn.) until 663, 694, 713, 720, 727, 735, 828.

neu conj. or 91, 383, 433, 434, 437, 514, 916.

neuad nf. hall 101, 114, 264, 329, 513n., 531, 773.

neut pre-verb. affirm prt. 878: xxii.

neur pre-verb. affirm. prt (neu + ry) 1028n: xxii.

newyd adj. new 607, 818.

newyn nm. hunger 308.

ni pers. pron. simple indep. pl. 1. 546, 560, 883, 948, 1089; dep. affix. aux. pl. 1. 127, 382, 860, 1086, 1093, 1094.

ni neg. pre-verb. prt. 80, 83, 237: also **ny.**

niuer nmf. host, force, company 99, 144, 1024, 1041, 1043n., 1052; pl. **niueroed** 1060.

ninheu pers. pron. conj. indep. pl. 1. 383; dep. affix. aux. pl. 1. 138

ninneu 967.

no(c) conj. than 65, 143, 239, 321, 401, 415 etc., **nocet** 97 (R **no chyt ac**).

nodi vn. note, name; pres. sing. 1. **nodaf** 163, 173, 570; pret. sing. 3. **nodes** 312, 950; plup. sing. 3. **nottayssei** 1020, impers. **nodydoed** 1141n.; subj. pres. sing. 1. **nottwyf** 568, 2. **nottych** 163, 171, 569 (R **mynnych**), 3. **notto** 157, 171; imper. sing. 2. **not** 162, 171, **nod** 568.

nodi vn. protect: subj. pres. sing. 3. **notho** 766.

nos nf. night 307, 376, 384, 385, 529, 620 etc.; adv. at night 751.

nu adv. now 756. Cf. GMW 221.

ny neg. pre-verb. prt. 91, 96, 102, 112, 127, 135 etc.; also **ni; nyt** 394, 396, 400, 415, 425, 445 etc., **nyd** 38, 212, 309, 421, 432, 442 etc., **nys** (ny +'s infix. pron. obj. sing. 3.) 45, 141, 621, 625, 629, 670 etc., (obj. pl. 3.) 590, 664.

ny(t/d) neg. pre-verb. prt. in rel. clause subj. 421, 764, **nyt** 393, **nyd** 95; in rel. clause obj. 578, 584, ?907, **nys** 729.

ny(t/d) neg. prt. + n. 40, 49, 662, 834, 834, 1020, 1236; + vn. 828; + adj. 108, 833, 833, 1219, 1220; + adv. 87, 87, 835, 1170.

nychdawt nm. languor 249.

nyt amgen adv. not otherwise, namely 85.

o conj. if 408, 483, 484, 507, 854, **ot** 103, 507, **or** 128, 153, 275n., 1081, 1222, **os** (o if + **ys** it is) 268, (o if + 's infix. pron. obj.) if ... it 505, 561.

o prep. from 5, 41, 64, 65, 70, 79 etc.,
+ vn. 892, of 8, 29, 78, 102, 107,
148 etc., because of 1217, on 71, 71,
72, 72, 864, 1185, 1185 by 1172;
sing. 1. **ohonof** 919, 2. **ohonot** 41,
3. masc. **ohonaw** 145, 175, 442,
605, 640, 818 etc. fem. **oheni** 459,
459, 470, 767, 817, **ohonei** 463,
854, 867, pl. 2. **ohonawch** 908,
1082, 3. **ohonu** 4n, 414, **onadunt**
109, 510, 558, 782, 1003, 1044,
1138, **ohonunt** 476, 920, 921, 951,
1183, 1223: xx, xxi.
o barth prep. on the side of 222.
o bell adv. from afar 959.
o blith prep from among 492–3.
o bop parth adv. on all sides 1068.
o ureid adv. scarcely, with difficulty
246.
o hediw allan adv. from this day
forth 110.
o hynny adv. from that 249, **o
hynny allan** from then on 984,
1202.
o lywenyd adv. with joy 460.
o pleit prep. on the side of 205.
ochwinsa adv. immediately, soon 451
(R y chwinsaf).
odif vn. throw, hurl 523, 537, 538,
551, 551, **odi** 523.
oduch prep. above, around: sing. 3.
masc. **ody uchtaw** 1184, fem.
oduchti 619.
odyma adv. from here 1093.
odyna adv. then 975, 1011, 1148,
1158, 1197, 1200, from then on
1035, from there 1128, thereafter
1130, 1156, 1158.
odyno adv. from there 715, 920,
1024, 1104, 1150, 1174, 1203.
o'e cheissaw adv to seek her/it 376n.,
405, (R y cheissaw).
o'e uod adv. willingly 580, 586, 591,
621, 625, 629, 648, 659, 664, 670,
691, **o'e uod ef** 615.
o'e vywyt adv. of his life, while he
lives 703.
oet nm. time, age 49, 116.
oen nm. lamb 420.
oer adj. cold 266, 310.
oes nf. age, life 243.
ouyn nm. fear 1061.
ongyl nf. corner 352. Cf GPC **ongl**[2].

oia interj. ah! 449, 797, 913.
olrein vn. trace, track: pret. sing. 3.
olrewys 355: xxi.
oll pron. (used adverbially following
the word it modifies) all 373, 482,
508, 575, 744, 754, 795n. etc. Cf.
GMW 98.
ony(t) conj. if not, unless 640, 652,
655, 702, 898, 965, 1027, **onyt** but,
except 579, 685, 890.
onys (ony +'s) conj. if . . . not . . .
it/her 103, 154, 533. GMW 240–1.
o'r pan conj. from the (time) when
1103, 1188.
o'r tu draw y prep. from beyond
291–2.
or nm. limit, boundary, edge 416.
osp nm. guest 765; pl. **ospeit** 151.

pa interr. adj. what? 476, 775, 912,
pa beth what thing?, which? 826,
pa du what side? where? 931, **pa le**
what place? where? 1202, **pa ueint
bynnac** indef. rel. however much
506.
paladyr nm. shaft 800, 801.
palueu npl. of **palf** palm 492 (R
dwylaw): xii.
pan(n) conj. when 6, 66, 98, 119,
122, 123 etc.
pan conj. whence? 445n, 762; that
(after **o** from) 151n., 189, **pan yw**
that it is 434n.
par nm. spear 62: xvii.
parchell nm. pigling 1073.
paret nm. wall 850.
parth nm. side 71, 71, 72, 72, 1002,
1185, 1185, direction 125.
parth a(c) prep. towards 944, 955,
958, 959, 1095, 1208.
pawb pron. subst. all, everyone 140,
226, 379, 411, 468, 619, 663, 1243.
pawl nm. stake 1241.
pebreit adj. peppered 93, 132:
xviii.
pechawd nm. sin 502, 600.
pedeir num. f. four 74, 74, 76, 497,
534.
pedryal nm. four corners 155.
pedwar num. masc. four 74, 534,
1113, 1224, 1224.
pedwar gayaf adj. of four winters
60.

pedwar troedawc adj. four-footed 238.

pedestyr nm. walker 405.

pei conj. if 301, 347, 619, 745n., 874, 1039, 1045n.

peidyaw vn. endure: pres. sing. 3. **peit** 271n. Cf. GMW 165.

peir nm. cauldron 635, 1037, 1044, 1047, 1050, 1054, 1056.

pell o amser n. a long time 886n.

pellach comp. of **pell** far 239.

pellen(n)igyon n.pl. people from afar 95, 151; sing. **pellenhic** 765.

pen(n) nm. chief 431, head 83, 87, 165, 308, 326, 481 etc., mouth 35, 62, 157, 171 top 79, 887; adj. chief 142, 299n.

penn y tir nm. headland 585.

penkynyd nm. chief huntsman 697n.; pl. **penkynydyon** 287n.

pendoll adj. big-headed 540.

pendro nf. giddiness 555.

pengrych adj. curly-headed 469.

pennguch nm. cowl 326.

penlluchlwyt adj. with light-grey head 60.

pennhynef nm. chief elder 222.

pennllat nm. the best drink 613n.

pennlliein nm. veil 608.

pensaer nm. chief craftsman 1125.

pentan nm. hearth 469.

peri vn. cause, bring about; pret. sing. 3. **peris** 1237.

peth pron. thing 133, 796, 840, that (which) 855, some part (of) 898, 1035; adj. some 520; pron. interr. what? 687, 1074.

pieu interr. to whom is/are? who owns? 432n., 433, 763; rel. who owns 434, 451n., 764, 765. Cf. GMW 80–81.

pigaw vn. peck: imperf. sing. 1. **pigwn** 888.

plant n.pl. children 37n, 38, 44.

plygu vn. bend: pret. sing. 3. **plygwys** 243: xxi.

pob pron. adj. every 21, 23, 48, 53, 70, 77, 77 etc., **pob tri nawyr** every thrice nine men, 27 men at a time 618n., **bob un bob deu** one by one two by two 941n.

poeth adj. hot 93, 132.

pont nf. bridge 281.

porfor adj. purple 76.

porth nm. gate 81, 85, 99, 100, 103, 105 etc. support 838.

porthawr nm. gate-keeper 82, 85, 511n., 770, 774, 778, 786, 798.

prenn nm. tree 387, 422, piece of wood, log 460.

presennawl adj. worldly 918n.

pressen nm. world 715: xvi.

priawt nmf. wife 432, 436.

prid nm. soil, earth 423.

prouedic past. prt. pass. tried 1175.

pryt anterth nm. tierce 98n.

pryt diwlith nm. time of no dew, when it had dried 573: xvi, xvii.

pryt na conj. since . . . not 833.

pryuet n.pl. insects 308.

puchaw vn. desire: imperf. sing. 3. **puchei** 1231.

pwll nm. pit 971, 973.

pwy interr. pron. who? 165, 167, 435, 437, 452, 798, which? 791; interr. adj. what? 44n., 89n., 772 (R **pa** 44 **py** 89, 772): xx.

pwyll nm. sense, reason 7.

py interr. pron. what? 832, why? 54. Cf. GMW 76–77.

py interr. adj. what? 54, 241, 686, 693, 765, 934.

py . . . bynhac indef. rel. however much 111–12.

pymhet ord. fifth 1069n.

pyr conj. that 83, 771n. Cf. GMW 77 (R **py rac** 771): xvii.

pysc nm. sing. fish 924.

'r def. art. 9, 16, 25, 29, 46, 65 etc., **a'r rei = a rei** 843.

rac prep. for 99, because of 308, 390, from 946, because + equat. adj. 80, 226n., 229, 244, 668n., 1026, lest, for fear that + vn. 502, 714, 1192; sing. 1. **ragof** from 45, 2. **ragot** for 94, 99, 149, on ahead 756, 3. **racdau** in front of 69, 139, because of 1061, pl. 2. **ragoch** for 438, in front of 858, 3. **racdu** on, ahead 513: xxi, **racdunt** 847; **rac ouyn** through fear of 8; **rac dy deulin** adv. before you 98 (R **rac dy vronn**), **rac vyneb** in front 270.

rackaer nf. outer wall 831.

racco adv. yonder 425n., 957, **racko** 965.

racloyeit n.pl. of **raclawf** deputy 85.

racllauyn nm. blade 67.

rat nm. grace 146.

ragot vn. waylay 1174n.: xviii–xix.

ran(n) nf. part 266, 1069.

rannu vn. divide: subj. pres. sing. 1. **ranhwyf** 150.

recdouyd nm. dispenser of gifts 17n.: xvii.

redec vn. run 459, 1194.

rengi bod vn. please, satisfy the will of: pres sing. 3. **reinc** 794; imperf. sing. 3. **ranghei** 814n.; **ranc bod yw genhyf** I am content with it 815.

rei pron. pl. subst. some 131, 662, 843, 1119; with art. and adj. ones 474, 598, 744, 817, 840.

reit nm. need, necessity 40, 535, 638, 651, 783, 984, 1236.

reit nm. tine 864.

restru vn. range 1109.

retkyr nm. pig-run 11: xvi, xvii.

rethri n.pl. boards 321.

rewinnyaw vn. ruin, destroy 715.

rieni n.pl. parents 375.

rith nm. shape, form 934n, 934, 940n, 1031, 1078n.

rithaw vn. form, transform: pret. sing. 3. **rithwys** 599n., 857, 870, 1076n: xxi.

rodi vn. give, place, put 12, 441, 465, 794, 813, 838, etc., **roti** 443; pres. sing. **rodaf** 837, 2. **rody** 533, 3. **ryd** 590, 625, 629, 659, 664, 670, 690, 748, pl. 1. **rodwn** 486, 2. **rodwch** 485; pret. sing. 3. **rodes** 1063, 1085, **(kyuarth)** 1112, 1116, 1129, pl. 3. **rodassant** 1064; subj. imperf. sing. 3. **rodei** 1045, 1045, imper. sing. 2. **dyro** 816, **doro** 532, 561.

ruchen nf. jerkin 418.

rud adj. red 318, 489.

rudeur adj. of red gold 70 (R **rudem**), 77, 488.

rwng prep. between 1090, **rwg** 260.

rwy adv. too much, excessively 381.

rwyf nm. course 319.

rwygaw vn. rend, break through 925.

ry affirm. pre-verb. prt. 25, 37n., 41n., 53, 55, 374, 379, 401, 436, 456, 464, 472, 548, 784, 1141n., re 478. Cf. GMW 166–8 R **a** 27, 55, 379, 464, 472, 548: xvi, xxi, xxii.

rybuchaw vn. desire 552.

ryd adj. free 928.

rynhet equal of **ryn** stiff 668n.

rysswr nm. warrior, champion 251, 958, 960, 1113; pl. **rysswyr** 1180.

ryw adj. such a 470.

Sadwrn n. Saturday 481.

saethutta vb. imper. sing. 2. shoot at 546, 560.

sangharwy nm. stirrup 79n.: xi.

salwen read **salwett** equat. of **salw** mean 1026n.

sawl pron. subst. those (who) 1231.

sef subst. 30n., 732, 1049, + a 15n., 23, 394n., 806, 894, 938, 1139, 1172; adj 2, 1000, 1085; adv. +y 7n., 18n., 1029. Cf. GMW 52–3; also **yssef.**

seuydlawc adj. bristling 328.

seuyll vn. stand 301, 831; subj. imperf. sing. 3. **safhei** 301.

seint n.pl. of **sant** saint 1062.

seith num. seven 25, 348n., 353, 355.

seithlydyn moch n.pl. seven young pigs 1067n., 1079–80n. Cf **llwdwn** 420.

serch nm. love 52, 465, 465, 497.

sidan nm. silk 488.

sorri vn. be displeased, grow angry: pret. sing. 3. **sorres** 981.

sugnaw vn. suck up: imperf. sing. 3. **sugnei** 317.

sur adj. sour 310.

suraw vn. turn sour: pres. sing. 3. **surha** 664.

swllt nm. treasure(s) 1054n

swyd nf. office, job 1049.

swydvr nm. officer 273n.

sych adj. dry 318.

sychu vn. dry: pres. sing. 3. **sych** 157.

syllu vn. see, look at: imper. sing. 2. **syll** 957.

synhwyr nm. sense, feeling 454.

syr n.pl. stars 888.

syrthaw vn. fall: pret. sing. 3. **syrthwys** 548: xxi.

tat nm. father 53, 57, 205, 223, 354, 503, 505, 996, 1001.

tauawd nm. tongue 157; **-t** 171.

tangneued nmf. peace 999, 1000.

tangneuedu vn. make peace 982.

tal nm. front, end, top, 332, 469.

talueinc nf. high seat 500.

talu vn. repay 154.

tan nm. fire 271, 304, 392, 946, 958, 1050.

taraw vn. beat, strike 972, 1213, 1227; imperf. sing. 3. **trawei** 320; **taraw llygat** adv. in the twinkling of an eye 1097n.

tardu vn. spring out: pret. sing. 3. **tardawd** 539: xvii, xxi.

tarren n. crag 833.

tebygu vn. think, suppose 414, 892; subj. pres. sing. 2. **tybyckych** 582.

tec adj. fair 126; **nyt dec** 1219; equat. **tecket** 229; comp. **tegach** 494.

teil nm. manure 572.

teir num. fem. three 104, 235, 334, 335, 338, 339n. etc. **teir oes guyr** three generations 371–2.

teithiawc adj. rightful 91n.: xvi, xvii.

telyn nf. harp 627.

teneu adj. thin, lean 310.

teruyn nm. place, spot 480.

teu poss. pron. sing. 2. subst. 116; adj. 83, 770, 793n.

teulu nm. force, war-band 123, 1070.

tew adj. fat 310.

tewi vn. be, become silent 629 R pres. sing. 3. **teu**.

teyrnas nf. kingdom 172, 648, 722.

teyrndynyon nn. pl. kingly men 126.

teyrned pl. of **teyrn** lord, prince 142.

ti pers. pron. simple. indep. sing 2. 156, 162, 163, 171, 172, 383, 451, 501n., etc.

ti pers, pron. simple dep. affix. aux. sing. 2. 41, 44, 54, 54, 89, 99, etc.

tir nm. land 33, 571, 579, 590, 607, 1062, 1188.

tirioni vn. grow fond, tender 166.

titheu pers. pron. conj. indep. sing. 2. 83, 93, 104, 435, 568.

titheu pers. pron. conj. dep. affix. aux. sing. 2. 58, 146, 148, 170, 426, 580 etc.

tlysseu n.pl. of **tlws** treasure, jewel 822n., 1025, 1027, 1032, 1092, 1190.

tom nf. mound 1240.

ton(n) nf. wave 491, 690.

torch nm. collar 678, 679, 681.

torri vn. break: imperf. impers. **torrit** 135.

tost adj. painful 528; equat. **tostet** 915.

tostes vb. pret. sing. 3. pained, hurt 527, 541.

tra conj. while, so long as 241n., 242n., 276n., 314, 852, 925, 965, 1243n.

tra'e geuyn adv. from behind 270n. Cf. GMW 210.

traean nm. (the) third part 1028n.

traeth nm. strand 318.

trafferth nm. difficulty 1222, 1223n.

tranhoeth adv. on the morrow 559, **trannoeth** 1070, 1099; also **drannoeth**.

trawst nm. rafter 328; pl. **trostreu** 321.

trebelit adv. clear, brilliant 1018.

tref nf. town, township 35, 275.

treiglaw vn. turn, wander, travel pres. sing. 3. **treigyl** 882.

treigyl nm. turn, time 890n.

treis nm. oppression, force 580n., 587, 591, 615, 629, 648, 665, 749.

treissaw vn. force, compel 622, 625, 660.

treulaw vn. wear away 854.

tri num. masc. three 335, 335, 336, 336, 337 etc.

tri meib ar ugeint n.pl. twenty-three sons 472. Cf. GMW 47.

trigaw vn. dwell, stay: pret. sing. 3. **trigwys** 248, xxi; subj. pres. sing. 2. **triccych** 156.

trimut adj. thrice-mewed 494n.

trist adj. sad 324, 455.

tristit nm. sadness 42.

troet nmf. foot 301, 303 (R **traet**); pl. **traet** 87, 244, 330, 971, 1183, 1188.

trossi vn. turn 956.

trugein num. sixty 647.

trum nm. ridge 64.

trw yt prep. + prt. whereby 27n.: xx. Cf. GMW 244.

trwst nm. noise 459.

trwy prep. through, by means of 4, 351, 523; also **drwy**.

trychan num. three hundred 78;
  trychant 275: xix.
trychanherw n. three hundred acres
  298: xix.
trychanllong n. three hundred ships
  317: xix.
trychantref n. three cantrefs 306: xix.
trydyt ord. third, one of three 313,
  550, **trydyd** third 877, 1072.
trydydyt nm. third day 545.
trydygwr nm. one of three men 230n.
trywyr n.pl. three men 235n., 743
  761. GMW. 16, 47.
tu nm. side 292, 686, 694, 864, 931,
  1109n.; **pa du** what side? where?
  931, **py tu** 686, 693–4.
tulatheu n.pl. of **tulath** side beam
  321.
tuth nm. canter 80.
twrch nm. boar 1194.
twyllaw vn. deceive, betray: sing.
  pres. 1. **twyllaf** 484.
twym adj. hot, warm 303, 310, 665.
twympath nm. bush 422; **twynpath**
  anthill 946.
ty nm. house 35, 467, 499, 529, 933,
  1001, 1042, 1055; pl. **tei** 275n.
tybygu vn. think, suppose: imperf. pl.
  3. **tybygynt** 227, **tebygynt** 229:
  xix.
tykyaw vn. avail: subj. pres. sing. 3.
  tyckyo 717.
tyfu vn. grow; imperf. sing. 3. **tyuei**
  497n.; pret. sing. 3. **tyuwys** 248:
  xxi, 865; subj. imperf. sing. 3. **tyffei**
  22, 24.
tyghet nf. destiny 50n.
tyngu vn. swear 50; pres. sing. 1.
  tyghaf 50; pret. sing. 3. **tygwys** 55:
  xxi.
tymp nm. appointed time 6n.
tynnu vn. draw, pluck, drag 1215;
  pres. impers. **tynnir** 640, 702, 966;
  imperf. sing. 3. **tynnei** 1193, 1196,
  impers. **tynnit** 1192; pret sing. 3.
  tynnwys 893: xxi; subj. pres. sing.
  3. **tynho** 643; imperf. impers.
  tynhet 303: xvi.
tyno nm. plain 302.
tywarchen nf. clod 74.

'th pers. pron. infix. obj. sing. 2. 112,
  1081.

'th poss. pron. infix. sing. 2. + nn.
  92, 92, 104, 144, 144, 144 etc..

uch prep. above, before; sing. 3.
  masc. **uchtaw** 75.
uch benn prep. over, above 1079,
  vch pen(n) 819, 1031.
uch y benn adv. above him 75.
uch y law adv. before his hand 389.
uchaf superl. of **uchel** tall, high 387.
uchet nm. height 889.
ucher nm. evening 853, 888.
uchot adv. above 905.
un num. one subst. 29, 398, 522,
  575, 782, 864 etc., adj. 32, 42, 238,
  298, 301, 301, 951, 1073; same 397,
  415, 598, 822, **un uam** by the
  same mother; only 806, 1243; pron.
  one 70, 274, 512, 865, 908, 932.
unben nm. chieftain 147, 156, 374,
  379, 381, 400, 766.
unllofyawc adj. one-handed 396n.

vb interj. ah! 438.
wedy prep. after 949; also **gwedy**.
weithon adv. now 18, 888n., 929,
  985, 1205, 1235. Cf. GMW 227.
wers vawr adv. for a long while
  893n.
whedleu n.pl. news, stories 779: xix.
  Cf. GMW 11.
wrth prep. to 44, 265, 809, 839, 951,
  1168, at 77, 140, 946, 1141, for
  240, 331, 967, against 50, of 783,
  according to 619, 1045, in order to
  + vn. 651; sing. 2. **vrthyt** 166, 3.
  masc. **vrthaw** 16, 47, 54, 57, 115,
  562, 762, 807, 896, 933, 947, 1219;
  fem. **vrthi** 501.
vrth dayar adv. earthwards 87–8.
vrth hynny adv. because of that
  248.
vrth nef adv. heavenwards 87.
vrth parth y dwyrein adv. towards
  the east 124–5.
vy pers. pron. simple indep. pl. 3.
  536; **wy** 668, 912, 1053.
wy pers. pron. simple dep. affix. aux.
  pl. 3 309, 414, 458, 521, 529, 543,
  759, 811, 920.
vyneb nm. face 571, honour 154n.,
  380n.; **vyneb yn vyneb** adv. face
  to face 564.

wynt pers. pron. simple indep. pl. 3. 355, 535, 805, 955, 1029, 1030, 1097, 1142, 1143, 1157, 1160.

vynt pers. pron. simple dep. affix. aux. pl. 3. 410.

wynteu pers. pron. conj. indep pl. 3. 827.

vynteu pers. pron. conj. dep. affix. aux. pl. 3. 510, 947, 969, 1064.

vyntvy pers. pron. reduplic, pl. 3. 410. Cf. GMW 49.

vyr(y)on (n.pl. of **wyr**) grandsons 334, 737, granddaughters 339n.

wystyn nm. stump 867.

y affirm. pre-verb. prt. 34n., 83, 95, 114, 129, 139 etc.

y prt + infix. pron. obj. 28, 278n., 480, 500n., 528, 655n., 702, 810, 876, 865, 1201, 1224; infix. pron. obj. 151, 451, 527; affirm prt. + **h-**: **y harchaf** 1082n. Cf. GMW 23.

y rel. pre-verb. prt. 5, 275, 317, 324, 562, 620, 667, 1084,.

y def. art. 3, 4, 8, 8, 9, 9 etc. ?poss. pron. sing. 3. masc. 57, 61n., 87n., 444n., 488n., 1183n., 1239n., 1240; after a vowel 1135.

y indef. art. 350, 352, 377. Cf. GMW 24–5.

y bore adv. in the morning 263, 349, 573.

y byw nm. the living 633.

y gwedi adv. **(yg gwedi)** to prayer 3n.

y gwr nm. the man, one, he (who) 37, 1237.

y gyt adv. together 626, 598, **y gyd** 475.

y gyt a prep. along with 400.

y llall pron. the other 376, 597.

y lleill pron. sing. subst. the one 596; adj. 325, 793n.

y marw nm. the dead 632.

y mywn adv. in 92, 112, 129, 141, 447–8, 778, 781, 784–5, 786, 802, 805, 805–6, 892, 1211; prep. in 530, 937; into + def. nn. 809.

y neb pron. the one he (who, whom) 451, 561–2, 913.

y neuad (< **yn neuad**) in the hall of 90.

y peth pron. that (which) 36.

y rei pron. those (who) 432.

y rwng prep. between 982, 999, 1003, 1025–6, 1166, 1178–9.

y ryn for **yr hyn** that (which) 25.

y sawl pron. subst. he (who) 129, 496; adj. as many as, all the 422n.

ychen n.pl. of **ych** ox 589n., 596n., 599.

ychydic adv. a little (while) 988.

yd nm. corn 92.

yt affirm. pre-verb. prt. 27, 41n., 381, 389, 541, 556, 795n.; **hyd** 386n.: xxii.

ytuot vn. be, become; subj. pres. sing. 3. **ytuo** 136.

ydrych vn. look, see 23; also **edrych**: xix.

yd affirm. pre-verb. prt. 5, 34, 100, 136, 158, 158 etc.

yuet vn. drink 1044.

yuory adv. tomorrow 98.

yg prep. in 28n., 106, 106, 229, 653, 822, 892, 914, 922, 923, 975, 1051, 1198, 1204, 1207, into 28; **yng** in 1024; **y (yg(h)-)** 117, 121, 125, 126, 226, 229, 261, 322.

yg karchar adv. in prison 831.

yg gordwy adv. by force 37n.: xvii.

yg gwyllt pred. wild 996n.

ygder nm. tightness 542.

yghongyl (**yn + congyl** indef. nn. corner) 1107.

ygwylldawc sub-pred. wild 5n.

ygyt a prep. along with, besides 838, 1124.

ym prep. in at 25, 35, 78, 105, 106, 107, 107, 155, 262, 585, 772, 938, 1041, 1055, 1098, 1126; + indef. nn. 460; into 52, 1096.

ym bronn prep. at the point of, close to 1119.

ym pell adv. far (from) 956.

ym penn prep. at the end of 25, 377, **ympen** 377, **ymphen** at the end of 822, into the head of 820.

ym penn gwers adv. after a while 268.

yma adv. here 836, 850, 851, 860, 863, 864 etc.

ymadrawd nm. word, discourse 1078.

ymadws nm. high time 1238.

ymauael vn. lay hold of 1047, 1182, 1212, **ymauel** 1213; pret. sing. 3. **ymauaelawd** 1238–9: xxi.

ymardisgwyl vn. watch 959.

ymchoelut vn. return, turn back/on 920n., 1170, 1215; also **ymhoelut**.

ymdaraw vn. fight, engage in combat (with) 1027.

ymdeith vn. go, travel: pres. sing. 1. **ymdaaf** 526, 3. **ymda** 87, 935; pl. 1. **ymdawn** 515, 2. **ymdewch** 515 (R **doethawch**): xvi, xvii, xvii.

ymdianc vn. get away, escape 894.

ymdidan vn. converse 1082.

ymdiret vn. trust: pres. sing. 1. **ymdiredaf** 646.

ymdwyn vn. bear, carry 1050; imperf. sing. 3. **ymdygei** 279.

ymeneinaw vn. bathe oneself 1203.

ymgeis vn. seek, search for 1029n.

ymgolli vn. lose, lose sight of: pret. pl. 3. **ymgollassant** 1131n.

ymgribyaw vn. wrestle 1220.

ymgyffret vn. reach, stretch; pres. sing. 3. **ymgyffret** 158: xix.

ymgynghori vn. consult 535.

ymhoelut vn. return, turn back; pres. (fut.) sing. 3. **ymhoelawd** 109, pl. 1. **ymhoylwn** 479; imper. pl. 2. **ymhoelwch** 478: xv, xix.

ymlad nm. fight, battle 119, 918, 919.

ymlad vn. fight 370, 925, 926, 991, 1002, 1052, 1089, 1211; pres. sing. 3. **ymlad** 1089; pret. sing. 3. **ymladawd** 1068, 1070, 1072: xxi.

ymlit vn. chase, pursue: pres. sing. 1. **ymlityaf** 1171.

ymolchi vn. wash oneself: subj. pres. sing. 3. **ymolcho** 481.

ymordiwes vn. overtake, catch up with 1100; pret. sing. 3. **ymordiwedawd** 1034, 1119, 1125, 1153, 1197: xxi.

ymrithaw vn. transform oneself 1030.

ymrodi vn. try hard, do one's best 1145n.

ymual < **ym mual (bual)** adv. into drinking horn 90n., 773.

ymwelet a(c) vn. see 1097; plup. sing. 3. **ymwelsei** 1143n.; subj. pres. sing. 1. **ymwelwyf** 563.

ymwyt < **ym mwyt** adv. into food 89n.

ymyrru vn. be concerned, involved with: pret. sing. 3. **ymyrrwys** 983: xxi.

ymys < **ym mys** adv. into (the) finger (of) 443.

ymysgytyaw vn. shake oneself 1034.

yn poss. pron. prefix. pl. 1. 137.

yn pers. pron. infix. pl. 1. 136.

yn prep. in 11, 35, 48, 61, 63, 75 etc. + indef. nn. 380, 984; involved with 969; into 813, 973, 977, 1054, 1176, 1177, 1186; + indef. nn. 480; sing. 3. masc. **yndaw** 229, 240, 249, 318, 450, 605 etc.; fem. **yndi** 64, 68, 69, 275, 277, 320 etc.; pl. 3. **yndunt** 658, 658, 664.

yn pred. prt. + nn. 59, 227, 229, 265, 302, 326 etc., **yn y gyuarws** as a boon 312n.

yn pred. prt. + adj. 144, 372, 390, 414, 554, 573 etc.; adv. part. + adj. 43, 109, 162, 172, 271, 351 etc.

yn pred. prt. + vn. 7, 26, 73, 81, 166, 284 etc.

yn drws prep. at the entrance of, before 127–8, 780.

yn erbyn prep. against 554–5; **yn y erbyn** to meet him 1167, **yn eu herbyn** to meet them 459–60, 461; **yn erbyn allt** uphill 542.

yn eu kyuereit adv. for their needs 306–7.

yn eu kylch adv. around them 955, **yn y gylch** around him 73.

yn eu gwyd adv. in their presence, while they looked 1054.

yn uarw adv. dead 966.

yn vyw adv./pred. alive 640, 965, 1138, 1150, **nyt a mi yn uyw** not while I am alive 1170n.

yn gwbyl adv. completely 974.

yn gyntaf adv. first 829, 930, 1092, 1182–3.

yn hyt prep. during, throughout 243.

yn y gyueir adv. straight ahead 1201.

yn y mysc adv. in their midst 1161.

yn y ol adv. after him 1240, **yn y hol** after her 498, **yn y hol hi** 511.

yn lluydd adv. on the march 305 (R **yny llud**).

yn llwrw prep. in the mode, manner of 915.

yn llwyr adv. entirely 973, 1141, 1233.

yn ol prep. after 1194.

yn rat adv. for favour, for nothing 748.

yn teir nossic adv. when three nights old 686, 849, 862, 873-4, 885, 904.

yn wastat adv. always 1049.

yna adv. then 384, 957, 961, 977, 985, 1017 etc. there 763 (R racco).

yno adv. there 95, 96, 127, 426, 427, 858 etc.

ynteu pers. pron. conj. indep. sing. 3. masc. 20, 246, 354, 443, 517, 525 etc.

ynteu pers. pron. conj. dep. affix. aux. sing. 3. masc. 46, 284, 524, 538, 551, 552 etc.

yny conj. until 880, 1183, 1227n.; affirm. pre-verb. prt. 911. 959. Cf. GMW 244-5.

ynyssoed n.pl. of **ynys** island 121.

yr def. art. 24, 75, 118, 120, 121, 128 etc., + cons. 26n, 598 **(yr rei hynny)** n.

yr affirm. pre-verb. prt. 901.

yr prep. for, for the sake of 438, 835, 982, 983, 1017, 1081, 1087; in exchange for 917, 917, 917, 918; in spite of: **er hynny** adv. nevertheless 1069; **yr duw** for God's sake 37, 477, 848; + vn. in order to 87, 152; sing. 3. masc. **yrdaw** 135.

yr awr honn adv. at this hour, now 128.

(y)r hwn(n) pron. dem. the one (that/who) 71n., 72n., 127.

yr hynn pron. dem. that (which) 390, 898, 948.

yr hynn = **yr hwnn** he (who) 393.

yr hynny hyt hediw from that day to this 867, 879, 889.

yr mwyn prep. for 356.

yr pan conj. since (time) 247, 1142-3.

yr un (a) pron. the one (who) 1003.

yr ys prep. since 886n. Cf. GMW 142-3.

yscar vn. prt. separate 1156; pres. (fut.) impers. **yscarhawr** 883n.; pret. sing. 3. **yscarwys** 231 (R yscarwn): xxi, xxi.

ysgawn adj. light 1041n., equat. **yscawnhet** 80; **yskafned** 244 (R ysgawnet): xix.

yskithyr n. tusk 646, **ysgithyr** 1020.

ysglyffyaw vn. snatch 1032.

ysgrybul n. coll. animals, stock 936n.

yscubawr nf. barn 319, 322.

yscwyt nf. shield 161n (R taryan): xii, 335, 737.

yscwyd nf. shoulder 908, 909, 924.

yskyuarn nf. ear 71, 669n. (R glust): xvi.

yskynuaen nm. mounting-block 140: xii.

yslipanu vn. furbish 782, 789.

yslipanwr nm. furbisher 775.

yspytty nm. hospice 94n.

ys(s)ef (ys is + ef it) 800n., 908n.; also **sef**.

yssu vn. consume, devour 968, 995; imperf. pl. 3. **yssynt** 308, 309.

yssyd (ys + yd GMW 63) 42, 47, 48, 54, 57, 107n.

ystauell nf. chamber 510n.

ystlys nmf. side 50.

ystrodur nf. saddle 62.

ystyr nmf. reason 44, 89, 772, history, significance 1074n.: lxvii.

Indices

Names of Places

Aber Cledyf 933, 936; Aber Deu
  Gledyf 932; Deu Gledyf 1101
Aber Gwy 1179
Aber Hafren 1168
Aber Tywi 1128
Affric 121
Allt Clwyt 1114
Amanw, Dyffryn 1149; Mynyd 1145
Annwuyn 714

Bannawc, Mynyd 597

Caer Anoeth 125
Caer Brythwch a Brythach a Nerthach
  122
Kaer Loyw 906, 923
Caer Neuenhyr Naw Nawt 126
Caer Oeth ac Anoeth 125
Kaer Paris 278
Caer Se ac Asse 117
Kaer Tathal 204
Camlan 226, 229, 231; Cat Gamlan
  297
Carn Gwylathyr 954
Kawlwyt, Cwm 872
Celli Wic y Gherniw 261, 351, 975,
  1024, 1204
Kelli (a Chuel) 297
Kerdin, Porth 1055
Keredigyawn 1159
Cerniw 261; Kernyw 106, 223, 297,
  313, 975, 1024, 1167, 1170, 1190,
  1201, 1204
Kerwyn, Cwm 1112
Cilgwri 847
Cledyf, Aber see Aber Cledyf
Cleis, Porth 1098
Corsica 121
Cum Kawlwyt 871, Cwm Kawlwyt
  872
Cwm Kerwyn 1112
Cymry 1095

Deu Gledyf 1101, see Aber Cledyf
Din Tywi 1158

Dinsol 106
Dyfneint 297, 313, 1167
Dyffryn Amanw 1149
Dyffryn Llychwr 1136
Dyuet 1056, 1098

Egrop 120
Eskeir Oeruel yn Iwerdon 107, 350;
  Esgeir Oeruel 1030, 1066
Euyas 1166, 1174
Ewin, Llwch 1152

Fotor 118
Freinc 202, 277, 294, 720, 1058, 1130

Gamon, Pentir 253–4
Garth Grugyn 1160
Glynn Nyuer 1112; see Nyuer
Glynn Ystu 1131
Gogled, Y 107, 997, 1012, 1208
Groec 124
Grugyn, Garth 1160
Gwern Abwy 882, 883
Gwlat yr Haf 1059
Gwy, Aber 1179
Gwylathyr, Carn 954

Hafren 1174, 1176, 1178, 1183, 1187;
  Aber 1168

India Uawr 118
India Uechan 118
Iwerdon 107, 295, 299, 350, 636, 644,
  697, 1010, 1011, 1029, 1037, 1040,
  1042, 1046, 1054, 1061, 1062, 1066,
  1069, 1143

Lotor 117
Lliwan, Llyn 1179; see Llyn Lliw
Llwch Ewin 1152
Llwch Tawy 1156
Llychlyn 120
Llydaw 216, 1007, 1058, 1163, 1164
Llyn Llyw 891, Llyn Lliw 902; cf.
  Llynn Lliwan 1179

EPITHETS

(The first appearance of each personal name is alone cited; where epithets are untranslated the reader is referred to the notes)

Alarch ('swan'): Gwen 361
Allt Clwyt: Tarawc 1114
Amhynwyedic: Custenhin 435
Ardwyat Kat: Vchdryt 186
Astrus: Gwyden 316
Atuer: Eli 1115
Arwy: Reidwn 221

Baruawc ('bearded'): Dillus 960; Llawurodet 223
Baryf Draws: Vchdryt 327
Baryf Trwch: Nodawl 223–4
Beidawc: Anoeth 322
Bernach: Conul 179
Beuthach: Lluber 179
Brenhin ('king'): Doget Urenhin 31; Iona urenhin Freinc 202; Flergant brenhin Llydaw 216, Dunart brenhin y Gogled 254; Peris brenhin Freinc 277; Guilenhin brenhin Freinc 720; Aed brenhin Iwerdon 295; Odgar brenhin Iwerdon 1045–6; Hir Peissawc brenhin Llydaw 1164

Canhwch: Kynwal 361
Canllaw: Canhastyr 190
Cant Ewin: Cors 190
Cawr ('giant'): Wrnach 747 (*see* Penkawr)
Keinuaruawc ('Fair-bearded'): Kynyr 264
Keudawc: Kynuelyn 342
Clauyryawc: Hettwn 708
Clememyl: Unic 359
Clof ('lame'): Tecuan 255
Coeshyd ('stag's leg'): Gilla 298
Cof: Kimin 185
Conyn Cawn: Eskeir Culhwch 191
Corr ('dwarf'): Grudlwyn 333; Guidolwyn 657; Gwdolwyn 364–5
Curyuagyl: Cynwas 186

Kyuarwyd ('guide'): Cyndelic 177; Elidir 329
Kyuwlch: Kledyf 334; Kilyd 736
Cyllelluawr ('Big-knife'): Osla 278
Kyn Croc: Neol 371
Kyruach: Gwawrdur 189; Gwaredur 363

Dallpenn: Datweir 197
Dathar Wenidawc: Gweir 288
Diessic Unben: Dwnn 343
Diuwlch: Cledyf 334
Du ('black'): Mil 123
Dydwc: Drwc; Hwyr 337; Llwyr 338
Dyuet: Alun 185

Eidin: Clydno 362
Emys: Llygatrud 251
Escob ('bishop'): Bitwini 356
Ewingath ('cat's claw'): Ispervr 187

Flam ('flame'): Flewdwr 182

Gauaeluawr ('mighty grasp'): Glewlwyt 111
Galldouyd: Greidawl, 176
Garanhir ('long shank'): Gwydneu 618
Godeith: Gwadyn 300
Gododin: Gwlgawt 624
Gouynnyat: Gallcoit 188; Llwydawc 1137
Gossol: Gwadyn 300
Gotyuron: Gwynn 288
Gwallt Auwyn: Gwruan 294
Gwallt Eurin ('golden hair'): Gwar(a)e 315; Grugyn Gwallt Ereint ('silver hair') 1136–7
Gwarthecuras: Gwrhyr 186
Gwineu: Gwlwlyd 589
Gwledic: Kyledon 1; Anlawd 2; Casnar 215; Flewdwr Flam 182; Tared 670

Gwrhyd Enwir: Gweir 290
Gwrych Ereint ('silver bristle'): Grugyn 1083
Gwydel ('Irishman'): Diwrnach 635; Garselit 697; Llenlleawc 253
Gwyllt: Kynedyr 708; Cyledyr 994
Gwyn ('white, fair'): Mygdwn (march Gwedw) 1177
Gwyn Paladyr: Gweir 290
Gwyr: Gwydawc 1155

Hael ('Generous'): Iscouan 224; Morgant 256
Hanner Dyr ('half man'): Pwyll 342
Hen ('old'): Gouynyon 250; Gwrbothu 252; Teithi 245; Hen Vyneb 274
Hir ('long, tall'): H. Atrwm 306; H. Amren 323; H. Eidyl 323; H. Erwm 305; H. Peissawc 1164; Arwy Hir 365
Hyuar: Gwynn 296

Llaw Ereint ('silver hand'): Llud 367
Llawwynnyawc: Lloch 192; Llwch 291
Lledewic ('Breton'): Glythmyr 1009
Lletlwm: Gwrgwst 993
Llygat Cath ('cat's eye'): Gwiawn 351

Marchawc ('horseman'): Dillus 700
Mawrurydic: Eidon 221
Melyn: M. Gwanhwyn (ych) 593
Minsych ('dry lip'): Samson 214
Moel ('bare, bald'): Dyuynwal 254
Mordwyt Twll: Echel 196
Mygdwn ('dun mane'): see Gwyn Mygdwn
Mynawc ('slender neck'): Moren 184
Myngul ('fair neck'): Essyllt 372
Mynwen: Essyllt 372

Oeruedawc: Moro 718
Offeirad ('preist'): Kethtrwm 347

Ordu ('very black'): Y Widon 652
Orwen ('very white'): Y Widon 653
Ossul: Gwadyn 300

Pebyr: Ruawn 183
Penbagat: Panawr 296
Penn Beid ('Chief of Boars'): Yskithyrwyn 639
Penn Beird ('Chief of Bards'): Teliessin 214
Penkawr (Chief Giant'): Yspadaden 51
Penlloran: Eiryawn 1128
Penn Uchel ('High Head') Sawyl 344
Pryt Angel ('Angel's form'): Sande 228

Reget: Uryen 366
Rin Baruawc ('stiff beard'): Rinnon 663
Ruduyw: Rys 1161
Rudwern: Run 286
Rwyddyrys: Reu 286

Saer ('craftsman'): Gluydyn 263; Gwlydyn 1124–5
Sant ('Saint'): Cynwyl 230
Scawntroet ('light foot'): Scilti 235; cf. Yscawntroet 239
Seueri: Gwrgi 1010

Tal Aryant ('silver brow'): Kadellin 289; Hettwn 344
Talgellawc: Tegyr 255
Tec ('fair'): Gwenlliant 366
Twr Bliant: Teyrnon 255
Twyll Goleu: Tathal 177

Unllenn ('one mantle'): Hyueid 220

Yscawntroet ('light foot'): Scilti 239